Return to It

Return to Ithaca

Glyn Iliffe

First published in the United Kingdom in 2017 by Canelo

This edition published in the United Kingdom in 2019 by

Canelo Digital Publishing Limited
57 Shepherds Lane
Beaconsfield, Bucks HP9 2DU
United Kingdom

A CIP catalogue record for this book is available from the British Library.

Print ISBN 978 1 78863 155 6
Ebook ISBN 978 1 91159 178 8

For all those who have faithfully followed Odysseus and Eperitus, from the slopes of Mount Parnassus to here, their final adventure

Book One

Prologue

Ogygia

Odysseus sat staring into the darkness. The beach was pale and the starlight gleamed on the black sea. The soothing rush of the breakers encouraged sleep, but he resisted the heaviness in his eyelids and threw another piece of driftwood onto the fire. A puff of orange sparks flew up into the blackness.

She had not come for two nights now. Sometimes she would not come for a whole week, but that was rare. She never left Ogygia – the island of which they were the only occupants – so he did not know where she went on those days. But she would come tonight. He felt the dread of her in his bones.

He ran his hands through his hair and scratched at his bearded cheeks in an effort to keep himself awake. Slumping back onto his elbows, he stared up at the stars and picked out the great constellations: Bootes the ploughman, pushing the Great Plough; the Seven Sisters; and Orion, slain by Artemis for becoming the lover of immortal Dawn.

He seemed to remember that they had been different once, in the world he had come from. But that had been a lifetime ago, and the memory of it faded a little more with each passing day. He fought the closing of his eyelids and tried to sit up again, but dropped back onto the goatskin that served as his bed. Then, as his eyes closed and he began to sink into unconsciousness, he sensed her.

'*Odysseus*.'

The fire shrank back like a cowed dog, its heat swept away by a breath of cold air. He sat up and pulled a burning log from the flames, holding it before him like a sword. Calypso stood at the edge of the ring of firelight, the sea breeze blowing strands of her blonde hair across her face and pressing her dress against her body. She was beautiful, even in the darkness, and her laugh was light and deceptively childlike.

'Odysseus, my love.'

She waved her hand and the flaming brand was extinguished.

He threw it at her with a grunt, but she was gone.

'*Leave me alone*!' he shouted.

'Why?' she asked.

He twisted round to see her standing behind him.

'Why do you resist? Am I not pleasing to look at? Does my lovemaking not satisfy you? I know it does.'

She unslipped the cord from around her waist and shrugged off her garment. It fell around her feet like a shadow and she stepped from it, her naked skin orange in the firelight. Though she was older than the mountains of Ogygia, her body had never known the corruption of old age. Shamelessly she stood before him, savouring the feel of his gaze on her flesh. She held a hand towards him.

'Come, Odysseus. Sleep with me.'

He looked at her with hate-filled eyes, as a prisoner stares at his gaoler, knowing that her control over him was very nearly absolute. She was a demigoddess, a powerful seductress who had used her sexuality to expunge his memories of home and family, erasing everything he loved and had fought for until only an instinct remained. And she would not be happy until even that was taken from him. He pulled away from her, mutely shaking his head.

'I *command* you,' she insisted, her eyes flashing red. 'The gods sent you to me. You are mine to do with as I please.'

'I don't belong to you!'

Calypso's eyes narrowed, and with a snap of her fingers she was gone.

Odysseus turned, looking for her in the shadows.

'I don't want you,' he shouted after her, his voice falling flat in the darkness.

'But I want *you*.'

The fire leapt up suddenly and went out. Startled, he fell backwards onto the sand. A spectre of grey smoke trailed up from the ashes, but instead of being carried away by the breeze it drifted towards him, thickening into the shape of Calypso. She crouched before his open legs, smiling lustfully.

'You *are* mine, Odysseus. You cannot escape Ogygia, and you cannot escape me.'

As quick as a snake, she gripped his knees and forced them apart. He tried to pull away, but her strength was irresistible. She lowered her lips to his right thigh and kissed it gently, before running the tip of her tongue up the long white scar he had been given by a boar when he was a boy. But the woman before him now was more dangerous than any boar. With a playful laugh, she slid her hand down to his genitals.

'Still don't want me?' she asked. 'Something tells me you're lying.'

'You're not her,' he hissed, trying to twist away from her hold on his legs. 'You never will be.'

'Who, Odysseus? *Who*? Do you even remember her name?'

Calypso pulled herself on top of him and, holding his wrists to the sand, lowered her face to his. He could feel the weight of her breasts upon his chest and taste her breath on his lips.

'My wife.'

'What's her name? Say it and I'll let you go. Say it.'

He could not remember. He had been unable to recall her face for a long time, but now even her name refused to come to him.

'Get out of my head. This is sorcery.'

'Say your wife's name and I'll release you. I'll even give you the tools to make a boat and sail away from Ogygia.'

Her control over him was almost complete. The slow, rhythmic rubbing of her body against his had made him erect, and now her mouth hovered over his, poised to subdue the last of his resistance.

'Say it!'

But he could not. Only one name was in his thoughts now, a name both hateful and compelling.

'*Calypso*.'

He felt the victorious smile on her lips as she kissed him. Her perfect mouth moulded to his and their tongues met, sparking his treacherous lust. He took her by the waist, intending to throw her off, but instead found his hands had moved to down to cup her buttocks. She slid back onto him with a sigh and sat up, her eyes closed and her face half-hidden by her hair as she moved her body against his. Her terrible beauty consumed him, as it had done so many times before, and his weak defiance surrendered to his desire.

When she had finished with him, she slipped off and lay at his side, breathing deeply.

'Marry me,' she said after a while, as if to herself. Then she turned to face him, propping her head on one hand as she ran her fingers over his chest. 'Marry me, Odysseus, and I will make you immortal.'

'I don't want to be immortal.'

'All men want immortality. Achilles exchanged long life for a name that would endure for eternity. I'm offering you more than that: to live with me here forever, until the gods fall and the world ends.'

'I saw Achilles's spirit in the Underworld. He hated the choice he had made.'

'Because he longed to feel the blood in his veins again,' she said. 'Marry me and your spirit will never have to suffer the torture of Hades, as his does.'

'No. Achilles hated that he had rejected a simple, happy life for something false and unfulfilling. I won't make the same mistake. I want to go home. That's where my heart is; that's where it's always been.'

Calypso sat up and stared at him with disdain.

'Why do you still cling to that false hope? You couldn't find the way to Ithaca before you came here, so why do you expect to find it now?'

'I would still try. What else is left to me? You've imprisoned me on this island of empty beauty; you've robbed me of my courage, strength and manhood; and you've hidden me away from the world that I knew. I'd rather die than remain your plaything.'

She pushed herself to her feet and stepped away. Her teeth were clenched and her eyes were fierce with anger.

'Why do you insist on denying me?'

'Because I don't love you. I will never love you, Calypso.'

She thrust a hand towards him, and though he was beyond her reach, he felt an unseen force around his throat, lifting him from the sand as it choked the flow of air to his lungs. He clutched at his neck, trying to pull the invisible fingers away but only finding his own flesh.

'You forget I am a goddess,' she snarled. 'I could kill you right now if I wanted to. What good are you to me if you refuse to give me your heart? Why should I let you live, Odysseus? No one would know if I ended your worthless life. No one would care!'

'No one except you,' he croaked.

Her hand dropped to her side and the hold on his throat was released. He fell back onto the goatskin, gasping for air.

'You're pathetic,' she said, glaring at him. 'Even if you knew the way, how would you sail to Ithaca? You don't have a ship. What's more, you're terrified of the sea. Do you think I haven't watched you as you stand on the beach, staring in fear at the waves with your hands trembling at your sides? Or heard you moaning in your sleep about storms and drowning shipmates? You're *half* the man you were when you first washed up on this island. How can a creature like you refuse the love of a goddess, and all for the sake of a woman whose name you don't even remember? Damn you, Odysseus!'

She snatched up her dress from the sand and walked down the beach towards the sea, giving him a last glance over her shoulder before disappearing into the darkness.

Odysseus found his cloak and curled up beneath it. He pondered her words and knew they were true. He was no longer the man who had conquered Troy or outwitted the Cyclops. His muscles had gone to waste and his stomach had seen too many easy meals. He lacked the courage to face the sea's treachery or brave Poseidon's anger. He had lost his fleet, his men and his greatest friend, Eperitus. He could not even tell how many months he had been imprisoned on Ogygia for.

But one thing remained. He had remembered her name.

Penelope.

Chapter One

The Stranger

The sea was as black as pitch in the moonless night. Countless stars watched the breakers roll one after another upon the shore, but there was no other light.

Eperitus stood on the lonely beach, the waves breaking up around his sandalled feet before being sucked back with a rush through the shingle. The wind howled around his ears and whipped his cloak ferociously against his thighs, though he remained upright beneath its assault. Out at sea rows of jagged rocks defied the waves with insolent boldness, as they had done for years beyond count. He watched them in silence, thinking of the time when he had first seen this shore from the deck of a Phaeacian galley. It had pulled him from the ocean after his own ship had broken apart in a storm and been sucked down to the depths, taking the crew with it. Sometimes he wished he had died along with them.

But the gods had not allowed it – whether out of benevolence or malice, he could not tell – and the Phaeacians had brought him to their ruler. King Alcinous had asked few questions, and Eperitus had responded with nothing more than his name and that he was returning from the siege of Troy. The king had accepted him as a suppliant and even offered him a place in the palace guard, but he had declined, saying that his fighting days were over. Instead, he served the king as a steward, and from that time on the Phaeacians had accepted him and he had been content to live among them.

But he had not found rest. Every night since setting foot on the island he had come to this beach to question the voices in the wind, to look up at the stars and seek the will of Zeus. And every night for seven years he had returned unanswered. But tonight something was stirring within him. Thoughts of Troy churned through his mind. He pictured the great kings and their beaked ships, the vast armies and the walled city that had kept them from their homes for ten years.

And his mind turned naturally to Odysseus, his king and friend, a man beloved of the gods and, ultimately, cursed by them. His stratagems had led to the fall of Priam's great city, but his reckless desire to return home had doomed himself and his followers to destruction. Of the six hundred who had sailed to Troy with him, only Eperitus and Omeros, the bard, remained; and Omeros could remember nothing, not even his own name. But Eperitus had not forgotten. He would never forget.

As his thoughts drifted through memories of long ago, the wind changed and a voice came to him across the waves. He ran out into the surf, straining his ears against its roar and squinting through the spray. Faintly he heard it again: a man's voice calling his name. It cried out again and he shouted back, but the wind stole his breath away. The voice came once more and then was gone, carried into oblivion by the storm.

Waves crashed against the rocks, throwing white flecks of spray high against the black sky. Half-remembered faces drifted before his eyes: Odysseus, Antiphus, Polites and other comrades; his wife, Astynome, and their child. All of them dead, their faces fading with the fall of the spray. He called their names through cupped hands, as if they would hear him in the cold places where they dwelt. As if he could bridge the bitter years and tell them of his anger and regret, and how he longed to be free of it.

But there was no response, so his fury remained, raging inside him like the sea. It was something he could not quench, not here on Phaeacia. If he was ever to find peace from it, he had to face his past. But that was impossible. The past was gone.

Stubbornly Eperitus waited, waist-deep in the waves, listening intently to the lonely howling of the wind. It was some time before he turned and walked back up the beach, wiping the seawater from his eyes and squeezing it from his beard. He passed the river where the Phaeacian women washed clothing, and walked along the road that led to the walled city of King Alcinous. The farmsteads on either side were silent but for the shifting of animals in the darkness and the occasional bark of a dog. As he walked, the night air carried the sound of the sea to him across the fields, crashing and foaming in its unceasing motion. But he heard no more voices in the wind.

It was not long before he saw the city walls. The gate was reached by a causeway between two harbours, where the fishing boats had long since been drawn up for the night. The only people in sight were a pair of guards, who nodded and let him pass.

The dark streets inside were quiet and deserted as Eperitus climbed the gentle slope to the palace. The monolithic structure stood two floors tall, its great size distinguishing it from the single-storey buildings around it. Its brazen walls gleamed in the flickering light of numerous torches set within the surrounding compound, and though he had seen the palace countless times, he still paused to admire its beauty. A guard stood by a gate in the outer wall. He opened the gate without a word as Eperitus passed through into the courtyard beyond.

The enclosure was broad, and even in the deceptive torchlight it was easy to see that Phaeacia's king was a man of great wealth and importance. The doors to his palace were tall and awe-inspiring, their golden casings glowing red as if on fire. The only guards here were two giant dogs, one of gold and one of silver, set on either side of the great portal; locals claimed they had been made by the smith-god, Hephaistos, to act as tireless sentinels against any who bore ill will to the king. But the island had few visitors, and Alcinous had no enemies that Eperitus knew of.

A side entrance led to a room where twenty hand mills stood vacant. A fine dust of ground barley was being swept up by a young slave, whose quicker friends had already finished their allotment of work and gone to the kitchens for their food. The girl paid him no attention and he continued through to the storage rooms and then into the kitchen. Here a large group of servants had gathered round the blazing hearth to share their evening meal, where they were being joined by their children and some of the off-duty guards. Without thinking, he kissed his fingers and touched the feet of a terracotta statuette of Demeter, which stood in an alcove by the entrance. There was no feast in the palace tonight. The king and his wife were away, so the usual gathering was swelled by a mixture of squires, wine stewards and meat carvers, whose normal duties were not required.

A young, long-haired soldier stood at the edge of the circle. He eyed Eperitus disdainfully, and as he passed caught him forcefully with his shoulder, knocking him into a group of male slaves.

'Watch where you're going, stranger.'

The Phaeacians still referred to him as *stranger*, because few knew his name and he minded nobody's business but his own. His preference for solitude made many think of him as aloof, and won him few friends. Not that he cared. He had always given his friendship sparingly.

Avoiding the soldier's gaze, he straightened himself up and turned to leave.

'Did I say you could go?'

'You heard Acroneos,' said another soldier, a short, ugly man with several missing teeth. 'You owe him an apology, stranger.'

Eperitus took a deep breath and stared hard at the stone floor. Acroneos stepped in front of him and pressed his face close to Eperitus's.

'You filthy coward,' he hissed.

Eperitus sensed the other soldier step up behind him. By now the room had fallen silent. A few looked on with sympathy; others watched in anticipation, enjoying his humiliation.

'I heard tell you were a deserter from the war,' Acroneos continued. 'That you ran away and left your own king to be slain, and that you've been hiding here ever since.'

'A man like him doesn't know the meaning of honour,' said the short, ugly soldier. 'Snivelling worms who always find their way into the rear rank of any fight.'

Eperitus's hands balled up into fists and he had to force them flat against his thighs again.

'Leave the stranger alone,' said a hunchbacked man from among the crowd. 'You know he won't fight, Acroneos. That's why you always pick on him.'

'Shut up, Pontonous,' Acroneos replied. 'Cripple or not, I ain't above giving you a bit of pain either, if you annoy me.'

'If you want an apology,' Eperitus said, 'then I'm sorry.'

'Sorry's not enough any more. You spilled my wine,' Acroneos said, dropping his cup on the flagstoned floor. It broke into several pieces and splashed Eperitus's shins. 'I want you to clean that up.'

Eperitus continued to avoid Acroneos's stare, knowing that to make eye contact with him would only escalate matters. Slowly, he knelt down and picked up the shards from around the soldier's feet.

'Now lap up the wine, like the dog you are.'

The short, ugly soldier and a few others laughed. Eperitus stared at the pool of dark liquid, focusing away from his anger. Acroneos was half his age and wanted to fight him, not realising that if Eperitus chose to, he could kill him with his bare hands right there in front of most of the palace servants. They would not laugh at him then, he thought. But he had sworn to the gods never to kill again, and he would not risk breaking that oath in a fight. Acroneos and his friend could beat him to the edge of death for all he cared. He would not fight.

'Enough now,' said an old woman. 'We're here to enjoy ourselves, Acroneos. Leave the stranger alone and go back to your drinking.'

Before the soldier could object, she had knelt beside Eperitus and mopped up the wine with a cloth. Catching his eye, she nodded to a corner of the room.

He stood and walked away, followed by the laughter of the two guards.

Pontonous, the king's chief steward, pushed his way through the crowd towards him and offered him a bowl of hot porridge.

'Why do you let them treat you like that, Eperitus? It just provokes them. Half the guards in the palace are desperate to get a reaction from you. It's like bull baiting to them: they know you're better than them, and at heart they're terrified of you, but they think it makes them look like real men.'

'There are no real men in the palace guard.'

'So rough one or two of them up and buy yourself a bit of respect – and peace.'

Eperitus took a spoonful of porridge, tested the temperature against his lips, then put it in his mouth.

'I've taken a vow...'

'I know, I know – a vow never to kill. But d'you think the gods would mind if you taught young Acroneos a lesson? Zeus loves to see justice – he wouldn't hold it against you, even if you killed the little rat.'

Eperitus shook his head and put the empty bowl of porridge on the floor.

'Yes, he would. And if I knock Acroneos on his backside and humiliate him, he'll draw his sword and it'll end in one of us dying. Besides, my fighting days are over. I gained nothing from being a warrior, Pontonous. *Nothing*. And you can take it from me, those who died at Troy gained nothing either.'

'That's rubbish,' Pontonous said, waving to a female slave. She brought two cups of wine and was repaid with a slap on the buttocks from the hunchback. 'Would Achilles say that if he could hear the tales Demodocus sings about him?'

Eperitus laughed.

'Achilles most of all.'

Pontonous shook his head.

'Well, my friend, you take it too far. I've spent my whole life being mocked and beaten because of this hump and my twisted spine. What I wouldn't give for muscles and courage like yours. I'd show the Acroneoses of this world a thing or two.'

'Courage?' Eperitus said with a smile. 'I'm a filthy coward, didn't you know?'

'Ah, shut up and drink your wine. I'm just saying there's a balance to be struck. Sometimes a man has to fight for what is right, and that's my last word on it. Anyway, how was the beach tonight?'

'Stormy,' Eperitus said, looking into his wine cup. 'I heard the voice again. Clearly this time, though. It wasn't in my head and it *wasn't* the wind.'

'Still think it was one of the gods?' Pontonous asked, peering sidelong at him. 'Maybe there's a link with the dreams you've been having. About Ithaca.'

'They're just dreams.'

'But you have them every night. The same dreams, and always involving Odysseus. Have you ever thought the gods might be calling you back there?'

'No.'

'Why not?' Pontonous insisted. 'You're tormented about something. I don't know what happened to you on that voyage back from Troy, and if you haven't told me by now then I don't want to know. But you'll never have peace until you stop running away and confront it. And you can't do that on Phaeacia. If you want my opinion, I think your past is waiting for you on Ithaca.'

'The past is in the past, Pontonous. There's nothing for me on that island any more, not since the king died.'

'What about the queen?'

'Penelope? It would be good to see her again,' Eperitus said with a smile, half-remembering something that he did not share with Pontonous. 'Though she'll have remarried by now, if she has any sense. And Penelope always had sense. But you're right about one thing. If the gods have remembered I'm here, then perhaps it's time to leave Phaeacia.'

Three more soldiers entered the room, shouting for wine. The chief steward waved a pair of slave girls over to serve them. Others followed in threes and fours, joining the growing crowd about the hearth. Three maids of princess Nausicaa began to sing while a group of the smallest children danced. Others clapped and one of the meat carvers called for a song. Amid the hubbub, Pontonous made his excuses to Eperitus and went to instruct one of the wine stewards to mix more wine. Before long the room was thick with the babbling of alcohol-loosened voices.

A young man with light, curly hair and effeminate good looks pulled down a tortoiseshell lyre from the wall and tested the strings. A group of women mocked his preparations, taking courage from the wine and accusing him of not knowing which end was which – until he struck the first few notes and the room fell into a hush. As he toyed with a melodious tune on the battered instrument, the carver who had requested a song called to him.

'What will you sing, Ocyalus?'

'What do you want me to sing?' he asked. 'What will the children have?'

A boy, whose father was captain of the guard, demanded the story of Perseus and the gorgon, but Ocyalus apologised and admitted he had not yet learned it all, meaning it was too long and scary for the young ones. Finally he sang the tale of the birth of Aphrodite, which particularly pleased the children and womenfolk.

While he sang, Eperitus felt the last of the seawater leaving his tunic and woollen cloak. The wine moved his thoughts back to the voice on the beach, and he knew that something irreversible had changed in him. There was a quality in that voice that reminded him of Odysseus.

Ocyalus's song had ended and the men were asking for a story from the Trojan War. Eperitus did not hear them. He was lost in the fog of his own thoughts, increasingly convinced that the voice on the beach was a call to wake him from his slumber.

Pontonous sat down beside him and poured some wine into his cup.

'Here, cheer up and have a bit of the good stuff. Just for you and me, you understand,' he added with a wink. 'Straight from the king's own store – not the bull's piss I serve those dull-witted guards.'

Eperitus took a sip and nodded.

'It's good. Though not as good as the wine we were given by Maron, after we raided the land of the Cicones.'

Pontonous waved his hand dismissively.

'Keep your stories for Ocyalus; he might even might make some of them into a song. You can tell me this, though: were you serious about leaving Phaeacia? Do you really think you can hide from the gods?'

'Hide? No, but I can keep running. The dreams, the voice in the wind – *something* is about to happen. I can feel it in the air, like the heaviness before a storm breaks. And I don't want to be here when it does. The gods have brought me nothing but trouble, and if they're calling me, then it's time to get as far away from them as possible. Will the king still honour the Phaeacian promise to all foreigners – to take me wherever I want to go?'

'If that's what you want, then he will. You must ask him when he returns. But where will you go? The outside world is a violent place. Your vow won't be as easy to keep as it has been here.'

'I'll go to the Peloponnese and find my way northwards to Alybas, the place where I was born. A few might remember me there.'

'But will they welcome you?' Pontonous asked. 'Didn't you say your father murdered the king? You may not have supported his cause, but…'

'I'll tell them my father is dead. They will be grateful for the news.'

'And Ithaca? Perhaps the people there are still waiting to hear what happened to their menfolk. Your tidings may not be received with joy, but at least they'll allow them to grieve. And perhaps Penelope hasn't been as sensible as you suggest. Perhaps she still watches the ocean for her husband's return.'

'Perhaps,' Eperitus said. 'But that's not my concern any more.'

'No, you're wrong,' Pontonous said, laying a hand on his friend's shoulder. 'It *is* your concern, all of it: Penelope, Ithaca, the gods. And this thing you're running from. Listen to me. You're one of the few real friends I have here, and I don't want you to leave. But you must, for your own sake. If the gods are calling you back to Ithaca, then go there and face your past. Unless you do, you'll never be free of it. You'll never find the peace you need.'

The hunchback looked him in the eye, then stood and went to find more wine.

'And so they sat in the wooden belly of the great horse,' Ocyalus said, 'each man clutching his bronze-tipped spear and listening to the Trojan revellers celebrating outside. Then, as the warriors waited for night to come and their bloody harvest to begin, they heard voices outside. Helen, beacon to the Greeks and doom-bringer to the Trojans, had come with her maids. Deiphobus was with her, her husband after Paris had been killed. They circled the horse, rapping at its hollow legs and calling up as if they knew what lay inside.

'By now the townsfolk had returned to their homes, or lay asleep by the fires where they had celebrated their apparent victory over the Greeks. And so the warriors could hear the soft voice of Helen, calling their names as if she knew who was inside, mimicking the voices of their wives…'

Eperitus heard Helen as if it was yesterday. He remembered how, with unnatural skill, she had made herself sound like the women many of the waiting warriors had left behind in Greece, making them yearn for their homes.

'Menelaus, on hearing Helen's voice, was determined to fling open the hatch and leap down from the belly of the horse, ready to kill his adulterous wife with a blow from his sword – or embrace her as he had wanted to do for so long. But the wily Odysseus, whose scheme it had been to build the Wooden Horse, held him tight and placed a hand over his mouth...'

That was not true. It had been Eperitus who had stopped Odysseus from crying out when Helen called to him in the voice of Penelope. Of course, Eperitus was used to hearing the inaccuracies, embellishments and outright untruths sung by poets about the events he had witnessed. But tonight he had no appetite for it. He took his wine and removed himself to the back of the room by the ovens. Here the walls were still warm, and with the gentle murmur of the poet's voice in the background, he leant back and closed his eyes, his thoughts drifting to events of long ago.

Chapter Two

The Gods' Decree

Odysseus sat naked on the sand, his arms folded about his knees as he looked out at the horizon. The morning sun glimmered on the sea, so bright it forced him to squint. He felt its heat drying his hair and skin and driving the chill from his flesh. The water had been cold as he had waded out into it. As his feet had reached the edge of the shelf of sand and he had slipped beneath the surface, he had sensed its emptiness below him, waiting for him to stop kicking and slip down into oblivion.

But at the surface, the sea had been full of sunlight, the golden glow of life that bore no resemblance to the pale twilight he remembered from the Underworld. He realised then that his life was not so empty yet that he was ready to join the shades of forgotten humanity in their kingdom below. So he had swum back, hating the weakness in him that could not face death, and loathing even more the joyless existence that the gods had made his lot.

He looked down at the sand on his feet and the footprints that led up from the water's edge. The beach was a wide crescent shape, fringed with trees. It took a whole morning to walk from one horn to the other, and there was not a rock or clump of seaweed to mar its grinning beauty. He gave an ironic laugh as he remembered his first sight of the wide bay, and how he had thought it a paradise. After his galley had been destroyed he had reached Ogygia by chance on a piece of wreckage, pulling himself up on a narrow beach between rocky headlands in the south of the island. It was Calypso who had found him and brought him here, giving him the bay for his very own.

But for all its size and beauty, it was still a prison. And though he had often accused her of keeping him there, his true gaoler was Poseidon, lord of the oceans. Without a ship or a crew to sail it, he was doomed to remain on the island. Indeed, even if he had a ship, he doubted he still had the courage to risk another voyage. When he had left Troy, it had been at the head of a fleet of twelve galleys, crewed by over six hundred men. But the sea had claimed every vessel and every soul but his own. And it was still waiting for him. Patiently. Menacingly.

He sensed a presence and reached for his discarded tunic, slipping it over his head and pulling it down to cover his nakedness. A shadow fell across him and he turned to see Calypso. She wore a grey mantle that shone like silver in the sunlight, and about her waist was a golden belt. Her sandals looked plain on her perfect white feet, and though she wore her hood up against the heat of the sun, Odysseus could see the striking beauty of her immortal face in its shade. But her cheeks were glistening with tears, and the black powder with which she always lined her eyes had smudged and run. Her bottom lip protruded in a pout like a child's, making her look so pathetic that, for a moment, he felt his resentment of her recede.

'What is it?' he asked, rising to his feet.

He had never seen Calypso cry before. Indeed, he thought tears were impossible for any immortal, but as he stood before her she broke down in sobs and fell into his arms, burying her face in his neck.

'What's wrong? Are you hurt?'

'What do you care?' she sniffed. 'You hate me, don't you? You hate me because I love you so much that I have to force myself upon you. Surely my tears are a joy to you!'

'What I hate is being held captive on this island, but I can hardly blame you for that. You're as much a prisoner as I am.'

'But you're *not* a prisoner. Not any more.'

'What do you mean?'

She thumped his shoulder with the flat of her fist.

'I mean you're free to leave Ogygia, you stupid oaf. You're free to leave me.'

He pulled back her hood and looked into her angry blue eyes. The sight of the proud demigod with shining cheeks and trembling lip made him laugh out loud.

She punched him indignantly in the chest and stamped on his foot, screaming at him in her frustration, but it only made him laugh even harder.

'How dare you laugh at me? Do you know what I could do to you if I wanted to?'

'Can it be any worse than what you've already done?' he said, his laughter drying quickly. 'But don't be offended, my lady. I'm not laughing at you, but at what you're saying. Who are you to tell me I'm free to leave? It's

Poseidon who keeps me here, not you. Look out there. I couldn't even reach the horizon without his permission. And he hates me for what I did to his son, Polyphemus the Cyclops, who would have eaten me if I hadn't blinded him. Even if you could summon me up a ship and a crew, how far would I get before he turned those gentle waves into ocean walls? How far before he smashed our wooden decks to kindling and pulled me down to the seabed with a sail for a shroud?'

'You don't understand...'

'*What* don't I understand?' he snapped. 'That even if I could slip past Poseidon unnoticed, I wouldn't fetch up on another gods-forsaken island and become prey to some flesh-eating monster or find myself trapped like a fly in another immortal's web? Or perhaps I don't understand that this is some new trick of yours to make me marry you?'

He was trembling with anger now, a fury he had not felt in a long time. And for a moment he sensed a little of his old self returning. Calypso stepped back, a look of fear on her face. But he had no power to harm her. She was immortal and he was just Odysseus the prisoner, no longer Odysseus the king and favourite of Athena. He unclenched his fists and let his shoulders slump. The moment had passed.

'What are you talking about?' he sighed.

She wiped away a tear.

'Hermes came to me this morning. The instant I saw him in my cavern, I knew something was wrong. He never visits me, so it had to be at the command of Zeus or one of the other Olympians.'

'So, what did he want?'

Her jaw set and her nostrils twitched, as they always did when she was angry.

'He came to tell me the gods have made a decision. You are to be set free. It's time for you to return to your home.'

Odysseus felt his flesh turn to goosebumps. His knees went suddenly weak, as if the bulk of his great torso was too much for them. He reached out and placed a hand on Calypso's shoulder to steady himself. She misread his intention and placed her own hand on his wrist, bending slightly to kiss the heel of his thumb.

'I don't understand. Why would they say that? Why now? I thought they'd forgotten me.'

'All I know is that Zeus himself has decreed your release. You still have advocates on Mount Olympus, Odysseus.'

Athena, he thought. *Athena has forgiven me at last! I've served my penance for taking the Palladium, and now I'm free.*

He looked about himself in disbelief, staring down at his open palms and the shell-smattered sand as if the proof of what Calypso was saying might lie there. He looked at the lush trees, swaying in the breeze, and behind him at the open ocean. And there the surge of euphoria was checked. He saw the white-capped waves breaking up around the headlands and the hazy horizon in the distance; he imagined the great depth of the water beneath and the creatures that filled it, small and large, gentle and lethal; and he remembered the vastness of the sea, the many days sailing that could lie between one landfall and the next, and the dangers of starvation and storm that haunted every passage. And he knew the gods were laughing at him still.

'And how am I to sail back to Ithaca? Did you think about that when Hermes told you to release me? Did he bring a ship and a crew with him, or does Zeus intend to transform himself into a whale and carry me home on his back?'

'You shouldn't mock...'

'Why not? You immortals have mocked me since the day I was born. And besides...' He turned and stared at the ocean for a long moment, before dropping back down to the sand and letting his forehead fall onto his knees. 'Besides not having a ship, I don't think I have the courage any more. There was a time when I was stout and brave, when I had the power of a fleet at my command and the strength of loyal friends around me. In those days, I felt I could do anything, even change the fate the gods had decreed for me. But they've shown me my foolishness, that really I'm *weak*. And now that man has gone. He's gone and what remains can never be free again.'

Calypso knelt beside him and placed an arm around his shoulders.

'Stop grieving, my love. Father Zeus has given me a command and I must obey it, but the choice to leave is still yours. If you can find the courage to take to the waves again, then I will help you, even though my heart is against your going. I can give you tools to make a sturdy raft – there are more than enough trees on Ogygia – and I can supply you with all the provisions you will need for a long journey. I will even send a following wind to start you on your way, though my control of the elements is limited.

'But if wisdom convinces you the sea is too perilous, then you still have another choice.' She laid her hand on his bearded cheek and turned his face to hers. 'Remember my offer to you. You can stay with me – forever –

and become an immortal like myself. I will submit to you as my husband and surrender dominion of Ogygia into your hands. You will be a king again, Odysseus, greater than any mortal ruler; crowned with honour like Heracles, whom the gods made into one of themselves. But so long as Zeus has commanded me to aid your return to Ithaca, the choice to stay has to be yours.'

He looked into her eyes, which had been open to the world almost since it began, and realised the intelligence and power behind them. The power to grant immortality. And yet with the smudges of black powder and the pink flush in her cheeks, she looked like a young girl, vulnerable and naïve, in need of the protection of a man. She was offering herself in place of Penelope, Ogygia in place of Ithaca, and eternal life over the everlasting misery of death. How could he refuse? Though he could barely remember Penelope's face, he knew his wife's looks could not compare to the beauty before him. And what was Ithaca but a windswept rock compared to the golden shores and soaring mountains of Ogygia? As for death – he had been to Hades, and had no wish to return.

'Come back with me to my cavern,' she said, taking his hand. 'I will cook you a meal and you will make your decision.'

He followed her into the trees that hemmed the bay and they took the well-trodden path to her home. They soon found the cliff face with the tall, lopsided arch of the cave entrance dominating it. The scent of the surrounding cypress trees mingled with the smell from the fire within, which made Odysseus's stomach growl at the thought of food. Birds were singing in the treetops, their voices rising above the trickling of the little streams that tumbled down the face of the cliff to form small pools in the meadow below. He stepped over the stones that crossed the marshy grass to the cave's entrance, plucking a bunch of grapes from the overhanging vines as he passed beneath.

The interior was gloomy after the bright sunshine outside, but the glow of the hearth fought the shadows back into the corners of the lofty cavern. At the back was the bed that Odysseus had shared with Calypso many times, and to the right was a large table with a chair at either end. She turned and kissed him briefly on the lips, then indicated one of the chairs.

He sat eating the grapes and watching her as she took a fish from a basket on the table and began gutting it. She moved skilfully about the kitchen, putting the fish over the fire, tossing a handful of flatbreads into a bowl and filling another with fruit, before sliding the elements of the finished meal towards him. He ate slowly, despite his hunger, conscious of her eyes on his every movement. As usual, she ate nothing. Before he finished, she went to a corner of the cave and fetched a bundle wrapped in cloth, which she laid before him. He pulled away the folds of cloth to reveal an axe and an adze.

'You'll need them if you're to make a raft. Assuming you know how.'

He picked up the axe and weighed it in his hands, feeling its keen edge against his thumb.

'I know,' he replied.

But it seemed a very long time since he had handled a tool of any kind, and the axe felt heavier than he remembered. The strength in his arms had faded through lack of use. When he had first arrived on Ogygia, his muscles had been hard and clearly defined, but too much easy food and too little work had made him soft. The thought that he might return to the woods, fell several trees and shape them into something capable of reaching beyond Ogygia's horizons seemed more preposterous than ever. And even if he could, there was still Poseidon to be reckoned with.

He thought of Ithaca and of his family – distant memories now – and of the dream of returning to them that had kept him alive for so long, and he wondered that he had never seen the reality of it. That was the point of Calypso giving him the axe, he supposed – to challenge whether he still had enough fight left in him. And she must have known he would fail.

'Shall I come with you to the forest?' she asked. 'I know where the largest trees are, if you have the strength to fell them *and* drag them to the beach.'

She had shed her mantle to reveal a white chiton of gauzy material, through which the broad circles of her nipples were clearly visible. She stood and walked to his side, leaning her stomach against his arm so that her breast pressed against his shoulder.

'Come, Odysseus, it is time to make your choice. Will you risk the ocean for her, or will you stay with me?'

She took the axe lightly from his hand and threw it onto the table with a clang. Then she leaned over him and pressed her lips to his.

'How does she compare to me, Odysseus?' she whispered. 'Do her looks exceed mine? Will her body excite you as much as mine does?'

'She is mortal and you are immortal. There can be no comparison.'

'But is she worth dying for? Only death awaits you if you leave these shores.'

'Death awaits all men, whether great or small. It's something I share with her that I never could with you, Calypso – a life spent knowing that our fate is to die. It's what makes you and I so different.'

She hid her frown behind a laugh.

'But you *can* share immortality with me, if you choose it. The gift will be freely given.'

He shook his head.

'You can make me live forever, but my mind will still be that of a mortal, conditioned to the expectation of death. Eventually I will tire of living and cry out for the end, driven mad by the prospect of eternity. And I will never learn to think like you gods do. You haven't lived under the shadow of mortality. To you, life is a game that can't hurt you; for us, it is short and brutal. For ten years I was kept away from home, fighting a war that it pleased the gods to inflict on mankind. Then they punished me for another two years, driving me from landfall to landfall, pitting me against one danger after another until it amused them to strand me here. And now they finally remember my existence and decide to release me, as if whatever offences I had caused never meant a thing to them in the first place.'

'It isn't for you to question the gods, Odysseus,' she said, glancing nervously upwards. 'Zeus does nothing without a purpose.'

'Oh? Then how am I to accept his gift of freedom if he hasn't given me a means of escape?' he said, banging his fist on the table. 'Does he even care that his brother won't rest until I've paid for the Cyclops's eye with my life? It seems to me the only freedom I've been offered is to choose between death at the hands of Poseidon and eternity spent in the sweet horror of your bed!'

She slapped him hard across the face.

'You think you know so much, and yet you know nothing! Poseidon is being feasted by the Aethiopes on the far side of the world. That's why Athena petitioned Zeus for your release now: because she knew her uncle wouldn't be back for weeks. So how dare you dismiss the father of the gods as a meddler, or sneer at the goddess of wisdom for "forgetting" your plight all these years? You don't deserve to become one of us!'

Odysseus looked at her through narrowed eyes.

'You knew this all along, but didn't tell me? You let me believe I would die the moment Poseidon saw me set sail, while knowing he was away at the ends of the earth?'

Calypso realised her mistake. She sank down before him and slipped her arms about his knees, resting her head on his thighs.

'Forgive me. I just wanted to save you from a terrible mistake. How could you, a simple mortal, understand what immortality *really* means? I couldn't just let you refuse eternity with me, not knowing what you were doing...'

He pulled her hands away and stood.

'Even if Poseidon was looking down from his throne on Olympus right now, I'd gladly sail to my death rather than stay here with you. You say I don't deserve to become one of you, but it's *you* that doesn't deserve *me*.'

He took the axe and the adze from the table and walked to the cave entrance.

'Don't leave me, Odysseus,' she pleaded. 'Stay and make love to me. Lie here in my arms and think about what you're doing.'

'My mind is made up. I have a wife and a son, and I am going to find my way back to them, or perish in the attempt.'

'I will come to you tonight and *make* you love me,' she shouted.

Odysseus laughed.

'That is not love, Calypso. Indeed, that's one of the great gulfs between mortals and immortals. Love requires self-sacrifice, and mortality is all about being prepared to give everything up. What can you gods know about that?'

He reached the edge of the shadow where the sunlight lay bright on the grass outside, then paused and turned to her.

'How long have I been here? A year?'

'A *year*?' she scoffed. 'Do you really not know? Odysseus, you have been on Ogygia *seven* years.'

He felt his blood run cold. Could he really have spent so much of his life shut away on this island? It seemed impossible, but then he remembered how quickly a year had passed with Circe, where only the position of the constellations had told him and his crew how long they had been there.

He felt his black mood coming back, turning his muscles to lead and stealing the gleam from the sunshine around him. Penelope would have heard of the other kings returning from Troy, and she would have wondered why her husband had not come back also. Then she would have waited, her patient, enduring character refusing to believe he had perished. And in her waiting, she would have been beset by worries, unaware of his fate and unable to grieve without news of his death, until eventually she would have forced herself to accept that he would never return. So, if he did find a way back to Ithaca, it would be destitute and without friends, to a kingdom that had forgotten him, a wife who had remarried and a son who had become a man in his own right.

As the terrible thought ran through his mind, he sensed an echo of something deep and forgotten. Words formed in the fog of his depression, words he had first heard in another cave thirty years before. *If ever you seek Priam's city, the wide waters will swallow you. For the time it takes a baby to become a man, you will know no home. Then, when friends and fortune have departed from you, you will rise again from the dead.*

And so it was that Odysseus recalled the oracle that had been given to him, and saw that the cruel prophecy had almost been fulfilled. For it was twenty years since he had left Ithaca for Troy, and now, alone and broken, the gods had decreed he must return.

Chapter Three

Telemachus Decides

Telemachus stepped onto the portico and rested his spear against the wall by the open doors. The smell of woodsmoke and roast pig floated out from the shadowy hall, mingled with the odour of fresh sweat. A lyre was playing and someone was singing, though the music was drowned beneath the shouting and laughter of many voices. By the light of the blazing hearth and the torches on the walls he could see a large number of men seated at tables or lying on cushions on the floor. They were being served food and wine by several maids.

He lowered his head and lifted the young boar from his shoulders, dropping it gently onto the floor. With a sigh, he turned to his companion, a tall youth with red hair and a face full of freckles.

'Sounds like they're half-drunk already. Don't come in, Peiraeus: they'll only mock you or try to pick a fight.'

'Like they do with you from sunrise to sunset?' Peiraeus said, peering into the gloom. 'Why should you put up with it alone? Let me stay, and we'll endure them together.'

Telemachus shook his head.

'I'm the master of this house and I won't have my guests abused. And I want you to take our boar with you to your uncle's house.'

'You killed it…' Peiraeus protested, but Telemachus held up his hand.

'We stalked it together. Besides, I'd rather you and your family enjoy its meat than let it be wasted on my mother's suitors. The moment I crossed the threshold, they'd be pulling it from my shoulders and chopping it up for their own plates.'

'You're right, of course,' Peiraeus agreed, laying his own spear against the wall temporarily while he picked up the boar and slung it over his shoulders. 'Bastards! I'm just looking forward to the day when Zeus takes his retribution on them. And the day's coming, my friend. You'll see.'

'We'll see,' Telemachus said, with a sceptical smile. 'Perhaps I'll come over to your uncle's house later and have a slice or two of our prize. What d'you say?'

'I say watch yourself among that lot. I know it's your home, whatever your mother chooses to do, but you can't fight them over everything they say and do. You're too proud, and they know it. That's why they keep provoking you.'

Peiraeus took Telemachus's chin in his fingers and tipped his head back, looking at the bruise on his left cheek. 'It's fading to yellow now, and the cuts on your knuckles are healing well. No need to reopen them, eh?'

'I'll do my best,' Telemachus said, slapping his friend on the shoulder. 'Now take your spear and go home.'

Peiraeus glanced again into the shadows and caught the eye of Melantho, one of Telemachus's maids. She gave him a smile, then returned to her duties.

'Watch that one,' Telemachus warned him. 'Her morals don't match her looks.'

'Worry about yourself and those suitors,' Peiraeus said with a wink, before heading back out of the courtyard.

Telemachus's eyes adjusted quickly to the darkness as he stepped into the great hall. The muralled walls were as they had been since he was a child: warlike scenes of the Olympians defeating the giants and the Titans, and of the fight between the lapiths and the centaurs. But it was the mural on the east wall that drew his attention. It depicted the battle to liberate Ithaca from the usurper, Eupeithes, and his army of Taphian mercenaries. Telemachus paused to look at the figure of his father, Odysseus, an oversized warrior at the centre of the fight, and wondered – as he did every time he looked at it – whether Ithaca's king would ever come back again to free his homeland from the new tyranny it had fallen under.

'Ah, our lord and master has returned!' Antinous's loud and arrogant tones rose above the clamour that filled the hall. 'My friends, stop your troughing and show some respect. Leocritus, get your lazy arse out of that chair and make way for our mighty host and soon-to-be stepson.'

Howls of laughter filled the hall and Telemachus turned tight-lipped to stare at the rabble of nobles that lounged around the burning hearth. Antinous sat on Odysseus's throne, his legs hooked over one arm while Melantho refilled his cup with wine. His broad chest and muscular arms bore no resemblance to the slack-shouldered, pot-bellied physique of Eupeithes, his ageing father, but his pale eyes, high forehead and beaked nose distinguished him as the old traitor's son. He waved his hand at Leocritus, a slightly overweight youth sitting on Penelope's throne, who sprang out of the chair and rolled onto the floor, waving his arms and legs in the air.

'Forgive me, Lord Telemachus,' he squealed, to guffaws of laughter. 'I didn't recognise your great and bushy beard as you entered.'

Telemachus put a hand self-consciously to the downy hairs on his chin, hating the tear-filled eyes and pointing fingers of the suitors as they wallowed in drunken amusement. A few months short of twenty-one – so nearly a man – and he *still* could not grow a beard. Burning with shame, he walked through the crowd of thirty or forty suitors – barely a third of those who were hoping to marry his mother – to the back of the hall. A few pieces of half-eaten bread and meat were flung after him, but he calmed his temper and found a seat next to Phemius. The bard stroked his fingers across his tortoiseshell lyre and began a new tune.

'Don't let them provoke you, my lord,' he muttered. 'See, they're already forgetting about you and returning to their food.'

'Now they've had their sport,' Telemachus replied. 'Gods, I wish I could be a bard instead of a prince.'

'Doesn't everybody?' Phemius replied with a wink.

'Something to drink, my lord?' asked a maid, who without waiting for an answer handed him a silver cup and filled it. 'It's one of your father's best wines. Antinous chose it himself from the storerooms.'

'It's wasted on them, but what can I do?' Telemachus said. 'Shouldn't you be attending my mother, Autonoe?'

'She's asleep, so I thought I'd come and help down here. The maids are hard-pressed with so many guests in the palace. And I've had some of the best wine moved to one of the grain rooms. They'll never look for it there.'

'You're a clever woman. I hope my mother appreciates you.'

'She does,' Autonoe replied with a smile, moving away to answer the shout of one of the suitors.

Telemachus watched her go. She was plain to look at, but she was cheerful, intelligent and loyal – a quality that was becoming less common among the palace slaves. She also liked her master, if only because they shared a willingness to stand up to the men who had invaded their home. Some were determined to marry Penelope, but most were hangers-on. The latter expected Antinous to claim the queen's hand – and Odysseus's crown along with it – but did not care so long as they could attend the nightly banquets and eat and drink at another man's expense.

The feasts had started three years ago, after the Kerosia – the council of elders – invited a few noble families to present their sons as suitors to Penelope, whose husband had still not returned from the war against Troy. Seven years before the invitation, she had promised to remarry if Odysseus had not returned within a time foreseen by the oracle at Mount Parnassus. A delegation was sent to speak with the Pythoness, reaching her cave on Apollo's feast day. There they were told that the king would return to Ithaca within ten years. The invitation to the first suitors had been Eupeithes's idea, hoping to pressure Ithaca's queen into choosing a new king since she showed no intention of giving up on Odysseus's return before the predicted date.

And so the handful of suitors came back week after week, then day after day as their numbers increased and they became a force none of the Ithacan elders dared oppose, until now more than a hundred of them occupied the palace. It was bad enough for Telemachus that his mother's oath had denied him the chance to inherit his father's kingship by right. But the palace and all the wealth that Odysseus had accumulated would still come to Telemachus when he became a man, so to see his inheritance consumed so voraciously for three years had been a bitter twist of the knife.

His only consolation, if it could be called that, was that Apollo's feast day was now only three weeks away. After that, the ten years stated by the Pythoness would have expired and Penelope would have to remarry. The successful suitor would take her back to his own house and the rest would have to leave the palace in peace. But the thought brought Telemachus no joy. Indeed, his father would be officially considered dead, his mother would have betrayed their marriage bed, and his beloved homeland would fall under the rule of one of the vile beasts before him.

He stared at them with contempt as they ate his food and drank his wine, despising the fact that one of them might soon be king. His mother had explained to him many times as a child why she had sworn to remarry and give away his birthright – the throne – before he came of age. To prevent civil war and buy time for his father to return, she had said. To let the more treacherous nobles like Eupeithes believe their sons could become king without first having to assassinate Telemachus. To keep her only son safe.

But he had been safe in Sparta, where she had sent him after Eupeithes had first made his ambitions clear. She could have left him there instead of gambling his right to the throne on the cacklings of some old hag on Mount Parnassus. And that was what he had come to resent: that she had sold his inheritance so that she could have him by her side. She did not even realise it herself, believing everything had been done for his protection. He did not expect her to see the truth behind her motivations. She pretended to be a strong queen, but she had all the weaknesses of a mother.

He watched as one of the suitors lifted his cup for Autonoe to refill. As she poured the wine into his cup, another man thrust his hand up her dress. She let out a yelp of surprise, then, grabbing the cup from the first suitor's hand, turned and threw the contents in her assailant's face. He leapt to his feet and slapped her hard. She fell to the floor with a scream, almost rolling into the hearth. The man leapt after her and pulled her to her feet, raising his hand to hit her again. But the maid struck first, scoring her fingernails across his cheek. He gave a shout and released her, clutching at his wound. She turned and ran, only for Antinous to block her escape.

'I've got the bitch, Elatus,' he yelled, seizing her arm. 'Now, teach her a lesson.'

Elatus removed his hand from his cheek and looked in mute rage at the blood on his palm.

'If this were my father's house, you'd hang,' he hissed, slipping off his belt and playing out a length between his fingers. 'Turn her round and tear open her dress!'

The suitors' laughter fell away and was replaced by ugly grunts of encouragement. Two men held Autonoe's arms while Antinous tore open her dress, exposing her back and breasts. Elatus gave a sneer of anticipation and drew back his hand, but before the first stroke fell, the makeshift whip was yanked out of his hand.

'But this *isn't* your father's house,' Telemachus said, throwing the belt into the fire. 'This is *my* father's house, and if anyone is going to strike his servants, it will be me. Autonoe, go up to the female quarters and change your clothes.'

Such was the authority in his young voice that the men holding her released her at once.

'No, my lord,' she said, covering her breasts with her arm. 'This isn't worth your trouble. You know what they'll do to you.'

'Go now,' he commanded and, with a last look of regret, she left the hall. 'You too, Elatus. Leave the palace and go back home. I won't tolerate guests who mistreat my maids.'

He stared at Elatus, who had ten years on him and was both taller and heavier. The suitors closed round him, their shocked expressions turning to anger. Though he was lord of his father's house, he had no power to enforce Odysseus's rules. The true master here was brute strength, as Telemachus had found out many times before.

'I've given your mother more than enough gifts to stake my claim on her,' Elatus said in his slow, gravelly voice. 'So I'm staying. If you want me to leave, you'll have to make me.'

'Form a circle, lads,' said Eurymachus, the largest of all the suitors. 'You know the routine. The little lord wants to play at being daddy again, so we need to remind him he's not a man yet.'

The suitors backed away to form a ring, while Elatus and Telemachus bent their knees and raised their fists.

'I'll kill you this time, you little...'

Before Elatus could finish, Telemachus moved in and swung his fist up into his jaw, throwing his head up with clack of teeth. He stumbled backwards, spitting blood, and was caught by two of his comrades. They shoved him back into the ring, which was suddenly alive with shouts of support and advice. Elatus gave a shake of his head and, with a menacing smile, raised his fists again.

He advanced quickly and lashed out with an awkward right hook, which Telemachus deflected, followed by a straight left. The blow caught Telemachus above his right eye and sent him reeling back, to the cheers of the suitors. Several hands caught hold of him and hurled him straight back at Elatus, who launched his right fist at the youth's head. Telemachus sensed the blow and ducked beneath it.

Through the clamour of voices, he heard Mentor's advice at the back of his mind. *Don't let your anger take control. Use it.* Staying low, he dashed forwards and rammed his head into Elatus's broad chest. He gave a grunt of pain and crashed back into the wall of suitors, who swayed back beneath his weight.

'Stop fooling around, Elatus,' one of them said. 'He's just a boy. Keep your guard up and go for the body.'

'Just a boy is he, Ctessipus?' Elatus growled, wiping the sweat from his eyes and standing up. 'I remember he taught *you* a thing or two last month, so keep your advice to yourself. I can handle him.'

He moved forwards, and Telemachus advanced to meet him. Given the space, he would have worn the bigger man out before knocking him down. But the suitors had become used to that tactic, so they kept the ring tight, forcing him to slug it out with Elatus. But a close-quarter fight with someone of Elatus's size could only end one way. His best hope was to hit him hard and fast. Closing quickly, he threw a double punch, but neither blow penetrated Elatus's guard. The suitor followed with a blow that caught him painfully on the shoulder, throwing him off balance. A second passed just over his head, leaving Elatus's guard open. Telemachus lashed out clumsily, but his opponent had the measure of him now and easily turned the blow aside.

'You've been a thorn in our flesh for too long, boy,' Elatus said. 'Now I'm going to knock your spirit right down into Hades, and claim your mother *and* this palace of yours for myself.'

He signalled for the men behind Telemachus to move back. Seeing the intent in his eyes, they shuffled away to form a corridor that ended at the hearth. Telemachus glanced behind himself at the blazing fire and, in that moment, Elatus attacked.

Sensing his mistake, Telemachus turned to see the suitor's fist filling his vision. The rank of knuckles thudded into his cheek and eye, and sent him crashing to the dirt floor. The pain was immense and his senses reeled; his ears rang and the faces of the suitors and the roof above seemed to tumble together, as if they were crashing in upon him. He felt more than heard the dull thud of Elatus's foot landing on the earth beside him, followed by a second explosion of pain as his other foot crashed into the side of his head.

The force of it rolled him over. He felt the dirt sticking to his sweat-soaked skin, tasted the coppery blood in his mouth and nostrils. The corners of his sight went black and he felt a sudden panic that he would succumb to unconsciousness. He tried to push himself up on all fours, but a second kick caught him in the ribs and turned him onto his back.

His right arm flopped out at full stretch and he could feel the hot ashes that had fallen from the fire under the back of his hand. The heat from the flames was close, and as he caught the blurred outline of Elatus bending down towards him, he knew the suitor's next act would be to throw him alive onto the fire. Fear gave speed and sudden clarity to his thoughts. He clutched at a handful of the ashes and threw them into his attacker's face.

Elatus gave a cry and staggered backwards, clutching at his eyes. Fighting the pain that wracked his body, Telemachus forced himself to his feet and swung a badly aimed punch. It caught Elatus on his raised forearm. Blinded though he was, he gave a bellow of rage and thrust both hands before him, finding Telemachus's tunic. The fingers squeezed hold of the wool and Elatus gave a victorious roar, lifting the youth from his feet and lurching with him towards the hearth. Telemachus's blurred vision cleared and he sensed the intense heat of the flames behind him. Quickly he locked his fingers around Elatus's throat, but he might as well have been strangling a bull.

Suddenly, a figure tore through the ring of cheering suitors and crashed into Elatus's side, bringing both him and Telemachus to the floor.

'What in Zeus's name do you think you're doing?'

Telemachus pulled himself away from the tangle of bodies and looked at the man who had saved him from the fire. His hair and beard were fair, and he had the looks of a god, though he was shorter and older than most of the suitors. At the same moment, Antinous pushed his way through the crowd of onlookers and pulled the man from Elatus.

'Zeus's beard, Amphinomus! Whose side are you on, ours or the boy's?'

'He's not a boy any more,' Amphinomus said, pushing Antinous away. 'And you should be thanking me, all of you. I can't believe you'd stand by and let Elatus throw him in the fire...'

'It was a fair fight,' Elatus protested, still rubbing the ash from his eyes. 'He'd have got what's been coming to him for years, if you hadn't interfered.'

'You'd have killed him, you idiot,' Amphinomus exclaimed. 'And that would have been the end of any of our hopes of marrying his mother. She'd have demanded justice and retribution from the Kerosia, and there isn't a man on Ithaca who wouldn't have been ready to throw us out of the palace – if they didn't hang us all for murder first.'

'I doubt that,' Antinous told him. 'A mob of farmers and old men against a hundred and eight of the best nobles in the kingdom – not to mention our servants. But you're right, of course. Telemachus knows how to provoke a fight, and it's hard for his elders and betters not to let our tempers run away with us. Come on Elatus, you've taught the young pretender a lesson. Now, shake hands the pair of you, and we'll go outside and play at dice. A shadowy hall on a summer's day depresses the spirits. Melantho! Bring some wine and tables into the courtyard.'

Elatus offered his hand to Telemachus, though the look on his face was less than friendly. Telemachus took it reluctantly, burning inside at Antinous's declaration that Elatus had won the fight. Elatus made an attempt to crush his hand, then released him and spat in the dirt. The crowd of suitors made a noisy exit, followed by servants carrying furs, tables and kraters of wine. Only Amphinomus remained, and a figure in the shadows whom Telemachus guessed was Autonoe.

'You must learn to stop rising to their bait,' Amphinomus told him, 'or they *will* kill you. What would have happened if I hadn't arrived when I did?'

'I'd have been put out of my misery,' Telemachus sulked.

'And your mother? Hasn't she enough to be unhappy about with all these men in her home?'

'I doubt she cares what happens to me.'

Amphinomus shook his head.

'Well *I* care. I'm going to be your future stepfather – mark my words – so take my advice and accept the world as it is. Now, clean yourself up and come and join us. You're still master of the house, after all, and we *are* your guests.'

He smiled and slapped Telemachus on the arm, making him wince, then strode out to join the others, who had already resumed their usual clamour. Autonoe came over and began dabbing at Telemachus's wounds with a bowl of water and a damp cloth. She had replaced her torn dress with another equally drab garment.

'He's right, my lord,' she said. 'It's dangerous to keep fighting them. And look, that old cut under your eye has opened up again. Your knuckles are bleeding, too.'

'Not to mention three or four cracked ribs and enough bruises coming through to make me look like an Aethiope.'

'But a skin that's whole and not crackling over those flames like a hog. You were lucky they didn't kill you. But if you carry on like this, they will.'

'It won't be for much longer. Mother will remarry on Apollo's feast day and then she'll go to live in happiness with her new husband, and we'll have peace again.'

'You judge her too harshly, my lord,' Autonoe said, glancing up as she dabbed at the blood on his knuckles. 'How could she be happy with one of these animals, remembering the husband she used to have? Not to mention being parted from her only son.'

Telemachus chose not to reply. He sat in silence while Autonoe washed away the dirt and blood from his body and rubbed one of Eurycleia's ointments into his wounds. She was right, of course. Even if he felt betrayed by his mother's promise to remarry, it was too harsh of him to wish one of the suitors on her. He could never have peace, though, knowing Antinous or one of the others had taken his place as king. But what could he do? Fist fights with the suitors would only get him killed, just as Amphinomus had warned.

Autonoe finished rubbing the ointment into the cut under his eye. She draped the cloth over her shoulder and picked up the bowl of water, but as she turned to leave he reached out and took her hand.

'What would you do, Autonoe? In my situation, what would you do?'

'I'm just a slave, my lord. If you want advice you should ask Mentor or maybe Halitherses...'

'But I want your advice. You have a clear mind and a strong will. More than that, you have the sort of wisdom only a good heart can give. If you were me, what would you do?'

She hesitated, then placed the bowl and cloth on the floor and sat on a footstool. After a long look at the suitors in the courtyard, she turned to her master.

'I couldn't kill them all, and I don't have friends powerful or numerous enough to help me. And I can't make the queen go back on her oath. So where does my hope lie? In the gods, as always, and in the return of the king. I would find a ship and sail to the mainland. Someone there will know what has happened to Odysseus, one of the noble lords who fought alongside him at Troy, perhaps...'

'Nestor,' Telemachus said. 'King Nestor's palace is only a day's voyage away. They say he was the wisest of all the Greeks at Troy...'

'Then go to him,' Autonoe said, closing his hand in hers. 'There's still time to find news of your father. And if you hear he's still alive, come back at once and tell your mother and the elders. They'll be forced to stop the wedding and wait for his return.'

'But my mother's oath...'

'Will be meaningless if her true husband is still alive.'

The thought excited him, but his doubts pulled him back. He looked once more at the unruly mob in the courtyard, hating them and at the same time fearing them. It seemed impossible that they could be stopped in their ambitions. Indeed, the easiest thing would be to endure another three weeks of their presence and wait for the wedding that would rob him of his mother, his right to become king, and what little remained of his self-respect.

'And if I learn my father's bones are rotting at the bottom of the sea or on some forgotten island? What then?'

'Then you will have tried.'

There were shouts from the courtyard where more suitors were arriving. Antinous and the others left their games, and with loud voices and raucous laughter led the newcomers into the great hall. Within moments the place was filled with sixty or seventy suitors and half as many slaves answering calls for food and drink. The walls echoed with snatches of songs, the shrieks of maids and cries for more wine. The racket quietened for a while as the first of the food arrived but revived again as Phemius was called on to play a tune. He struck up a popular melody and the suitors began to sing along. A dozen jumped to their feet and danced together in the space between the rows of tables. A few of the slave girls joined in, some more willingly than others.

Telemachus watched them with disdain and knew that Autonoe shared his feelings.

'You'd better go attend to my mother,' he said. 'It's not wise for you to be around the suitors in their current mood.'

'Don't forget the oracle, my lord,' Autonoe said as she stood. 'The gods do not lie: your father *will* return. Perhaps it's your task to go find him.'

She bowed and left, leaving him to ponder her words. To find a ship and a crew without the suitors knowing about it would be difficult, but to come back with news his father was still alive was beyond any expectation. And yet he deplored the feeling of helplessness as he sat in the great hall day after day watching the suitors consume his inheritance. The inertia alone was destroying his soul. He had to get away from Ithaca and pursue the hope – however forlorn – that his father was still alive. And the more he watched the suitors, the greater his enthusiasm to leave became.

He called over to Phemius, who had just finished his song, and told him to sing about the end of the war and the return of the kings. The request was met with catcalls and boos from the suitors, forcing Phemius to look to Antinous, who was seated once more in Odysseus's throne. Antinous thought for a moment, then smiled and nodded at the bard.

'Yes, Phemius, do as young Telemachus asks. The boy's missing his father and wants encouragement that he's coming back. Isn't that so, Telemachus? So, sing to us of Agamemnon, that tragic man, and how he returned home to find a treacherous wife and her lover waiting for him.'

Phemius gave an apologetic glance at Telemachus and began to sing. His skill was such that even the suitors forgot their revelry and fell silent, listening to the soft voice as it told of the king of Mycenae returning with his doomed lover, Cassandra, to the palace he had not seen for ten years. It was a long song, but as it approached its climax, with Agamemnon in his bath and Clytaemnestra, his spurned wife, approaching with her axe, the side door opened and a woman entered, followed by Autonoe and another maid. She wore a veil over her face, though it hid little of her tragic beauty.

'Stop this song, Phemius,' Penelope commanded. 'Stop it at once.'

Chapter Four

Penelope

Penelope was woken by a hand on her shoulder. She opened her eyes to see the bright light of morning streaming in through the white drapes, which moved gently in the breeze blowing up from the sea. Birdsong was coming from the trees beyond her window and there were voices deep within the palace.

She had been dreaming that she was at sea on a large, well-built raft. There was an island on the horizon with tall, purple mountains capped with snow. The shores were dense with trees and she knew she had to reach its yellow beaches. But she did not know how to angle the sail or steer the rudder, and watched helplessly as the island slipped farther and farther away. Waking up gave her no relief. Remembering where she was only brought a flock of dark thoughts crowding down upon her, like vultures that had been waiting eagerly for her to open her eyes. She felt the tears welling up inside her.

'My lady, it's time to wake and get dressed. The sun's halfway to noon already.'

Autonoe was sitting on the bed beside her, smiling. Hippodameia, her other maid, stood behind her with a hairbrush in her hand and a look of concern on her face.

'Why, Autonoe? Why should I show myself before those apes? Why tolerate it any longer?'

'Because one of them will be your husband in less than a month, my lady.'

'Thank you, Hippodameia, for reminding me of my own stupidity. Why don't you go and prepare a bath?'

'Yes, my lady.'

Penelope turned on her pillow so that she was facing the white ceiling, then closed her eyes. She remembered now. Odysseus had been on the island, that was why she had had to get there. But she had failed to find him. It was strange that in all her dreams she never saw his face. Sometimes she would see a distant figure, under the eaves of a wood, on the deck of a far-off galley, or in the shadows of the great hall – always beyond the reach of her memory. For she had forgotten what he looked like.

Autonoe stroked her hair, letting her fingertips run across her scalp in a way that soothed her thoughts.

'What are you thinking, my lady?'

'Whether I would still love him, if he ever came back.'

'Of *course* you would. You love Odysseus as much as any woman has ever loved a man. Even I can see that. He's your first thought every morning, and your last at night – and has been every day for twenty years.'

'I wonder,' Penelope sighed. 'Is that love, or is it habit? Desperation, perhaps. Or just the desire to be saved from these cursed suitors? But if he came back now, today, how would I feel? Everything inside me seems so dead. It's as if my flesh has turned to wood, or stone. Oh, Autonoe...'

She sat up and the tears came at last. The maid put her arms about her in a motherly embrace, wordless and comforting. What would Odysseus see in her if he did return, she asked herself? An old, forgotten love? A woman he hardly recognised or knew, separated by twenty years of war and adventure? Surely other women would have laid claim to his heart in that time. Was that not the reason for his absence: that his great and passionate heart had been won by another? Or perhaps her anguish was wasted because he was already dead, killed by one of the assassins Eupeithes had planted among the Ithacan army. Or were his bones lying at the bottom of the ocean, jumbled up with those of his crewmates? So what did it matter whether she loved him or he loved her any more? He was never coming back.

She wiped the tears from her eyes.

'Let's go down to them now,' she said.

'The suitors? But your bath...'

'I'll feel more like a bath *after* seeing them. Just do something with my hair, Autonoe, and Hippodameia can put on some face powders. Then I won't need to show myself to them again until the evening feast.'

Music had hushed the noisy conversation in the hall by the time she descended the steps from the women's quarters, and the only voice that could be heard was that of Phemius. She paused to lift the veil across her face, as was her custom in the presence of the suitors, and heard the name of

Clytaemnestra rise up in threatening tones. Running forwards, she pressed her ear to the door of the great hall.

The bard was describing how Clytaemnestra, having helped her lover, Aegisthus, murder Agamemnon's companions at the homecoming feast, was now approaching her husband as he lay in the bath she had prepared for him. The axe was in her hand, rising slowly with each silent, barefooted step. Penelope could almost hear the trickle of overrunning bathwater and the bated breaths of the notorious murderess. Then, as the curtains were torn aside and the axe was held high over Agamemnon's head, she grappled with the door handle and pushed it open.

'Stop this song, Phemius. Stop it at once.'

The axe that hung in their imaginations dropped with a discordant note, and the bard fell silent.

'Why do you have to sing such a tale?' she asked, sparing a glance for the suitors as they lounged on their chairs or lay on furs. 'It's hideous. Aren't there happier songs for a bright morning?'

'What would you have then, Penelope?' Antinous asked. 'A love song? What better way to remind us that we will be married in three short weeks.'

The suitors laughed and shared a few remarks among themselves, which Penelope had no doubt were crude and at her expense. The leering looks on many of their faces spoke of what was in their minds. She suppressed a shudder and wondered how she would ever be able to betroth herself to one of them. Again she cursed herself for having made that rash promise so long ago, believing she was buying time for herself and Telemachus while Odysseus found his way home. But now he was either dead or in the arms of another woman, and in a few days she would be compelled to take one of the vile suitors into her bed.

She wondered briefly whether it was any worse than Odysseus returning and her being forced to sleep with a man she had fallen out of love with, or who had fallen out of love with her. She swept the thought aside, not wanting to let it settle and put down roots. No, if Odysseus returned, they would learn to rebuild their marriage and love each other again. Had not Menelaus and Helen re-established their relationship, despite everything that had passed between them?

'Any song is better than that one, Phemius,' she said. 'You know it upsets me to hear of the war and the kings who failed to find the homecoming they'd longed for. It reminds me of the husband I lost, a man without equal.'

'Let him finish his song, Mother,' Telemachus said, stepping out from the shadows at the back of the hall. 'If some of the Greeks met a tragic end, then how is that Phemius's fault? Surely we should blame the gods, who decide every twist and turn of a man's fate. Besides, I like to hear about powerful women who follow their heart. Not forgetting,' he added, looking at Antinous, 'the son who avenged his wronged father.'

'Stop flexing muscles you don't have, Telemachus,' Eurymachus sneered, his voice rising above the sudden uproar of protests from the suitors. 'You're no Orestes. If you can't beat Elatus in a fight, how do you expect to oppose the rest of us?'

Penelope looked across at her son and felt her misery deepen. He was tall like herself, well-built, and possessed his father's looks and voice. But he was young and naïve, and despite his hot temper he lacked the confidence and self-control to master his circumstances. It would have been so different if he had grown up knowing Odysseus. Though Mentor had taught him to fight, handle weapons, debate and speak in the Assembly – and all the other things a young nobleman should know – it could never replace having the authority and protection of a loving father.

Instead, he had become used to being mocked daily in his own home by men who were neither his friends nor his guests, and who held the advantage of age and numbers. But the fault was not Odysseus's, who had simply honoured the oaths he had taken. It was hers. She had crushed his spirit when she had gambled away his right to become king. The decision to marry before Telemachus came of age had been forced on her for his protection, because Eupeithes would have contrived to kill her son if there was any chance he could inherit the throne. She had had no other choice. But she hated herself for her weakness. A weakness that she still felt every day when she presented herself before the suitors who had invaded her husband's home. A weakness for which she sensed her own son also hated her. And his resentment was perhaps the most unbearable of all her woes.

Eurymachus's mockery had roused the suitors to jeers and laughter, with some even throwing scraps of bread at Telemachus. But there was a defiance in his eyes as he raised his head and walked towards his mother. He took her by the hands and kissed her briefly on the cheek.

'Father is still alive,' he whispered. 'I know he is.'

Penelope shook her head.

'We must stop holding on to such hopes. The oracle was wrong – he isn't coming home.'

'What if I can find proof that he lives? You wouldn't have to honour your oath then, would you? You wouldn't remarry if you thought he might come back.'

'And what if your father lives but has decided he doesn't *want* to come back? Have you ever thought he might be happy in the arms of another woman? That he might even have a new family to replace us? No, Telemachus, I am bound by my oath to remarry unless Odysseus returns within the next three weeks.'

'You wouldn't marry one of these oafs if I could prove to you Odysseus lived,' he snapped. 'You wouldn't dare!'

'*You wouldn't dare*,' Antinous mimicked. 'It's about time you grew up and accepted your father's dead and your mother's going to choose one of us to take his place.'

'In her bed!' shouted Eurymachus, to the laughter and taunts of the others.

'You can't change the will of the gods, boy,' Antinous added.

'The will of the gods?' Telemachus retorted. 'What would you and your pack of thieving friends know about the will of the gods? You help yourself to my father's food and wine, never thinking to repay us or bring your own livestock to the palace. You're just as liberal with his slaves, apart from the few who've still got enough pride and loyalty to resist your demands. You're an affront to the gods, all of you!'

'Telemachus,' Penelope said, laying a hand on his arm.

'No, Mother. Why do you tolerate their presence? This is your husband's house; you still have the authority to throw them out, don't you? Tell them to go back to their own estates, until Father returns or the day comes when you're forced to choose one of them.'

'Throw us out?' Antinous said with a laugh. He stepped up to Telemachus and stared him in the eye. 'The Kerosia invited us here. They're concerned this kingdom doesn't have a king, and so they want your mother to choose a new husband. Someone to make Ithaca strong again.'

'*They*?' Telemachus said. 'You mean Eupeithes! And what moral right does the Kerosia have to order that my father's house be devoured by locusts?'

'Moral right, he says. We have *every* moral right to be here. Your mother has been playing us along for three years, promising herself to each of us in secret and encouraging us in our ardour to give her gift after gift. Perhaps she thinks she's being clever, stringing us along, or wants to enhance her reputation for having a shrewd mind. Didn't she promise to choose one of us once she'd finished her father-in-law's shroud?' he asked the rest of the suitors. 'Spending her days at the loom, letting us believe she was creating a masterpiece worthy of the old crone, only to unpick each day's work again at night. It was almost three years before we learned what she was really doing.'

He glanced at Melantho, who dropped her gaze to the floor and tried to hide her smile.

'I tell you now, Telemachus, we will only leave if your mother chooses her husband now. What do you say, Penelope? Will you pick one of us to be your groom right this moment, if only to save a little of your son's fast-dwindling inheritance?'

Penelope looked at Antinous with loathing. She wished she had the courage of Clytaemnestra, who had murdered her despised husband and all his entourage with him. Could she not poison the suitors? Did she have the audacity and wickedness to create a name for herself that would outdo even the infamy of Clytaemnestra? She shared the same blood as Helen and Clytaemnestra – it was only right that she should take her place alongside her notorious cousins.

She looked at Antinous's arrogant, mocking face and imagined him thrusting into her on their wedding night, his wine-soaked breath rasping in her face and his sweaty hands pawing at her naked flesh. The thought was enough to make her want to snatch a knife from one of the tables and stick it in his chest. But killing him and his vile friends was as dangerous as leaving them alive. Their families would seek vengeance on her and Telemachus, and all she had fought so long to preserve would be destroyed.

'I will not choose between you until I have to,' she said. 'My decision will be made on the morning of Apollo's feast day, by which time my husband will have returned.'

The suitors laughed at her pathetic bravado. She turned away, wanting to give a last glance at her son but knowing she could not face him. Autonoe opened the door and Penelope walked out of the great hall with her head held high, until she heard the click of the handle shutting behind her. At once, she tore off her veil and ran up the stairs to her room, where she knelt by her bed and sank her face into her pillow. Moments later she felt Autonoe's hands on her shoulders and heard her ask Hippodameia to fetch a drink. But there was no other comfort her maids could offer her.

She thought again of Odysseus. Whether or not there would be any rekindling of their former love, she wished he would come back with his fleet behind him. Then the suitors would taste the justice of the gods! But she knew in her heart that would never happen. She had always known she would feel it in her blood if he was coming back, but she felt nothing. No, this was her own mess and nobody was going to save her from it. She was the one who had to sort it out, or live with the consequences.

There was, of course, one option. It had stalked her like a phantom ever since she had taken her rash oath to remarry, haunting her nightmares and mocking her hopes. But it did not rely on Odysseus returning. It was a solution she could bring about without the help of anyone else. It would save her from marrying any of the suitors, and it would mean Telemachus becoming king of Ithaca. But did she have the courage for it?

She pushed herself up from her pillow.

'No, I will not. I can't.'

'My lady?'

She looked up to see Hippodameia standing beside her with a cup of wine in her hand. Autonoe took it from her and raised it to Penelope's lips.

'Here, drink this. It'll make you feel better.'

-

'What's your name then?'

'Theoclymenus,' Eperitus answered.

'From where?'

'Alybas. It's in the north.'

'Never heard of it,' the chief steward said, craning his neck to count the sacks on the back of the wagon. 'Some dreary hovel in the middle of nowhere, is it?'

'Something like that.'

A fine drizzle was beginning to fall from the pale-clouded skies, and in the courtyard where they stood the slaves and guards were moving away to find shelter. It was a week since the Phaeacian ship had brought Eperitus to the Peloponnese and it had taken him all that time to find his way to Pylos. He had tried for work in other towns, but things had changed in Greece since he had left twenty years ago, and none seemed willing to trust a stranger.

'Here, give me a hand with this.'

Eperitus reached up and took hold of the top corners of the sack the man was indicating, lifting it down from the cart without help. The chief steward gave him a sizing look, then opened the sack and peered inside.

'Here,' he said, fishing out a green apple. 'How's that taste to you?'

Eperitus took a large bite. The flesh was crunchy and the juice sweet, his senses savouring every drop.

'Good,' he answered. 'But farmers always put the best ones at the top. It's what's at the bottom you want to worry about.'

'No need to tell me my job,' the chief steward said. 'Good or bad would have done. So, you were a steward in the king's palace there, were you? Well, we don't need stewards here.'

'All I'm asking for is my food and a place to sleep. I've no family to look after.'

The chief steward reached out and felt Eperitus's upper arm with his thumb and forefinger.

'You've muscles like an ox, man. I can get you a job in the guard easy enough.'

Eperitus shook his head. 'I'm not a soldier.'

'But you were. Any fool can see that.'

'Not any more.'

The chief steward lifted himself onto the back of the wagon and opened a few of the other bags. Eperitus finished the apple. It was the first food he had eaten since the provisions the Phaeacians had left him with had run out the evening before.

'Here, have another,' the chief steward said, tossing him a second. 'I can tell you're famished. So, did you fight in the war? I can always find work for an old soldier. The king's holding a big sacrifice in a couple of days and I might need a few extra hands for the feast afterwards. Do well and you can stay on.'

'I was at Troy from the start,' Eperitus answered, biting into the apple. 'And you?'

The chief steward nodded and pointed to the pink scar running across his forearm.

'The Aethiope who gave me this didn't get a second chance. My armour kept me from too much other damage. What about you? Who were you with?'

'I fought for Diomedes.'

'You're no Argive,' the chief steward said, pausing to look at him. 'And your face is familiar, now that I think about it. I don't recall anyone called Theoclymenus, but weren't you with... let me think... Odysseus! That's it, you were with Odysseus.'

Eperitus did not reply, but eyed the other man cautiously.

'So why would an Ithacan say he's an Argive? What are you running away from?'

'I wasn't a deserter, if that's what you mean,' Eperitus said. 'I just want to put all that behind me.'

The chief steward gave a knowing nod.

'There's a lot of men think of the war that way. Want to forget all about it. Then it wasn't the glorious affair we were led to believe it'd be, was it?'

'No, it wasn't. Do you want these sacks carried somewhere?'

'Leave them for the slaves. There were supposed to be six sacks of pears in this lot, but I can only find five. Try one of these for me, will you?'

He tossed him a dark-skinned pear. Eperitus bit into it and gave a nod of approval.

'You know Odysseus and his fleet were never heard of again,' the chief steward continued. 'Just like they sailed off the edge of the ocean.'

'Perhaps we did. The last bit of familiar land we saw was Cape Malea, ten years ago. After that, it was one uncharted landfall after another, each one taking its toll until only one galley remained. That went down in a storm, taking every man with it. Except me and one other.'

The chief steward forgot about his missing bag of pears and sat on the tail of the wagon. For a few moments, he simply stared at the stranger.

'So, they all perished, even Odysseus?'

'All of them. I hung on to a piece of wreckage until I was rescued by a passing galley. The crew took me to an island where I've lived for the past seven years, until I asked them to return me to Greece.'

'It seems you have a few tales to tell.'

'None that you'd believe, or that I'd be willing to share. As I said, the past's behind me now, and all I want is a fresh start with the years I have left.'

The chief steward gave him a shrewd look. 'Then why come back? Wouldn't you have been better off staying with your rescuers on their island?'

'I think my past had found me there. Anyway, thanks for the fruit. I should be moving on.'

'Running away again, Theoclymenus – if that is your name? Well, I'm not letting you, and don't think of refusing me, either. You'll stay and eat your fill with us tonight, sleep on something soft and dry, then in the morning you'll start working for me as a steward. And I'll get a couple of the girls to give you a bath, too. You need one.'

Eperitus shook his head.

'If an old soldier like you can recognise me, then Nestor's going to know me the moment I serve him a cup of wine.'

'You won't be serving him,' the chief steward said, jumping down from the wagon and clapping a friendly hand on Eperitus's shoulder. 'That's been my job since he sailed to Troy, which is how I recognised you: you came to Nestor's tent several times with Odysseus. But you've nothing to fear. The old man's grown forgetful and his eyes are none too good nowadays. If you're that concerned, though, we can come up with a disguise. I've got something in mind, if you can tolerate it.'

He walked across the courtyard towards a small door in the side of the palace, signalling to two men sheltering in the nearby stables as he went. The men ran to the cart and began unloading the sacks of fruit. The drizzle had turned to rain now, and Eperitus was faced with the choice between a good meal, a dry bed and the possibility of some unwelcome questions, and another night spent under an open sky. He remembered his first evening on the Peloponnese, looking up at the constellations and realising they were back as he had remembered them before they had reached the land of the lotus eaters, where the stars had assumed unfamiliar patterns. But the ground had been hard and stony, and the air cold. He ran to where the chief steward was waiting in the doorway.

It led into a narrow, torch-lit passage. He followed his guide past open storerooms and rooms where slaves were milling grain, then left into another corridor where he caught glimpses of glowing ovens through open doors, and the air was filled with the aroma of fresh bread. When they reached a large kitchen, the chief steward called to two slave girls and ordered them to prepare a bath. After glancing at Eperitus's chest and muscles and sharing a smile with each other, they went off to heat water and find towels. The chief steward turned to look at Eperitus.

'Do you have any plans to return to Ithaca?' he asked. 'I know you say you're putting the past behind you, but when a man has been away from home for a long time, he's naturally inclined to be curious about the people and places he used to know.'

'Ithaca holds nothing for me now.'

'It's just that I heard a rumour – several rumours, in fact – that the queen... what's her name, now...'

'Penelope.'

'That's it, Penelope. Well, I hear her palace has been overrun by suitors vying for her hand. With her husband dead and her son not yet of age, they say these suitors are pressing her to remarry so one of them can become king. I thought you might want to know, being an Ithacan yourself. I would.'

'I'm not an Ithacan any more,' Eperitus said, as one of the slave girls took him by the elbow and led him away.

But as he reached the small, steamy room where her companion was pouring hot water into a bath, he felt a strange stirring in his stomach. The mention of Penelope had pricked his emotions. Perhaps he was not as immune to the past as he had hoped he was. Odysseus's actions had led to the death of Astynome and the last of his comrades, and he would never forgive him for that. But the king was dead. Could he then ignore the plight of Penelope, who had been a friend for so long? She was not to blame for what her husband had done.

The maid knelt before him and untied his sandals. She slipped them from his feet and removed his belt. Last of all, with a wry smile, she pulled his tunic over his head. Laying her hand on his shoulder, she pointed him to the bath.

The pungent aroma of herbs lifted the tiredness from his mind, and as the hot water washed over his body he felt the stiffness being eased from his limbs. He lay back and closed his eyes while the slaves washed him clean, their fingers massaging the knots out of his muscles. The words of the chief steward returned to him briefly, and for a moment he wondered whether the gods were trying to lead him back to Ithaca. The thought jarred in his mind. His old sense of duty and conscience were stirring, but his anger fought it back down. The past was the past. Let the gods make their plans; he would make his own.

-

Odysseus woke to the feel of rain on his face. His raft was pitching and yawing on rough waves, and as he opened his eyes he could see great continents of cloud moving across each other in the dark skies above. Seventeen days at sea working sail and rudder single-handedly had wearied him so much that the pale glimmer of dawn had failed to wake him. Alarmed, he sat up and loosed the leather bonds that tied him to the deck. All around him the surface of the sea was being whipped up by powerful crosswinds. They tugged hard at his clothing and blew his hair across his face, so that he was forced to tie it in a knot behind his head.

Then, as he stood and steadied himself against the mast, he looked to the dark horizon and glimpsed a dark smudge sandwiched between the grey sea and the blackening sky. A wave lifted his raft violently upward and plunged it down into a trough. As it rose again, he squinted against the rain and caught another sight of the smudge: a line of mountains, far off still, but within reach of his little craft if he could master the rough seas that lay between.

His heart jumped with excitement, banishing the tiredness from his mind. For a moment, all he could think of was home. On Ogygia his memories of Ithaca and his family had faded almost to the point of being forgotten, but now all that was needed was one last effort to be with them again.

He loosed the ropes that held the sail in place, letting it drop to half the length of the mast. Immediately the canvas sheet that Calypso had woven for him billowed out and propelled the raft forwards. With difficulty he secured the stays and staggered across the small deck to the rudder. Leaning his weight on the rail, he unlashed the bar and held the rudder straight with all his strength. The wind howled around him and the rain began to drive into his back, further drenching his cloak and the tunic beneath. His sodden hair hung heavy on his head and he was almost blinded by the water pouring in rivulets down his face, but he kept his narrowed eyes on the distant mountains, willing the fragile craft forwards.

A sudden flash of lightning caught him unawares. A boom of thunder followed, tearing open the skies above and filling him with fear.

'No!' he shouted. 'Not again! Not now!'

He recalled the day his galley had been struck by lightning and sent to the bottom of the ocean, taking his crew with it. The memory of it had fuelled his nightmares for seven years. Now the gods had found him again, helpless prey to the forces of nature at their command. A second bolt hit the sea some way ahead of him, with a peal of thunder close behind. The waves were growing in size and ferocity, drenching his little vessel again and again, tossing it about like a leaf in a gale.

The raft he had spent four days building and shaping was no galley, and even a ship with a full crew would have struggled in this storm. The mountains had disappeared behind the thick curtains of rain, and he no longer knew whether he was heading towards them or away from them. The canvas snapped in the wind, and as the stays strained and the mast bent under the pressure, he knew he had to furl the sail or lose it altogether.

Then a wall of water rose up out of the sea ahead of him, filling his vision and deafening him with its roar. It broke over the raft with a force so great it tore the rudder from his hand and threw him overboard. Before he hit the water, he saw the mast snap in half and the sail and yard come crashing down onto the deck where a moment before he had been standing.

The sea closed over him and sucked him under. The down-rush of the wave tugged at his clothing, pulling him deep into a darkness punctuated only by black shadows and the jellyfish-like bubbles of air escaping his lips. He felt the pressure on his flesh and the pain in his lungs; the terrible cold of the water penetrating his skin, and the panicked, claustrophobic terror of impending death. He saw briefly but clearly – as clear as if they were drowning with him – the spirits of the dead he had encountered in Hades, then the beautiful face of Calypso, mouthing the offer of eternal life he had foolishly rejected.

And then he saw Eperitus in the water above him, stretching out his hand and calling to him. He had often dreamed of Eperitus, always with sadness and regret. But now he was as he had been when they had fought alongside each other on the plains of Troy – fierce, determined and loyal. Odysseus reached up to take his hand, but it was gone.

With his lungs burning for air, he felt the desire to live take hold of him again. He began to swim, pulling against the weight of the water until he exploded from the surface into the murky gloom of the storm. He gulped down a lungful of air and was washed under by another wave before emerging again to see the mast-less remains of his raft floating a short way off. He swam towards it and pulled himself onto the planks. Spewing out brine, he dragged himself to the stump of the mast and clung on with the last of his strength as the storms dragged him farther out into the darkness.

Book Two

Chapter Five

Sacrifice at Pylos

The early-morning sun rose pale above the mountains, its gentle warmth drawing the chill from Telemachus's flesh. He stood in the prow, watching the waves break over the cheeks of the galley and feeling the spray on his face. It was an exhilarating sensation, made all the sweeter by having escaped the confines of the palace and the suitors that had made it their own.

But his escape had not been an easy one. To keep his voyage a secret from Antinous and the others was one thing; to find willing help in obtaining and crewing a galley was another. Too many Ithacans, including many of the slaves in his own household, would be quick to tell the suitors of his plans to sail to Pylos. Many more were too afraid to do anything that might bring the anger of the noble families down on their heads. The only Ithacan he knew that would lend him a ship was Noemon, whose father, Phronius, was rumoured to have been thrown from a cliff by Antinous, and so bore nothing but hatred for the suitors.

Finding a crew had been even harder, but he had managed to recruit twenty lads of his own age keen on a bit of adventure. Several had been taught to sail by their fathers, but there had been no chance to train together as a crew before they had slipped anchor the previous night. The darkness had been essential for them to get away unnoticed by the suitors, but without Mentor's captaincy they would surely have foundered on Ithaca's rocky shoreline within moments of leaving.

With his one remaining hand on the tiller, he had steered a true course around the eastern edge of the island, calling out instructions to the oarsmen and making them work as a team as they rowed the ship out into deep water. Then, at the right moment, he had ordered the more experienced handful to lower and set the sail, making a few adjustments as the vessel ploughed through the black waters into the night. And there he had stayed, watching the wave caps in the moonlight to judge the currents, and keeping the coast of the Peloponnese at a good distance to port while the galley headed south and the crew slept.

Telemachus looked back at his old teacher. He was still a handsome man with very little grey in his black hair and beard, and with a strong physique that showed no signs yet of turning to fat. He wore an old leather breastplate that could be glimpsed beneath his cloak, and had laid his two spears and his specially adapted half-moon shield on the deck by the bow rail. His good hand remained firmly on the tiller, barely moving as he watched the distant shoreline slipping by, while the leather-encased stump of his left wrist hung idle at his side. The loss of his hand thirty years before had prevented him from joining the expedition to Troy, something he had regretted every day since. Not that he had said as much, but Telemachus knew his teacher well enough to see the pain in his eyes every time Odysseus and the war were mentioned.

At least Mentor had some memory of his father to draw on, though. Telemachus had nothing. He had never known the man who should have protected him as a child and shaped him into manhood, the man from whom he should have drawn his confidence and identity. It was that hole in his life that he was so desperate to fill, and which he would pursue to the ends of the earth if he could.

But what if Nestor told him that Odysseus was dead? Would he then return to Ithaca and inherit what remained of his father's estate while his mother remarried and her new husband became king? Could he endure the struggles of an unhappy homeland and a life dispossessed of his rightful place in it? Or would he set out to find a new life for himself? If so, where would he go and what would he do? There was no Trojan War for his generation to test itself in. No powerful enemy to win a name against or plunder great wealth from. Or would he return to Ithaca and fight the suitors, to perish and be forgotten?

A distant sound made him look up. The coast was closer now, and he could see a wide, sandy bay ahead of the galley. There were no ships in the water, but the beach was thronged with crowds of people. The vast majority were seated on the sand in orderly companies, each containing several hundred men, like the divisions of an army ready to spring to their feet and march into battle. Indeed, he could see the gleam of helmets and spear points on many of the distant figures, but no enemy, unless they intended to make war on the sea itself. Several columns of smoke rose up from the beach, and as he watched a cheer rose up from the ranks of seated men. Telemachus looked behind him. His crew were standing and staring at the spectacle, while in the helm Mentor was shielding his eyes with his forearm as he steered the galley towards the beach.

'What is it?' Telemachus asked, joining him.

'A sacrifice,' Mentor answered. 'I count nine fires, and around each I can see groups of men flaying dead animals and offering their thigh bones to the flames. Heifers or bulls I'd say, by the size of them.'

Telemachus looked on in wonder.

'But there's so many. I've never seen anything like it, even in Sparta when I was a boy.'

Mentor laughed.

'But Menelaus was away on the shores of Ilium when you were there. The war finished ten years ago, and the king of Pylos is making an offering to the Olympians that befits his wealth and status.'

'Nestor's there?'

'Certainly. Look to the centre: the white tent with the row of figures seated before it. Nestor is most likely the one presiding over the sacrifices. But that's good. No need to wait to present your question to the king. You can go straight up…'

'I'm not sure, Mentor. I mean, he's a king and many times my senior, whereas I'm not even a man yet. What right do I have to…?'

'The right of any honoured guest, Telemachus. A pious man like Nestor isn't going to ignore a visitor who arrives in the middle of a major sacrifice, is he? For all he knows, you could be a god. And if you ask me, the gods are with you right now. We could have landed on an empty beach, tired ourselves out on the long trek up into the mountains where the palace lies, and then been made to wait until the morning. Instead, we're about to walk right into the king's presence.'

His smile faded as he looked at Telemachus.

'Just remember everything I taught you about xenia. A show of good manners will get Nestor's attention, and when he finds out whose son you are, he'll make you an honoured guest and give you all the help he can – though whether he knows anything about what happened to your father is another matter.'

Mentor called for the sail to be furled and the oars shipped out. There was a flurry of activity, and then the crew settled on their benches and rowed. As they reached the beach, the oars were withdrawn again and three anchor stones were tossed into the water. Mentor slung his shield onto his back and picked up his spears, indicating that Telemachus should do the same. The young Ithacan adjusted his ill-fitting cuirass, tossed his cloak over his shoulder and took up his shield and spears. Mentor had already leapt into the shallow blue water and was striding up the beach.

'Let me come with you,' Peiraeus said.

Peiraeus had been his closest friend for much of his life. Both had grown up without their fathers, and when Telemachus felt frustrated and oppressed by the presence of the suitors, Peiraeus was always there to restore his mood. Glancing nervously at the gathering on the beach, he nodded. Peiraeus grabbed his shield and spears and leapt down into the shallow waves. Following as quickly as he could, Telemachus jumped and half-fell into the water – to the laughter and jeers of his friends on deck – then jogged up the beach in the wake of the others.

The air was full of voices as they approached the assembly, and the aroma of roasted meat was already mingling with the smell of woodsmoke. Several men were pointing at them, and a group of a dozen spearmen had formed a line at the edge of the nearest fire. A young noble stood at their head, watching the newcomers approach.

'Welcome, friends,' he said, taking first Mentor, then Peiraeus and finally Telemachus by the hand. 'Will you join us?'

He did not wait for an answer, but led them across the crowded beach towards the white tent. The soldiers followed, boxing them in but keeping their distance. On every side slaves were jointing the sacrificial bulls, skewering the meat and roasting it over the many fires. More men were setting up tables and laying them with a rich array of foods, while others were busy mixing wine or slicing meat on large boards as it was brought to them. It promised to be a feast far more varied and sumptuous than anything the great hall back on Ithaca had ever offered.

Telemachus noted their guide was about his own age, but wore an air of authority and absolute confidence. Every guard or slave that he passed paused and bowed before him in a formal recognition of his position that would have been unthinkable on Ithaca. When they reached the largest of the fires, the flames of which were contained within a circle of stones and burned high into the sky, he called over a wine steward. The man brought him a golden cup, which he handed to Mentor.

'My name is Peisistratus, son of Nestor. Here, take the cup of libation and raise a prayer for us to Poseidon, whom these sacrifices honour; and to all the gods on whom men depend.'

'Hear me, Poseidon, lord of the oceans, and answer my prayer,' Mentor began in a loud voice, tipping some of the wine on the sand. 'Give glory and honour to our hosts, King Nestor and his sons, and in accepting these sacrifices, grant the people of Pylos their wishes.'

He passed the cup to Telemachus, who held it towards the flames. The cup was beautifully crafted, with dolphins pulling a sea-borne chariot and Poseidon at the reins. What was a mere trinket to Nestor and his sons would have been an item of great value in his own country. He glanced round at the crowds of worshippers and the many slaves preparing and roasting the sacrificial meat; at the sand running red with the blood of the animals; and the skies dark with the smoke of the numerous fires. He sensed hundreds of eyes upon him and felt out of place, like a child among gods. Peisistratus's eyes narrowed slightly, questioning his hesitation, and Telemachus felt his hands begin to tremble. Then, forcing himself to concentrate, he tipped a little of the wine out in libation and invoked the name of Poseidon.

'Give your blessing to this great nation, its people and its king. Repay them for this sacrifice given in your honour. And grant also that I will accomplish the mission that brought me to the shores of Pylos.'

Peiraeus followed with his own libation and prayer, before a slave took the cup from his hands.

'Come with me,' Peisistratus said, leading them to a large table where six men were seated.

The food piled upon it could have easily fed fifty men. At the centre was a man with a grey beard that reached down to his lap. His brown face was a web of wrinkles and his eyes were almost shut, giving the impression he was half-asleep. He must have been tall and well-built once, but now he was bent low and listed to one side, as if he was made of wax that had slightly melted in the sun and would soon fall away completely. Despite the warmth of the late-summer morning, he wore a heavily embroidered double cloak that lay piled about him in numerous folds, and from which his long-fingered hands protruded to cling to the arms of the chair.

So, this was Nestor, Telemachus thought, the famous charioteer whose wisdom and experience had guided Agamemnon and the Greek kings through the Trojan War. From what remained of him, Telemachus could barely imagine the man his father had once fought alongside, so heavy had been the toll of the past ten years on him.

To the king's left sat three of his sons, and to his right two more, with an empty chair for Peisistratus at the end. The latter directed two slaves to lay fleeces in the sand for his guests to sit on, then went to assume his own seat at the table. Stewards appeared with a selection of meats, followed by others with golden cups and skins of wine. The man who served Telemachus seemed old for a servant and showed all the signs of having been a soldier: brown scars criss-crossed his muscular arms and legs, and though one eye was hidden by a leather patch, the other revealed a hard and formidable character. The man's gaze lingered on Telemachus a moment longer than was polite; then he bowed his head and stepped away.

Telemachus ate ravenously, savouring the tender meat and mopping up the thick grease with his bread until he had eaten his fill, after which he lay on his side and nibbled at pieces of cheese. A young woman rose from another table where several females were seated and approached the seat of Nestor. She glanced across at Telemachus as she passed, letting slip the faintest hint of a smile. The cup he had been poised to drink from remained hovering at his lip, and all he could think of was how beautiful she was. She stood behind the old king's chair and bent down so that her black hair spilled over his shoulders. Her eyes caught Telemachus's again, and he felt both surprised and pleased at the realisation that she was flirting with him.

She whispered something in Nestor's ear and the old man rose from his slumber. Up to that point he had not eaten a morsel of the food that was piled before him, or moved to sip at his bejewelled cup, or speak to the sons either side of him. But at the sound of the girl's voice he slowly pushed himself up from the folds of his cloak and groped at the air with his hand. The girl took it and his gnarled fingers wrapped around hers.

'Well, who are they?' Nestor asked impatiently, and a little too loudly. 'More merchants with their ships full of useless baubles? Though pirates are more likely in this day and age! Let them eat their fill, Polycaste, and send them on their way.'

Peisistratus shrugged his shoulders in silent apology to Telemachus, while Polycaste hid her smile behind her fingers.

'My lord Nestor,' Telemachus began, provoked to throw off his diffidence by the old man's dismissal and the girl's amusement. 'We are neither merchants nor pirates, but men of Ithaca. We seek news of our king, Odysseus. I am Telemachus, his son, and these are my companions, Mentor and Peiraeus. The fate of every king and prince who sailed to Troy is known, except my father's. You fought side by side with him during the long years of the war; I'd hoped you might know something of what happened to him.

If he's being held somewhere against his will, or if you've heard rumours of his death, then tell me and bring an end to my misery.'

Nestor was facing him now, and there was a glimmer of light between his half-closed eyelids. His wiry hair had caught the sunlight and hovered about his head like a mist, but a new keenness seemed to have stiffened his spine and given energy to his limbs, so that Telemachus could sense the intelligence still inhabiting his decrepit form.

'Yes, your father and I fought at Troy, curse the name. We were great allies. With my wisdom and his intelligence, it was rare that we didn't reach the same conclusion in any matter. It was as if we spoke with a single voice. But the war was a great maker and breaker of men. The greatest of our generation and for many generations past. May such a fate never befall our sons. It conquered the mightiest, like great Achilles, and broke the spirits of the strong, such as Ajax. My own son, Antilochus, fell there too.'

At this his strength seemed to fail. His daughter tightened her grip on his hand, and a look of concern darkened her beauty. She knelt beside him and whispered something in his ear, and his chin lifted again.

'Yes, the gods took many, as was their will. But they also raised many up, and none more so than Odysseus. In their wisdom, the Olympians chose to humble the powerful and honour the lowly. We dashed ourselves against those merciless walls for nine years, but it was your father who overcame them in the end – not by force of arms, but by the zeal of his mind. And now that I look at you and hear your voice – though as if through a fog and at a great distance – I'm minded of him. Ah, Odysseus...'

He reached for his cup with a shaking hand. Polycaste took it and raised it carefully to his lips. He sipped at it loudly, spilling much and staining his beard red, then nodded slowly when his thirst had been satisfied.

'But even those the gods raise up, they can dash down again at whim. They gave the victory to the Greeks, then struck us down with such madness that we were ready to draw our swords against each other. The Atreides started it. Even as the Council of Kings was summoned for a last time on the field of victory, Menelaus called on us to head home at once. But Agamemnon opposed him, demanding we appease the wrath of the gods before we set sail. To my mind – and your father's – Menelaus's proposal seemed best. But Agamemnon resented his younger brother taking charge, and wanted to stamp his authority. We defied him, though. The oath that bound us to him had been fulfilled, so the next morning half of us pushed our galleys into the water and struck out for home. Odysseus was with us.

I'd never known a man so eager to put the war behind him and return to his family. That's why I couldn't understand why he turned back.'

'To Troy?' Telemachus asked.

Nestor gave the faintest of nods.

'That was the last any of us saw of him. The gods put some unhappy thought in his head, I suppose, for if he'd stayed with us he would have made it safely back to Ithaca ten years ago. Many reached their homes without incident: Diomedes, Philoctetes, Neoptolemus, Idomeneus...'

He reeled off the names of the survivors one by one, with no sign of having forgotten a single name. 'But many did not. Little Ajax, Oileus's son, was drowned by the gods for his arrogance. Agamemnon, the conqueror of Troy, was another. He reached his home city of Mycenae without incident, only to be murdered by his faithless wife. As I said, the gods can shower a man with glory and wealth one moment, then throw him down the next. His death didn't go unavenged, though. His son saw to that.'

'Orestes,' Telemachus said, looking into his wine. 'His fame sweeps before him, even to lowly Ithaca. If only the gods would help me as they helped him.'

Nestor eased himself forwards, assisted by Polycaste, and stared at Telemachus.

'Tell me, my friend: why is it you come searching for your father now? Is it because of the rumours I hear about your home? That the quick-minded Penelope is besieged by suitors, who've little respect for the gods and even less for the rules of xenia? Then, are the rumours true? And do you meekly submit to the rule of these men, without calling on the people to aid you against this injustice? Or are you pinning your hopes on finding Odysseus, thinking he will deliver you from your predicament?'

'It's true our home is overrun by my mother's suitors, who've heaped one humiliation after another on me, helping themselves to my inheritance and disregarding what is right and honourable. But what can I do?' Telemachus felt his frustration building. 'The people fear these brutes and won't lift a finger against them, and the few soldiers my father left to protect us returned to their homes long ago. As for Orestes, at least he only had one man to deal with – I have over a hundred! In answer to your question, the gods inspired me to come here in search of my father. And if he's still alive, then I hope he'll come back and reclaim what is his. But perhaps the gods are mocking me.'

'The gods do many things, good and bad,' Nestor said, 'but they do not mock. If you believe they sent you to find news of Odysseus, then perhaps there is news to be had, eh? Your father was a resourceful man, driven by a fierce love of your mother. And you, Telemachus; you were always in his thoughts. But he would not give up his life easily, or allow himself to be imprisoned without a fight. If it comforts you, I believe he still lives and will one day find his way back to Ithaca. And I will give you this advice, too: go visit Menelaus in Sparta. His own return was a hard one, with great loss of ships and men. He was driven to the remotest corners of the ocean and had many strange adventures before he returned home. And when he and I met last year, he hinted he had heard something about your father's fate, though he would say no more. Maybe he can give you news of Odysseus that will restore your hope.'

Telemachus felt his spirits rise. It seemed unlikely Menelaus would know any more than Nestor, but he would go to Sparta and ask. He stood and bowed.

'Thank you, my lord. And now I must leave you and return to my galley. It's a long voyage to Sparta, and my crew are weary from a night and a morning at the benches.'

'Is my palace the hovel of a pauper that you should prefer to sleep under a ship's bench and let the waves rock you to sleep?' Nestor asked. 'I have spare beds enough for you and all your men, and you will find our hospitality worthy of the gods. In the morning, my son will lend you his chariot and driver and you can go overland to Sparta. You'll arrive there as quickly as if you had gone by sea.'

Telemachus consented and sat back down. Mentor raised his empty cup and the one-eyed steward refilled it.

'Peiraeus and I will not come with you to the palace,' he told Telemachus in a low voice. 'Our place is with the crew, and you'll be safe with Nestor – though be careful of *him*.'

He nodded towards the steward with the eyepatch.

'Him?' Telemachus said. 'Why?'

'Because his gaze hasn't left you since you said your name.'

Chapter Six

The Storeroom

Autonoe dried her hands on the front of her dress. The crowded kitchen was busy with slaves roasting meat, preparing dough, mixing wine and a dozen other chores. The warm, humid air was filled with shouted orders and curses as a constant stream of maids and stewards entered, filled wooden boards and baskets with a variety of foods, refreshed kraters of wine and left again for the great hall. Penelope had retired for the evening, so Autonoe had come down to help the other servants who were hard-pressed by the demands of the suitors. But the clamour from the hall was beginning to die down at last. Handful by handful, the drunken nobles were drifting off: the Ithacans to their family homes, and the men of Samos, Dulichium and Zacynthos to the lodgings they kept in town.

'There you are,' said Melantho, entering the kitchen and running up to her. 'The suitors are demanding some of that vintage wine Telemachus keeps in the storeroom in the eastern corner of the palace. You know the one I mean. Would you please do me a kindness, Autonoe, and go fetch a jar? They've got me so busy chasing after this and that I can't go get it myself.'

Melantho was older than Autonoe, and though Eurycleia was in charge of the servants, she could give orders to her juniors. What surprised Autonoe was that her commands were usually delivered with a shout and a frown on her pretty face, not with a soft voice and a smile.

'Would you rather I go to the hall and let you have the quieter job of fetching the wine? I don't mind.'

'No, you go, Autonoe. I've already got half a dozen things they want me to do. You know the storeroom I mean, don't you?'

Autonoe nodded and followed a slave carrying a selection of meats out into the dimly lit passage. One of the boards nearly slipped from his hands.

'I've got it,' she said. 'Come on, I'll carry it for you.'

They reached the great hall, where thirty or forty suitors were singing and dancing and making enough commotion for twice their number. In the shadowy corners, Autonoe glimpsed two or three others with Telemachus's maids, their white buttocks moving up and down between the open legs of the girls. The steward she had been following told her to place the board on top of the others he was carrying, then entered to a chorus of shouts from the crowd of young men.

Autonoe returned the way she had come, past the kitchen door, then right and left again to another corridor. The torch here had died out and not been replaced, leaving the narrow space cold and black. The storeroom she needed was at the end in the old palace archive, which had been converted before the war to provide storage for Odysseus's growing stock of wine. Being the only son of an only son, the king had inherited the undivided riches of two royal generations, and had added much to that before leaving for Troy. Despite the insatiable greed of the suitors, a half of his wealth at least still remained, though Autonoe doubted he would ever return to claim it.

For a moment, she thought about returning to the kitchens to fetch a fresh torch so that she could find the right wine. Then she saw a faint line of shifting orange light beneath the storeroom door at the end of the passage. Perhaps the torch had not died out after all, but had been taken into the storeroom by another slave and left there. She walked to the heavy door, pushed it open and stepped inside.

The storeroom was cool and shadowy. The torch in the bracket by the door flickered rhythmically, and by its wavering light she could see many jars of wine stacked against the right-hand wall. Dozens of sacks of grain had also been stored there, a few of which had been left in a disorderly heap on the floor. The room smelled of burning fat, dry earth and barley, but there was something else, an odour that her instincts told her was out of place before her mind could identify it. Sweat.

The door shut behind her and the bolt was pushed in with a metallic click. Autonoe turned and saw several figures moving towards her from the corner. She opened her mouth to scream, but a hot, powerful hand closed over the bottom of her face, stifling her cry and pushing her back against the stacked grain. She raised her fists and began beating the man's hulking torso, but to no effect. With his other hand he took her painfully by the throat, squeezing it so hard she felt certain he meant to murder her there and then.

'I'm going to take my hand from your mouth now,' Eurymachus said. 'If you scream, it'll be the last sound you ever make. Do you understand?'

She nodded, and slowly the clammy fingers were peeled from her mouth. A moment later the pressure on her neck eased and the hand was taken away. She bent over, holding her hands against the bruised flesh and feeling like she was going to vomit.

'That's it, get your breath, girl,' said another voice, which she recognised as belonging to Antinous. 'We've just got a couple of questions and then you can go back to your duties. Am I clear?'

She nodded and raised her body a little, propping herself up with her hands on her knees. There were five men, though she could not identify the others silhouetted against the torchlight.

'Melantho says she saw you and her father loading bread, wine and other stores on a wagon the other night. Is she right?'

'I'm not a thief.'

'Then you'll be the first honest slave I've ever met,' Antinous said, to the chuckles of the others. 'But you know the punishment for theft, don't you, Autonoe?'

'Dolius and I were acting on the orders of Telemachus. What business of yours is it what goes on in his household?'

He slapped her hard and she gasped in pain and shock.

'Don't get above yourself with me,' he warned, his voice cold and clear. 'A slave should respect her superiors or learn the consequences. Now tell me where you and Dolius took the wagon.'

'That's my master's business, and his alone.'

She closed her eyes, expecting another slap. None came.

'Elatus,' Antinous said.

Autonoe opened her eyes again and saw the suitor who had molested her in the great hall a few days before. He stepped forwards, and she could see the marks her fingernails had left on his cheeks. There was a smile on his lips that scared her more than Antinous's threats of violence.

'You owe Elatus a favour, after you bloodied his cheek,' Antinous continued. 'He and Leocritus and Agelaus' – he indicated the other two figures in the corner of the room – 'have all been spurned by you and think you need a lesson in humility. You're a little plain for my tastes, so I'm happy to let you go unharmed. But you have to answer my questions. Do you understand me, Autonoe? Tell me what I want to know and I'll let you go; refuse and – well, that's your problem.'

'If any of you touch me, my lady will know about it. Some of the other girls might have given themselves to you, but if you take any of her maids by force Penelope will take it to the people for justice.'

'Who was that other girl, Agelaus, a year or so ago? The one who threatened to report you to Telemachus and Penelope when you had your way with her?'

Agelaus stepped forwards. His good looks were marred by the cruelty in his eyes, and there was an air of seedy brutality about him.

'You mean little Chloris. She was a sweet girl, much too flirty for her own good, though. Ran away, didn't she?'

'Fell off a cliff in the fog, I heard,' Elatus said.

Autonoe thought of the feisty maid who had been born to slaves after Odysseus had sailed for Troy, but who had been brought up loyal to his household. She had always questioned the rumour that Chloris had escaped to the mainland on a visiting merchantman.

'You murdered her!'

'And we'll murder you, too, if we have to,' Antinous retorted. 'Now tell me where you were taking those stores.'

Autonoe hesitated, but Elatus moved forwards and took hold of her dress.

'To a ship,' she gasped. 'A galley that was sailing that night.'

'Who was on the galley?'

'I don't know!'

Elatus ripped her dress, the same one she had repaired after they had torn it open in the great hall. She could smell his foul breath on her face and turned away in disgust.

'All right! It was Telemachus and his friends.'

'Where were they going?'

Again, she hesitated. This time Elatus gave a growl and tore the dress down the middle, pulling the two halves apart so that her white breasts hung free. She tried to cover them, but Elatus's hands moved to her arms and held them apart.

'That's it,' said Agelaus. 'That's what we want.'

Leocritus gave a short laugh that trembled with nervous excitement. Autonoe felt their exhilaration building and her own little resource of courage running dry. She did not want to betray her master, but she felt suddenly and terribly afraid.

'He was going to Pylos, to see King Nestor,' she said. 'Now, will you let me go? I've got a lot of things to do in the kitchens. They'll miss me and come looking…'

'Why did he want to see Nestor?' Antinous insisted, his tone uncompromising. 'To bring soldiers back to Ithaca?'

'To ask what had happened to his father, that's all. Now, will you let me go? I've answered your questions.'

Antinous reached out and took her left breast in his hot hand, running his thumb over her nipple.

'You can go after you've paid Elatus what you owe him.'

'No!'

Elatus pushed her. She tripped over one of the grain sacks and fell backwards. A moment later he was kneeling over her, ripping her dress from her in short, hard snatches until she was naked. She felt the rough material of the sacks chafing her skin and the hard little grains digging into her flesh. She sensed the horrible strength in his hands and arms as he pulled her legs apart. And for an instant she was filled with terror, the terror of knowing her virginity would be taken from her in the most brutal way, and that she would share the fate of poor Chloris.

Then the terror succumbed to a sudden swell of fierce anger. She fought to close her legs, to squeeze out the hand that was grabbing at her vagina. Elatus shouted, his face and voice frightening in their fury. She clawed at his face with her fingernails, aiming for his eyes. Elatus pulled back before she could reach them and brought his fist crashing into her face. The pain was immense. The room grew darker and her head felt like it would burst. She heard herself screaming, screaming despite the pain, screaming as loud as she could. Then a hand closed over her mouth and she felt warm breath against her ear.

'Don't make us kill you,' Agelaus said.

She lay still. There was blood running back into her nostrils and she felt her jaw grating. She hoped it was not broken. There were fingers on her thighs, pushing them apart. She felt the air between her legs and knew she had to keep her thighs together, as tightly as she could, but nothing happened. It was as if her legs no longer belonged to her. Somewhere below her she sensed Elatus pulling his tunic over his head so that he, too, was naked. Something nudged against her, something hard. She closed her eyes and felt it pushing against her, then into her. She felt a terrible pain and wanted to scream again, but Agelaus's hand was still over her mouth. All she could think about as the tears filled her eyes was how much it hurt.

'And what if he returns with news that Odysseus is still alive?'

'He won't. My father's assassins killed him long ago. Or perhaps the whole fleet perished. What does it matter? He won't be coming back in the next two weeks, and by then it'll be too late.'

'Hurry up, will you? You've more than had your turn.'

'Piss off. I'm almost there.'

'*Think* about it. If he comes back saying his father isn't dead and is trying to find his way home, Penelope will refuse to honour her oath. She'll claim she can't remarry while her husband lives and snub us all.'

'Hm. Perhaps you're right.'

'About time. Get out of the way, will you?'

'Hey, it's my turn.'

'Get your hands off me or you'll regret it.'

'Stop fighting, you fools! Let Leocritus go first; he won't last a moment anyway. So, what are we going to do, Antinous?'

'Ready a ship of our own and man it with the best fighters among us. Then we'll set a watch day and night on Mount Neriton. As soon as we spot his galley – any galley – we'll launch our own to intercept it. And that'll be the end of the matter.'

'You mean you'll kill him?'

'Of course we will, Elatus. And his entire crew with him. What choice do we have?'

'I don't think she had time to realise you were in her, Leocritus. Now watch this. I'll make her sing. Won't I, little bird?'

'I'm not sure.'

'Put it another way, then. With Telemachus dead, his estate will stay with Penelope. Whoever marries her will get everything: throne, palace, the lot! But listen, to be fair to the rest of us, here's what we do: whoever gets Penelope gets the throne and the palace, but the estate gets divided up between whoever's in on the plot with us. Agreed?'

'You mean us five and anybody with us in the ambush?'

'She's not singing. She's not doing anything. You don't think she's… you know.'

'Shut up, will you. You're putting me off.'

'Absolutely. No Amphinomus or any of the weaker ones; they'll just give us away.'

'Agreed then.'

'Agreed. Now, let's go.'

'Are you done?'

'I'm done.'

'Come on then. Bring the torch with you.'

Agelaus stood and pulled his tunic down. He kicked Autonoe hard in the ribs, but she did not move. Then he took the torch and followed the others out, shutting the door behind him and leaving her in darkness. She lay there and listened to their voices fade away down the corridor.

Chapter Seven

Nausicaa

Despite the comfort of his bed in the echoing porch of Nestor's great hall, Telemachus slept fitfully. Thoughts of what was going on at home mingled with concerns about how he would be received by Menelaus, so that his dreams were shallow reflections of his anxieties, and when he awoke to the first glimmer of dawn he hardly felt as if he had slept at all. As he lifted his head from the pillow, he found a young slave girl waiting at the side of his bed.

'My lord Nestor has requested that you attend a sacrifice with him before you leave for Sparta,' she said. 'Your bath is waiting for you.'

He pulled aside his blanket, slipped on his sandals and threw his cloak hurriedly over his shoulders before following the girl into the great hall. She led him to a side door and then through wide corridors to a room in the east of the palace, where the sunlight was pouring in through a high window. The room was filled with steam and the smell of herbs. As his eyes adjusted to the brightness, he saw the silhouette of a woman waiting beside a stone basin filled with water.

'Leave us, Tyro,' she commanded.

When his guide had left and closed the door behind her, the other woman stepped into the light.

'Polycaste,' he said, unable to contain his surprise. 'What are you doing here?'

She smiled boldly. 'I'm here to bathe you, my lord.'

His heart beat fast as he looked at her slender figure and the dark eyes so prominent in her pale face. Then he remembered she was the daughter of his host and dropped his gaze to the flagstone floor.

'That is too much of an honour, my lady. I'm happy to be bathed by one of your maids, but…'

'You'd rather a slave wash you than me?'

He looked at her, caught her smile and laughed gently.

'No, of course not.'

'Don't be shy, then. Here, sit down.'

She knelt beside the bath and patted the seat of a three-legged stool. As he lowered himself onto it she untied his sandals and slipped them from his feet, her warm hands soft and calm. His own were shaking, and he was almost forced to sit on them. Then she unclasped the brooch that held his cloak together and slipped it to the floor, before beckoning him to stand.

She's the daughter of your host, he told himself, trying to stop himself from becoming aroused. *The daughter of your host. The daughter...*

She rolled his tunic upward, her fingertips brushing his pubic hair and stomach, then slipped it over his raised arms and tossed it in a pile on top of his cloak. For a moment they looked at each other – he only a little taller than her – and he struggled against the desire to hold her and kiss her. Then she stepped back, and with a smile – a small, disappointed smile, to his reckoning – she took his hand and guided him to the bath. The moment had passed and, daughter of his host or not, he silently admonished himself for a timid, witless idiot.

Her gaze followed him down into the water, though, and as she pulled the stool up beside him he sensed his cowardice had not deterred her. She picked up a sponge from a wooden pail beside the bath and dipped it in the water.

'I'm embarrassing you,' she said as she washed his neck and shoulders. 'I'm the daughter of your host, not just some slave girl, and I have you at a disadvantage.'

'You have. Though not an unpleasant one.'

Why had he said that? But her smile told him he had not offended her. She pushed the sponge down to his chest and stomach.

'I had to see you before you left, and this was the only way. My father won't allow me to attend the sacrifice, but I have to say something to you.'

She pushed the sponge lower. He caught her wrist gently and took the sponge from her hand.

'I can do there.'

This time she laughed and raised her hand to his jaw, rubbing her wet fingers through the soft hair of his beard. She was only a little older than himself, he guessed; and yet Nestor would have been an old man when he sired her.

'I heard what you said to the king yesterday, and it shamed me that he didn't offer you more help. Feasts and parting gifts might be what are required, but they're not what you *need*.'

'What do I need?'

'Soldiers.' Polycaste said it almost as a whisper. 'I feel for you, Telemachus, having all those brutes filling your house and not being able to do anything about it. And I know Peisistratus feels the same way, too. We're the youngest and we know what it's like not to have any power.'

'And yet he has a lot of respect and authority.'

'Only what he's earned. And he's ready to lend you spearmen, if you need them. I persuaded him that you're in an impossible situation, and he agreed that if you can't find news of Odysseus, then send word to him and he will come himself to Ithaca with fifty men, or a hundred, if you need them.'

Telemachus sat up, spilling the bath water onto the floor and Polycaste's dress.

'You'd do that? For a man you hardly know?'

'For the son of a king whom my father loved, even if his manners have forgotten it. And for a man who… who I would like to know better.'

Telemachus's mouth opened to speak, then shut again. He felt excited, elated even. He wanted to stand up and shout his happiness to the high ceiling above. Then he remembered his nakedness and felt suddenly awkward.

'It seems you already know a lot more about me than I do you,' he answered, looking down at himself. Then the smile withered on his lips and he felt his joy lose its lustre. 'But I can't accept.'

'Why?'

'I can't invite foreign soldiers into my palace to massacre the suitors, even if they deserve it and much worse. It's not like they're Taphians, whom my father defeated with the help of a few Spartan warriors. They're men of Ithaca, nobles, each one the son of a powerful lord. If I used your brother's spearmen to fight my battle, the whole kingdom would unite against me; they'd forget the crimes of the suitors and join forces with them. Can you imagine what your people would do if a foreign army landed and started killing the heirs of every noble family in Pylos?'

'They would rise up and resist,' she said. 'Forgive me… And yet, what other hope do you have?'

'Only one: that my father still lives. The people loved him once and honour him still. If I bring news of him back from Sparta – that he's alive and on his way home – that might put a stop to the suitors' ambitions. If not...'

'If not, then forget your homeland and stay with us,' she said, taking his hand in hers. 'We will welcome you and honour you, and love you as one of our own.'

'Love me?'

She leaned forwards and kissed him on the lips. It was soft and warm and all too brief, but when she pulled away again and looked at him there was a new understanding in her eyes. Something secret had been acknowledged and become a secret shared.

'Yes, go to Sparta, and if you hear nothing, come back; I will be waiting.'

He looked at her and saw the beauty of her character, and he knew he wanted her. But he did not want her as a poor, exiled prince, running meekly away from troubles he could not fix. How could she ever respect a man like that? How could she truly love a weakling?

'No,' he said. 'I will not come back here. I will send the chariot back to the palace and return to Ithaca in my galley. And whether I have news of my father or not – whether he is dead or the gods are sending him back as we speak – I will settle matters at home myself. Then and only then will I return to Pylos. To you, Polycaste.'

She looked both happy and sad – happy at his desire for her, and sad at the impossible obstacle he had placed between them. But she nodded.

'I understand. You're a man, after all, and you must prove yourself. I will wait.'

She stood and unwrapped the towel from around her waist, holding it towards him and – after a last glance – looking away.

Telemachus ate his parting feast with Nestor and his sons and thanked them for their hospitality. He poured libations with them, and Peisistratus prayed the gods would protect him and help him find what he was looking for. All the while, Telemachus was looking for Polycaste, hoping she might appear one last time to say goodbye. But she did not. Peisistratus alone accompanied him to the stable yard, where a chariot and a fine team of two horses were waiting for him. The horses were restlessly awaiting the journey, stamping their hooves and raising their heads as the two men approached.

'Where's the driver?' Peisistratus asked the slave holding the horses steady.

'He'll be here soon, my lord. He was called away with an urgent message.'

'My apologies, Telemachus. He's a good man, and an excellent charioteer. Until we meet on your return.'

He held out his hand and Telemachus took it with a firm grip. Then Nestor's son departed, striding across the yard to the door by which they had entered. When he had gone, a man left the stables and walked towards the waiting chariot.

'I'll have those,' he said, taking the reins from the slave's hand. 'The chief steward wants you in the kitchens at once. At once, I said.'

The slave looked at him uncertainly for a moment before running off. It was then that Telemachus noticed the leather patch over the newcomer's eye.

'You were my steward last night.'

The man nodded.

'Yes, my lord. And now I'm your driver.' He unslung two skins from his shoulder and placed them next to a sack of food inside the cab. 'My name is Theoclymenus.'

'Isn't it unusual for a charioteer to serve his master's wine, too?' Telemachus asked, placing his spears and shield inside the chariot. 'Are you sure about this?'

'I'm sure, my lord.'

He stepped up into the cab and held his hand out to the prince. Telemachus hesitated a moment, then took it and climbed into the chariot. Theoclymenus seized the reins and the whip and gave a shout. The horses sprang away towards the open gates, leaving a cloud of dust behind them.

-

Odysseus woke to gentle laughter. Nymphs, he thought as he began to drift upward from the depths of sleep. He could feel warm air on his skin and sense the sunlight through his eyelids. Shifting a little, he felt something soft beneath him. He closed his fingers around a handful of dry leaves, which crumbled at his touch. The nymphs laughed again, excited by something.

Their voices reminded him of the goddess in his dream. He had been lying on the wreckage of a raft, being tossed about by a murderous tempest, when she had landed beside him in the form of a seagull, carrying a pale-blue sash in her beak. Commanding Odysseus to tie it about his waist and swim for the shore, she had flown away again. The next thing he remembered was being naked in the sea, fighting the fury of the storm as he swam towards a distant island, knowing the sash would protect him.

After what seemed like an eternity, he heard the waves crashing against rocks and was almost dashed to death against them himself. Striking out again, he swam on until he felt the current change and knew he was near the mouth of a river. He swam towards it and pulled himself up onto a pebbled beach, nearly dead from cold and exhaustion. Tossing the goddess's sash back into the water, he stumbled up the shore towards a small wood, its trees tall and black against the night sky. Here he threw himself down beneath the shelter of some olive bushes and fell into a deep sleep. Or so he had dreamed.

As his senses awoke to the world around him, he forced his eyes open and looked up at a dense mesh of interlocked branches and leaves. The canopy was only an arm's length above his face, and looking around he could see he was cocooned inside a natural shelter. Its thick walls filtered out the sun so that the only light came from the narrow archway at his feet, through which he must have climbed the night before. This was the place beneath the olive bushes that he had dreamed about. Recognition brought back his other memories – of the storm that had torn his raft to pieces, and of the two-day fight for survival that had followed. None of it had been a dream, except perhaps the sympathetic goddess and her sash. And the laughter of the woodland nymphs.

Then he heard them again, and he knew he was not dreaming. He thought he heard a clear voice singing, too. They were all female, but he questioned the wisdom of showing himself. He had found little welcome in the strange lands he had wandered in since leaving Troy, and even those who had treated him with apparent friendship had too often proved to be enemies. But as he lay on his bed of olive leaves looking up at the tightly wound branches, he was suddenly aware of his thirst and hunger. He had not had a sip of water or eaten a morsel of food for two days and two nights, and his body was desperate for nourishment. And if he was to find his way home, he first had to learn where he was, and discover what help might be available. Reluctantly, he turned about and crawled out.

He staggered to his feet and surveyed his surroundings. The late-summer sun shone brightly through the trees above, warming his skin and making him squint against the light. The sound of waves rolling in on a pebble shore came from his left. The laughing voices also came from there so, driven by his hunger, he stumbled through the undergrowth to the edge of the copse.

The grass sloped away before him towards a shingle beach, with the mouth of a wide river to his right. A covered wagon was parked on its far bank, where two mules munched lazily at the grass. Along the edge of the watercourse were a number of large rocks, on which were laid brightly coloured dresses, rich tunics, cloaks and a few heavily embroidered drapes. A fine steam was rising from them, and on the beach beyond Odysseus could see five young women tossing a ball from one to another, while a single voice kept time with a song. An excited yell was followed by a splash as the ball overshot and landed in the river. Odysseus ran forwards into the water and picked it up before it could be washed out to sea.

A high scream rang out and was followed by several more. Odysseus looked up to see four of the girls running away, as if a lion, rather than a mere man, had sprung snarling from the trees. One dived beneath the wagon while two more jumped into the back. The fourth ran along the beach without stopping. The fifth, though, remained where she stood, staring wide-eyed at him with her chest rising and falling in rapid breaths. She was young – barely more than a child – and very tall, with black braids that fell down past her hips. Her dress was simple and practical and she wore no jewellery, but from her determination not to flee – despite the obvious fear in her large brown eyes – he knew at once that she was high-born.

'My lady,' he said with a bow. 'Forgive me for startling you and your friends. I'm a stranger here and...'

'Sir, is it any wonder you scared us?' she replied. 'When a naked savage leaps from the trees, how else are civilised women supposed to react?'

Odysseus glanced down at himself. The days spent building the raft and sailing it on half-rations had burned away his flab and restored his muscles to something like their former tone. But his skin was smeared with a combination of brine, sand and dirt, and he had thrown off all his clothing in the storm when he had leapt from his raft to swim for shore. He lowered the leather ball to cover his manhood and stared awkwardly back at the girl.

'Again, I ask your forgiveness, my lady. I washed up on these shores last night after nineteen days at sea, two of them in the water after Poseidon destroyed my raft, and now I'm starving and exhausted. But not all the gods can be against me if they've brought me into the presence of such matchless beauty.' The girl's mouth twitched into a smile, which she quickly suppressed again. 'And it's obvious by your speech that you're a lady of high birth and noble mind; doubtless a respecter of the laws of xenia, which the gods decreed to protect poor unfortunates like myself. Will you tell me what place this is? And would you show me the kindness of a drop of water and a few rags to cover my shame?'

The girl's breathing had steadied and her look of fear had mellowed into one of intrigue and mild disgust.

'Sir, you have arrived on the island of Phaeacia, where King Alcinous reigns in wisdom and majesty, and is idolised as a god by his people. I am Nausicaa, his daughter, and you have my word that no suppliant has anything to fear here, where xenia and the gods are held in high respect. Come, my maids will bathe you and clothe you with a tunic and cloak, though I have no sandals for your feet. And you are welcome to what few provisions we have brought with us before you go on your way.'

'Thank you, my lady. You are kind as well as beautiful, and I pray the gods will bless you with a handsome husband, a fine home and many children. As for my own family and home, the gods separated us twenty years ago, and I have been trying to find my way back to them ever since. Perhaps there is a ship on Phaeacia that would allow me to earn my passage back to Greece?'

'Sir, only my father can decide who leaves Phaeacia, even if they arrive uninvited.'

'Then perhaps you will tell me how to find his palace, so I can put my case before him?'

'He isn't known for his sympathy towards beggars and vagabonds,' Nausicaa replied, though there was a look of pity in her eyes now. 'But it seems to me you could be a man of noble blood, despite your vulgar appearance. You certainly display good manners, and I can see from the stubble what the harvest was like, even if Zeus has cast misfortune in your path. When you've satisfied your hunger and are more presentable, I will tell you how to find my father's palace. He is a busy man but may listen to your entreaties – in time.'

She turned and called to her maids, admonishing them for running away and deserting her. Slowly they emerged from their hiding places and approached Odysseus, as much out of curiosity as in response to the command of their mistress. She told them to take him to the river, wash him and rub him with olive oil. But as soon as he had descended the bank and stood in the shallow water, out of sight of Nausicaa, they threw him a sponge and a flask of olive oil.

'Wash yourself, you old tramp,' said one. 'Then put on that tunic and cloak before you come before the princess again. You're lucky she took pity on you.'

Lucky indeed, he thought. After all, what right did a naked beggar have to expect anything from a princess? But she was his best hope of entering her father's presence so he could request passage home. He waited for the maids to go, then threw the ball that had been covering his modesty over the bank onto the grass and began washing. He had to work hard to scrub the scurf from his skin and wash the dried salt from his hair, but after he had finished he rubbed himself with the oil and oiled his hair.

On the rocks nearby were several tunics and cloaks that were drying in the sun. Some were of plain wool, like the one the maid had told him to wear, but others were richly dyed and embroidered. Ignoring the clothes the maids had left him, he chose a fine blue tunic and a cloak of rich purple. Once he was dressed, he climbed up the bank to find Nausicaa and her maids standing by the wagon.

They looked at him in disbelief, shocked that the beggarly figure who had rushed out to them from the woods now stood before them looking like a king. After a few giggles and nudges from her maids, Nausicaa came towards him.

'Forgive me, sir. When I first saw you, I found you… well, I misjudged you. They say the gods sometimes visit the earth dressed like beggars to test what is in a man's heart.'

Odysseus laughed.

'I can assure you, I'm no god.'

'And I'm no man, sir, or I might have recognised your noble status and treated you with more respect and kindness. As it is, I'm just a girl and still learning my manners. But perhaps I can earn your forgiveness by taking you to my father's palace. You can walk beside me while I drive the wagon back – not before you have satisfied your thirst and hunger, though.'

She gave him a last look – though whether it was still disbelief at his transformation, or something deeper, he did not know – then called to her maids to bring food and drink. Two of them pulled a box from the back of the wagon and brought it over to him, while the third spread a fleece over the grass and the fourth fetched a skin of wine. In the box he found a few flatbreads, some fish and a little fruit. It was only the leftovers from a meal Nausicaa and her maids had eaten earlier, but he ate it greedily until nothing was left. He slaked his thirst on the wine, but left half for the journey back to the palace. Meanwhile, the others folded up the clothes and stacked them in the back of the small wagon, then harnessed the mules ready to go.

The chariot of the sun had passed its zenith by the time they set off, and the breeze from the sea cooled them as they followed a dirt track into the foothills of the purple mountains. Sunlight gleamed from their snowy caps, and with new clothes and a full stomach Odysseus felt better than he had done for a long time. He remained anxious about what sort of people the Phaeacians would turn out to be but, judging by Nausicaa's character, he hoped they would be civilised and gods-fearing. The thought that they might provide him passage home left him feeling sick with anticipation, but also revived ingrained fears of the inevitable sea crossing that would require. Poseidon had not yet satisfied his desire for revenge – Odysseus still lived, after all – and the thought of embarking on another voyage filled him with despair.

He tried to encourage himself with what memories of Ithaca remained to him, but his recollections were stale and joyless. So, instead, he imagined how Penelope and Telemachus would welcome him when he walked unexpectedly back into their lives. He pictured Penelope, her face a blur, sitting on her chair in the great hall and working on her loom. He wondered whether she would stand and run into his arms, or stare at him in shock before coming to him in tears. Or would she look at him with eyes that had long since been emptied of love, resenting his return and shaking her head at the sight of him? And Telemachus? He would be a man in his own right by now, a man who had grown up without Odysseus's love and influence. Would his son honour him or loathe him?

'Did you fight in the great war?' Nausicaa asked him after they had been travelling for a while.

'The war against Troy? What do you know about it?'

'Demodocus, our bard, sings about it often. I think he might have been there, though he never speaks of his own part in it. He makes the war seem terrible and tragic, not glorious and exciting like the other poets.'

'Then he must have fought at Troy, for no one who had witnessed that slaughter would sing of it as glorious and exciting.'

'Then you *were* there! When you said you were parted from your family twenty years ago, I wondered if it was the war that had separated you. But it's been ten years since the walls of Troy fell. Why are you only going back now?'

'My dear Nausicaa,' Odysseus said with a laugh, 'I've been trying to find my way home for all that time. But the story of my adventures is a long one, and now is not the time to tell it. I'd prefer to hear about your father. Is he a kind ruler, or is he difficult to please? Will he listen to a foreigner who has lost everything on his travels and only seeks to find his way home again? His own daughter should be able to advise on how to win his sympathy.'

Nausicaa gave the mules a touch of her whip, then glanced over her shoulder at the maids walking behind the wagon. She gave a shrug.

'Kind, difficult to please, godlike, stern, generous – he's whatever my mother tells him to be, if you see my meaning, sir.'

'I think I do.'

'They are often together in the great hall, her at her loom and my father drinking wine until she tells him he's had too much. I would take you directly to them myself, but it wouldn't be good for me to be seen entering the city with you. The gossips would say you are to be my husband, or worse rumours. Instead, with your permission, I will leave you at Athena's Grove outside the city walls. When I've had enough time to reach the palace myself, you should enter the city and make your own way there. Anyone can tell you how to find it, but be careful who you ask. We Phaeacians are proud, and someone may ask who you are or insult you.'

And so they travelled on between cultivated fields, orchards, stone-walled sheep pens and lonely farmsteads. As he walked, Odysseus asked questions about the island and its people, and Nausicaa answered freely and fully. She had already come to trust the stranger, despite his appearance at their first meeting and the fact he had neither given her his name nor his heritage. An observer seeing them chatting and laughing together might easily have mistaken them for father and daughter, rather than would-be lovers, as Nausicaa had feared. And all the time, Odysseus was wondering how he would convince her father not only to let him leave Phaeacia, but also to provide him with passage home to Ithaca.

Chapter Eight

The Road to Sparta

It was the second day of the journey to Sparta. Eperitus and Telemachus had stayed the night at the house of a friend of Nestor, whom Peisistratus had promised would give them a warm welcome and good lodging. With an early start, they were able to reach the top of the pass through the Taygetus Mountains by late afternoon. As they passed a final bend in the road, the broad plain of Sparta opened up below them. Half was under the shadow of the mountains, cast by the westering sun behind them; the rest was a haze of browns and greens where the remaining sunlight lingered on the farmsteads and olive groves.

'That's the Eurotas,' Eperitus said, drawing the chariot to a halt and pointing to the broad river gleaming in the distance. 'And that's Sparta.'

'I know it well,' Telemachus said. 'I stayed there for a while when I was a boy.'

Eperitus glanced at him, wondering why he had spent time away from his homeland, then returned his gaze to the city. His eyesight – like all his senses – had a supernatural quality, given to him many years before by Athena. Despite the irritating eyepatch he had adopted as a disguise, he could see every detail of the city walls and their watchtowers, with the sun gleaming from the shields and helmets of the soldiers that guarded them. A swathe of hovels lapped against the battlements, while inside were the well-built houses of the nobles and merchants.

At the highest point was the citadel, the beating heart of the city with its high walls and stone temples, and the palace complex at its centre. Eperitus looked at its broad courtyard and the bright, many windowed walls, and remembered the weeks he had spent there as a companion of Odysseus. The king had gone to Sparta to court the beautiful Helen, but had returned with Penelope – a humble princess next to Helen, but Odysseus's match in intelligence and guile. That had been thirty years ago, though to Eperitus it seemed as if he had lived through many lifetimes since then.

'I also know it, my lord,' he said

'Then have you seen Helen? Is she as beautiful as they say?'

'*More* beautiful, though I wonder how the years have treated her.'

'The years and her husband,' Telemachus added, raising an eyebrow at Eperitus. 'After all that passed between them, I expect forgiveness hasn't come easily.'

Eperitus laughed and shook the reins, encouraging the horses on down the winding road towards the shadows below.

'She was just an unhappy girl, really,' he said. 'Desperate to escape the pressures of palace life and find freedom and obscurity. Not easy to do when you're the most beautiful woman in the world.'

'How do you *know* that?'

'She told a good friend of mine,' Eperitus lied.

He recalled his meetings with Helen in Aphrodite's temple all those years ago. She had been a young maiden then, desperate for freedom and idealistic about love. They had met to discuss the possibility of running away with Odysseus, and over time they had formed their own friendship. She had even once offered herself to him, to be his wife if he would take her away from Sparta.

'There's more to you than meets the eye, Theoclymenus,' Telemachus said, looking him up and down with a half-smile on his lips. 'And yet you say so little about your past. I almost had to bully it out of you that you were at Troy, though you won't say who you fought for, other than it wasn't for Nestor. And if I mention the great kings who took part in the war, it's almost like you knew them personally. You don't say as much, but I can see it in your face – just like when we spoke of Helen a few moments ago.'

'You have your father's intelligence,' Eperitus said, smiling despite himself. An instant later he cursed his slip.

'You knew him, too?'

'Only by reputation.'

He pulled on the reins as they reached a tight bend in the road, guiding the horses carefully around it. Another sloping stretch of road lay before them, with the side of the mountain on the right and a drop down to the next level of the road on the left. He could see the stony track doubling back on itself several times as it wound its way through the trees that covered the lower half of the mountainside, down to the floor of the valley far below.

'And yet,' Telemachus continued, 'when you helped me up into the chariot yesterday morning, my first thought was you might be an assassin sent by the suitors to do away with me. Mentor warned me against you at the banquet the day before. Said you were staring at me.'

Eperitus felt the edge to Telemachus's questions. The lad suspected something about him, but did not yet know what it was.

'Then why did you get into the chariot? If you're afraid of assassination, you should be more careful. *Much* more careful.'

'So why *were* you staring at me?'

Eperitus gave a flick of the reins, urging the horses on to the next bend in the road. He felt suddenly awkward. He had enjoyed his time with Telemachus, who reminded him of Odysseus in the days before the war had corrupted everyone who took part in it. But now the moment he feared had come: he was asking questions that Eperitus was not sure he could answer without divulging who he really was. And the last thing he wanted was to reveal that he had been a friend of Odysseus, which would oblige him to explain to Telemachus that the father he was so desperate to find had actually perished long ago. All he wanted was to forge a new life for himself, not be dragged back into the old one.

'When you mentioned the men who've taken over your home and how they treat you and your mother, I was offended,' he said. 'After ten years of war, a man expects to return to a civilised world where there's peace and justice. So to hear that your father's kingdom has succumbed to chaos and the rule of brute force... Well, it angered me.'

They reached the next bend in the mountain road, and turning it entered the darkness of the tall fir trees that clung to the steep slope. Eperitus thought back to how he had felt when he first set eyes on Telemachus: the shock of seeing the shadow of Odysseus's face in his; and when he spoke, hearing the echo of the king's voice. It had been like the jolt of a knife wound, ripping suddenly through his nerves and knocking the strength out of him. He had not understood his feelings then – joy, pain, hope, regret, relief and anger, all tumbled into one – and even now he still did not understand the meaning of how he had felt.

But he knew it was no coincidence that Odysseus's son had come to Sparta a few days after he had arrived there himself. It had to be the call of the gods, telling him to return to Ithaca. He had tried to escape the past, but the past would not let him. And so he had resolved to accompany Telemachus on his journey to Sparta and then escort him back to Ithaca, if Telemachus would have him. If, indeed, there was anything that a man who had vowed never to kill again could do.

And then there was Penelope. Could he stand idly by while a woman he had respected and loved as a sister offered herself to someone who could violate the rules of xenia in such a way? Inexplicably, the thought of her remarrying sickened him more than anything, even if there was little he could do to intervene. The more he thought about it, the more powerless he realised he was to make a difference on Ithaca. But go there he must. It was his fate, and he had learned that Fate was unavoidable.

'Have you thought what you'll do if Menelaus tells you your father's dead?' Eperitus asked, peering into the gloom ahead of them.

'I'll return home and sort matters out myself. I couldn't call myself a man unless I tried.'

'But they'll kill you.'

'Better death with honour than life with shame.'

'You remind me of somebody I used to know,' Eperitus said. 'Perhaps with hindsight he would have advised you to forget honour and cherish the life you have.'

'A wise man, by the sounds of it,' Telemachus said. 'But he wasn't born in the shadow of Odysseus. Not only do I have that to live up to, but I've promised someone special that I'll face up to the suitors.'

'Penelope?'

'Mother? She doesn't care about me or anything I do.'

'I doubt that.'

'There you go again,' Telemachus said, glancing at him from the corner of his eye. 'But if you must know, it's a girl.'

'A girl!' Eperitus mocked, a wry smile on his lips. 'A *girl*. So you won't do it for yourself, but you'll do it for some nobleman's daughter who fluttered her big eyes at you. She probably doesn't care if you die in the attempt, and certainly wants something from you if you succeed.'

'It's not like that,' Telemachus said with a shy grin.

'Of course not. It's different.'

'Anyway, I thought perhaps you might want to come back to Ithaca with me. You know, help me put matters in order. You're a fighting man, after all.'

'I used to be.'

'*Used* to be?'

'I took a vow never to kill again.'

'You did *what*?'

He stared at his companion, but Eperitus was suddenly focused on the road ahead of them.

'What's that? Whoa!'

Eperitus pulled the horses to a halt and peered into the shadows. A tree had fallen across the road, its thick trunk flat against the ground and its dense branches sticking up like a wall.

'It must have fallen,' Telemachus said. 'Do you think we can move it?'

'It didn't fall. It was chopped down. Do you see?'

Eperitus pointed to the stump where the pale flesh of the tree was clear in the gloom. He pulled the reins to one side, guiding the horses into a tight turn, but before they could face the chariot about, several men emerged from behind rocks and trees. Two seized hold of the horses while the rest surrounded the chariot. They wore woollen tunics that came to below their knees and around their shoulders were the skins of long-haired goats. By the dirt on their skin and their unkempt hair and beards, it was plain to Eperitus they were used to sleeping rough. Though none wore any armour that he could see, they each had a weapon of some kind, ranging from daggers and swords to clubs and spears. Eperitus reached down and picked up the food bag and a skin of wine, throwing them on the ground.

'Here. Now let us pass.'

A man stepped forwards. He was tall and broad-shouldered with a beard that hung down to his stomach. His arms and legs were so thick with muscles that he seemed barely able to bend elbow or knee. In his hand was a large club with a dozen arrowheads embedded in the wood, point-outward.

'We want the chariot and your cloaks,' he said in a lazy, foreign-accented voice.

'Do as he says,' Eperitus whispered to Telemachus. 'If we comply, there's a chance they'll let us live.'

'There're just twelve of them. We only have to kill two or three and the rest'll run.'

Eperitus stepped down from the chariot and unclasped his cloak.

'Look at their eyes, Telemachus. They aren't runners, any of them. Now get out of that chariot and take off your cloak.'

He knew their chances were slim, and that if he let them have his cloak he would have nothing to snag their weapons in if they attacked. But he had no choice. He rolled it into a bundle and threw it to the leader. Telemachus did the same.

'Now your weapons.'

Telemachus picked up his shield and spears before the horses and chariot were led away, leaving the two men at the centre of the circle of brigands. He lifted the shield onto his arm and planted one of the spears into the dirt.

'Not the weapons,' he said.

Eperitus turned round so that he was back to back with Telemachus. Since his vow, he had been the victim of a few beatings in which he had never lifted a hand in his own defence. Even when he had felt his life was under threat he had been happy to keep his promise to the gods, and in return they had allowed him to survive. But if he refused to fight now, then he would surely die and Telemachus would perish with him. Did he have the right to decide Telemachus's fate for him? A small voice in his head dared to utter that it would be one way to pay Odysseus back for Astynome, but he cut it off immediately.

'Have you ever killed a man?' he asked Telemachus in a whisper.

'No.'

'Have you been in a battle before?'

'With weapons?'

'Of course!'

'No, but I know how to use a shield and spear. And there's a spear for you, too.'

Telemachus pointed to the spear point-down in the dirt. Eperitus looked at it, tempted to hold it in his hands and feel that never-forgotten power that a weapon gives a man. Then he shook his head.

'My oath can't be broken.'

The leader of the brigands pointed his heavy club at Telemachus.

'Give us your weapons now and we will let you go.'

'Give us yours first,' Telemachus responded.

The man gave a nod and four of his followers stepped forwards, two facing Eperitus and two opposite Telemachus. Eperitus looked at the short swords in the hands of his grinning opponents and tried to think how best he could use his bare hands and body to protect Telemachus's back. Then one of the men raised his sword with a snarl. And instinct took over.

He snatched the spear out of the dirt, tossed it in the air and caught the base with both hands. The man gave a fierce cry and launched his attack. Eperitus swung the spear round in a wide arc and caught him in the side of the head before he was within arm's reach. There was a crack of bone and a grunt as the brigand dropped his sword and fell unconscious in the dirt.

The second swordsman charged, his weapon held in both hands above his head. Eperitus dropped to one knee and swept the spear low over the ground, catching the man hard on his ankle. He came crashing down, rolling onto his shoulder and jarring the weapon out of his grip. As he struggled to regain his feet, Eperitus stood and kicked him in the side of the head. The blow knocked him onto his back and he did not move again.

A loud shout behind Eperitus was followed by a clash of bronze. He turned and saw Telemachus force aside the blade of one of his opponents, opening his unarmoured body to an easy spear-thrust. Telemachus stabbed the point of his weapon into the man's liver and pulled it out again. The man dropped to his knees – blood gushing from the wound and his mouth – and fell face down in the dirt. Eperitus saw horror and doubt flash across Telemachus's face, to be swept aside as he took a blow from his second attacker's club with his shield. The training Mentor had given him had taken over, and Eperitus knew he would not have to carry Odysseus's son through the fight.

He turned and saw four more brigands fan out before him. They had seen the quick demise of their comrades and edged toward him with caution.

'Take him!' their leader snapped.

Eperitus looked down at the discarded sword of one of his victims, which lay in the dust at his feet. He could throw the spear at one of the men, then snatch up the sword and deal with the other three. If his fighting skills had not grown too rusty, he knew he could kill them all in a matter of moments. But the violent impulse that had seized him – sparked by the instinct to protect Telemachus – had receded, and he remembered his vow. He would not take up the sword and he would not kill his enemies. He even considered holding up a hand for parley, but negotiation had not helped before and it was too late for words now. The four men were coming closer, none keen to be the first to attack, but each seeking an opening in his defences. Eperitus knew what he had to do.

He lowered his spear and pointed to their leader, beckoning to him with a flick of his fingers. The man's small eyes narrowed, then he spat on the fallen tree trunk and waved the others back. The sound of fighting ceased behind Eperitus and, glancing over his shoulder, he saw that the three men who had been pressing Telemachus hard had lowered their weapons and fallen back. Their chieftain strode forwards, swinging his club in a circle above his head so that a single blow would crush Eperitus's skull, if it did not remove his head entirely.

'Throw your spear at him,' Telemachus urged. 'Or stand aside and let me face the brute.'

Eperitus waved him back. Crouching low, he watched the brigand chieftain come steadily closer. The slightest misjudgement would mean death, and perhaps that would be the price he must pay for not breaking his vow. But death did not scare him. He dashed forwards and rolled beneath the downward swing of the club, knocking the chieftain's legs from under him and bringing him down into the dirt. He gave a loud grunt, but twisted aside and staggered to his feet again, the club still clutched in his hand.

Eperitus was already up. As the brigand blinked and glanced around to find him, he brought the shaft of the spear down fast and hard onto his wrist. The club fell from the man's hand and he gave a howl of pain. Eperitus dropped his spear and sprang forwards, punching him first in the stomach, then swinging his fist up hard into his jaw, snapping his head back. The chieftain staggered backwards into the semicircle of his men, who held him as he steadied himself. He blinked and shook his head, then turned his fierce stare on Eperitus.

'Now I'm going to kill you,' he grunted.

He lunged forwards and threw his arms about Eperitus's body. The air was squeezed from Eperitus's lungs and he felt the pressure on his ribs and back threatening to break his bones and crush his insides. He cried out with pain and punched his attacker repeatedly in the face, but that only made him tighten his grip.

Out of the corner of his eye, Eperitus saw Telemachus move to help him, only to have his advance blocked by several brigands. His senses were succumbing to the pain and the lack of air now, and he knew he did not have long left. In desperation, he seized the chieftain by the hair and sank his teeth into his cheek. He felt the wiry hair of his beard and smelled the combination of fresh sweat and rank breath. The skin beneath his teeth was rubbery in its resistance, before suddenly succumbing and filling his mouth with the taste of blood. He bit harder, forcing his teeth deeper into the flesh. The man's grip about his body grew tighter in a last attempt to kill him, then Eperitus felt the man's cheek coming away in his teeth.

At the same time, the arms that held him let go and the brigand pulled away, clutching at his cheek and crying out at the top of his voice as he fell backwards on the dirt road and began to kick out in his pain. Eperitus fell to the ground and spat the bloody mess from his mouth as he gasped for air. Breathing was hard, his chest bruised and painful as he forced the muscles to move, but he knew the fight was not over. As his senses returned, he saw the spear lying among the dead pine needles beside him. He reached out and seized it, then forced himself back onto his feet. When he turned, he saw his opponent pushing himself up onto one knee, his other hand still clutching at his face. Eperitus swung the spear hard into his face, snapping the shaft in half. The chieftain fell onto his back and lay still.

Seeing their leader defeated, the others turned and fled into the trees. Telemachus ran forwards and caught Eperitus by the arm as he stumbled, helping him to his feet.

'Zeus's beard!' he exclaimed. 'I thought you were dead for certain.'

'I don't die that easily,' Eperitus gasped, lowering himself onto the fallen tree trunk.

He clutched at his sides, feeling the pain of each breath and wondering if any ribs had been broken. His heavy muscles had probably saved him from worse hurt, he thought. Then he looked around at the scene of the battle. The other brigands he had felled had either regained consciousness or been taken away by their comrades. Only their chief and the man Telemachus had slain remained.

'You'd better find some rope, my lord,' he said, 'and bind him before he wakes up. And then we'll have to harness the horses to that trunk and pull it out of the way before we can move on again. Give me a moment to catch my breath and I'll help you.'

He pushed himself to his feet, took two steps towards Telemachus, and collapsed.

Chapter Nine

King Alcinous

As the sun was setting, Odysseus and Nausicaa crested a ridge and saw two harbours before them. Both were filled with a mixture of fishing boats and merchant galleys; the smaller vessels drawn up on the pebbled beaches for the night and the larger anchored out in the middle of each bay. The road continued on a causeway that separated the harbours, then ran up a slope between a stone temple on the left and a poplar wood on the right. Outside the temple was a painted wooden statue holding a fishing spear, reminding Odysseus that even if he convinced Alcinous to grant him passage home, he still had Poseidon's wrath to contend with.

A little farther on was a city built on a hill. It was surrounded by a thick wall punctuated with several square towers, and though not particularly large, Odysseus noted that it looked wealthy. The sort of wealth that only a trading city that had not suffered war could enjoy. There were many well-built, flat-roofed buildings, but the largest of them all sat on the crown of the hill and seemed to blaze with fire as the last rays of the sun caught its bronze-covered walls. He was reminded of his first sight of Aeolus's palace, nearly ten years before, and hoped it was not a bad omen.

Nausicaa paused to look at her home and Odysseus saw the faint smile of satisfaction on her young face. He wondered whether he would ever enjoy the same satisfaction for himself again. Then she tapped the whip against the mules' flanks and they continued down the slope and across the causeway, stopping when they had reached the wood. Dusk had already fallen, but in the twilight he could see a clearing through the trees and hear the trickle of water.

'This is Athena's Grove,' Nausicaa announced. 'There's a spring that you can drink from, and if you wish you can sit in my father's royal garden and rest before you enter the city. And remember, if you want to return to your home, then seek out my mother, Queen Arete, and win her over. Goodbye.'

Odysseus smiled and bowed slightly. He watched Nausicaa and her maids continue up to the city gates, which had been left open and seemed unguarded, then follow a path through the trees to the garden. The brightly coloured flowers were rapidly turning to grey, but their mingled aromas still filled the cool evening air. The spring came from a large rock set to one side of what looked like a man-made pool. He sat on a wooden bench opposite it and listened to the music of the water, praying quietly to Athena until darkness descended.

By now a thin mist was creeping between the boles of the trees and sitting low on the grass. Odysseus rose to his feet and pulled his hood up so that his face was lost in its shadow. As he left the grove, the temple of Poseidon had half disappeared beneath the fog, and all he could see of the harbours were the masts of the different ships. He followed the road up to the city walls. Two guards were standing within the shadow of the gates, but did not challenge him as he passed through into the city. Here the flagstoned streets were quiet. A few Phaeacians were returning to their homes at the end of their day's labours, and though some glanced at the hooded figure with suspicion, none spoke to him.

He followed the upward incline of the road, but could not see the palace through the thickening fog. Then a child appeared, carrying a clay pithos on her shoulder. She was perhaps no more than ten years old and was struggling beneath the weight of her burden, yet gladly agreed to take him to the palace. She led him to a broad avenue lined with white-plastered houses. It curved upwards, and as they passed the angle of the bend Odysseus saw Alcinous's palace ahead of him. It was clad with bronze and topped by a frieze of blue enamel. Though night had fallen and a dense fog surrounded it, the walls glowed with a dull sheen cast by torches in the compound below.

His guide, who seemed indifferent to the magnificent sight, continued on to the gate in the outer wall. Odysseus pulled his hood forwards and followed, wondering how he would get past the guard and wishing Nausicaa was still with him. But the guard was leaning against the wall with his cloak pulled about his shoulders, fast asleep. He turned to thank the girl, but she had disappeared.

Walking quickly and silently past the soldier, he entered a compound lit by several torches that gave the walls of the palace their glow. The enormous golden doors that barred the entrance were open. On either side were figures of gigantic hunting dogs, one of silver and one of gold. They were so perfectly detailed that Odysseus could almost have believed they were alive. The doors were otherwise unguarded, and he stepped through into the great hall.

Golden statues of young men stood in the corners of the vaulted chamber, holding burning torches that illuminated the hall with yellow light. Tall chairs were ranged about the walls, each draped with ornately embroidered covers, and long tables were set before them on which were left the remains of a sumptuous feast. Dozens of slaves were busy clearing away the scraps of food and the dirty plates, bowls and cups, while in the centre of the hall, gathered around the large hearth, a crowd of Phaeacian nobles were calling on the name of Hermes as they poured libations into the flames.

Set a little back from the circular fire were two high-backed chairs. A man was slumped halfway down one, a wine cup in his hand and a bored expression on his face as he watched the group around the hearth, some of whom were giving their cups to slaves and throwing cloaks around their shoulders in readiness to leave. In the other sat a woman so tall that her head and shoulders were above the back of the chair. She was using a spindle and distaff to spin yarn, and behind her a group of maids were seated by a stone pillar doing the same. Recognising the king and queen from Nausicaa's description, Odysseus threw back his hood, swept his cloak back over his shoulder and crossed the hall.

'Can I help you, my lord?' asked a steward as he passed.

Some of the nobles turned to look at him.

'Who's that?' asked one.

'The feast's over, friend,' said another.

The queen looked up at the sound of raised voices, then dropped her spindle in surprise as Odysseus walked past her husband and dropped to his knees before her. He threw his arms about her legs in a sign of supplication and looked up at her. She stared back, her large, square-jawed face blank with astonishment.

'My lady Arete,' Odysseus began, 'may the gods increase your happiness and grant you long life! I'm a stranger on Phaeacia, a shipwreck who has suffered long at the hands of the immortals, and I throw myself at the mercy of your husband, yourself and your guests.'

With tears in his eyes, he released the queen's legs and crawled away to sit in the ashes that had spilled from the hearth, his head bowed. The guests had fallen silent and were staring intently at the newcomer. King Alcinous stirred from his stupor and looked at Odysseus in confusion.

'Who's this? How did he get into my palace?'

A young man stepped out of the crowd and took Odysseus roughly by the arm.

'Leave him alone, Laodamas,' Arete commanded. 'For all we know this man could be a god. Alcinous, has the hospitality of your hall fallen so much? Lift your guest out of those ashes and give him a chair to sit on. Then tell Pontonous to mix more wine – we must offer a libation to Zeus, the protector of suppliants. And bring some food!'

The queen had found her voice again, and at the sound of it the men around her became charged with life. The king – a short man with a ruddy face – left his chair and offered his hand to Odysseus, while all around them the guests removed their cloaks again and returned to their seats, eager to find out the identity of their strange visitor. Odysseus took Alcinous's hand and felt the strength in the grey-haired king's arm as he pulled him to his feet. Without concern for either man's dignity, Alcinous patted the ashes from the back of Odysseus's cloak and led him to the seat closest to his own, where the young man who had seized Odysseus by the arm had just sat down.

'Come now, Laodamas, give up your chair for our guest. There are plenty more at the back of the hall.'

'Yes, Father,' Laodamas said, standing reluctantly and glaring at Odysseus.

'Pontonous!' Alcinous hollered. 'Now where is that lazy, hunch-backed...?'

'I'm here, my lord.' A stooped man with a long chin and black hair appeared at his side. A group of stewards stood behind him, one carrying a mixing bowl and the others jars of wine or water. 'I'll have the wine mixed shortly.'

A maid came with a basin and some water for Odysseus's hands, followed by an old slave with baskets of food, which she laid on the table before him.

'Eat your fill, my friend,' Alcinous said. 'And if you *are* a god in disguise, then forgive your servant if I was a little slow in welcoming you. You took us a bit by surprise, you know.'

Odysseus smiled.

'I'm no god, my lord, just a man desperate to find passage home. I have been told you will be able to help me.'

'That depends,' Alcinous replied, cryptically. 'Now, eat up while I get rid of these hangers-on. No doubt my wife'll want to question you alone.' He turned to the rest of the hall and clapped his hands. 'My friends, don't remove your cloaks or make yourself comfortable again. It's late and we're all tired; go to your homes and return in the morning, when we'll entertain our guest and test his quality. Off you go now.'

After the last man had gone and Odysseus had eaten his fill, Pontonous brought cups of wine for him and Alcinous. They poured libations to the gods while a slave set Odysseus's chair down in front of the thrones of the king and queen. Arete had returned to her spindle and distaff, but put them aside again and turned her attention to Odysseus as he sat before her.

'Now, sir, tell me who you are and where you come from. And where did you get such fine clothes? Didn't you say you were shipwrecked?'

In Greece it was an outrage for a woman to speak before her husband; and for a queen to question a suppliant while the king remained silent was unheard of. But Odysseus could sense the keen intelligence behind the large, unattractive face – an intelligence that Alcinous appeared to have accepted was greater than his own and must long ago have been happy to accede to. Odysseus met Arete's gaze, aware she was searching for more than just his name and background.

His old instinct to bend the truth stirred within him. Should he reveal his name, or mention the trials that had kept him from home for ten years – a tale she was unlikely to believe anyway? Should he disclose his meeting with Nausicaa and risk her parents' wrath that she had been unaccompanied in the presence of a man? Or was it easier to claim he was a mere merchant who had fallen victim to a storm? All these options rushed through his mind in an instant, and immediately he knew the answer. He had passed through life on a light wind of deceit, relying upon trickery and a quick mind to get his way. But dishonesty required unshakeable confidence – something he had lost while a prisoner on Ogygia. The exciting impulse to resort to cunning – the unexpected glimpse of his old character – faded away again; he decided to place his trust in the truth.

'Indeed, I was shipwrecked, my lady,' he said, his shoulders slumping, 'but that was just the most recent of my misfortunes. The man before you has been cursed by the gods to wander the seas from one landfall to the next, enduring terrible suffering and misfortunes. Seven years ago, Zeus sent a thunderbolt that destroyed my ship and all the men in it, except myself. For days I clung to a piece of flotsam until, half-mad with thirst and hunger, I reached the island of Ogygia. There I became the prisoner of a goddess, Calypso, who made me her lover against my will, even offering me immortality if I would agree to marry her. But I refused to accept.'

'You *refused* immortality?' the king asked, leaning forwards on his knees and frowning.

'Be quiet, Alcinous,' Arete said. 'Please, carry on.'

'Yes, my lord, I refused for seven years until the gods who marooned me on her island remembered me and had a change of heart. They ordered her to let me go, so I built a raft and set sail, hoping against hope to find the home I've not seen for twenty years. And a foolish hope it was. The moment I saw the mountains of your homeland, Poseidon spotted me and took vengeance for what I did to his son.'

'What *did* you do to his son? *Which* son?'

'Alcinous!'

'He sent a storm that destroyed my raft,' Odysseus continued, at a nod from Arete, 'but by the strength of these arms and a little good fortune, I reached shore. And it was there, this very morning, I met your daughter. Her friends fled at the sight of me, naked and covered in brine, but she refused to run, showing character far beyond her years. Instead, she fed and clothed me. You recognised the tunic and cloak I'm wearing the first moment you saw me, did you not Queen Arete?'

'I embroidered them myself for my oldest son,' she said. 'Her gift was a generous one, to a man she did not know. And lesser men might have taken more than was offered.'

'Her gifts were good enough for me. Nausicaa is a credit to herself and her parents.'

'She's generous to a fault,' Alcinous said, 'but I'll be asking her why she didn't bring you direct to us herself. It would have saved you a lot of trouble.'

'And caused plenty for herself, you old goat,' Arete said, giving the king a gentle nudge on the arm. 'She knows the sort of gossip that would go around the city if she was seen entering the gates with a man beside her – and a foreigner, too.'

'Well, perhaps it wouldn't be such a bad thing,' Alcinous retorted. 'After all, the girl will need to find a husband soon, and our guest here strikes me as better than most of the young hotheads we breed on Phaeacia.'

'He's already married,' Arete said, giving Odysseus a knowing look, 'and it's clear he loves his wife more than life itself. Am I wrong, sir? Why else would you refuse an offer of immortality from a beautiful goddess?' She sat back and looked Odysseus up and down. 'There's more to you than you're telling. A man away from home for twenty years must have left to fight at Troy – that much is clear to me. But what kept you from returning to your wife, I wonder, before the gods washed you up on Ogygia? Perhaps you'll take the time to tell us tomorrow; and perhaps we'll find out then who you really are.'

'Gladly, my lady, and all I ask in return is for a ship to take me back to Greece. Nausicaa tells me visitors to Phaeacia cannot leave without the king's permission. That's why I came to you tonight, to beg passage back to my homeland.'

'It seems our daughter has sympathy for you – I assume it was she told you to come to me first, rather than my husband? But she hasn't told you everything about Phaeacia, it seems. We are a secretive people – our happiness depends on it. Though our galleys sail far and wide, mastering the seas and buying and selling goods to our profit, our small kingdom remains hidden from foreign ships. We are blessed by the gods, who protect us from the wars of other lands, from raiding and piracy, and from the ships of those seeking new homes. Sometimes the gods send us survivors of shipwrecks, like yourself, but they rarely return to their own countries again.'

'Rarely?' Odysseus asked, feeling the first fronds of despair creep into his heart.

'Most stay because they love our homeland, and we are prepared to tolerate their presence if they are peaceful. Some ask to leave.'

'Of these, only those of the highest character are permitted to go,' Alcinous added. 'Men who will swear never to return, and who can be trusted to keep their word. We do not want them coming back to Phaeacia at the head of a fleet, to rob us of our wealth and take our women and children into slavery. That's the way of your world, is it not?'

Odysseus nodded, shamefully.

'Then you understand,' Arete said. 'We will give thought to your request, but now it is time to sleep. A bed will be set up for you here in the hall, and tomorrow you will be our honoured guest. Perhaps you'll find our island to your liking and you will want to remain with us.'

'Not if I don't have a choice, my lady,' Odysseus replied.

Chapter Ten

A Proposition

The great hall was quiet without the suitors. Penelope sat in her chair, running her fingers repeatedly through the fleece that covered it. She looked at the familiar murals that ran around the walls, which seemed to dance in the pulsating glow from the hearth except near the open doors, where the hazy afternoon sunlight slanted in and drove the shadows away. She glanced at the weapons hanging on the walls and watched the smoke trailing up to the aperture in the high ceiling. She even looked at the dirt floor where the footprints of slaves had ruined the regular lines that had been raked into it that morning. Anywhere but at the seat to her left. Though the formal meeting of the Kerosia was over and its members had gone home, one of the small circle of seats remained occupied.

'What difference does it make whether you announce your decision tomorrow or on Apollo's feast day?' Eupeithes asked, a little impatiently.

'I will make my choice on the morning of the day I'm to be married, and not a day earlier,' she answered. 'The wedding can take place in the afternoon.'

Eupeithes sighed as if he were dealing with an obstinate child. He was still the pot-bellied, pale-skinned, mole-covered toad Penelope seemed to have spent her life fencing with, though he had lost the last of his hair over the past few years. He sat in the chair and observed her coldly, his thick purple cloak wrapped around himself despite the late-summer warmth and the heat from the fire.

'That doesn't leave long for Ithaca's future king to prepare himself.'

'Let him wait. Besides, there's still time for the oracle to be fulfilled. Do I need to remind you that the Pythoness predicted my husband – the *true* king of Ithaca – would return within ten years? That was on Apollo's feast day a decade ago, so I will wait until the day arrives before I honour my promise.'

'Odysseus perished long ago, Penelope,' Eupeithes said. 'You know it in your heart, and yet you insist on hurting yourself. If you'd chosen a new husband three years ago, you would have saved yourself all the trouble of these nightly feasts and so many mouths to feed. Yet you insisted on the trick with your father-in-law's shroud, and even now stubbornly refuse to name Odysseus's successor.'

She looked at him angrily.

'And if I had chosen then, I would have created an expectation of marriage. No! I want the people of Ithaca to know that I am still awaiting their king's return. And I want my son to know it, too. He has little enough faith in me since I sold his inheritance.'

The closer the day of her marriage came, the more she felt Telemachus's resentment at the oath she had taken. She could not expect him to understand she had acted for his safety, or that she hated herself for the decision she had taken. Instead, he thought she was betraying his father by remarrying, and so their once-close relationship had become distant and cool as a result. Indeed, she had not seen him since that day he had insisted Odysseus was still alive.

'You only yielded his right to the throne,' Eupeithes said. 'His other inheritance, his father's estate, still remains – though your suitors are eating into it while you put off your choice. But what does the timing matter any more, with so few days to go? The important thing is *who* you will choose. Surely you've given that some thought.'

'How can I be expected to choose from a pack of wolves? Isn't one as bad as another?'

'They may appear so, my queen, but a moment's consideration will show the advantages of one particular wolf – as you call them – over the rest.'

'You mean Antinous, of course,' she said. 'And you're correct. Your son *is* the greatest of them all – the greatest bully, the greatest braggart, the greatest thief! Do you think I could even contemplate allowing that arrogant buffoon into my bed? The thought repulses me.'

Eupeithes gripped the arm of his chair, then pushed himself up and walked to the back of the hall. Penelope watched him from the corner of her eye as he looked at the mural depicting his own defeat at the hands of Odysseus thirty years before. *How he must long to remove that reminder of his humiliation*, she thought. It amused her slightly to think of how she insisted his seat at the Kerosia was always placed facing that wall. But part of her also wondered whether it had only served to fire his ambition to have the last laugh. And once Antinous was king, Ithaca would be ruled from his own house, a palace to rival the home of Laertes, Odysseus and Telemachus. He turned from the mural and gave a dismissive shrug.

'Penelope, you think like all women. What does it matter if you don't love Antinous? And I'd be the first to agree that he lacks certain charms, not to mention that our families have been opposed to each other for so many years. But you'd only have to allow him into your bed once or twice, just enough to give him a male heir. By Hades, you could even make him sleep with a slave girl and pass the child off as your own! It matters little, as long as the people believe it's his and yours.

'And if you were to choose Antinous, I could make it worth your while. I am very rich, Penelope. If you were to help my son become king, I would help your son restore his estate by compensating him for all that the suitors have taken over the past three years. Every pig, sheep or goat they've eaten, every jar of wine they've drunk, I will replace. And more – much more! Just name your price. Within reason, of course,' he added with a small laugh.

'Do you really think I can be *bought*, Eupeithes?' she responded, rising to her feet. 'What sort of queen do you take me for? In all my years have I ever acted out of self-interest where the people of my husband's kingdom are concerned? Do you think I would betray them now by placing a monster on the throne? I'd sooner marry the lowliest and most destitute of all my suitors if he showed the slightest inclination towards serving the people rather than himself. Even if Antinous had shown me the respect due to his queen, let alone a woman he wanted to marry, I will never hand him the crown. So damn you, Eupeithes, and damn your son!'

The merchant looked at her sternly, then turned and began following the circuit of the walls.

'I thought that might be your reaction,' he said, stopping in front of a pair of crossed spears and picking one from the hooks that held it in place. He felt the weight of it in his hand, then looked down the shaft and turned it in his fingers, checking its straightness as if he were a warrior. 'Which is unfortunate, because as determined as you may be not to marry Antinous, I am *more* determined that you should. My offer to restore your son's inheritance was a kindness on my part, one that I didn't have to make. But now you've put me in a more desperate position, requiring a more desperate solution. And I think you know what I'm capable of when I really want something.'

'Are you proposing another failed coup?'

'Nothing quite so clumsy this time, my queen. But surely you know Phronius did not just *fall* off that cliff; and that the assassin who was sent to kill Telemachus all those years ago was not hired by Nisus. So, if you don't choose Antinous, then another assassin will come for him. And this time he will *not* fail. Indeed, a man has already been chosen and is merely awaiting my signal. So you see…'

'Get out! *Get out*!'

Penelope picked up the cup from the table by her chair and threw it at him. It crashed into the wall, spattering him with wine and making him drop the spear in surprise.

'Get out of my home at once, or I'll take that spear and kill you myself.'

'As you please, my queen. But your anger alone won't remove my threat. Choose Antinous, and Telemachus will be compensated for his loss; choose another, and he will pay with his life.'

She watched him walk out of the shadowy hall and into the sunlit courtyard beyond. Then, with a sudden lightness in her head, she groped for the arm of her chair and collapsed back into it. Her head reeled with the thought that she had gambled everything for Telemachus's safety, but they were planning to murder him anyway. Panicked, she knew there was only one thing she could do: she had to agree to Eupeithes's terms at once, before he could leave the palace and return to his home on the other side of the island.

She jumped up and ran to the porch. The sunlight was dazzling and forced her to throw her arm in front of her eyes. Squinting, she looked around the courtyard, only to see that he was not there. She ran to the open gates in the outer wall and stopped. Low voices were coming from the other side. Recognising them as belonging to Eupeithes and Antinous, she hid herself in the shadows and listened.

'She will choose you, just like I said she will,' Eupeithes said.

'How can you be sure? She shows me nothing but contempt.'

'That's because she loathes you, Antinous, and I expect you've done everything in your power to earn that. But I've made her an offer she won't refuse. I'm surprised she isn't running after me now to accept it.'

'What offer?'

'A bribe, of course, to reimburse her son's estate for everything you and your friends have helped yourself to.'

Antinous laughed.

'Much good it'll do him.'

'What do you mean?'

A short bark interrupted their conversation.

'I hate that flea-ridden hound,' Antinous said. 'The damned thing should have died years ago, but the gods keep it alive to torment me. Every time it sees me, it barks. Go on, damn you!'

Penelope heard a muffled thump followed by a pathetic whine. A moment later a dog limped slowly in through the open gates. Its fur was thin and patchy and its skin hung from its bones, making it look pathetic. She remembered Argus when Odysseus had first brought him to the palace as a puppy, and it pained her to see the old dog clinging on to life out of faithfulness to its master. Argus looked over his shoulder to see if Antinous was going to follow him with another kick, then saw Penelope. Turning slowly round, he hobbled towards her and lay down at her feet, his rheumy eyes staring up at her. She pressed a finger to her lips as she heard the conversation recommence.

'Where is the boy?' Eupeithes asked. 'I'm told nobody's seen him for days.'

'Gone to find news of his father. Didn't tell anybody; just took a galley with some of his friends and sailed to Pylos.'

Penelope covered her mouth with both hands. Telemachus had told her he had gone to Samos with Peiraeus.

'He's getting audacious,' Eupeithes said. 'It's to be expected, I suppose, as Apollo's feast day gets nearer. He won't come back with anything, though.'

Shocked tears rolled down Penelope's cheeks as she thought of her son sailing to the Peloponnese. She had lost her husband to the sea; she could not bear the thought of losing her son also. The thought pained her so much she did not hear Antinous's reply, though the tone of his father's response regained her attention.

'What do you mean? Of course it's important. If he comes back with so much as a rumour Odysseus is still alive, Penelope will contrive a way not to honour her oath.'

'I said don't worry. We've prepared an ambush for him. The moment his sail appears on the horizon, we'll go out to meet it, and neither Telemachus nor his crew will survive to bear witness to what happened.'

The sound of a hard slap announced what Eupeithes thought of his son's plan.

'You fool! Everything depends on Telemachus being alive when his mother picks her husband. Don't you understand that? By threatening her son's life I can persuade her to choose you over the other suitors; if you kill him, then all our leverage is gone.'

'*Never* hit me again, Father,' Antinous said, his voice low and hard. 'In a few days I'll be your king and then *I'll* have the whip hand, so you don't want to lose my favour. As for that bitch, there are other ways to make her choose me. Even if Telemachus gives us the slip and comes back with news his father's still alive, what of it? I'll make her honour her oath, whether she likes it or not.'

'And the people?' Eupeithes challenged. 'You think they'll stand by while you force their queen to marry against her will?'

'They haven't done anything so far, have they, other than complain that we've invaded the palace and helped ourselves to the king's estate? They're too afraid. And when Telemachus doesn't return from the mainland – when they think their little prince has run away forever – then they'll be quick enough to honour me as their king. If not, they'll feel the weight of the king's authority.'

'Antinous, my son, don't be rash!' Eupeithes said in a pleading tone, his voice receding as the two men began to walk away from the gates. 'Why do you think I've been so careful not to seem to impose my will on the people…?'

As the conversation faded from earshot, Penelope leaned back against the wall and slid down to her haunches. Shock at Telemachus's secret departure and disbelief at the suitors' plot to murder him had numbed her. She had to send word to Pylos and warn her son about the ambush – *if* he intended to come back. But what about herself? The now near certainty of becoming Antinous's wife in just six days was unendurable. Anything was better than such a fate.

She reached out to touch Argus's bony head, her shoulders shaking as the tears flowed freely down her cheeks.

Chapter Eleven

Helen of Sparta

Memories of long ago came back to Eperitus as he drove the chariot through the streets to the royal palace. Little appeared to have changed in Sparta in the thirty years since he had accompanied Odysseus, then a suitor to Helen. There were still merchants selling their wares, household slaves browsing the many stalls and going about their ordinary business, idle soldiers, children playing and throwing stones at stray dogs, and the dogs barking at shambling flocks of sheep and goats as they were driven along by their herdsmen. The city walls were still tall and strong, the buildings in the citadel still large and impressive, and the palace itself still decorative and opulent.

And yet a shadow seemed to have fallen across it, as if it had lost its former confidence and naivety. That was the effect of the war, he supposed, and the pressure of the settlers from the north, clamouring for land that they would one day take by force. Sparta felt like a city quietly awaiting its doom.

His first test on arriving at the palace was Eteoneus, the king's herald, who had known Eperitus during the war. If he recognised him there would be questions about Odysseus's fate; questions he did not want to face. Eteoneus was waiting in the courtyard as the chariot entered, clearly forewarned about the visitors. He welcomed Telemachus warmly, and then his gaze fell on Eperitus. But his attention was momentary and showed no sign of recognition. Instead, he ordered the horses to be unharnessed and fed. Then, after briefly questioning Telemachus, he led the two visitors away to be bathed. He promised to return soon and take them to the feast, which was being held in honour of the impending weddings of Menelaus's son and daughter, Megapenthes and Hermione: he to a Spartan girl, while she was being sent away in the morning to marry the son of Neoptolemus. There the king would welcome them at his table and they could put their needs to him.

The hot bath soothed Eperitus's aching muscles, almost lulling him into sleep. His first fight in over seven years had left him tired and aching, reminding him that his body was not all it had once been. But he had enjoyed himself. The thrilling nearness of death and the satisfaction of surviving had made him feel more alive than he had for seven years. And at least he had not killed anyone. His promise to the gods remained intact, and he was determined it would remain so. Telemachus had not exulted over his first combat victory, either. Rather he had seemed subdued by it. After his concern for Eperitus's injuries had been satisfied, he had fallen silent. When Eperitus had asked him how he felt about killing a man, he had simply replied it had been necessary and he hoped he could do the same to his mother's suitors.

Eteoneus returned and escorted them to the feast. The last time Eperitus had seen the great hall it had been filled with the mightiest heroes of Greece: Great Ajax, Diomedes, Patroclus, Little Ajax, Philoctetes, Agamemnon and many others. All of them had been full of youthful confidence, as if no one could ever stand against them or do them harm. None had suspected that within ten years they would sail away to a bitter war from which many would not return. Now the hall was filled with a new generation of young men and women, dancing merrily as if the peace that reigned in Sparta would last forever.

Eperitus paused at the threshold, listening to the music and singing and watching the crowd of dancers in the torchlight. They were not the equal of their forefathers, he thought. But could any generation, past or future, have matched such men? He looked across to the dais where the king of Sparta was seated. There were streaks of grey in his red hair and his girth had expanded, but seeing him brought back emotions he thought he had forgotten. In that moment, all Eperitus wanted to do was embrace his old comrade and reminisce about the war and the comrades they had left on the shores of Troy.

But he had turned his back on that life long ago, he reminded himself, and said a prayer to Athena that Menelaus would not recognise him. Adjusting the large eyepatch and brushing his hair down about his face and beard, he turned to Telemachus. The Ithacan prince stood staring at the feast, reluctant to move.

'My lord?' Eteoneus asked him. 'The king has instructed me to bring you direct to his table.'

'Lead the way,' Eperitus replied, laying a hand on Telemachus's shoulder and giving him a small push.

'Sorry,' Telemachus said in a low voice as they followed the herald through the crowd. 'I'm not used to such large gatherings.'

'You mean you lack confidence,' Eperitus said. 'The suitors have made you feel that way. But you're a man now, Telemachus. You killed for the first time today, and when you did that you crossed a threshold into a new world. A *hard* world of being responsible for your actions. You can't just take a man's life and then give up on your own! Better to have let him kill you so he could go on living. Have faith in yourself.'

Eteoneus leaned over and spoke into Menelaus's ear, who turned to stare at the two newcomers. The king smiled as he rose unsteadily to his feet, though Eperitus thought he caught a hint of recognition in his old comrade's eyes.

'Welcome, friends. Sit with me and eat your fill. There's nothing like a long chariot journey to shake the bones and give a man an appetite. Then there'll be time for you to tell me your names and the names of your fathers, though I can see by your looks and bearing that you're both men of noble stock.'

They took their seats on Menelaus's right and washed their hands. The king offered them meat from his own board and they helped themselves gratefully. If Menelaus had recognised Eperitus in that first glance, he hid it well. Nevertheless, Eperitus thought it best to keep a clear head and made sure his stomach was full before starting on the wine.

Telemachus hardly touched his food, despite having eaten little since that morning. Rather, he kept his eyes on the table as if in deep thought, while the king of Sparta gave him occasional sidelong glances.

'Say something,' Eperitus urged in a whisper. 'It's not just the host that should show good manners, you know.'

Telemachus nodded uncertainly.

'This is a feast worthy of Olympus, my lord,' he ventured, turning to Menelaus.

'What's that, son?' the king asked. 'The music's a bit loud.'

Telemachus repeated the compliment and Menelaus smiled.

'One of the advantages of being disgustingly wealthy. Sparta's always been rich by Greek standards, of course, and I had my fair share of what was left of Troy's treasures. But we had a wayward journey home and visited many exotic lands, amassing a fortune as we went. I was one of the luckier of the kings who sailed to Troy.'

Menelaus paused to take another mouthful of wine, looking thoughtfully at Telemachus as he raised the cup.

'When I think of the others that perished in the war, like Achilles, or on the homeward voyage, such as Ajax, Oileus's son, I count myself blessed. Not to mention the greatest of us all, Agamemnon, murdered by that bitch of a wife after he'd crossed the threshold of his own home. He and I didn't part on the best of terms, and I'll regret that for as long as I live; but my brother should have enjoyed the rewards of his victory and died in peaceful old age, not cut down in his own bath!'

Menelaus took a carving knife and thumped it down into the meat board, where it vibrated with the echoes of his anger. But the moment passed quickly and he took another swallow of wine.

'And then there was Odysseus. I still remember the day he arrived at Aulis, where the Greek fleet was gathering for war. Those ships he'd begged and borrowed and the paltry force he brought with him! Really, his contribution should have gone unnoticed among the other grand and powerful kings, with our hundreds of ships, our thousands upon thousands of men, our great wealth and our boastful lineages. And yet, do you know my friend – *he* outdid us all. While the stout hearts and strong walls of the Trojans checked all our efforts, it was the poorest and weakest among us who led the way to triumph. That astute mind and his desire to return home gave us the victory. And what was his fate, after all he'd done? Nobody knows! A watery death, probably. Or murdered by barbarians, after they'd robbed him of everything he had. The gods are cruel.'

Menelaus stared at Telemachus, who was looking down into the dregs of his wine.

'You're his boy, aren't you?' he asked unexpectedly. 'When I first glimpsed you, my heart almost stopped. For a moment, I thought you were him. Telemachus, isn't it? We met once, when you were a baby. Indeed, it's thanks to you that the war was won. Your father…' He gave a laugh and slapped the table, making the cups and plates jump. 'Your father was feigning madness to avoid going to war. He was ploughing a field with an ox and an ass, sowing the furrows with salt, when Palamedes snatched you from your mother's arms and laid you in his path. He turned aside to save you and his trick was exposed. So you see, Telemachus, without you Odysseus wouldn't have won the war for us and covered himself in glory. Not that he wouldn't have surrendered all that fame to return to his family a single day earlier. Used to talk about you and your mother all the time. It made me feel most guilty!'

'It's not your fault, sir,' Telemachus said, raising his head and looking Menelaus in the eye.

'My wife's then, perhaps,' the king replied. 'But I forget myself. What brings you and your quiet friend...?'

'Theoclymenus, son of Polypheides,' Telemachus said.

'What brings you and Theoclymenus to Sparta? I understand you spent time here with your mother's family some years ago, hiding from assassins.'

Telemachus opened his mouth, but before he could speak the clamour of voices and the sound of dancing faltered and all movement in the room seemed to slow down. Heads of nobles and slaves alike turned towards a corner of the hall. Eperitus followed their collective gaze, but could not see through the wall of bodies. Then the lull was over and the dancing resumed its frenzied pace, and the voices rose to an even higher volume than before.

'That will be Helen,' Menelaus said in a tired voice, raising his cup for a steward to refill.

Her unseen entrance had been like a stone dropped into a calm pond, and her progress through the room could still be marked by the small ripples as heads turned and conversations were momentarily stilled. Eperitus recalled the astonishing beauty of the woman so many had died to win back for Menelaus, and wondered what toll the past decade had had upon her looks.

Then she was there, standing over her husband and looking down at the two guests. And to his eyes she had not changed. Her hair was deepest black and her skin as white and as smooth as any girl half her age could boast. Her features were perfect in their proportion and position, and beneath the white chiton – with her slender arms bared and the wool parting across one exquisite thigh – he could see that her figure had lost none of its allure. Only her eyes had changed. They were the same icy blue, but seemed a little kinder than he remembered them. It made her appear almost accessible. And that only made her more desirable.

She leaned down and kissed her husband on the cheek.

'Please sit down, my queen,' Menelaus said, indicating the chair to his left. 'This is Theoclymenus, son of Polypheides, and...'

'Telemachus,' Helen said, 'Odysseus's son. Yes, it's unmistakeable. You have his eyes.'

'So I'm told, my lady,' Telemachus replied.

He was barely able to keep his eyes from her as he bowed. She met his helpless gaze with a smile.

'There were few men as brave or cunning as your father. I remember a time when I was held in Troy...'

'Held?' Menelaus queried, his smile a little forced.

'Held by my own foolishness and the fog Aphrodite had thrown over my eyes,' she continued, 'when Odysseus entered the city disguised as a beggar. He fooled everyone, even me to start with, but I can never be deceived for long.' Here her eyes flicked towards Eperitus, then back to Telemachus. 'I questioned him, but he was too clever to let slip his true identity. Only when I insisted on removing his rags and bathing him was he finally exposed.' Menelaus finished his wine and banged the cup down on the table. Helen gave a slight smile and continued. 'By that time, I'd lost all desire to stay in Troy and wanted nothing more than for the war to end. Instead of giving your father away to the Trojans, I helped him steal the Palladium that gave Troy its divine protection. If we hadn't succeeded then, Troy would still be undefeated today.'

'Odysseus deserves the credit for conquering Troy, it's true, and in nothing more than the ruse of the Wooden Horse,' Menelaus said. 'Though his plan was almost undone, dear wife. We were waiting inside its belly for night to fall when you arrived with one of your husbands. What was his name?'

'You know who it was, my dear. You've tortured me enough times for marrying Deiphobus, even though it was done against my wishes.'

'So you say. But do you remember how you walked around the base of the Horse, calling up to the Greek kings in the voices of their wives? Some nearly leapt out in response, and that would have given us all away and ended the war very quickly. As I recall, Odysseus himself wanted to open the trap door, but Eperitus threw a hand over his mouth at the last moment and stopped him.'

'My lord and lady,' Telemachus said, 'I don't know this man you talk of with such fondness, though he is my father – or was. But I come seeking news of him. His wife is besieged by over a hundred suitors who for three years have helped themselves to his livestock and stores of wine, happily consuming his wealth and ruining his estate while they await Penelope's decision. Nobody dares do anything to stop them. But in six days she'll be forced to choose one of them to be her husband. Is there nothing you can tell me that might send me back home with hope in my heart? Even a rumour that Odysseus is alive might be enough to put fear in these suitors' hearts and stop the wedding.'

Menelaus leaned back in his chair and crossed his arms.

'What do you mean, nobody dares stop them? Are you not the master of your own house? Tell them to go, Telemachus, and if they refuse, then take your appeal to the elders and the people.'

'With respect, my lord, these things I've done, and they've ignored me.'

'Then find a way to remove them by force. Do you think the gods won't approve of your action or assist you? Take my nephew, Orestes. He didn't hesitate in carrying out divine justice on those who had slaughtered his father. And let me tell you this: *your* father wouldn't have sat there complaining! He'd have *done* something. He certainly wouldn't have run away.'

Telemachus's cheeks reddened beneath his downy beard, but he let show no other sign that he had felt the slur.

'You're right, sir,' he said. 'I should have done something a long time ago, regardless of the number or power of my enemies. I'm sure the much-vaunted Orestes would have faced up to the problem. And if all I've heard from you and Nestor is true, the father I've never known would have acted swiftly, justly and with deadly effect. But you're wrong if you think I'm running away, or if you believe I intend to stand by and do nothing! Yes, I'm seeking my father, and it was my hope to find him alive so we could sail back together and overthrow these men who would usurp his place as king of Ithaca and husband to my mother. But whether I hear he is dead or alive – or if I hear nothing at all – I am resolved to return and deal with the enemies in my own house. And if it pleases you, Lord Menelaus, I am tired and would like to retire, even if it is to sleep on the streets of Sparta.'

He stood, bowed to the king and then the queen, and turned to leave. Eperitus gave a last look at Menelaus, who remained seated and showed no signs of apologising to his guest, then followed Telemachus from the hall. They reached the large portico, where the din from the feast was dampened by the cool night air streaming in through the open doors.

'I'm sorry, Theoclymenus,' Telemachus said. 'I don't know why I spoke to him like that. All I've done is earned us a night under the stars and an early-morning chariot ride without breakfast. I told you I'm not used to such gatherings.'

'Nonsense,' Eperitus replied with a smile. 'That was a greater achievement than your victory over the brigand this morning! Besides, you only gave Menelaus what his wine-dulled wits deserved.'

'I don't think it was the wine. It was the presence of his wife. From the moment she arrived, he was a different man. I expect the war opened a great gulf between them. Makes me wonder how things would've been between my father and mother if he'd returned safely from Troy.'

'Different from before, perhaps. But at least Penelope didn't leave Odysseus for another man, and he didn't have to fight a war to get her back.'

'Telemachus, wait!' Helen said, emerging from the crowd and joining them in the portico. 'Please wait. The king spoke much too harshly, and we apologise. Beds will be arranged for you, and in the morning my husband will offer you whatever help you need. Zeus is the protector of suppliants and guests, and Menelaus will not risk offending the father of the gods again.'

They looked at her standing before them like a goddess, her perfect looks made human by the concern in her eyes.

'Thank you, my lady, but the only help I need is news of my father. If Menelaus knows nothing of Odysseus's fate, then there's little he can do for me. I will return to Ithaca and deal with the suitors alone, if I can.'

'You will not be alone,' she said, looking at Eperitus. 'If only Theoclymenus is with you, I feel sure your goal is closer than you think. But I insist that you stay here tonight. It's already late and the feast is coming to an end, so I will arrange for beds to be set up here in the porch. And while you wait here, perhaps Theoclymenus will help me find a little more food and wine for you to enjoy before you go to sleep. Come, Theoclymenus.'

Eperitus looked at Telemachus, who sat on a stone bench by the wall and nodded that he should go. Reluctantly he followed Helen back into the thinning crowds. The king had already vacated his seat and many of the guests were offering libations to the flames before retiring. Slaves were busy clearing away what remained of the food.

'What do you think you're doing?' Helen said, taking him suddenly by the arm. 'Do you think I'm blind, Eperitus, or just too stupid to recognise you after all these years?'

'I fooled Menelaus.'

'Who's both drunk and stupid.'

'It's nice to see you too, Helen.'

He could not help but smile, though whether it was relief at being able to be himself again or just the pleasure of speaking with an old friend, he could not tell. She frowned back at him.

'Come with me.'

She led him through the side door by which she had entered earlier and into an empty passage. To his surprise, she threw her arms about him and held him tightly. As he returned her embrace, he felt as if they were both young again, meeting secretly in the temple of Aphrodite as they had done thirty years ago.

'It's good to see a friendly face, Eperitus. Someone who doesn't judge me – one way or another.'

'You don't know how good it is to see you, too. We were good friends, once.'

'We were,' she agreed, smiling at him. 'What happened to your eye?'

'This?' he asked, lifting the leather patch so it rested on his forehead. 'It's just a disguise. Sometimes it's easier when people don't recognise you.'

'Do you think it'd work for me?' she said with a small laugh.

'How are you, Helen? What's it like being back here again?'

'Dull. Confining. The same as it ever was, really. And then there's Menelaus.'

She leaned back against the wall, where a nearby torch cast deep shadows in the hollows of her face and the folds of her clothing. He could see the curves of her body beneath her soft woollen dress.

'It was bearable for a time, while we sailed back from Troy. The voyage was a long one – years – and we visited many exotic places I'd never seen or even heard of before. You should see the land of the Egyptians, Eperitus! Palaces and tombs as big as mountains; more gold than you could ever imagine; and the women, with their dresses and jewellery, and their hair like this.' She demonstrated with strands of her own hair, and for a moment she seemed like the young girl he had known a lifetime ago. It made him smile to glimpse her happiness. 'I have three Egyptian dresses and a necklace that hangs around the neck in bands. Perhaps I could wear it for you...'

Her words faltered as her imagination gave way to reality.

'Perhaps you could have done,' he said, 'if the world had turned out differently.'

'Do you ever wonder...' she began. 'Do you ever wonder what our lives would have been like if I had talked less about Odysseus during those secret liaisons and thought more of you? No, don't shake your head, Eperitus.

You're the most decent man I've ever known. You're honest and kind, selfless and noble. What if you'd accepted my offer in the temple of Aphrodite? What if we had run away together and become lovers? I still think about it sometimes.'

He looked at her, and for a moment there was an understanding between them, an acceptance that it might have worked. But only then. Never now. And then he smiled at the thought and they both laughed, as only old friends can.

'I don't think I could have withstood the combined armies of Greece for very long.'

'It would have been worth it, even if only for the short while it lasted,' she said, stroking his shoulder and smiling at him. 'But the gods never give us what we want. Do they?'

He shook his head.

'No, they don't, Helen, so don't even think it.'

She looked him up and down.

'We would have been good together – still could be – but don't be concerned. I would not insult you by trying to take you to bed.'

'Insult me?'

'Does sex have any other purpose any more? I haven't made love to a man since Paris was killed. Deiphobus used to force himself upon me from time to time. Menelaus takes me occasionally, when his lust for me outweighs his hatred, briefly tipping the scales enough for him to rape me. It helps him to let me know who is master in our marriage. And I will sometimes find myself a slave or a young noble to meet my needs and take a little bit of vengeance on him. I would never pull you into that vicious circle, Eperitus.

'But now you must tell me about yourself. What happened after you sailed from Troy, and where is Odysseus? They say he sailed off the edge of the world, and yet here you are. That you're not at his side makes me fear the worst.'

'It's a story that needs longer than a few hurried moments in a dark corridor, Helen. And your fears are true. We, too, had a long voyage, but the lands we visited and their inhabitants were horrible beyond my power to describe. I and one other were the only survivors from the Ithacan fleet. And yes, Odysseus perished in the end.'

'How?'

'Zeus struck our ship with lightning. Odysseus and the whole crew went down with it. Our bard and I were rescued by a passing galley, though he was blinded and the gods took all memory from him. Now only I remain with any knowledge of that voyage and its terrible outcome.'

Helen raised a hand to his cheek. Her eyes were full of concern.

'I'm sorry for you, Eperitus. But why this disguise? And why do you travel with Odysseus's son, remaining silent while he searches for a man you know to be dead?'

'Odysseus and I were no longer friends when the storm took him. I'd lost my wife and our unborn child days before, and I laid the blame on him. It… it changed me, Helen. I decided to turn my back on who I was and seek out a new life. And that's what I've been doing ever since. Running away, I suppose. But…' He laughed. 'But what did you say? The gods never give us what we want? Not our cruel gods! I tried to hide from my past, so they crossed my path with Telemachus's. They must have known I'd take pity on him and want to return with him to Ithaca. Though I can't tell him who I am – not if I want to keep my past behind me.'

'Then your experiences haven't changed you as much as you think,' Helen said. 'You still seek justice for the weak, just like you sympathised with me when I was a young girl, desperate to escape from my father's plans. But are you sure about Odysseus?'

'What do you mean?'

'I overheard something Menelaus said to old Nestor once. He was drunk, as usual, but he said he knew where Odysseus was. Perhaps he just meant the Underworld or the bottom of the ocean, but I don't think so.'

'Then it was a lying boast,' Eperitus said. 'Who doesn't enjoy knowing the answer to a riddle, or pretending to? And it won't do Telemachus any good if Menelaus tries to feed him such fantasies.'

'Won't it? All the boy seeks is hope. Perhaps a rumour that his father still lives will give him the confidence he needs to face the suitors by himself. Menelaus owes him an apology, so tonight I will swallow my disgust and sleep with him. If only to ensure he tells Telemachus what he knows.'

Chapter Twelve

The Phaeacian Games

Two men held the boar while King Alcinous cut a tuft of its hair and threw it into the flames, offering up a prayer to the Olympians. Then he held the knife to the struggling animal's throat and drew the blade backwards with a tugging motion. The boar squealed briefly, then collapsed as its blood sluiced out. Alcinous quickly and skilfully cut out the thigh bones and a layer of fat, which he threw onto the flames in honour of the gods. A slave stepped forwards and took the knife from the king's hand, while another untied and removed his gore-spattered leather apron. Yet more slaves approached with a bowl of water and a cloth, which Alcinous used to wash and dry his hands and forearms before joining his sons and Odysseus at the table.

The boar's carcass was cut up and roasted along with the meat from the other boars, sheep and oxen that had been sacrificed that morning. The aroma filled the hall, making Odysseus's stomach rumble and his mouth water. Many other tables and chairs were occupied by the hundreds of Phaeacian nobles who had come to see the rare spectacle of a newcomer to their island. But there was little welcome in their faces as they stared at him and talked among themselves. The women eyed him lasciviously, while the men regarded him with arrogance, distrust or open hostility.

Not least among the latter was Laodamas, Alcinous's eldest son. He was tall and handsome, with muscles that had been developed on the sports field rather than through the demands of the plough or the oar. He looked at Odysseus as if he were an object of fascination or revulsion, commenting to his brothers in whispers that provoked scorning laughter. But Odysseus ignored them. He had faced worse trials than simple derision. Alcinous said nothing about it, if he noticed at all.

Slaves brought plates of piled meat to the long tables. Wine was served and baskets of bread brought from the kitchens, along with platters of cheese, fruit and other delicacies. Odysseus rolled a slice of roast boar into a piece of flatbread and raised it to his lips. Then he forgot his hunger and stared blankly at the doorway to the great hall.

A man with girlish looks and light-coloured curly hair had entered, leading a second man by the hand. The second man carried a tortoiseshell lyre over his shoulder; his eyes were tightly closed and his steps hesitant. But despite his blindness, Odysseus recognised Omeros at once.

'My lord Alcinous,' he said, 'who is that man with the lyre?'

'His name is Demodocus, my royal bard. The gods have robbed him of his sight, but compensated him with a voice that surpasses all others.'

'Was he born blind?'

'He lost his sight during the storm that sent his galley to the bottom of the ocean. One of our ships found him clinging to a piece of wreckage the next morning.'

'And did he ever ask to be returned to his homeland?'

'You seem very interested in him, my friend,' Alcinous commented. 'If you'd like to question him further I can...'

'No. No need for that, my lord. I was only interested because he and I are both survivors of shipwrecks.'

'He never asked to leave Phaeacia, because he can't remember anything of his past – not even his real name, or where he came from. Though if his memory ever restored itself, it would be a sore test to let a bard of his skill leave us. You'll understand what I mean when you hear him sing. Ocyalus!' the king called to Omeros's guide. 'Lead Demodocus to his accustomed seat and lay a table with wine and bread before him. And when you are ready, Demodocus, I have a guest here who very much desires to hear you sing.'

Omeros bowed in silence and allowed his squire to lead him to his seat. When he had wetted his lips, he took up his instrument and stroked his fingers across the strings. As the first notes reverberated across the smoky hall, the mingled voices of the guests fell silent. Soon the only sound to be heard was the gentle plucking of the lyre. Its music continued alone for a while, seeping into the minds of the listeners and driving away all thoughts until they acknowledged no other master but the bard before them.

Then he began to sing, and his voice was such that it did not jar with the music, but seemed part of it. It was the same voice Odysseus remembered from before, except its owner had mastered it so completely that it no longer seemed to belong to the Omeros he had known. It was like the voice of an unseen god, commanding and beautiful to listen to. At first his words did not register, but settled like tender flakes of snow on the mind. But when the story began to reveal itself, Odysseus remembered all the words that had gone before it. And then, like a blast of cold rain on the face, he realised the song was about himself.

It was a small matter in the great events of the time: a petty quarrel between himself and Achilles at a festival to the gods, which had resulted in drawn swords and near bloodshed. The argument had taken place in the early years of the war, before Omeros had arrived, but his storyteller's mind must have heard it spoken of and stored it away in a place where – unlike everyday facts such as his name and homeland – it was readily accessible. His words conjured up the Achilles Odysseus had known and honoured, bringing him fresh into his mind's eye. They also reminded him of himself as he had once been: a man of confidence and action, quick-witted and courageous, pining for the home and family he loved. Tears came uncalled to his eyes and rolled down his cheeks. He wiped them away with a corner of his robe, hoping his hosts – Laodamas in particular – would not see.

When the song was finished, Alcinous called on the Phaeacians to rise and make for the place of assembly on the slopes beyond the city walls that overlooked the larger of the two harbours.

'There you will witness the prowess of our young men,' the king said to Odysseus, as they led the procession out of the palace gates. 'If you still wish to leave, and should we decide to grant it, you can tell your countrymen that the greatest sportsmen in all the world come from Phaeacia.'

'It's certainly true they have splendid physiques,' Odysseus conceded, looking at Laodamas and the others. 'Like peacocks in mating season. But how can you claim they're the greatest wrestlers and runners in the world if they only ever challenge other Phaeacians?'

'What's that, my lord?' said Laodamas, though the word *lord* was grudgingly spoken. 'Perhaps you'd care to try your hand against us? You're well-built and plenty strong enough, I'll wager, even if you are an old man.'

Odysseus shook his head.

'I'm not in the mood for sports, sir. I've been wearied by weeks at sea and being shipwrecked. All I hope for is to be granted passage home to Greece.'

'Did my father not tell you? That gift is only given to men of honour, who can be trusted when they promise never to return to Phaeacia or tell others how to find our home. And a man of honour would rise to a sporting challenge, not run from it.'

'Laodamas!' Alcinous said. 'Leave our guest alone. If he says he is too tired, then take him at his word. Go now, or the foot race will begin without you.'

His son gave Odysseus a parting look of disdain, then ran down the road to the city gates, followed by the crowd of young nobles. Odysseus, Alcinous and the others followed them out to where seats and benches had been placed on the sloped grass overlooking a stretch of level ground beside the harbour. Several slaves had run ahead to set markers for the race, and on the city walls behind hundreds of Phaeacians were gathering to watch the games. The runners had removed their cloaks, tunics and sandals and stood naked behind the starting rope, jostling each other for position. A slave raised a white cloth in one hand and looked up the slope at the king.

Odysseus smarted at the accusation of cowardice from Laodamas, but the weariness in his spirit was like a great weight on his shoulders. In his youth and during the long years of the war, he would have accepted any challenge, whether sporting or otherwise; but his imprisonment on Ogygia had extinguished that old fortitude, replacing it with self-doubt and lethargy. And yet if he had any hope of seeing his home again, he knew he had to impress on Alcinous that he was a man who could keep his word never to return to Phaeacia. Without that, he would simply have exchanged his imprisonment on Ogygia for imprisonment here.

Alcinous gave a small nod and the slave dropped the cloth. The pack of runners sprang away, elbowing each other aside as they tried to get ahead of the rest of the pack. One fell almost immediately, bringing two more down in a cloud of dust and raising an ironic cheer from the city walls and the watching nobles.

Odysseus saw Laodamas leap over the tumbling figures and press on, neck and neck with a thickset man whose short legs worked furiously to hold off the challenge. The two lashed out at each other's ribs and arms until the runners closing behind them forced them to give up their personal battle and concentrate on the race. A scrawny-looking youth who had not yet grown a full beard edged away from the chasing pack and drew up alongside the two leaders. Laodamas glanced over his shoulder at him, then swerved aside, intending to shoulder barge him out of the race. Then the course turned away from the watching crowd, following a curve in the line of the harbour, and the runners were lost behind the cloud of dust kicked up by their feet.

Odysseus craned his neck to see who was in the lead as the track doubled back on itself and headed towards the white post that marked the finish line. A figure emerged from the dust, arms and legs pumping as he pulled away from the others. To Odysseus's delight, it was the scrawny youth. Laodamas was close behind him, recklessly throwing himself into the pursuit. Then he lost his footing and fell beneath the legs of the others. The leader passed the finishing post to wild cheers from the onlookers.

'Clytoneus wins!' shouted a herald.

The crowd shouted his name and Alcinous nodded with satisfaction, telling Odysseus that Clytoneus was his youngest son. They watched the remaining runners finish, some collapsing with exhaustion, others placing their hands on their hips as they tried to regain their breath. Their sweat-damp skin was filthy with dust, and some, including Laodamas, sported scuffed elbows and knees that were smeared with fresh blood.

After they had been washed down and freshly oiled, a selection of spears was brought over and a group of slaves began pacing distances and setting markers. The youths tested the weight of the spears in their hands and twisted them in their fingers, checking their straightness. Then the first throws were cast. One by one, spears arced through the air and thumped into the grass to cheers from the watching crowds. Odysseus was less impressed by the Phaeacians' throwing skills than he had been by their running. Observing their efforts, he felt a nagging desire to join the contest and show Laodamas and his friends how it was really done. He resisted the temptation, though, and applauded with the rest of the crowd as Laodamas claimed victory with his second and final throw.

Ropes were now brought out and laid in wide circles on the grass. Eight men were selected by the herald and called forward to have their knuckles bound with strips of leather. Lots were drawn and the competitors were sent in pairs to the four rings. The contests started almost simultaneously. The fighters advanced quickly on each other, throwing and dodging punches, grunting as fists connected with heads or bodies, their bare feet shuffling up clouds of dust from the dry ground. The dull thuds of the blows and the responding groans were drowned out by the frenetic shouting of the spectators. None dared stand, though, for fear of obstructing King Alcinous's view, leaving the naked fighters clearly visible to all.

Odysseus had a knowing eye on each fight. Though the Phaeacians were skilful boxers, they lacked the aggression his fellow Greeks would have shown. Only Laodamas seemed eager to close with his opponent, who was a small man with a short reach. As a result, he boxed defensively, constantly dancing away from Laodamas's attacks. Then Laodamas threw a wide punch that left his guard open. His opponent did not read the clever feint, as Odysseus had done, and moved in to deliver a body blow. Immediately, Laodamas corrected himself and swung his fist into the shorter man's face.

His head rocked sideways, ejecting a line of red spittle, and he fell shoulder-first onto the ground. Laodamas showed no signs of exhaustion as he pounced on his fallen victim, kneeling over him and delivering punch after punch. After a few more moments, the match overseer stepped in and gripped Laodamas's wrist. He pulled him to his feet and raised his arm in the air to the rapturous applause of the spectators. His adversary remained where he lay until he was carried off by two slaves.

The four victors went on to face each other, their opponents chosen by lot. The fighters were slower now, tired by their previous exertions, and the contests were less mobile with the men choosing to slug it out. Eventually, the remaining winners – Laodamas and the short, thickset man he been shoulder to shoulder with in the opening stage of the foot race – were pitted against each other.

After the blood was washed from their faces and knuckles and their cuts treated, they closed on each other with determination. Laodamas scored the first hit, crashing one fist after the other into the man's broad chest. Despite his dislike of Alcinous's arrogant son, Odysseus could not help but admire his skill and belligerence. Again, he found himself wishing he had entered the contest at the start, eager to try himself against Laodamas in particular.

A flurry of punches were thrown by both men, some finding their target and eliciting short grunts. Cuts were quickly reopened and Laodamas's opponent's left eyebrow was red with blood. It trickled down into his eye so that he was forced to box half-blind. From that point, the match was short-lived. Laodamas reigned in his aggression and used his speed and skill to deliver punch after punch until his challenger received a final blow to the face and his knees buckled beneath him. The overseer stepped into the ring and, taking Laodamas's hand, raised his arm in a sign of triumph.

'Well fought, son!' Alcinous called. 'Well fought indeed.'

Laodamas cupped his hands into a bowl of water offered by a slave and washed the blood and sweat from his face. Taking a towel and dabbing himself dry, he walked over to stand before Odysseus.

'Have you changed your mind yet, my lord? Or do you lack sporting prowess? Any beggar can look dignified in clothes stolen from a prince, but sport shows the true quality of a man.'

'Enough, Laodamas,' Alcinous warned.

His son held up his hand in a silencing gesture.

'Come and join us, my lord, and show us your mettle. If you *are* a man of substance and quality, you'll soon be able to prove yourself. But if you're just another lying vagrant, as my friend Euryalus tells me you are, then we'll soon find you out. What do you say, nameless one? Will you compete with us to earn your passage home, or will you continue to plead tiredness and throw yourself at my mother's knees again, hoping she won't toss you out into the streets to beg crusts of mouldy bread for the rest of your life?'

Odysseus watched him through narrowed eyes. The insult was arrogant and calculated. Laodamas was Alcinous's heir, Phaeacia's next king, and he was used to being deferred to in all things. He was also a bully, who wanted revenge for the affront of being made to give up his seat for Odysseus the night before. And he was a fool. But his challenge woke something in Odysseus that Calypso had taken from him. His determination. He cared little for the insults of a boy, but Laodamas had offered him the chance to compete for his passage home. And he would take it.

'Your friend, Euryalus, must reckon himself a keen judge of men. Without speaking to me, he declares me a fraud and a beggar. In some respects, he is right, for I have defrauded many over the years, and I once begged my way into the most heavily defended city in the world to steal its greatest talisman. But I am not the low-born scoundrel your friend thinks I am. Indeed, anyone who thinks of me that way is a fool. A man may be unimpressive to look at, but the gods can still grace him with speech and intelligence that puts lesser men to shame. Other men are handsome and well-built, with oiled hair and fine clothing, but the moment they open their mouths they are revealed to be vulgar, rude and of a base mind. Don't you think, Laodamas?

'But come, your friend's accusations have stirred me to anger. Wearied though I am, I accept the challenge. I may prove a better sportsman than you guess, and in so doing will prove the quality of my breeding.'

He stood and unclasped his purple cloak, letting it fall in a heap around his feet. Then he removed his sandals and belt and walked across the grass to where the rest of the young Phaeacians had gathered for the next contest. They greeted him with sneering looks and muttered jibes. A length of rope had been laid in the grass, facing a stretch of field where a line of distance markers had been laid. Beside the rope was a pile of circular lumps of iron of differing sizes.

One of the youths was called forward by a slave and told to choose a discus. He picked one of the lighter ones and tested the direction of the sea breeze. Spreading his feet apart with his left flank towards the markers, he twisted his body round from left to right until the discus was behind his left shoulder, then swung it back hard and released it with a shout. It flew high and to the right for a good distance, the sun gleaming from its smooth surface as it spun, before dropping to the grass with a thud.

The thrower punched the air and gave a victorious bellow, before being pushed aside by the thickset man who had lost to Laodamas in the final boxing match. Odysseus heard the name Elatreus from among the other youths and, judging by their silence as he made his preparations, it seemed he was the man to beat. He picked up a large discus, tested the weight, then switched it for the largest. A moment later it was hurtling across the field, passing the first man's throw until it hit the ground with a puff of dust. The crowd cheered and the next man stepped forwards to select a discus. But Elatreus's throw was not surpassed by any of the subsequent competitors, though Laodamas's came close to it.

Finally, it was Odysseus's turn. There were a few smirks and nudges among the ring of Phaeacians, and sounds of mock awe as he checked the shape and felt the weight of each discus.

'He's fondling them like they're his wife's tits.'

'They're much too firm and round for that.'

'Perhaps they're too heavy for him to lift.'

'Do you want us to help you, old man?'

Odysseus had found a discus that balanced nicely in his hand but, irked by their mockery, he deliberately tossed it aside. It landed on Elatreus's toes, who gave a shout of pain before lunging angrily towards Odysseus. Laodamas grabbed his elbow and pulled him back.

'Now then, Elatreus, don't do anything that would displease the gods. The stranger's our guest, after all.'

'Are these the biggest you have?' Odysseus asked, standing and looking at the overseer.

The man had a grey beard and skin that was lined with age, but from his size and muscles, he must have been a capable sportsman in his day.

'We have a box with a few more, my lord. Nobody uses them, though; they're too ungainly.'

'Let me see them.'

At a wave from the overseer, the box was brought and the contents tipped onto the grass. All four discuses were larger than the first selection, and three showed signs of wear. The fourth, however, seemed only to have been included for mockery. It was large and its rough edges had not been polished with use. Odysseus knelt and ran his hands over it to the hesitant laughter of the onlookers. The crowd of spectators on the benches and city walls talked excitedly, their tone overwhelmingly doubtful.

Then he lifted it into his hands and stood. Silence fell. He clasped the edge with his fingertips. The opposite rim reached up to the angle of his inner arm. He felt the weight of it straining at his muscles. But those same muscles had carried heavy spears through many a full day of battle, and the memory of that old vigour revived the latent strength in his arm, emboldening him to the challenge.

'Step back, Elatreus. You wouldn't want me to drop *this* one on your toes.'

'Put it down, you old fool,' Elatreus snarled, 'before you do yourself an injury you'll never recover from.'

Odysseus gave him a half-smile and took up his position. Shifting his weight to his right leg and placing his free hand on his bent knee, he twisted his body round to the right so that the heavy discus was pulling him backwards. Then with a burst of strength and a practised movement of his feet, he swung it back round a half turn to the left. The weight of the iron seemed to want to pull his fingers out of their roots and take his whole arm with them. A blur of faces whirled past his vision. A voice in his head chose that moment to remind him he had not thrown a discus since the funeral games of Achilles ten years before, when he had come second to the throw of Great Ajax. Then he released his grip on the rim of the discus and, with a great bellow, watched the black shape spinning higher and higher as if lifted by an invisible hand. It passed Elatreus's marker easily before hurtling into the ground and throwing up a large clod of earth.

'The stranger wins!' shouted the overseer.

The shocked whispers of the seated Phaeacian nobility were swallowed up by the roar from the city walls. Odysseus turned to the youths around him, who stared in disbelief.

'Does that satisfy you, Laodamas?' he asked, singling out Alcinous's son. 'Or must I face other challenges to prove my quality?'

'A lucky throw,' said a young man beside Laodamas.

'Luck, Euryalus?' Elatreus scoffed. 'That was the greatest display of strength and skill I've ever seen with a discus, and there's not a man in Phaeacia who can beat me in the sport. I apologise, sir, for insulting you, and hope you can forgive me.'

'I can and do, Elatreus,' Odysseus replied, accepting his hand. 'But what does Laodamas say?'

'You told my father we only ever challenge other Phaeacians, and you're right. But should we then allow you to boast that you've never been beaten by a Phaeacian? Should we stand by while you claim superiority over us, even as a beggar in our own country? Our pride and dignity won't allow it, my lord stranger. So, I give you a final challenge. If you succeed, my father will certainly grant you passage to whatever savage land you call home; but if you fail, you will remain a beggar in our palace until the end of your days.'

'What is this challenge?'

'To compete in the king of all sports – wrestling – against Phaeacia's undefeated champion. Do you accept?'

'And if I win, you will grant me passage home?'

Laodamas glanced at his father, who nodded.

'Then I accept,' Odysseus said. He looked first at the youths gathered before him, then at their fathers and brothers on the benches behind. 'Where is this giant among giants?'

Laodamas stepped forwards.

'Here. Prepare yourself, old man.'

There was a roar of approval from Laodamas's friends and brothers, who patted him on the back as they went to sit on the grass behind the two competitors. Only Euryalus remained. He took a flask from a slave and, pouring some of the contents onto his hands, began to rub Laodamas's shoulders and back. Odysseus, knowing he was slathering Laodamas with oil to make it harder to grip him, pulled off his tunic and stepped forwards. Euryalus quickly poured more oil and rubbed the rest of Laodamas's torso, but the prince gestured for him to go.

'Three falls for victory,' Laodamas said.

Odysseus nodded and advanced, making a grab for Laodamas's arm while throwing his other hand over his shoulder and neck. Laodamas did the same, though where Odysseus's fingers failed to grip his opponent's oiled skin,

Laodamas's gained a firm hold. Within moments he had thrown Odysseus on his back. As the crowd cheered, Odysseus looked up at the victorious Phaeacian and realised he had underestimated his strength. He also knew he had to find a way to keep his hold on Laodamas if he was to have a chance of winning. Feigning tiredness, he discreetly tore away the grass beneath his hands and scraped up fistfuls of the dry dirt beneath.

'Come on, old man,' called a voice.

'Throwing that discus took up the last of his strength,' laughed another.

Odysseus pushed himself to his feet, staggering slightly as if weak with exhaustion. Laodamas approached and the two men threw themselves at each other. Odysseus pushed his right shoulder under Laodamas's chin so that their heads were locked side by side while their hands sought a hold on each other. Opening his fists, Odysseus spread the dirt over his rival's shoulders and upper arms.

As Laodamas pushed against him, trying to take him beneath his armpits, Odysseus slipped his head under the Phaeacian's chest and pushed upwards, throwing him off balance. Laodamas staggered sideways and Odysseus took hold of his knee, lifting him off his feet and driving him onto his back in the grass. The overseer raised his hand, signalling the point was his. There was a cry of angry despair from the onlookers on all sides and, leaping back to his feet, Laodamas ran off to remonstrate with the overseer. The man shook his head and pointed to Odysseus.

Laodamas did not wait, but rushed straight at his opponent. They grasped at each other's arms, then Laodamas slipped inside Odysseus's hold so that they were side by side. The young Phaeacian's arm was now around Odysseus's neck in a powerful embrace that he could not shrug off. Then, with a skilful sidestep, Laodamas brought his foot up behind Odysseus's heel and kicked away his leg. Using his weight, he pulled Odysseus down onto his back to another tumultuous cheer from the watching assembly. The overseer signalled a second point to the Phaeacian prince.

Odysseus raised himself onto one knee and stared down at the grass, gathering his strength. If he suffered another throw the contest would be over and he would live out the rest of his years as a beggar in King Alcinous's palace. His fragile dream of returning to Ithaca – so recently revived after his escape from Ogygia – would be dead forever. He would never see his wife or son again. He gave voice to the thought in his head, hoping it would stir him back to action. Instead, he felt his weakness and the acceptance of defeat taking hold of him.

'Get up and fight,' Laodamas goaded him. 'One more throw and it'll all be over.'

Odysseus thought of the hardships he had endured to find his way home: the battle against the Cicones, the storm off Cape Malea, the Cyclops and the Laestrygonians. He remembered the twin horrors of Charybdis and Scylla, and the wrath of Zeus that had destroyed his ship. He saw the faces of the friends who had died: Antiphus, Eurybates, Polites and Eperitus. He thought of their spirits in Hades, that most terrible place – the place he had endured in the desperate hope he would learn the way back to Ithaca. Had it all been for nothing? Would the man who had done such things, who had even brought about the destruction of Troy, weakly submit to an arrogant boy, who not so long ago he could have defeated with an arm tied behind his back? Was he going to give up on Penelope just because he was tired and had lost his self-belief?

He realised the crowd were booing him now. Raising his head, he looked at Laodamas and slowly got to his feet.

'You'll soon by eating crusts from my plate, old man,' he said, with a grin. 'And on feast days I'll even toss you a bone. I'm looking forward to having you as my dog.'

'You'll have to tame me first.'

Laodamas advanced, throwing his arms around Odysseus's back and reaching forwards with his foot to trip him. Odysseus passed one arm over his opponent's shoulder and the other beneath his armpit, locking his hands together behind his back. With a grunt, he pulled Laodamas's head under his neck, turned him sideways and pushed his hip into the Phaeacian's groin. Laodamas's whole body was lifted from the ground and in another instant Odysseus had thrown him onto his back, pinning him there with his own weight.

The overseer called out another point to Odysseus and was greeted with a clamour of protest from all around. The other youths surrounded him, appealing with open palms and raised voices. Laodamas pushed them aside and seized the old man by his beard, dragging him to his knees. Pulling the man's ear close to his mouth, he whispered something through gritted teeth then shoved him onto his back. Shamed and frightened, the overseer regained his feet and bowed submissively to Laodamas before calling the two contestants together for the deciding bout.

Laodamas approached more cautiously this time. Their hands met, fingers interlocking as they tested each other's strength. There was power in Laodamas's arms and a ferocious desire to defeat his foe, but Odysseus's stamina – built up over years of war – was a match for it. Both men dug their feet into the grass, their muscular legs holding fast and refusing to give ground. Then Odysseus slipped his hand behind Laodamas's neck, forcing his head down. Laodamas resisted, pushing back with such force that when Odysseus released his hold the Phaeacian's upper body was thrown upward, exposing his chest and stomach. Odysseus instantly threw his arms about Laodamas's waist and butted his head into his stomach, driving him backwards and into the dirt.

'No!' the Phaeacian shouted, slamming his fist onto Odysseus's back.

Odysseus looked across at the overseer, whose arms remained by his side. He shook his head and signalled for the two men to stand. The crowd cheered, though one or two voices on the city walls called for the point to be given. Laodamas wriggled free of Odysseus's hold and got to his feet.

'What's the matter? Get up and fight, old man.'

Odysseus stood and planted his feet firmly apart, lowering his centre of gravity. Laodamas edged toward him. They scrabbled for a grip and Odysseus took hold of the back of his opponent's upper arms, drawing him inward. Dropping to his knees, he grabbed Laodamas's right leg and pulled it into his body. The younger man tried to squirm free, but Odysseus thrust his shoulder into his ribs and stood, the strength in his legs enough to lift Laodamas off his feet. The next moment he was on his back with the Ithacan pinning him to the ground.

Both men now turned their head towards the overseer. He looked uncertainly towards Laodamas, then over his shoulder at Alcinous, who shook his head. The overseer signalled the wrestlers to their feet again, but this time the cheers from the seated onlookers were half-hearted, while the townsfolk on the walls above began to boo and jeer.

'So, what will it take, son?' Odysseus said, as the two men faced each other again. 'Do I have to kill you to get back home?'

'Kill me and you'll pay with your own life.'

Odysseus's confidence was returning. His muscles had remembered their strength and his victories had fanned the dying embers of his self-belief. He looked around at the few guardsmen who had accompanied the nobles to the field, doubting any of them had ever seen combat before. And he took note of the spears that had been used by the Phaeacian youths earlier, still piled on the grass.

'Do you think so?' he asked, staring at Laodamas. 'After Achilles fell, it was me who held off the armies of Troy while Ajax carried his body back to the Greek camp. When the oracles said the Palladium had to be stolen from under the Trojan's noses, I was the one who took it. And it was me who came up with the idea of the Wooden Horse and sat in its belly while the Trojans celebrated their false victory, waiting for night to come so I could steal out and put their city to the sword. Now, Laodamas, do you still think a pack of unarmed youths and a couple of inexperienced guardsmen are going to stop me?'

'*You're...*'

Odysseus sprang forwards, ducking his right shoulder beneath Laodamas's chest and lifting him from his feet. He rolled the Phaeacian onto his shoulders then threw him down onto his back as if he were nothing more than a child. The nobles were stunned into silence, while those watching from the battlements let out a great cheer. Again Odysseus looked at the overseer, who this time refused to meet his gaze and stared in silence at the grass.

Alcinous stood and threw his golden wine cup at the man.

'Another foul throw. Start the next bout at once.'

But Laodamas hauled himself to his feet and took hold of the Ithacan's wrist, raising it over his head.

'No, Father,' he declared. 'The stranger has won the challenge and will be given safe passage to his homeland.'

Chapter Thirteen

The Harbour of Phorcys

Telemachus woke to the feel of sunlight on his face. He squeezed his eyes open to see a rectangle of white stretching from the door of the portico to his bed. A figure was silhouetted in the open doorway, and at first he thought it was a slave, come to wake him for breakfast, or just passing through to rake the dirt floor in the great hall. Then he recognised the bulky outline of Menelaus.

He sat up and rubbed the sleep from his eyes.

'Good morning, my lord.'

'Ah, you're awake. That's good.' Menelaus walked to the corner of the portico, its stone walls echoing with his footsteps. He picked up a chair and set it down beside Telemachus's bed. 'You slept well, I hope.'

'Yes, thank you.'

Telemachus pushed the furs aside and sat up. The simmering anger and drunkenness of the night before were gone from the king's face. Instead, he seemed embarrassed by the memory of his insult. On the other side of the portico, Theoclymenus rubbed the sleep from his good eye and sat up.

'I had a little too much wine last night,' Menelaus said. 'Don't remember much that happened, in fact, so forgive me if I said anything out of place.'

Telemachus held up a hand and dismissed the event with a shake of his head.

Menelaus smiled broadly and patted his knee.

'Good! Wouldn't want to have offended an honoured guest. Now, I think I remember you were seeking news of your father.'

Telemachus nodded.

'I should have come before now, but I didn't like leaving my home in the hands of my mother's suitors.'

'Then perhaps I can offer you some hope.'

'What do you mean?'

'When you first told me about these suitors – news I'd already received from other sources – I was surprised at you. Here's the son of Odysseus, I thought to myself, the very picture of his father in looks; and yet, here he is in Sparta seeking news of his father when he should be back home, plotting an end to these parasites who're wasting his inheritance! But my anger was misdirected. Those men are the cowards, not you. Forgive me if I implied you were. That they should dare lord it over you in your own house is disgraceful! But even if you could slaughter them all, what good would it do you? Their families would soon make you pay the price for their deaths.'

'That's the problem,' Telemachus agreed, with a shrug.

'So your only solution is to go back with evidence that the rightful king still lives – something to make them think twice about marrying Odysseus's wife, or sitting on his throne. And I can give you the evidence you need.'

'What evidence?'

There was something in Menelaus's tone that gave Telemachus hope. For years, beggars and merchants had peddled stories of Odysseus, looking to earn themselves a meal or a rich gift by preying on the desperate hopes of a lonely woman and her son. But none of the rumours of Odysseus's imminent return had been fulfilled, leading to scorn of all such tales. But the word of a king – and the king of Sparta, at that – was different.

Theoclymenus stood and pulled over another chair, setting it down at the end of Telemachus's bed. Menelaus acknowledged him with a nod, then began his story.

'It was some years after we'd sailed from Troy when we found ourselves stranded on the island of Pharos, off the Egyptian coast, without even a breeze to carry us on our way again. We'd been there twenty days, and our supplies were running out when I dreamed I was visited by one of the immortals. She told me to seek out Proteus, the Old Man of the Sea, whose island home we were on. If we could catch him, he would tell us how to get off Pharos and anything else we should want to know. So, on the advice of the goddess – Proteus's own daughter – I and three of my men went to the secret cave where he sleeps. We killed four seals and covered ourselves with their skins. And a more powerful stench you will never come across in your life! We were almost sick several times, though in the end we became used to it as we waited for the ancient god to arrive.

'Then the time came, when the sun was at its zenith, and the black waters before the cave began to ripple. Like the rings made by drops of rain at first, then small stones, until soon the whole pool was bubbling like a cauldron. And that was when he emerged: pale and naked at first, his green beard and hair dripping with brine as he hauled himself out using his powerful arms. He had the strangest eyes, like pools of black water. Then we saw what passed for his lower body. From the waist down, he had the tail of a great seal, which was useless on land and had to be dragged up the shingle to the cave by the strength of his arms alone. We lay still, barely daring to move as he crawled into the cave, followed by the great numbers of seals that lay around him like a defensive wall. When the last one had settled down, he stretched out his arm and began counting them, touching each creature on the head.

'I lay there with Eteoneus, Diocles and Phrontis, knowing that if he suspected we were there, he'd slither back down into the water and disappear again. Then, when his hand touched the head of the skin I was wearing and he saw he had been tricked, I gave a shout and threw off my disguise. With the others, we leapt onto Proteus and took hold of his arms. At once he transformed himself into a formidable lion, covering me in spittle as his great jaws roared at us. But his daughter had forewarned us of his sorcery! She told us some of the shapes he would assume, cautioning us to hold on regardless until he resumed his former appearance.

'And so we swallowed our terror and held on to him with all our strength as he changed into a writhing serpent, then a panther, then a bear. Each time it was our fear that nearly undid us, as his strength was unchanged and he hadn't the power in himself to throw us off. Even when he transformed himself into water and we could feel the cool liquid running through our fingers, he still couldn't escape our grip. Last of all he became a living torch and we nearly lost him. Eteoneus and Phrontis let go, screaming with imagined pain, but though Diocles and I also saw our hands blacken and felt the intense heat of the flame, we forced ourselves to remember it was all an illusion. And at last he relented.

'When he assumed his natural form and lay on the shingle, panting with exhaustion, we looked at our palms and saw that no mark of fire had been left! When Proteus gave us his word that he would not try to escape and would tell us whatever we wanted to know, we released him and asked him how to leave the island. He told us that we were being punished because we'd failed to offer the proper sacrifices to Zeus and the other Olympians before we set sail from Troy, but that the gods would allow us to sail for

Egypt to make our sacrifices. After that, they would permit us to continue our voyage home.

'It was then I remembered his daughter's words,' Menelaus continued, 'that we could ask him anything once we'd subdued him. So I questioned him about the fate of my friends who had fought alongside me at Troy. He told me first of the drowning of Little Ajax and the murder of my brother. Tears flowed down my face as he described Agamemnon's death, but I insisted he continue with the fates of the other commanders. It was then that he told me about your father.'

Telemachus stood up and walked over to the open door of the portico. He looked out into the sunlit courtyard, where the chariot Peisistratus had loaned him was being uncovered. The horses were being fed and watered by two slaves, while two more were brushing them down. Soon they would make the return journey to Pylos. But would he set out in hope or despair? He turned to face Menelaus.

'And what did he say, my lord?'

'He told me that Odysseus lives.'

The last word was like a body blow. Telemachus seized the iron ring on one of the doors to steady himself.

'That's impossible,' Theoclymenus exclaimed.

'But it's true, my friend. Proteus is a sea god. He saw Odysseus with his own eyes, sitting on a golden beach on the island of Ogygia, beyond the realms of the known world. There he was held captive by the nymph, Calypso, without ship or crew to help him escape. And who knows that he isn't still there, alive in his body and yet dead to the world?'

Telemachus saw the disbelief on Theoclymenus's face, mirroring the disbelief in his own heart. He turned his gaze back to the courtyard, his thoughts a muddle as he tried to understand what it meant. His father was a prisoner on an island he had never heard of. But he was alive.

-

Odysseus awoke from a deep sleep and opened his eyes. He was lying on a sloping, sandy beach with a thick blanket covering him from his shoulders to his sandalled feet. He could hear the gentle lapping of water a short distance away and smell brine and seaweed. But he could see very little, for a thick fog had covered everything. Twisting his head back he saw steep cliffs in the shape of a horseshoe looming out of the white mist behind him. He was in a natural harbour, that much was clear. But where? The Phaeacians had promised to take him back to Ithaca, but nothing seemed familiar. He looked around at the alien setting and felt his heart sink. Was this Laodamas's revenge for his humiliation in the wrestling, to maroon him on yet another island peopled by monsters and savages? Had the nightmare started again?

He closed his eyes and let his mind drift back to the events of the previous two days. After his victory in the games, Alcinous had agreed to grant Odysseus passage back to his homeland, even insisting he stay another night so they could properly honour him with a feast and gifts. Indeed, all the nobles who had watched the games were called on to donate gold, fine linens and other precious items that had been stowed in a huge oak chest provided by Queen Arete.

The feast had been a lavish display of Phaeacia's wealth. He remembered the great hall packed with hundreds of nobles, and being served by an army of slaves. The air had resonated to the sound of music and singing, and the tables were creaking under the weight of food and drink. Then as the evening wore on and the wine made the guests sentimental, King Alcinous had called for a song. Omeros – Demodocus to the Phaeacians – told them the story of the Wooden Horse and the fall of Troy. His skill was such that his audience was in thrall to his every word. And when Odysseus heard the bard describe that terrible and glorious night as only one who had experienced it could, tears had flooded his eyes and rolled unchecked down his cheeks. Seeing his guest's reaction, Alcinous had suggested it was finally time for Odysseus to reveal his identity and tell them the tale of how he had reached Phaeacia.

At first, his claim to be Odysseus was met with incredulity. Some of the old resentment entered the eyes of those who heard him, silently accusing him of being a liar. And so, as he began the story of his voyage from Troy, he summoned the half-forgotten voice that had once been able to enthral any audience and bend them to his will. To his surprise, he found that – like his old strength and determination – his ability to captivate and charm had not been left behind on Ogygia. It had simply been awaiting the chance to be used.

He told them of the raid against the Cicones and the price they had paid; about their failure rounding Malea and the wind that had swept them beyond the world they knew. He mentioned the terrible secret of the lotus eaters and his narrow escape from their clutches. And by the time his tale had led the Phaeacians to the lair of the Cyclops, they no longer doubted who he was or what he was telling them. Their faces reflected their horror at the deaths of his comrades, followed by nodding approval of his outwitting of Polyphemus. They shared his anger at his crew's betrayal in opening the leather bag that Aeolus, the Ruler of the Winds, had given him, and his despair as the released winds blew the fleet away from the shores of Ithaca.

When his story took a darker turn, the silence of the Phaeacians told him their imaginations had been transported to the cove where the Laestrygonians had destroyed his fleet and eaten his men, and that they felt the grief of his loss and the relief of his escape. Almost from the start, Odysseus had seen Omeros and Ocyalus discussing his tale in whispers, no doubt thinking of the song they might make of it. *And why not?* he thought. It was a tale worth telling.

There was no question in the eyes of his audience as he described Circe turning his men into swine, or how he was able, with the aid of Hermes, to defeat her magic and reverse it. When he told of his descent into Hades – though he felt the limits of his ability to describe that most awful of trials – there was open weeping. The faces that stared at him were ashen despite the reflection of the firelight, reminding him of the crowds of phantoms that had clustered before his blood offering, their expressions forlorn but greedy for a taste of the life they had left behind. Not a single hand reached for a cup, not a whisper was heard. Their relief as his story returned to Circe's island was palpable, though the awfulness of the Sirens and Scylla and Charybdis soon captured their attention again.

Finally, when he shared the tragedies that happened on the island where Hyperion kept his cattle, followed by the destruction of his galley and his entire crew, there was widespread distress among the Phaeacians. By now their empathy for him was total. He heard voices openly discussing how they could help compensate his loss of treasure, or volunteering to man the ship that would take their visitor back at last to his beloved homeland. Only one man among them looked uncertain, as if silently questioning a point of detail – a wine steward with a hunched back, who had paused in his rounds to listen to the ending of Odysseus's story. It was only when Laodamas called for silence that Odysseus was able to conclude with his imprisonment on Ogygia and the storm that had destroyed his raft and thrown him onto the shores of Phaeacia.

The morning after the feast, Alcinous had insisted on making sacrifices to guarantee him safe passage back to Ithaca. This had been followed by another banquet, delaying Odysseus's departure until evening and increasing his desperation to set sail. When the meal was nearly over, Ocyalus had asked if he would speak with Omeros, as the bard hoped to make a song of his adventures and wanted to clarify a few points. Odysseus had agreed, half hoping the sound of his voice might trigger some memory in Omeros. But it did not.

Afterwards, Odysseus asked Ocyalus to accompany him back to his table.

'Does Demodocus really know nothing of who he was before the shipwreck that stranded him here?'

'Only that he was a soldier in the war at Troy, my lord,' Ocyalus answered. 'He doesn't remember his name or the king he served, but his recollections of the things he saw and heard are very clear. It only makes the mystery of who he is more tragic.'

'Ocyalus,' Odysseus responded. 'I know this man – who he used to be, I mean. He's an Ithacan. He fought beside me at Troy, and he was on my ship when Zeus destroyed it.'

'Then why haven't you told him?'

'Something holds me back. But a man should know who he is. Will you tell him, Ocyalus?'

The young man nodded.

'Good. But give me your word you'll wait until I've left Phaeacia, and that you'll not share what I tell you with anyone else. The information is for Demodocus, and for him alone, so that he can decide what to do with it. Do you promise by all the gods to do as I ask?'

'I do, my lord.'

And so Odysseus told him Omeros's name and the name of his father, adding a few details that might help the bard connect with the person he once was. Then Alcinous declared that his ship was ready. Libations were poured and Odysseus was escorted down to the harbour, where a sleek galley lay waiting on the moonlit waters. A more beautiful vessel he had never seen, and when he was told it was able to find its own way to Ithaca without need for a helmsman, he was amazed. But it still needed a crew to man the oars and trim the sail, and he noted that many of the men on the benches were the young Phaeacians who had competed in the games the previous morning. Then, as he was about to board, a hooded man stopped him.

'A word, my lord?'

'What is it?' Odysseus said, recognising the hunchbacked wine steward.

'Demodocus, our bard, was rescued from the sea seven years ago, about the same time you said your ship was sunk. It may be just a coincidence, but I've seen the way you look at him, and I wondered whether you were on the same ship.'

'If I was, what business is it of yours?'

'None, my lord. Except...'

'Pontonous!' Laodamas called, walking along the beach towards the waiting galley. 'Leave our friend alone and let him board.'

'Except what?' Odysseus urged.

'Except he wasn't the only man who was fished out of the water that day. There was another.'

'Another? Where is this man?'

'He asked for passage to Greece only a few days before you arrived.'

'What was his name?'

'Pontonous, go about your work,' Laodamas ordered, pushing him in the direction of the city gates. 'The king won't be pleased if he finds you've been shirking down here by the boats. Now go on.'

The steward turned and ran along the beach with his shuffling gait. Laodamas took Odysseus by the hand and spoke friendly words of departure, but all the Ithacan could think about was who else had survived the wreck that he once thought had killed every member of his crew. The last thing he remembered was lying down on a blanket in the prow and hearing calls for the anchors to be pulled up.

Odysseus sat up. The sun had risen at the far ends of the earth, thinning the fog to reveal a little more detail of the small harbour. The cliff behind him was of a soft, pale rock, and here and there shrubs had made their homes in its cracks and nooks. There was a path running along its foot, too, that he had not noticed before. He followed its course with his eyes until it was lost to the fog. He wondered who had made it, and whether they were hostile to strangers, or friendly. Then he remembered the gifts the Phaeacians had loaded him with – the gold, expensive fabrics, cauldrons and tripods given by the leading households. He looked about himself, but could see no sign of the treasure. It was then that the fronds of mist swayed back against one of the sloping cliffs that flanked the harbour, giving a momentary glimpse of an old olive tree and the tall, narrow mouth of a cave behind it. Then the milky vapour rolled down again and swallowed it once more.

Odysseus stood and picked up the blanket, throwing it around his shoulders. He walked up the beach to the grassy bank and followed the path round to the cave. The arched entrance seemed familiar, but he could not remember where from. He walked inside, taking care on the wet stones, and found his treasure. At least, the chest was the one Arete had given him. But the lid was open, and instead of fine linen and gold he found piles of seaweed, the fronds neatly folded, and heaps of small shells of different shapes and hues. On the floor around the chest were a few larger shells and a scattering of starfish.

'They stole it,' he exclaimed, his voice echoing back at him. 'They abandoned me on this gods-forsaken place and took my wealth with them!'

He picked up a handful of the shells and threw them into a corner of the cave, where they bounced off the walls and fell with echoing plops into an unseen pool. In despair, he sat on a rock and put his face in his hands. After a while he looked again at the casket, half expecting to find his treasures returned and that the seaweed and shells had been part of a bad dream. But there they were, glistening wetly in the shadows. Perhaps, he thought, Phaeacia itself had been a dream. Perhaps the whole of the past ten years had been one long, inescapable nightmare that he was just beginning to emerge from.

Then he heard the jingling of a bell. It was faint at first, but coming closer. And the closer it got, the more he realised it was not the sound of a single bell, but of several. Of the small kind that shepherds tie around the necks of goats.

He stood. Anxiously he put his hand to his side, only then remembering that he carried no weapon. Why had he not asked the Phaeacians for a sword before he left? And now he was unarmed in an unknown land where the people were likely hostile or savage. He moved to the mouth of the cave and looked out along the path. The fog was still thick and seemed to blow down from the unseen top of the cliff in billows. Through these slowly shifting curtains, a shape emerged. It was fat with long hair and horns that angled backwards across its body. Its shaggy coat shook as it jogged towards him. Soon it was followed by a second and a third, until suddenly a dozen or more creatures filled the path and spilled out onto the grass and the beach, their wool shining like strands of silver in the pale light.

Then a man strolled into sight. He was young and tall, with large eyes and a long nose. He wore a rough cap on his head, a goatskin jerkin and a cloak folded back over his shoulders. In one hand he carried a staff, and in the other a tall spear. Cautiously, not wanting to be trapped in a cave by a potential assailant, Odysseus stepped out.

'Good morning, friend,' he said.

The shepherd showed no sign of surprise as he looked up from his goats. He gave Odysseus a curt nod.

'Can I help you?'

His words sent a wave of relief coursing through Odysseus's tense body.

'Yes. Yes, you can. I'm a stranger here and... Well, I was wondering where *here* is, exactly.'

The shepherd frowned.

'You don't *know*? My friend, this is Ithaca.'

Odysseus's head became light. He felt that he was going to vomit.

'Ith...'

'Ithaca,' the shepherd repeated, stepping forwards and taking Odysseus by the elbow. 'Here, lean on this.'

He was surprisingly strong, and his hands were hot as he wrapped Odysseus's fingers about his staff.

'You're certain?'

'Absolutely,' the shepherd said, smiling. 'It may not be a large or populous island, but we want for nothing. There's no shortage of pasture for our herds of cattle and goats. We have plenty of corn and our grapes produce a fine wine, too, so we aren't counted among the poor nations. Indeed, the gods bless us with sun, wind and rain and protect our shores with the wide sea. You must have travelled far, sir, if you haven't heard of Ithaca.'

Odysseus sat on a rock that jutted out from the base of the cliff. He looked about himself at the short length of beach visible through the walls of fog. The waves were lapping over the sand, and the phantom outline of the slope-sided headlands were jutting out on either side. Was this really his homeland? He had once known every harbour, every path and every cave in his beloved kingdom but, enveloped in mist and obscured by his dimming memory, he could not be sure.

His chest welled up with a storm of different emotions, from relief to regret and elation to terror. Would his people welcome him back, alone and without their fathers, husbands and sons who had accompanied him? Did the Kerosia still govern his kingdom's affairs, or had some tyrant taken power? And would Penelope be waiting for him, or had she taken him for dead and moved on, filling the gap he had left with another man? These anxieties raged within him, an agony of unknowns with a crowd of hopes and joys pressing behind.

'Of course I've heard of Ithaca,' he replied, his voice shaking, 'if this really is that blessed island. Even in my country of Crete, men speak of its beauty and natural wealth.'

'You're a Cretan?' the shepherd asked, raising a sceptical eyebrow.

'I was, but now I'm in exile. The king's son tried to take my share of the plunder from Troy, so I killed him. After that I boarded the first ship I could find and bought passage to Pylos. As we were passing Messene, the winds became too strong to handle and we were driven off course, until, as night fell, we spotted land and rowed our way into this cove. Exhausted, we jumped onto the sandy beach and threw ourselves down to sleep. They must have slipped away before dawn, leaving me where I lay.'

The shepherd looked back at the beach.

'I see only the imprint of a single body, my friend. Surely the whole beach would be marked with footprints. Are you sure you weren't dreaming?'

'Of course not.'

'Lying, then?'

'How dare you…?'

The shepherd snatched his crook from Odysseus's hand and brought it down on the path. There was a tremor, and suddenly the ground heaved upwards, throwing Odysseus from the rock where he was seated. The cliffs above him seemed to sway and groan, releasing a shower of dust and large stones that fell all around him. He held his hands out before his face, terrified that the cliff would collapse and crush him. Then the quaking stopped and the earth grew still again, leaving the air smelling and tasting of dirt.

Slowly, Odysseus lowered his hands. The shepherd stood over him, untouched by the rockfall. The expression on his face was stern, but as Odysseus stared at him he noticed a pale luminescence in his complexion. His clothes, too, possessed an inner light that was growing in intensity, filling the dusty air around him with a white radiance. Slowly he stretched out his arms either side of himself and raised them upwards, lifting his eyes to the heavens as thin shafts of brilliant light spilled out from the folds of his clothing. Suddenly he arched his back and gave a deafening shout that rolled back from the surrounding cliffs, his whole body convulsing as beams of light erupted from his mouth and eyes. The air shuddered and a wave of energy exploded outward from him, throwing Odysseus onto his back and pressing him to the floor as a fierce wind blew over him. He closed his eyes and turned his face away, no longer able to look at the brilliance emanating from the figure before him.

Then, as quickly as it had begun, it was over. The light faded and the howling wind was stilled. Cautiously, Odysseus opened one eye and saw that the harbour was still shrouded in fog, pale and grey in the predawn light. He looked toward the shepherd, but he was no longer there. Instead, a woman was standing in his place, though she was much taller than any mortal female. Her skin was as white as milk, her face beautiful and grave, and her eyes large and grey. As she stared down at him, Odysseus felt as if she knew every thought in his head, could see every memory – even those that had been lost or purposely buried – and understood every ambition, desire, fear and motive that gave his existence purpose. And yet there was a bottomless vigour in those eyes that loved life and was fascinated by everything it had to offer.

'How dare I what, Odysseus?' Athena asked.

He stole a last glance at the face he remembered so well, surrounded by shining golden hair and crowned with a bronze helmet, then dropped his gaze to the path.

'I didn't recognise you, my lady.'

'My disguises have always been better than yours, don't you think?' she said, pulling him gently to his feet. 'My dear Odysseus, how I've missed you.'

The goddess drew him into a powerful embrace, crushing him against the breastplate she wore under the folds of her white cloak. Her hands were warm against his back and she smelled of clean linen and mountain springs. He dared to put his arms about her, but she quickly took him by the wrists and removed them.

'We forget ourselves,' she said, holding him at arm's length and looking at him with affection. 'Some gods, of course, can't resist the touch of a mortal, but I'm not one of them. It turns friendship into something more intimate. And as gods and men can't exist together in any form of intimacy, it means the end of their friendship – and usually the end of the mortal's life. I wouldn't want our friendship to end, Odysseus.'

'Then are we still friends, my lady? I thought when I disobeyed you and took the Palladium…'

'It did not end our friendship, Odysseus. It just… gave it a hiatus. An Olympian cannot tolerate defiance from anyone. Where would our authority be if we did? You had to be punished…'

'And I *was* punished. Again and again and again. I lost everything I had. Even my friends were taken from me. And I was kept from seeing my wife and son for another ten years. Years that I will never get back, not even if I were to live to a hundred.'

'Odysseus,' Athena stopped him, raising her fingers to brush against his bearded cheek and move a lock of hair from his forehead. 'Odysseus, I should have killed you, but I did not. I *could* not, even though some of the immortals advised me to. Being an Olympian is not like being a king. The gulf between us is immeasurable. Our rules are *absolute* – the existence of the universe depends on them. So, to let you live, to forgive you, Odysseus, was not the easy gesture you think.'

'Yes, my lady,' he replied, bowing his head and letting his anger subside.

'And I have helped you, too, though you may not have seen me. I was the little girl who led you to Alcinous's palace and put the guards to sleep. It was I who encouraged Laodamas to challenge you, knowing it was the best way to restore your qualities of courage and single-mindedness that were weakened by your imprisonment on Ogygia, and which you will need again soon. And it was I that encouraged the Phaeacians to shower you with gifts...'

'Gifts that they stole from me when they left me here! Replacing them with shells and seaweed to mock me in my loss. I should have known Laodamas's friends could not be trusted.'

Athena raised her hand.

'You are too harsh on them. They brought you here out of respect and remorse for their treatment of you; and they have paid for it with their lives. When Poseidon discovered the Phaeacians had given you passage from their homeland, he turned their ship – crew and all – to stone. It's as I said, Odysseus: an Olympian cannot tolerate defiance.

'As for your treasure, they did not steal a single tunic or talent of gold. They placed it in that cave last night, just where you found it this morning.'

'Then someone else took it.'

'No. What is real in the world where you have spent the past ten years is not real in this world. Tonight you will see the stars as you used to know them, before your voyage took you beyond the borders of this world. For you really are back home, Odysseus.'

She waved her arm and the fog rolled back, as if blown by a powerful wind. The angled cliffs were now revealed, as well as the harbour that they protected. Its waters were clear enough to disclose the dark plant life beneath and the schools of fish that swam above it. The cave now stood out clearly, and he knew it as a place where naiads were said to visit, and where he had made several sacrifices in his years as king. Rising above the cliffs in the near distance were the slopes of Mount Neriton that he knew and loved so well. The early-morning sun had lit its eastern flanks and he knew that his palace lay among the skirts of its northern end. The sight of it brought tears to his eyes.

'I know this place. This is the Harbour of Phorcys.'

He left the path and walked down to the beach, turning round and round as he took in his first sight of home in twenty years. It was like a dream, but he knew it was real. At last the barrier that had held back his emotions broke. His choking tears brought him to his knees, and then face down on the ground as he kissed the sand and clawed his fingers into its softness. The sound of the waves and the wind playing over the rocks and the smell of the sea and the vegetation hanging down from the cliffs was all too much to take in.

He stumbled to his feet and shouted at the top of his voice, enjoying the sound bouncing back from the cliff faces and the mouth of the cave. Then a thought occurred to him and he ran up the beach to the grassy bank. He searched the ground, pushing aside the long grass with his fingertips until he saw what he was looking for. A small white flower, nudging its way up through the dirt. He took it gently between his finger and thumb and lifted it from the soil.

'A chelonion,' he said, showing it to Athena. 'The native flower of Ithaca. I wore one in my belt for all the years I was at Troy.'

'Then I hope your sceptical mind accepts the evidence of your senses, Odysseus,' she said as he tucked the flower into the top of his belt. 'But be warned. Though you are now home, things are not as they were when you left. Ithaca has become a dangerous place, especially for its king. Penelope has promised to remarry on Apollo's feast day, just four days from now. I'd hoped to bring you back from Ogygia sooner, but I couldn't arrange it until Poseidon made his annual visit to the Aethiopes at the far end of the world. Even then he returned early and nearly put an end to you.

'Meanwhile, your son has travelled to Pylos and Sparta to seek news of whether you're still alive, in the hope he can annul his mother's promise. But you cannot just return to the palace and reclaim your throne and your wife, as no doubt you are already planning to do. Your home is filled with suitors, over a hundred of them, and they will gladly kill you before they give up their chance to become king.'

Odysseus frowned, his joy at returning to his homeland suddenly checked.

'A hundred, you say?'

'A hundred and eighteen, including their servants. You will have to kill them all.'

'But I only have four days before this wedding! Four days to assess the strength of my enemies and find out who my friends are.'

'And to do that you must hide your true identity while you make your plans. And not some feeble attempt like the one you made to fool me earlier. That was poor by your standards, Odysseus, which I put down to your being imprisoned by Calypso for so long. No, I will disguise you myself – a disguise that none will see through, even those who know you best. Only one feature will I leave that you can be recognised by: the scar on your thigh. Everything else, even your voice, will be changed.'

'And how long will this disguise last?'

'Until you kill the first of the suitors. Only then you will be revealed as Odysseus, King of Ithaca. But first you must go to the home of Eumaeus, the swineherd. Not all the servants you left behind have remained faithful to your memory, but Eumaeus detests these suitors who have taken over your home and are consuming your wealth. He will serve you loyally, but do not reveal your identity to him yet. Rather, use what he knows about these suitors to draw up your plans against them.'

'And can I count on you to help me, mistress, now that I have your favour again?'

Athena reached out and straightened a fold on his cloak, like a mother with her child.

'You are about to face your last great ordeal, Odysseus. Everything you love depends on it: your kingship, your home, the restoration of your family. And everything you have endured for the past twenty years has prepared you for this moment. I could strike the suitors dead for you and not receive a scratch in return, but this is not my battle. It's yours alone. You have to prove yourself to Penelope and Telemachus. You must show your enemies and your people that you are strong, even stronger than you were before you sailed to Troy. If you are to mark your authority and rule Ithaca again, then everyone must see that you have the determination, courage and strength to do it.'

'I'm not sure I do,' he said, looking back at the empty ocean. 'Even if I used to have those qualities, time and bitter experience have weakened them. Throwing a discus and winning a wrestling match prove nothing. Goddess, I *doubt* myself.'

'Odysseus, that is exactly *why* I will not do the job for you. A king must have faith in his abilities or he will not be king for long. So you must rediscover your strength and cunning of old if you are to win back your family and your kingdom. And you have four days in which to do it. Now, prepare yourself.'

She picked up the staff he had left on the path and touched his shoulder with it. Immediately he felt a chill creeping down his arm and up his neck, spreading from skin to flesh, muscle to bone, until his whole body shivered with cold. He raised a hand to the shoulder that had been struck and let out a gasp.

The skin was loose. Looking down, he saw that it was leathery and covered with liver spots. The once solid muscles were now soft, and the black hairs on his forearms had turned grey. The veins in his hands stood out and the fingers were gnarled and bony. The fine blue tunic the Phaeacians had given him had turned to coarse brown wool, threadbare and holed. It was held together by a belt made from a length of rope, in which his chelonion was still lodged, while hanging from a strap over his shoulder was a worn leather pouch. He stared at his legs and saw they had become bowed, the muscles sunken and flaccid. As he looked, he felt something like a hand on his shoulders, pushing him downward as his spine bent from the base of his neck to the top of his buttocks. Every limb became stiff and heavy. If he fell, he felt sure he would break into a hundred pieces.

'This is too much,' he cried out, his voice croaking hideously. 'I can't bear it.'

'It's necessary,' Athena assured him. 'And you will quickly become used to it. I have not dulled your mind or your senses, and you will find – when the need arises – that you are as strong and quick as you ever were. Go into the cave. You will discover a small pool near the entrance. There's enough light now for you to see your reflection.'

Odysseus tried to straighten his back and move his legs. It was painful, but step by step he made his way to the cave and went inside. The surface of the pool was like a darkened mirror, and the face that stared back at him was horrible to behold. The nose was swollen and lumpish, his lips had thinned to a narrow line, and his hair and beard were white. The small, milky eyes were lost in a bed of wrinkles that fanned out across the rest of his face. He turned away in disgust and staggered back to the cave entrance.

'Turn me back, mistress,' he pleaded. 'Give me another disguise or let me make my own. Anything but this.'

But Athena was no longer there.

Chapter Fourteen

The Swineherd

The hide of a stag lay folded on the grass with a gnarled staff beside it. Odysseus put the pelt about his shoulders and, leaning heavily on the staff, hobbled to a flight of steps cut into the low cliffs. They were flat and worn, but it was still a struggle for his decrepit body to reach the meadows above. At the top, he followed a path towards a wood that skirted a hill. The stippled shade of the trees was pleasantly cool, and despite his stiff limbs, he walked with a smile on his face. It seemed to his eye that nothing had changed. His dim memories were being slowly restored, so that as he reached each bend in the path, he began to remember what lay beyond it. The swineherd's hut, as he recalled, was positioned on a stony knoll in the middle of a wide clearing a short way ahead.

He toiled up the path towards the glade and paused in the shadow of the eaves. The hut was still there, but the outer wall had been built up to a greater height than he remembered and topped with a thick hedge. It was surrounded by a stockade made from sharpened stakes of oak, inside of which a few score hogs were lying on their sides in the sun or snuffling at piles of old vegetables.

The gates to the stockade and the outer wall had been left open, but four savage-looking dogs lay on the grass before the hut, their heads resting on their paws as they watched the path. A portly, middle-aged man was sitting on the porch, holding a piece of leather against his foot and marking out the shape of the sole. Odysseus recognised Eumaeus at once and, forgetting his disguise, stepped out from the shadows. The dogs leapt up and raced down the path towards him, barking ferociously with long dribbles of spittle trailing out from their jaws.

Odysseus raised his staff and prepared to defend himself. The dogs were nearly upon him, their teeth bared and their black eyes filled with a single desire: to rend his flesh until his bloody carcass was lying still and lifeless in the sunlight. Then a high whistle sounded and the dogs came to a skidding halt. They formed a semicircle around him, snarling and drooling until their master came up and ordered them back to the courtyard.

'Zeus's beard, old man!' Eumaeus said. 'You can't just go wandering across a person's land without a by-your-leave these days, you know. Times have changed: there are too many thieves about and too little respect for the property of others. Nowadays people will set their hounds on you first and ask who you are later.'

'I'm just glad I wasn't ripped to shreds.'

Eumaeus laughed.

'As if I haven't got enough troubles without adding an innocent corpse to them. Assuming you're innocent, that is.' He gave a wink and offered Odysseus his hand. 'Looks like you've got a tale to tell, friend, but not before you've had your fill of pork, washed down by a drop of wine. Come and join me in my hut.'

'I'll be glad to, sir. May Zeus grant you your heart's desire for your kindness.'

'Even *he* couldn't do that,' the swineherd answered, glancing at the heavens.

He led Odysseus into the enclosure. A dozen large pens had been built against the stone walls, housing hundreds of pigs. The grunting of the mothers and the high-pitched squeals of their offspring was loud. Odysseus followed Eumaeus into his hut, where a small fire was glowing in the middle of the room. The smoke trailed up to the roof and out through a hole in the thatch. There were a few goatskins scattered over the floor and a selection of cooking pots and wooden tools hanging from pegs in the stone wall, but little else. Eumaeus threw a handful of logs onto the fire, then lay a shaggy goatskin over a bundle of brushwood and invited his guest to sit down. Despite the sunshine outside, Odysseus's sagging flesh seemed permanently cold, and he held out his hands to the flames.

'I've travelled far and wide, friend,' he said, 'but found few welcomes that weren't grudging or hostile. I can't tell you how good it is to find some genuine hospitality.'

'You flatter me, stranger – I'm doing nothing more than the gods require. You'd have received a richer reception if times weren't so hard.'

'Are they really that bad?' Odysseus asked. 'You have a farm and plenty of pigs. It could be much worse.'

He plucked at the rags he was wearing and smiled. Eumaeus held up a hand in apology.

'I mean no offence. I'm only a slave myself, tending another man's herds. But if you'd seen how this place was when my master was here, you'd know what I mean. He treated his servants with respect and generosity, and me not least among them. Had he survived, by now I'd have been given a proper house of my own with some land to farm when I wasn't about my master's business, and a wife as well. *Then* you'd have received a proper welcome.'

'So what happened to this master of yours?'

Eumaeus sat on a block of wood. His cheerful demeanour had softened.

'He sailed to Troy twenty years ago and never came back.'

'Him and many others,' Odysseus said. 'But a warrior's death isn't to be despised.'

'I only wish he'd received such an honour. If he had, the whole of Greece would have raised a mound to him and spoke his name in the same breath as Achilles, Patroclus and Great Ajax. But he survived the war and sailed for home, and that's the last honest news we've had of him. I don't comfort myself with foolish optimism, though. He's dead. Carrion birds have feasted on his flesh, or the fish have picked his bones clean.'

He shrugged his shoulders, stood and left the hut. A short while later he returned with a young pig under each arm. They wrestled in his grip and complained loudly, until he knocked each one over the head with a piece of firewood and slit their throats. With expert skill, he chopped them up and slid the meat onto skewers, which he roasted over the fire.

As the squares of pork browned, the smell reminded Odysseus of his hunger. Eumaeus pulled a skin of wine from a peg on the wall and mixed it in a bowl with water from a clay jar. He paused to pick up the trotters he had laid aside and threw them out to his dogs. As they snapped and snarled over the titbits, the swineherd continued his preparations – turning the skewers, setting a small table between Odysseus and himself, and laying two wooden boards on it. When the pork was ready, he set a couple of spits before Odysseus and took the remaining two for himself, sprinkling them with barley. Finally he poured the wine into cups and offered a libation.

Odysseus followed his example and started on his meal. It was every bit as good as it smelled. Eumaeus had little to give, but he shared it freely and with no other motive than to honour the gods. Odysseus only wished the simple pleasure of that meal could have lasted longer. But his mind wandered back to Athena's warning on the beach. Within days Penelope was going to take a new husband. He did not blame her: she had waited longer than most, and it was good sense to remarry before her looks withered. But it still felt like a betrayal, though he knew he was a fool to take it that way. He was the one who had betrayed her, after all. And yet the thought she could forget him and marry another seemed impossible after the love they had shared. Maybe her affections had succumbed to the slow death of too many years apart. Or maybe she had fallen for one of the young nobles that courted her.

Odysseus took a swallow of the strong wine. The thought of the suitors irked him more now. Had one of them slept with Penelope already? More than one? Was that why so many hovered around the palace, because they knew she would not withhold her affections? He clenched his fists and wished he could march to the palace and kill the first suitor he saw. But he was now an old man, unarmed and without friends. Even if Penelope wanted him back, what hope would he have of defeating so many enemies? Despair and anger ran in equal measure through his veins.

'So who do you tend your master's herds for now, my friend?' he asked, his voice edged with bitterness. 'There seemed a lot fewer hogs outside the walls than the sows inside. Somebody hereabouts must have a ravenous appetite for pork.'

Eumaeus stared at him from behind the rim of his wine cup. Placing it down carefully, he leaned forwards and looked his guest in the eye.

'And there, my friend, you touch on the greatest of my woes. I still serve my master's wife and his son, as loyally as I used to serve the king himself. But the queen has decided to remarry. That's her choice and it's not for me to question it, though I wish she could be content with the memory of her husband, who was a man without equal. And yet some god put it in her mind to allow the young men of the kingdom to court her in her husband's house. One hundred and eight of them at my last count, not including their personal servants.

'For three years they've been there, and almost every night they've feasted on my master's estate. Goats, sheep, oxen, *my* precious pigs! No regard for the rules of xenia, no respect for the gods at all. They say they want a hog for the feast and I have to pick them the best or face a thrashing. I tell you, stranger, they show no respect for anyone, least of all us servants. The men they beat and the women they... well, I'm sure you can guess. My swine have better manners than these *nobles*. They know the king's not coming back so they steal with impunity. It doesn't bother them, because they know what's left of my master's wealth will go to his son. All they're interested in is the queen. You see, according to our ancient laws, if the king dies and the queen remarries, her new husband gets the throne.'

'What about the son?'

Eumaeus shook his head. 'Only if he's of age. And Telemachus won't become a man until next spring, months after the wedding.'

'Why doesn't she wait, then?' Odysseus asked. 'Doesn't she love her son enough to let him claim his birthright?'

Eumaeus poured more wine for them both.

'It's not my place to judge. She's been a good mistress to me and I've no understanding of how the rich and powerful think. I can't imagine she's fallen for one of these young men and wants him to be king ahead of her son. Some say she's long been sworn to remarry if her husband doesn't return by Apollo's feast day this year, though why she'd have taken such an oath I don't know. Or maybe she just wants to stay queen. Either way, the wedding takes place in four days and nobody can do anything to stop it.'

'Can't her son deal with these suitors?'

'He hates them more than anyone, and with good reason. But rumour says he's had enough. Took a ship to the mainland a few days back and hasn't been seen since. Perhaps he can't bear to see his mother married to one of those men. Can't say I blame him. The only comfort I take from the whole affair is that the suitors will all go back to their homes after the wedding and things might return to some sort of normality – whatever that looks like!'

Odysseus shook his head.

'It seems everyone who loved this king of yours has given up on him. Doesn't anybody think he might return and restore things to the way they were? You shake your head, my friend, but perhaps you should have some faith in the immortal gods, who right all wrongs and bring justice to the earth. Tell me what this country is called, and the name of its king. I fought at Troy, perhaps I'll have heard of him. I might have some news of his fate that can bring you hope, or help you to properly grieve his death.'

'Friend, don't spoil our meal,' Eumaeus said. 'I like you and I'd rather you didn't turn out to be another of those wretches who come here peddling stories about Odysseus's imminent return. They turn up from time to time, shuffling their way to the palace gates and demanding to see Penelope or Telemachus. And the queen invites them in and sits them down to a good meal while she listens to their made-up tales of how Odysseus and the fleet are at Pylos for repairs; or that her husband has escaped imprisonment and is at this very moment on his way home; or that he's been around the known world gathering vast wealth and is presently being feasted by the king of this kingdom or that kingdom before returning to his family. When they've finished, she nods and thanks them before giving them a new cloak and staff and letting them go on their way.

'When the first came six or seven years ago, she eagerly awaited Odysseus's return, only to be bitterly disappointed. She believed two or three others when they told different stories, and each time promised Telemachus his father would be back soon. And again they were left frustrated and disillusioned. Some counselled her to turn all future beggars away, but her hope had already died by then, and with it the potential for more hurt.

'So she took them in out of the goodness of her heart and obedience to Zeus, the protector of wayfarers like yourself. She's an enemy to herself, of course, because they just pass the word that there's a meal and fresh clothing to be had from the queen of Ithaca in return for news of her husband. Tell me you're not another of these unscrupulous folk. Even if she no longer feels the hurt, I do! Every man who says he's seen my master here or there, or knows of his imminent arrival, just makes me yearn for him more.'

Odysseus reached out and took the swineherd's hand.

'You've been good to me and I won't deceive you, but when you said the name of your master, I could barely keep myself from interrupting. For Odysseus *is* coming back. I swear it before all the gods, and may they strike me down if my words don't come true! Listen, I'm a man of honour. Like you, I hate these leeches who feed off the suffering of others, telling whatever fictions come to mind just to fill their empty bellies and earn a bed for the night. But I'm not one of them, and to prove it, I won't ask anything from you or your mistress in exchange for my news – not until Odysseus himself sets foot on these shores. When he does, perhaps then you can reward me as you see fit. And if he doesn't, then throw me from the nearest cliff as a warning to others.'

Eumaeus sighed and looked down at his feet.

'At least it's to your credit that you don't ask for payment up front. I even think you believe what you're saying. But I've welcomed you here out of respect for the rules of xenia, not for any news you might have about my master. As for throwing you from a clifftop, what good would that do either of us? After all, Odysseus has perished from this world and will not return, so let's forget this news of yours – and your oath – and drink our wine in peace. Tell me a little about yourself instead.'

Odysseus told him a story about being a Cretan noble and a veteran of the Trojan War. His hardships had started after the war, he claimed, when he led a raid against the shores of Egypt and was taken prisoner. After working his way into the favour of his captors, the gods subjected him to further misfortunes, leading him from one misadventure to another until he ended up in Thesprotia, a guest of King Pheidon.

'And that was where I heard about Odysseus. He was a guest of the Thesprotians, too, though his comrades had perished on the voyage back from Troy. He was planning to return to Ithaca after he had consulted Zeus's oracle at Dodona. He'd gone there by foot, but the oracle is on the mainland to the north of Ithaca, so it can't be long before he returns.

'As for myself, I took passage in a grain ship heading to Dulichium and then Crete, where I hoped to return to my family. But the crew robbed me of the clothes and gifts King Pheidon had given me, dressed me in these old rags and planned to sell me into slavery. Luckily, they stopped at a harbour not far from here for water and I escaped. I hid until dawn, then followed a track inland, which led me here.'

'That was the sail I saw yesterday evening as I was herding my pigs,' Eumaeus said. 'As for the rest of your tale, I don't doubt that it's true, either – except for the part about Odysseus. Perhaps it was another Odysseus, or maybe the king lied to you for reasons of his own.'

'It's sad that the end of your woes might be at hand, but you insist on clinging to your misery.'

'Misery indeed,' Eumaeus replied. 'As I listened to your story something struck me. Don't misunderstand me – I love my master and long for his return. But part of me doesn't want him to come back.'

The dogs barked briefly and were silenced by a whistle. The swineherd stood and looked out through the open doorway.

'My herdsmen are returning from the fields. You'll stay the evening with us, of course. It'll be crowded with an extra body to accommodate, but we'll find room. And I think we'll sacrifice one of the hogs. Give you a real feast, stranger – though the gods know we can't afford to lose another animal.'

'First tell me why wouldn't you want Odysseus back. You claim to be a faithful servant, yet you wouldn't welcome his return?'

'You misunderstand me,' Eumaeus said. 'It's because I love him that I hope he stays away.' He sat opposite his guest again and looked him in the eye. 'Think about it. If he came back today – without the army that accompanied him to Troy – what chance would he have against a hundred young nobles?'

'He'd have the help of his friends and his people, wouldn't he?'

'Less help than he might have hoped,' Eumaeus cautioned. 'I'd fight at his side, of course. I used to train with Odysseus when I was a boy, and I still know how to handle a spear. Mentor and Halitherses would join us, too, though I don't know what good a one-handed man and a greybeard could be. I'd ask my own men, but they only know how to whack a hog's backside, and would be throwing their lives away in a fight. As for the rest of the islanders, too many have no memory of the king, and most of the rest are too scared to face up to the suitors. If Odysseus returned, it'd be to a swift death and a lonely grave.'

'It'd be better than death in a foreign land away from his family,' Odysseus said

'His family?' Eumaeus asked, raising an eyebrow. 'A mother long dead; a father who refuses to leave his farm; a son who's run off to find a new life elsewhere; and a wife who, for all we know, might have stopped loving him years ago. And who can say whether she'd welcome him back? They were the perfect couple in those first years of life together. Not the usual arranged marriage that nobles admire so much, all power and wealth. No, they were in *love*. But that was twenty years ago. Now he's dead and she's ready to give her heart to another. So, if he *was* alive, he'd be better off staying where he is and forgetting all about Ithaca. My heart wants him back, but my head says "what's the point?"'

The swineherd's words filled Odysseus with despair, and it was with difficulty that he forced himself to smile at the new arrivals as they entered the hut. They greeted Eumaeus loudly and embraced him, then offered their hands to the beggar in friendship as Eumaeus explained his presence. They talked about their day in the fields – the idle chatter of simple men – then Eumaeus sent them out to fetch a fatted hog. After the animal had been killed, they ate together for a while and Odysseus made up a few more stories from the Cretan beggar's past. He drank heavily, hoping to wash away his sorrows, but only managed to deepen his feeling of misery. Eventually, long after the sun had set, Eumaeus made a bed for him and then went outside, it being his turn to sleep by the herds and keep watch over them.

Odysseus lay down and closed his eyes, his mind groggy with wine as he listened to the snores of the herdsmen. He thought about the suitors and the impossibility of defeating so many men in open battle. He considered calling the people of Ithaca to Assembly and openly declaring his return. But that would just lead to open war against the ambitious suitors, who were not likely to relinquish their designs on the throne. Besides, after twenty years away, he could no longer count on the people to support him. The best of them had gone with him to Troy and perished; those left behind had been too old or too young to join the army.

He might find support among the older generation, but they would be too frail now to be effective warriors. As for the younger men, would they not simply despise him for returning without their fathers and uncles and blame him for their deaths? Why would they feel any loyalty to a king they had never known, this generation who had grown up without figures of authority in their lives? All these concerns might be resolved if he could go among his people and gauge their thoughts, persuade them to support his return to the throne. But even if he dared to reveal himself openly to them, there was no time. No, Athena was right: he would have to prove himself to the people by defeating the suitors himself. And that would be suicidal.

His thoughts turned to his family. What sort of lad was Telemachus, he wondered? Did he long for the return of his father, or would he spurn the man who had abandoned him as a baby? Had he run away, as Eumaeus had suggested? The notion his own son was a coward did not shame Odysseus; rather it saddened him, that he had not been there to teach him courage or develop in him a sense of honour.

And then there was Penelope. Twenty years was a long time to be apart. Through all his trials in Ilium and on the voyage back, he had encouraged himself with the belief she still loved him. The assumption that they would one day be reunited and their lives would be as they had been before had carried him through every difficulty, even to the Underworld and back. Never had he considered that her love for him might die. Not then, at least.

And for her part, Penelope would have heard of the other kings returning from Troy and looked to the horizon in anticipation of seeing his sail. But it had not come. So time would have eroded her faith in his return, eating away at her love like a moth, leaving only the bare threads. Now he was but a memory. He could not expect to return home and find her love for him still alive. Instead, she would reject him for whatever new love had fanned the embers of her dying passions.

Only one choice seemed open to him now. To leave. To beg a place on the next merchantman to the mainland and never return. He would slink away and leave Ithaca to its new rulers, and Penelope to the new husband she had chosen. He would be cursed to remain in the old and withered body Athena had given him, but what did that matter? What did he care if he had to spend the rest of his life begging from one town to the next, living off the generosity of lesser men until merciful death took him?

He raised his head and looked around. The others were still sleeping. Finding his staff, he dragged himself wearily to his feet and pulled the deerskin cloak about his shoulders. Opening the door, he felt the contrast between the chill night air outside and the warmth from the hearth within. A half-moon sailed between silver-edged clouds, and through a cleft in the trees he could see the surface of the ocean, gleaming in the moonlight. It seemed to grin at him, mocking his despair. It had kept him from his home for ten years, and now it would take him away again. All his efforts against it had been in vain. Even when he thought he had defeated his great enemy by finding his way to Ithaca, it must have known his victory had already eluded him.

Indeed, defeat had been sown when Zeus's storm had sunk his ship and he had washed up on Calypso's island, there to rot for another seven years. He thought again of her offer of immortality. Had he rejected her for nothing? For a wife who had given her affections to another, or an ignominious death beneath the swords of a crowd of her would-be lovers? But no: spending forever with a woman he did not love would have been its own hell.

He stepped out onto the porch and walked slowly and painfully down the path towards the gates. Then, as he often had in recent years when gripped by the agony of his misfortunes, he thought about Eperitus. He wished his friend was still with him. He regretted all the terrible things that had happened; that they had argued and he had seen the hatred in Eperitus's eyes. And he realised how much he owed him.

He remembered what the wine steward had said on Phaeacia, and wondered if the gods had spared Eperitus as they had done Omeros. They had not, of course; he knew that in his heart. But how different things would have been if Eperitus was with him now. He would have had no fears about facing a hundred suitors then – even two hundred. And Eperitus would have told him to have faith in Penelope's love, to face whatever obstacles the years of their separation might have put between them. If her love for him *had* died, Eperitus would have told him to win it back again. In all the years of war, he had never given up on her. He had overcome every trial the gods had put him through because he believed he would one day be reunited with his wife. If Eperitus was with him, he would not have thought twice about facing these new barriers the gods had put before him.

And even though Eperitus was dead, he would face them anyway.

He turned his back on the grinning sea and returned to the hut. He had confronted his self-doubt and he had overcome it. Whatever lay before him, whether it be rejection and death, or reunion and victory, he would not look back again.

–

Penelope watched the suitors cavorting in the space beyond the fire. In their drunken state, they could barely keep time to Phemius's music. Not that they cared. The more steps they got wrong the funnier it seemed, until eventually they collapsed in a heap on the floor. The others on the benches threw bones, cheese rinds and half-eaten fruit at them, and drunken laughter filled the great hall to the ceiling.

She wished some god would pitch them into the roaring fire so that they burned to death or ran around in a panic setting light to each other. But the gods rarely listened to her nowadays. Instead, the suitors staggered to their feet and called for another tune. This time Antinous joined them, pulling a few of the serving maids into the dance with him. Some dragged themselves away to return to their duties, but most were happy to have the strong arms of the suitors about their waists, or feel their hands wandering over their breasts or down to their backsides. Already Penelope could see that Eurymachus and Melantho were in a corner of the great hall, rutting like street dogs without a care about who knew.

Autonoe was at the queen's side, seated on a low stool and working at a piece of embroidery. But her eyes were more on the suitors than the cloth, watching them with an anxiety that Penelope had not seen before in her maid. Indeed, she had lost her cheerful optimism of late, and hardly spoke unless spoken to.

'What's wrong, child?' she asked. 'You've barely added a stitch to that cloth.'

Autonoe gave her a startled look, as if caught stealing.

'Sorry, my lady.'

She picked up the needle, and with a shaky hand threaded it through the cloth.

'Are you sick?'

'No, my lady.'

'Have the suitors offended you? Have they hurt you?'

The maid's pause was too long not to have meaning.

'No, my lady.'

'Have it your way,' Penelope said, reaching out a hand and stroking her hair. 'But if any of them are threatening you, you must tell me. I'll deal with it.'

'Only five more days to go,' Autonoe replied with a weak smile. Then her expression changed to one of shock. 'Oh, my lady, forgive me. I didn't mean...'

'Don't apologise. I'm the one who should be sorry for subjecting you all to these men. I should've chosen one of them three years ago and ended this misery before it began.'

'You had to wait, though. You had to see if Odysseus would return.'

'A fool's vigil.'

They were silenced by angry voices. Elatus had seized one of the others – a brute by the name of Peisander – and was pushing him back against a table. Fists were thrown and benches toppled. A woman screamed briefly as several others jumped into the fight. Penelope's heart was beating rapidly. She gripped the edge of her chair and wondered how much more terrible a battle would be, with bronze ripping flesh and men falling to the ground with hideous wounds. She thought then of Odysseus, subjected to long years of such violence before the walls of Troy.

Then the scuffle was over. Elatus and Peisander were being held apart, their fists and faces blotted with each other's blood. Phemius began a jaunty tune and Leocritus performed one of his comic capers, breaking the sudden tension and bringing laughter back to the feast. The two men returned to their benches and found consolation in wine and the encouragement of their friends. Autonoe, Penelope noticed, was silently crying.

'That's enough for one night, don't you think?' she said, rising. 'Come on, Autonoe, let's go upstairs and find comfort in sleep.'

'Do you believe he's still alive, my lady?' Autonoe asked, discreetly wiping the tears from her eyes. 'Odysseus, I mean. Do you think one day he'll return to Ithaca and take back what's his?'

Penelope dropped back into her chair.

'The man I loved died long ago, some wretched, lonely death far away from everything he ever held dear. And we need to stop looking to him to solve our problems. Telemachus has sailed to the mainland for news of his father, hoping he'll come back and throw the suitors out of his home – as if these swine would go without an argument! But all he's doing is running away from his responsibilities. I only know because I've been doing the same for years. Trying to buy time for my husband to return, when all along I should have been looking for my own way to sort out this mess – a mess that *I've* created.'

Autonoe fell to her knees before her mistress and laid her head on her thigh.

'What could *we* do against such men? Apart from Mentor and maybe Halitherses, nobody would raise a finger to help us. And we're only women. I can barely lift a spear, let alone use one.'

'But we have different weapons,' Penelope said, stroking the maid's hair. 'And we must have the courage to use them. *You* must. I know they've upset you in some way, though you won't admit it. Don't let it weaken you. You're strong, Autonoe, and if you ask them, then the immortals will give you a chance to show that strength. I'm strong, too. There are things within my power to do that can still upset all their plans.'

Autonoe looked questioningly at Penelope, then took her hand.

'I don't feel very strong,' she said. 'I've prayed to the gods to strengthen me, and you; but you have to fulfil your oath in a few days and nothing seems to have changed. I've been hoping for something to happen, but nothing has.'

Penelope looked at the suitors and her eyes met Antinous's, who raised his cup to her. She guessed he had been watching her for some time. His face was flushed with wine and there was a smugness about his expression. He knew she had to choose him to be her husband. Some of the other suitors still believed they had a chance, but their fathers had not threatened to murder Telemachus if she did not pick them.

A handful were not completely objectionable, such as Amphinomus, Nisus's son. His father had been a strong ally until Eupeithes's schemes had forced him into exile, and Amphinomus had inherited a measure of his decency. But there was not a man among them who could compare to Odysseus. From the first moment she had set eyes on the Ithacan prince, she had known he was special. He had something that none of Helen's other bragging suitors could boast. It was more than his cunning, his intelligence, his wonderful voice. It was the potential for intimacy. Few other men had the ability to give of themselves like he did. That had made falling in love with him easy.

And if he *did* come back? Would he be that same man? Would she see him and feel her love for him revive? She smiled to herself. Of course she would not love him. But she would want to, and she would learn to again.

It was a nice thought and it comforted her for a moment. Then a different voice reminded her Odysseus was not coming back. If she wanted a solution to the suitors, she would have to find it herself. And find it she would, whatever the cost.

Chapter Fifteen

The Ambush

The sun had only risen high enough to cast its rays on the peak of Mount Neriton, leaving the rest of Ithaca in shadow, but even with one eye Eperitus could still pick out the familiar details of the place he had once called home: harbours and villages; trees and hills; the white specks of goats and sheep grazing among the rocks. A few fishing boats were in the coves unloading their morning catches. It was as if nothing had changed since that day when he had sailed away at Odysseus's side, heading for the great gathering at Aulis.

As he looked out from the prow of the galley, he asked himself again why he was returning. He owed nothing to Ithaca, or Telemachus, or Penelope. Part of him even resented the thought of going back and helping Odysseus's family. It was because of Odysseus that Astynome had died. Would it not be right to let Odysseus's wife suffer in vengeance? Should he not leave Telemachus to fight the suitors alone and fall beneath their swords, just as Odysseus's selfish decisions had led to the death of his own son?

His fists clenched as he endured the wave of anger that always followed when he remembered the tragic end of his family. Then the tension eased and the anguish faded away. It was not the fault of Penelope or Telemachus, of course. He had come to like Telemachus in their short time together and would not abandon him to face the suitors on his own. Neither would he stand by and let Penelope marry one of the men who had invaded her home. He had loved her as a sister once, and the thought of her surrendering to a life of misery was unacceptable.

But there was another reason for his return to Ithaca. The deaths of Astynome and their baby still tormented him, and always would as long as he had no scapegoat to vent his anger upon. There was an injustice to it that he could not reconcile. He had blamed Odysseus for so long, but Odysseus was just a phantom. He could not strike his former friend down to exact revenge; he could not close his fingers around his throat and punish him for taking away his family. His grief for their deaths was being dammed up behind his rage. And with no physical outlet for that grief, his suffering would go on and on until the day he died and took his unhappiness with him to the Underworld, where he might forget the reason for his misery, but never the misery itself.

But after years of this torment, the gods had remembered him. They had called him away from Phaeacia, and now – since the arrival of Telemachus at Pylos – they were calling him back to Ithaca. Ithaca, at last. There he would find a way to confront his inner rage, this fury that had never sat easily with him because his old loyalty to his friend had never really died. The few days spent with Telemachus – who looked and spoke so much like his father – had reminded him of the love he had once had for Odysseus. So first he must deal with his anger, and then he could find room to grieve. After that, he might be able to live again. That was why he had gone with Telemachus to Sparta. That was why he was answering the gods' call to return to Ithaca.

The more urgent question now was what could a man who refused to fight do? It was a question he had not yet answered. As he boarded the galley the evening before – thankfully Mentor had not seen through his disguise – he had looked at the young crew and wondered whether they could be made into an effective fighting force. They were nobles to a man, and each would have received weapons training from childhood. As friends of Telemachus they would be loyal to him – or should be. But they were young and naïve, there were only twenty of them, and it would take time to train them to fight as a unit. And time was not on their side. To Eperitus, it seemed destroying the suitors was not an option.

He looked back at Telemachus, who was talking with Mentor in the helm. The young prince believed he only needed to announce the news that his father was still alive and all his problems would fade away. The suitors would accept that they could no longer marry Penelope and would simply go home. But Eperitus guessed otherwise. The suitors were not interested in Penelope – only the power that marrying her would bring. And the lure of power was not an easy thing to ignore. Nothing except Odysseus's arrival with the fleet would make them relinquish their ambitions. But the fleet was dead and, despite everything Menelaus had heard, Odysseus was, too.

Only one course of action offered itself to Eperitus's mind. He would have to go to the palace and assess things for himself. A plan might present itself, or it might not. If not, he would find a way to get Penelope out. He doubted she would come. It would be difficult to persuade her to desert her home and leave a vacuum behind for some ruthless noble to fill. But she had to be stopped from marrying one of the suitors and making him the legitimate king of Ithaca. Better to find refuge on the mainland, perhaps with Nestor, and seek whatever help they could find. They could even buy help, if they had to. And one day they would return and fight to regain Ithaca. It was not an ideal plan – nothing compared with the sort of schemes Odysseus might have dreamed up – but it was all he could think of.

The island was much closer now, and the whole of its eastern flank was bathed in sunlight. The galley cast a long shadow over the surface of the water, and he felt an unexpected sense of excitement that he would soon set foot on Ithacan soil. Then he noticed something to the north of the island. A sail! It was small and distant at first, and a few more moments passed before a member of the crew cried out that another ship was rounding the northern end of Ithaca. By then Eperitus had been able to count around forty men on board, each one armed with a shield and a spear. They did not look like Taphians, whose spears were longer and who had a more aggressive look to them. But a galley full of armed men signalled two things to him: it was either a ship of war, or they were pirates.

He left the prow and ran back to the helm.

'Telemachus, that's a pirate ship, I'm sure of it. Order the crew to head south or they'll cut us off before we turn into the straits.'

Telemachus glanced at Mentor, who gave a slight shake of his head.

'It's not a Taphian vessel. I can tell that much from the sail,' he said. 'It looks like a merchantman to me.'

'It's not a merchant!' Eperitus insisted. 'There are at least forty men on board, wearing full armour and carrying spears.'

'How can you possibly see that?' Telemachus asked, shielding his eyes against the sun. 'I can't even pick out a single man.'

'Trust me. Whoever they are, they mean trouble, and they're gaining on us fast. Mentor, change course now. If you don't give the order, I will.'

Mentor stared at the approaching vessel, which was beating rapidly down the eastern flank of Ithaca with the southerly wind filling its sail. It was now clear they were on a course to intercept. Mentor nodded and cupped his hand over his mouth, shouting orders to change course to the south-east. The crew fumbled with the stays and angled the sail to catch as much of the wind as it could, while Mentor – shaking his head at their sluggish efforts

– leaned his weight on the tiller. Slowly – too slowly – the galley began to turn its prow to the south.

Telemachus threw himself against the bowrail and stared at the pursuing craft.

'It's the suitors,' he said to Eperitus. 'They must know by now that I left Ithaca. They want to make sure I don't return.'

'What would they gain by killing you?'

'With me dead, the man who marries my mother will also become master of Odysseus's palace, slaves, land, livestock… everything!'

Eperitus looked at the pursuing vessel. A tall, muscular figure stood in the prow shouting orders. The crew adjusted the trim of the sail quickly and skilfully, taking advantage of a change in the wind to give the galley a little more speed. More men sat on the benches, wearing expensive armour, with spears and shields at the ready. So, these were the young nobles who were seeking to replace Odysseus? Men whose ambitions were not limited to his throne and his wife, but even sought to possess what remained of his estate by murdering his only heir.

He glanced over his shoulder at the southernmost point of Ithaca. It was still some way off, and he knew they would not reach the headland before their pursuers caught them.

'Do you have bows and arrows aboard?'

'No,' Telemachus replied.

'Then we'll have to fight,' Mentor said. 'Because we're never going to make the straits before they cut us off.'

'But they outnumber us two to one,' Telemachus said. 'It'll be a massacre. Can't we head back to the mainland?'

'They'd catch up with us long before we could make it to safety,' Eperitus said.

'Then I'll give myself up if they try to board us.'

'Don't be foolish,' Mentor said. 'I haven't watched over you for twenty years just to see you butchered without a fight. Besides, do you think they'll leave the rest of us as witnesses to your murder? No, if they want you, then they'll have to kill us first.'

'Perhaps it won't come to that,' Eperitus said.

'What do you mean?'

Eperitus looked again at the men on the other ship. Soon they would be drawing alongside, leaping onto the deck with violence in their eyes and death on their spear points. Telemachus's young friends would be slaughtered within moments, followed by Mentor and Telemachus himself. And these suitors would not spare a stranger, even if Eperitus's oath kept him from resisting them. Then they would leave the galley to be wrecked on the rocky eastern shoals before sailing safely back to their own harbour. Within a day or two, reports would arrive at the palace to say the broken remains of Telemachus's ship had been found, and that every member of the crew had been washed overboard to their deaths. Penelope would wear black on her wedding day and Ithaca would have a murderer for its new king.

But if ten years of relentless war had taught Eperitus anything, it was when to fight and when to run.

'Mentor, turn the ship around,' he said. 'Head her back to the mainland. And Telemachus, take off your armour.'

-

'She's turning back,' Ctessipus said.

'I can see that for myself,' Eurymachus growled. He looked at the faces staring at him from beneath their plumed helmets. 'Well, what are you waiting for? Go after her!'

Ctessipus pulled on the rudders while several of the suitors adjusted the sail, turning the galley quickly to port. It was a simpler manoeuvre than the reversal in direction being carried out by the other ship – which was being executed clumsily and with less speed. Eurymachus grinned to himself. The forty men who had agreed to join the ambush included some of the best sailors among Penelope's suitors, and they would make quick work of overhauling their prey.

The moment the runner had arrived from the lookout on Mount Neriton, his instincts had told him the ship was Telemachus's. Twice they had sailed out to meet galleys that were foreign merchantmen beating their way northward to buy or sell goods from the Taphians or the Thesprotians. On both occasions he had been able to tell from a distance that the ship was not the one loaned to Telemachus by Noemon, a vessel he knew well from the time it spent moored in the harbour below the town. He had returned and beaten up the watchmen out of anger and frustration, but today's lookout had saved himself a whipping.

Eurymachus loosened the sword in his belt and bent down in his stiff armour to pick up his helmet and shield. Nervous excitement was stirring his blood. He had trained all his life in the use of arms, and this morning his training would be tested in combat. Not a single man on Telemachus's ship was to survive. That much had been agreed by all. No one would be allowed to bear witness to the murder of Penelope's son – the pleasure of which Eurymachus had reserved for himself. Should Penelope not choose him to be her husband, he would at least have a share of her husband's estate. Besides, he was looking forward to seeing the light leave Telemachus's eyes as he sent his spirit down to Hades. The boy's complaints had marred every feast that the suitors held, and no amount of beatings had persuaded him to shut up.

But death would.

He looked at the other ship. They had adjusted the trim of their sail and were building up speed. If the crew were slow and inexperienced, their helmsman at least seemed to know how to sail a galley. Using the currents to his advantage, he had steadied the distance between himself and his pursuers. And with half the number of men aboard, in time the lighter load would give him the edge and help him to escape his pursuers.

Eurymachus clenched his fists in frustration. Then he felt a change in the wind. Ctessipus sensed it, too, and called for an adjustment to the sail, which was carried out with smart efficiency. He glanced across at Telemachus's ship. The same order had been given, but was executed tardily, losing them precious distance.

Not only had the wind changed direction; it had also picked up in strength. Eurymachus felt the hem of his cloak pressed against his calves, flapping around his shins. Ctessipus gave an order to reduce the sail.

'No!' Eurymachus shouted, waving the men away from the ropes. 'Leave it.'

'But the wind's too strong. You'll risk tearing the canvas.'

'We need to close the distance. They're not getting away; not if I have any say in it.'

He clutched at the bowrail and stared across the waves. Telemachus's galley had shortened sail and was already losing distance to them. Nervously, he spared a glance at his own sail and saw how dangerously taut the material was. But he also felt the speed as the ship darted across the wave tops towards its prey.

The other ship's helmsman must also have seen that he was losing the race. Taking the same gamble as Eurymachus, he ordered the sail to be opened to its full extent. But his crew lacked the experience of

Eurymachus's, and the suitor watched with satisfaction as the canvas jerked and tore.

'Reduce sail,' he called.

He caught Ctessipus's eye and read the scepticism in it. But the risk had paid off and soon Telemachus would be at their mercy.

'They're not armed,' Agelaus said, walking over to stand beside Eurymachus. 'Surely they can see our spears and shields at this distance. What do you think: shall I send a few arrows over to let them know we mean business?'

'No. Why make this any harder than it needs to be? Let's get alongside them and get to work.'

Before long they were drawing up behind Noemon's ship. They could see the faces of the crew looking anxiously over their shoulders. Eurymachus thought he recognised Mentor at the twin rudders, but could see no sign of Telemachus. He must have guessed their purpose and hidden himself in the hold.

'Who are you and what do you want?' Mentor called, cupping his hand around his mouth.

Eurymachus walked to the prow, followed by Agelaus.

'I am Eurymachus, son of Polybus,' he said, removing his helmet. 'I have an urgent message for Telemachus. Let us board.'

To Eurymachus's surprise, Mentor ordered his sail to be furled and the oars withdrawn. As the suitors drew alongside, he even threw over ropes so the two vessels could be tied together, and laid a plank between the bow rails. Eurymachus took his spear and looked across at the other ship. Still the crew had not taken up their shields or spears, though they wore swords about their waists and some had armour. He hesitated, wondering whether he was leaping headfirst into a trap. Then he stepped onto the board and ran across, jumping down with a heavy thump onto the deck. Agelaus and several others followed, all of them fully armoured with their spears at the ready.

Eurymachus felt the adrenaline coursing through him. He was anxious for the fight to begin, but he could not see Telemachus anywhere among the crew.

'Where is he?' he demanded.

'Who?' Mentor replied.

'Telemachus, damn it! I have an urgent message for him.'

'If you tell me what it is, I'll take it to him.'

'I'm to give it him personally. Now, where is he?'

Mentor gave a half-smile.

'He's in Pylos with Nestor. He didn't want to return to Ithaca and watch his mother married off to thieving scum like you.'

Eurymachus gave his spear to Agelaus and crossed to the helm in a few strides, seizing Mentor by his tunic.

'Don't lie to me, old fool. Call him out now, or I swear by all the gods, blood will be spilt.'

Mentor held Eurymachus's gaze. His sword was hanging by his right hip, but his hand did not wander towards it. Eurymachus turned and nodded to Agelaus, who signalled for two of the other suitors to open the hatch. They threw it back on its hinges with a bang and peered into the hold before lowering themselves into the darkness. Agelaus followed. The remaining suitors formed a circle about the hatch, while on the opposite deck several more prepared to run across at a signal from Eurymachus. Sounds of banging and scraping came from the space below. A short while later, Agelaus and the others reappeared, shaking their heads.

'It's dark as pitch, but I'm certain he's not down there. He must be at Pylos.'

'Do you want me to take your message to him?' Mentor asked. 'If not, get your hand off me and let us go on our way.'

Eurymachus released his hold, shoving Mentor backwards as he did so. He looked about the small deck, then up at the mast and rigging, as if Telemachus might be hiding beneath one of the benches or clinging to a spar. But he was not aboard the galley. Eurymachus had been robbed of his share of Odysseus's estate. The nervous tension of the expected battle now turned to frustration and anger.

'What are you so happy about?' he shouted at Peiraeus, who was leaning against the bow rail with a look of mild amusement on his face. Eurymachus seized hold of his hair, dragging him violently down to his knees. 'I know you. You're Telemachus's friend, aren't you? Tell me where he is or I'll throw you over the side.'

'He's in Pylos,' Peiraeus cried, his face a mask of pain. 'We left him in Pylos. I don't know anything else.'

'You're lying!'

Eurymachus twisted the hair in his fist, enjoying Peiraeus's distress.

'Leave him alone.'

Eurymachus heard the slither of a blade being unsheathed. He turned to see Mentor with his sword in his hand.

'Release the lad and return to your ship. It's as I told you: Telemachus isn't here. Your *message* will have to wait.'

Eurymachus dragged Peiraeus forwards by his hair and drew his sword.

'I know Telemachus isn't on Pylos. Tell me where he is or I'll slit this pathetic runt's throat.'

In an instant, the point of Mentor's weapon was resting against the base of Eurymachus's neck. The suitor raised his chin nervously at the feel of the cold bronze and swallowed. He released his hold on Peiraeus, who slipped back to the benches. Mentor was momentarily distracted by the movement and Eurymachus pulled back from his sword point. In the same move, he brought his own weapon up and knocked Mentor's blade aside.

A wave of nervous energy engulfed him. He hacked down at Mentor's unprotected flank, but Mentor blocked the attack and twisted away. Again and again their blades met, slashing and parrying with quick, instinctive movements. Eurymachus's nerves faded as years of training took over. Attacks suggested themselves to his mind and were carried out without further thought, while each thrust or sweep from Mentor's sword was anticipated and met intuitively.

His mind absorbed and accounted for the rocking of the deck beneath his feet. It took in the closeness of the benches behind him, and understood that if he could drive his enemy backwards, he might trip on the step up to the helm. While his instincts handled the immediacy of the fight, his mind began to form a plan. As Mentor feinted to the left, Eurymachus moved to meet the blow, only for Mentor to bring the flat of his sword down hard on his knuckles. He cried out, almost dropping his weapon. But for all his experience, Mentor had underestimated Eurymachus's strength and determination.

He held on to his sword, and with his other hand aimed a punch at the old soldier. It slammed into his jaw and sent him flying across the deck to land in a heap beside the bowrail. An instant later Eurymachus's sword was pressing against the soft flesh of his throat. The slightest move from Mentor and the cold bronze would cut through his windpipe and send his soul down to Hades.

'Kill me if you have to,' Mentor said. 'But I swear by all the gods Telemachus is not here.'

Eurymachus glanced around himself and saw that the other suitors had their spears against the chests of Mentor's crew, whose puny swords were in their hands and whose faces were white with dread. All he needed to do was nod and twenty young men would be lying dead in pools of their own blood. But to what end? They had checked the galley and Telemachus was not on board. There was no point in murdering the galley's crew out of sheer frustration.

'Lower your weapons and go back,' he commanded the others.

'But the ship is ours!' Agelaus protested.

Other voices murmured agreement.

'Do as I say!'

Grudgingly they lowered their weapons and began returning to their own ship. Eurymachus looked down at Mentor, who stared back at him defiantly.

'Be warned, old man,' he said, sheathing his weapon. 'The next time you draw your sword against me, I'll kill you.'

Chapter Sixteen

Reunion

Telemachus waded up the beach, water streaming from his hair and tunic. Every muscle in his body was tired and heavy from the long swim. Several shallow-bottomed fishing boats had been dragged onto the shingle, though most of the crews had taken their catches to the small village that lay between the shore and the hills beyond. The few fishermen that remained – mending nets or making repairs to their boats – stared at him with casual interest. He turned and looked at the white breakers rolling into the small cove. Theoclymenus's head was just visible beyond the edge of the rocky spit that protected the harbour. Farther out, he was relieved to see that the two galleys were now travelling in opposite directions: the suitors heading north while Mentor and his friends sailed south.

Theoclymenus emerged from the water. His heavy muscles were stained white with brine, and he spent a few moments leaning on his knees spitting salty water out onto the shingle. Then he stood and looked round himself, a curious smile on his face, but one tinged with sadness.

'It's been a long time,' he muttered to himself.

'A long time since what?'

'What?' Theoclymenus asked. 'Oh, a long time since I've swam that far. So, this is your homeland?'

Telemachus looked round at the pale hillsides with the scrubby vegetation that clung to them. Goats were stumbling across the scree or standing on boulders, while here and there scrawny olive trees twisted up out of the dry earth like the fists of old men. The little fishing village was plain and rustic. Its sand-coloured walls were crumbling and had only a few, small windows. Plainly dressed women with baskets on their hips shuffled from stall to stall, haggling with leather-skinned fishermen over their morning's catch. As he imagined what the place looked like from Theoclymenus's foreign viewpoint, he realised how shabby it must seem. He felt a sudden twinge of embarrassment that he might have made it sound more than it was in his conversations with Theoclymenus.

'It's nothing compared to Pylos or Sparta – or Troy, no doubt – but it's all I've ever known. It's all I have.'

'It's beautiful,' Theoclymenus said, smiling more broadly now. 'Worth standing up to these suitors for. Talking of whom, you shouldn't go straight back to the palace. If they really were planning to kill you, then their blood will still be up, and who knows what they might do if you wander into the middle of them.'

'You're right, of course,' Telemachus agreed. 'Eumaeus's hut isn't far from here; I'll go there first. He's my father's chief swineherd, and a man couldn't ask for a more faithful servant. He'll give me a bed for the night and tell me what's been going on while I've been away. You'll be welcome, too, and between the three of us we can decide how to break the news that my father still lives – whether direct to the suitors, to my mother and the Kerosia, or publicly in the Assembly.'

'Then you still hope they'll accept a rumour heard by Menelaus?'

'Not the suitors, perhaps. But if the people believe he's still alive, perhaps they'll call for my mother's oath to be annulled. Then I can demand the suitors leave the palace...'

'At which point they may decide to defy you openly. If they feel their chance of power is slipping away, they might just take it by force. Have you thought any more about what I suggested last night?'

'Ask my mother to leave Ithaca until we can find support on the mainland?' Telemachus asked, shaking his head. 'She won't do it. She won't go back on her oath. And she won't desert her people and let Eupeithes step in.'

'Even though marrying one of the suitors will give them legitimacy as king?'

'I know you mean well, but the news my father is still alive will bring about a solution. Come now,' Telemachus said cheerfully, 'let's find Eumaeus and dry these wet clothes in front of a fire while we enjoy a meal of freshly cooked pork.'

He sat down on a rock, unhooked his sandals from his belt and slipped them on his feet. Theoclymenus did the same.

'You go to the swineherd's hut,' he said. 'I'll find my way to the palace. I want to size up these suitors you've said so much about. Besides, it won't do any harm to have a hidden ally listening in on their plans.'

'You're right,' Telemachus agreed. 'Go to the harbour first, though, and find Peiraeus when the galley arrives. He'll take you to his uncle's house and give you some fresh clothes and a sword.'

'I'll not carry a weapon, friend,' Theoclymenus said, rising to his feet. 'The temptation to forget my oath and strike down one of these arrogant guests of your mother's would be too strong.'

They set off through the village and embraced at a fork in the road before going their separate ways. After Telemachus had walked for a while along the dirt track he saw a column of smoke above the tree tops that he knew came from the swineherd's home. It was only then that he realised he had not told Theoclymenus how to find the harbour. Strangely, his friend had taken the left-hand path with the confidence of a man who already knew the way.

-

'He looked up at the battlements and there was Helen, just as the guards had said she would be. Like a goddess she appeared to him, more radiant than the sun's rising, and yet tinged with the sadness of its setting. Even without his beggar's disguise, Odysseus would have felt base and insignificant compared to her. A hush fell among the widows and orphans who had gathered below, hoping for a glance of her famed beauty – the beauty their husbands and fathers had given their lives to defend. And then the king of Ithaca shuffled forwards and raised his voice...'

Odysseus paused. A chorus of barking told him someone was approaching Eumaeus's hut, though it was not the furious clamour that had greeted his own arrival two days ago. This time the dogs were yelping with delight. He craned his head over Eumaeus's shoulder. He saw their tails wagging and heard their whimpering as they crowded around the newcomer. The young man knelt down to stroke them and let them lick his lightly bearded face, before rising once more and stepping onto the porch.

Eumaeus, who had been mixing wine as he listened to Odysseus's story, turned and gave a shout of joy. Dropping the bowls, he ran to the threshold and threw his arms about the visitor, hugging him tightly and planting kisses on his forehead and cheeks. Pulling away to look the youth up and down, he kissed both his hands, then wrapped him in another hug.

'You're back! Thank Zeus. Thank *all* the gods. When they said you'd sailed to the mainland, I feared the worst, but here you are, safe and sound again. Let me look at you, boy.'

Odysseus took a sharp breath. His legs seemed suddenly weak, and his hands began to shake. It could not be, he told himself. But as he looked at the smiling face of the young man, he knew it was. He tore his eyes away for a moment and stared down at his own shameful appearance. Were these bony wrinkled arms the arms of a great warrior; these rags the raiment of a returning king? He looked up and saw Eumaeus step back a second time to look his visitor over. The swineherd's eyes were brimming with tears, as if the man standing on his threshold were his own son and this was their first meeting after years apart.

'You're damp,' he said, ushering him inside. 'It hasn't rained, though, has it?'

'We met a galley full of suitors on the way back. Swimming ashore was the only way to save myself from being murdered.'

So, this *was* his son, Odysseus thought. The sight of his face, the sound of his voice – he did not know whether to stand and take him in his arms, or retreat into a corner of the hut and hide in the shadows. All he could think to do was sit on his hands to stop them shaking.

'Damn them! Curse them all,' Eumaeus hissed. 'At least you had the good sense to come to me. You can hide here until we work out what to...'

'Hide? I'm not *hiding*, Eumaeus. I've had enough of letting them rule my life. I've come to find out what's been going on in my absence, and then I'm going to confront them before this wedding can take place.'

Eumaeus's face was full of concern.

'Sit down and let's talk about it before you make any hasty decisions...'

'It sounds to me like your friend has made the right decision already,' Odysseus said. 'Evil can't be allowed to take root – it has to be faced with courage. I take it this young man is your master's son?'

He rose from his seat, but Telemachus immediately waved him back down.

'Forgive me, stranger, I didn't see you in the shadows. And please keep your seat. Eumaeus here will find something for me to sit on.'

'And something to eat, of course,' Eumaeus added, rolling a bundle of brushwood over beside the fire and covering it with a fleece. 'You've arrived in time for breakfast, my lord. There's meat on the spit and bread and fruit in those baskets on the side there. I was just mixing the wine when the dogs started up.'

After pouring them all a drink, he joined them by the fire and they ate in silence. Odysseus had lost his appetite, but forced himself to eat while he watched Telemachus tear into the chunks of pork and wash them down with wine. He could barely take his eyes off him. If he had feared his son might prove a coward, his decision to face the suitors suggested the opposite. But he could not let Telemachus march down to the palace and confront them alone. Indeed, desperate though he was for allies, he wondered whether he dared permit his son to risk himself in any battle.

He could see himself in the young man's features and felt a sudden and powerful affection that denied explanation. He took a swallow of wine and tried to quash the feelings stirring inside him, to contain them before they gave him away. But if he was to stop Telemachus forcing his own solution onto the problem of the suitors – if he was to bring him into his own plans – then he would have to reveal who he was sooner rather than later.

Telemachus leaned back and tossed the scraps from his plate out onto the porch, where the dogs fought over them. He washed his hands in a bowl of water that stood on a small table to one side, then looked at the beggar.

'Tell me, Eumaeus, where is your guest from, and what brings him to Ithaca?'

'He's a Cretan by birth and comes here after many hard adventures, but I'll let him give you his story himself. You'll soon see he's no mere tramp, but a man of noble blood whom the gods have heaped with misfortune. He was hoping to go down to the palace later today and throw himself on you and your mother's mercy.'

'And you were going to *let* him?' Telemachus asked, turning to the swineherd in surprise. 'If this man truly is high-born, why would you send him to me to care for? You know full well I can't protect him from the suitors…'

'Can't protect a guest in your own home?' Odysseus asked.

'At the very least they would insult you, my friend; probably give you a beating, too. And I can't let you fall victim to their violence. Let me have a set of fresh clothes sent up for you, a solid pair of sandals for your feet and a sword to hang at your side. And I'll arrange passage for you to the mainland. You'll be safer there than on Ithaca, to our shame.'

'I watched your father fight many times on the fields of Ilium,' Odysseus said. 'He wouldn't have stood idle while his home was being ravaged, as Eumaeus here tells me is happening under these suitors. Why then are you?'

The question was direct and harsh, but Odysseus had to test his son's mettle before he decided whether or not to confide in him. Telemachus nodded slowly.

'You're right to ask the question. I've asked it myself enough times. Am I a coward? Shouldn't I kill these men who help themselves to my livestock and wine, or at least die an honourable death trying? Have I not heard of Orestes and how he avenged his father? Am I not Odysseus's son?

'Indeed I am, or so my mother tells me. But how can a son be like the father he has never known? Indeed sir, if you were there at the siege of Troy then you've seen more of him than I ever did! As for my oppressors, there are one hundred and eighteen of them, and I dream every day of driving my spear into their stomachs, even though I wouldn't slay more than two or three before the weight of their numbers overwhelmed me. And what then? My mother and our slaves would be left totally at the mercy of the suitors. I won't give them that pleasure. But look here, and here.'

He showed Odysseus the marks of old scabs on his knuckles, and the scars and fading bruises on his jaw and forehead.

'Barely a week passes that I don't end up fighting with one or more of them. And before my mother can fulfil her oath to marry one of these thugs, I'm going to tell them the news I've brought back from the mainland. From the king of Sparta himself, no less. That my father lives.'

'What?' Eumaeus said. He glanced at Odysseus. 'How can he be sure?'

'Menelaus isn't a simple beggar, Eumaeus, peddling stories of my father to earn himself a crust. He had no reason to lie to me, and I believed him. Odysseus *is* alive, and one day he's coming back. My mother has to know before she rushes into this terrible marriage.'

'She'll also want to know you've returned safely from Pylos,' Eumaeus added. 'She's hardly slept since you sailed away, or so I've heard. And if these suitors have been planning to ambush you, I wouldn't be surprised if she's aware of their schemes. Can you leave her in such misery?'

'You're right,' Telemachus said. 'Put on your cloak and head to the palace. Let Penelope know I'm safe. And bring back the gifts I promised for our guest. He won't depart without knowing I'm a man of my word and a respecter of xenia.'

'I'll leave immediately, my lord.'

Eumaeus pulled on his sandals and took his cloak from a peg on the wall. His staff was by the door and, taking it in hand, he turned and bowed farewell before clumping over the wooden threshold and down the path. When he was gone, Telemachus turned to Odysseus.

'Eumaeus said you're a Cretan, but your accent…'

'I've not spent much time there, not since I was a boy. Most of my life has been lived abroad, fighting in foreign wars or travelling from one place to another. A plaything of the gods for most of it.'

'And you were at Troy? With my father?'

'Did it please you when you heard he was alive?'

'Of course it did! Who wouldn't want to see the father he never knew? All I've ever wanted was to put my arms around him and feel that sanity was returning to the world.'

'I thought you might…'

'What I wouldn't give, stranger, to overlap my shield with his and drive those suitors out of my house. I pray every day for that moment. Every day.'

There were tears in Telemachus's eyes now, forcing him to lower his head and cover his face. Tentatively, Odysseus reached out a hand. His fingertips hovered over his son's shoulder, wanting to touch him. To reassure him.

He pulled away.

'Surely he abandoned you, though? You and your mother. Wasn't his first duty to be a father and a husband, to protect you and love you? Instead he chose to fight another man's war…'

'Chose?' Telemachus asked, staring at the beggar. 'He didn't *choose* to go to Troy. My mother said he feigned madness when Agamemnon and Menelaus came to Ithaca, and only when they threatened my life did he abandon his pretence. That a king would give up his honour for the sake of his family says much, don't you agree? Think about it. If he'd succeeded, he would've been the only king in Greece not to go to Troy. His name would have been forgotten, only remembered in scorn. Odysseus the Shirker. Odysseus the Coward.

'He'd have suffered that for our sakes. And since he was forced to go, I believe every moment was spent in wishing he was home again; every thought and deed was given to ending the war so he could return to Ithaca. The songs say it was him who gained the Greeks their victory in the end – not the reckless courage of Achilles or the suicidal pride of Ajax, but the patient intelligence of Odysseus. Who wouldn't want a father like that to come home again?'

Odysseus felt the tears on his own cheeks now. He waved a hand at the fire.

'This smoke gets in a man's eyes,' he said with a small laugh. 'Perhaps you would share with a simple beggar what you've heard from Menelaus? I think of your father as an old comrade and have an interest in his welfare.'

Telemachus smiled.

'You're no simple beggar, my friend, and I wouldn't normally share a personal matter with a stranger. But something tells me I can trust you. Menelaus said my father was being held prisoner on an island by the name of...'

'Ogygia.'

Telemachus frowned at him.

'How could you possibly know that?'

'I know many things about your father, though I don't know how Menelaus learned his whereabouts.'

'A god told him. Phorcys, I think. Why didn't you say you knew where my father was?'

'Would you have believed me? Eumaeus didn't. He said beggars like me are commonplace on Ithaca, peddling fantasies about Odysseus in order to earn a meal and a new cloak. Indeed, you're only listening to me now because I named the same island Menelaus mentioned, a place you'd never heard of just a few days ago. Perhaps I heard the same rumour he did.'

'No,' Telemachus said. 'Phorcys told him he'd seen Odysseus on the shores of Ogygia. Menelaus swore he hadn't revealed that to anyone else, so how do you know? What else do you know about my father?'

'I know that on his return from Troy he reached as far as Cape Malea, then was blown south into waters that few have travelled before. There he journeyed from one strange land to another, losing men and ships along the way until his last remaining galley was destroyed by Zeus. All the crew except himself were killed, while he was cast up on the island of Ogygia, home of Calypso. She kept him there for many years until the gods commanded her to release him.'

'Then he's no longer a prisoner?'

'He reached the island of the Phaeacians, who brought him here.'

'Here? *Here*, on Ithaca? But how do you know this? How could you know this unless... unless you've met my father.'

'No, Telemachus. I *am* your father.'

Odysseus looked his son in the eye. His breaths were short and his heart was beating fast in the brief but tense moment that followed his revelation. Then he reached out and placed his hand on Telemachus's shoulder. The young man's skin was warm to the touch of his cold, gnarled fingertips. For a moment, Telemachus did not move. Then he flinched, as if noticing the beggar's hand for the first time. He brushed it away and sat back, staring and shaking his head.

'Don't be absurd. You're not my father. How could you be? Look at you. You've got to be... what? Seventy years old? You look more like my grandfather.'

'This?' Odysseus said, looking down at himself. 'No, you don't understand. This is just...'

Telemachus stood up and moved away.

'No, old man, *you* don't understand. It's bad enough that your kind comes begging at my mother's feet, making up stories that my father is waiting at Pylos, or that the fleet is being repaired at Crete. But to claim to *be* Odysseus...' He seized a spear from the rack by the door and held the point to the beggar's chest. His face was a mask of anger. 'I should kill you right now.'

'Your mother told you about the time I tried to convince Agamemnon I was mad.'

'She told me what my father did.'

'Your father, then. Did she also tell you that Odysseus ploughed the earth with an ox and an ass yoked together? That I... that he sowed salt? That they laid you down in front of the plough, making him swerve aside and prove he was in his right mind?'

The pressure of the bronze point against his flesh lessened. Telemachus's anger had morphed into uncertainty.

'Then who laid me before the plough?' Telemachus asked. 'Was it Agamemnon or Menelaus?'

Odysseus smiled.

'Neither. It was Palamedes.'

Telemachus lowered the spear.

'When you raced against Lesser Ajax to win my mother, how did you beat him?'

'I drugged his food and turned his bowels to water,' Odysseus said. He stepped towards Telemachus. 'Son, it really is me. All this' – he plucked at his rags and wrinkled flesh – 'is a disguise, a temporary transformation created by Athena to keep me safe from the suitors.'

He reached out and laid a hand on Telemachus's shoulder. It was not rejected. Slowly, Odysseus pulled him into an embrace. For a moment, his son was limp and unresponsive. Then his arms slipped around Odysseus's back and held him tightly.

'Father,' he whispered.

For years he had been the head of his house, struggling beneath a burden that should not have been his. Now the burden was lifted. Odysseus stroked his hair and kissed it, his sight blurred by his tears.

Odysseus did not know how long they had stood there, but the feelings of regret for the lost years soon succumbed to joy. He was home. His son was in his arms and did not hate him as he had feared. The problem of dealing with the suitors seemed far off, insignificant compared to their moment of reunion. He pulled away and held Telemachus at arm's length, looking him up and down and trying to familiarise himself with the features of his face, his hair, his height and stature, all things he had never known. He apologised that Telemachus could not see him as he really looked – not yet, at least – and apologised again for not coming back sooner, and for all the things he had missed over the years of his childhood. For a long time they sat and talked of things small and large until, inevitably, their conversation was drawn towards the present.

'How is your mother?'

'Sad, mostly. Bitter, perhaps. Fate hasn't been kind to her since you left. The suitors have only made matters worse.'

'I can't imagine her being sad,' Odysseus said, a distant look in his eye. 'She used to have the most wonderful smile. Not that I can remember what she looks like.'

'I remember she used to smile, when I was a child. Now she can hardly bring herself to look at me. It's guilt, I think. Guilt about promising to marry before I could inherit the throne. She made the promise when I was just ten to protect me from being assassinated, or so she says. She'd hoped you would return before she had to go through with it. But I haven't made it any easier for her. I was angry that she could think of giving it all away, that she could betray your memory and invite these monsters into our house; just so she could bring me back from Sparta to be at her side. I've wanted to leave Ithaca so many times. I would have done, too, but I couldn't bring myself to abandon her. Then one day I'd had enough. I decided to go to the mainland and seek news of you. I thought if I could find you I would find an answer to this mess. And now you're here, but… but you're *not* you.'

'You mean the disguise?'

'What you think of as a blessing – a protection from the suitors – I think of as a curse. If you still had your true appearance, we could go to the palace and have my mother withdraw her promise. You could throw out the suitors and call an Assembly so the people knew you were back.'

Odysseus shook his head.

'I wish it was that simple, Son. But the goddess is no fool. Would the people welcome back a king returning without an army? Over six hundred of their menfolk perished under my leadership – they won't easily forgive that. And you must know the suitors won't surrender their chance of power. If they were prepared to ambush and murder you, what would they do to me – a lone wanderer without friends or allies?'

'But we only have two days before Mother has to choose a new husband!'

'All the more reason to use our intelligence and plan carefully, Telemachus. The gods have given us a last chance to save Ithaca from these men, so let's not squander it. But of all the obstacles against us, it's your mother's reaction I fear most of all. What if she refuses me? What if her love for me has died? It's the one thing I don't think I could face. At least looking like this, I might find a way to learn her true feelings for me before I dare make myself known to her.'

Telemachus stood and picked two apples from a basket on a table. He threw one to his father.

'And when you find out she does still love you, what then? How will you reveal your true self to her? Or are you cursed to wear those wrinkles forever?'

'Not forever. Only until I've killed the first of the suitors, or so Athena told me. Up to that point, my identity has to remain hidden. You must not tell Penelope I've returned. In fact, you must tell no one at all until our plans are in place and we are ready to act.'

'But what *are* our plans, Father? If you won't declare your return to your people, or even to your wife, what are we to do about the suitors? What *can* we do with the wedding day almost upon us?'

'The first thing I will do is to go to the palace. I'll beg at the tables of these men and see their qualities for myself.'

'And when they've beaten and insulted you?' Telemachus asked. 'What then?'

'Then we will kill them,' Odysseus said. 'They've violated our home and offended the gods, and it's not likely they'll run away the moment I show my face. So you're going to get your wish – to fight shoulder to shoulder with your father. Bloodshed is inevitable.'

Book Three

Chapter Seventeen

A New Suitor

Eperitus stood in the deserted marketplace and looked at the long wall that protected the palace. The lime plaster had discoloured over the years and was flaking and cracked in many places. The familiar dung heap was still piled up by the gateway, waiting to be collected by farmers to spread on their crops. On top of the pile of used hay, rotting scraps of food and worse detritus was the body of an old dog. It must have been a proud beast at one point, Eperitus thought, but now the size and strength it had once boasted meant nothing.

The entrance was unguarded and the wooden gates had been left open, revealing the empty courtyard within. Eperitus remembered how it had looked before he had sailed to war – busy with life and purpose – but now it was tired and deserted, as if some terrible disaster had killed everyone inside or driven them away, leaving the palace to fall into decay.

His journey from the fishing village had been filled with anticipation, as if everything was going to be the same as it had been in those happy days of years ago. He had even found a chelonion flower on the way and tucked it into his belt. So to see the palace so empty and rundown left him with a feeling of melancholy. It was as if the long years of war, the horrors of the voyage back and all the sacrifices that he and others had made had been for nothing. He felt then that he could turn around, find a ship to the mainland and never come back.

But he did not. Somewhere inside the palace was Penelope. Though he would not admit it to himself, the loyalty he had once felt for Odysseus had transferred itself to her and her son. He had resolved to help them, even take them away from Ithaca if that was what was needed. But he would not abandon them.

He walked through the gates and crossed to the threshold of the great hall, where the paint on the cypress wood pillars was peeling. The door was ajar. He listened for a moment, but heard nothing. Looking down at the clean tunic of grey wool and the black cloak he had been given by Peiraeus, Telemachus's friend, he decided he was respectable enough to present himself before a queen.

Pulling up his hood, he pushed the door fully open and entered. The interior was dark and echoed to his footsteps. A fire still burned in the hearth, its orange light pulsing against the four columns that supported the high roof. His senses told him the place was empty, but had not long been vacated. The air smelled of roast meat and fresh bread, and the tables were littered with bowls of half-eaten food and abandoned cups of wine. The fire had only recently been stacked with wood, and the chairs and tables that were silhouetted by its flames were in disarray, as if many people had left in a hurry. To man the ship that had been sent to intercept Telemachus, he guessed.

Despite having come to learn the number and quality of Telemachus's enemies, for now he was pleased to have the great hall to himself. Folding his hands behind his back, he walked the circuit of the walls and studied the murals. It seemed many lifetimes ago that he had watched them being painted, shortly after Odysseus had become king. Now the once-vivid pictures were smoke-stained and had lost their boldness. Like ghosts, they strode about the walls re-enacting the battles of the past.

And then he found the figure that represented himself. His youthful pride had swelled thirty years ago when the artist had brought him to the main scene, showing Odysseus's defeat of Eupeithes's mercenaries. Eperitus was shown outside the palace walls, standing on the figure of a dead Taphian. The artist had even depicted him with the old-fashioned shield he had inherited from his grandfather. A small flake of plaster had fallen away, taking with it the top quarter of his shield and the tip of his spear.

Odysseus stood inside the palace walls. He was twice the size of all the other figures, and a diminutive-looking Eupeithes was kneeling before him in submission. Eperitus smiled at the sight of it, remembering how Odysseus had often laughed to see that part of the mural. But it seemed Eupeithes had won in the end. The king was dead, and – from everything Telemachus had said – it was likely Eupeithes would find a way to make Penelope marry his son. In two short days, his own line would replace Odysseus's on the throne.

He looked again at himself and remembered the exhilaration of the battle and the joy of victory. Pointless now, of course. It had all been pointless – the little skirmish that had liberated Ithaca for a single generation; the great war that had destroyed Troy and taken with it the mightiest of the Greek kings; the struggle to return to Ithaca that – in the end – had brought back a single man: himself, a foreigner by birth.

The side door opened and a slave girl entered, carrying a wooden bucket that she set down by one of the tables. She glanced round the hall, but did not spot the newcomer's black hood and cloak in the shadows. Then she fished out a cloth, wrung it out and began to wipe the table. As she worked – sweeping scraps of food into her hand and tossing them into the flames – she sang a sad song about a milking maid who lost her innocence to a god. Her voice was so delightful he could have listened to her all afternoon, but when she took one end of a table and began dragging it across the dirt floor, he felt obliged to help.

'Allow me,' he said, leaving the shadows.

She gave a short scream and retreated behind the table, holding her hand to her chest.

'Who are you? What are you doing here?'

'Isn't it for the master of the house to ask those sorts of questions?'

'The master has gone to the mainland,' she said, remaining behind the table and eyeing the hooded man with fearful suspicion. 'Not that I'm alone. There are plenty more servants within.'

Eperitus raised his hands.

'I'm not going to harm you. I'm a visitor to Ithaca. There was nobody at the gate, so I let myself in.'

The side door opened again and an old woman entered. She was short and round with large breasts and greasy grey hair tied in a knot on top of her head. Eperitus recalled her fretful face and remembered she had been a slave of long service in Odysseus's household, from before the time he had arrived in Ithaca. She looked at him and then at the maid.

'What's all this screaming about, Autonoe?' she demanded. 'And who are you? I hope you're not causing trouble among my maids, sir, whoever you are? I'll call the stewards and have you thrown out.'

'He hasn't touched me, Eurycleia,' Autonoe said. 'He surprised me when he stepped out of the shadows, that's all. Will you tell the queen we have a visitor?'

Eurycleia gave Eperitus a mistrustful look, then left the hall.

'Please, sir, take a chair while I bring some food and wine.'

'Let me help you with these tables first. Where do you want them?'

'I can do that, sir, thank you. It's my job. And I won't have my lady catching a guest doing my work.'

'Well, your lady isn't here yet. Where shall I put this?'

He took the end of the nearest table and pulled it towards himself. She shook her head and motioned for him to stop.

'If you insist on helping, they go in rows like this.' She signalled with her hand. 'And please finish as quick as you can, before the queen arrives. I'll fetch you something to eat.'

She wiped her hands on the front of her dress and picked up the bucket. Despite her plain looks and her initial nervousness in his presence, she had an air of self-assurance about her that he liked.

'Before you go, tell me why there are so many bowls and cups on the tables. Does your king have so many sons that every breakfast is a banquet?'

'Our king sailed to Troy twenty years ago and never returned. The master of the house is his only son, Lord Telemachus, though he's destined never to be king in his father's stead. The queen agreed to remarry before he comes of age – an arrangement that was forced upon her. The mess you see was left by her suitors.'

'And where are these gentlemen?'

'Gone to meet their friends, returned from a short voyage. It might not be my place to say, but they're not what I would call gentlemen. I'm pleased for you, sir, that they weren't here when you arrived. Doubtless they'd have found some insult to throw at you and make you feel unwelcome.'

'How many suitors are there? I count at least fifty wine cups.'

'And more still are in the galley they've gone to meet,' Autonoe replied, the resentment clear in her tone. 'Over a hundred men will feast here tonight and offend my lady with their lack of manners. It's the same every night.'

'So many? Then your queen must be beautiful beyond compare.'

'What beauty I had has been withered by grief and worry. They want to marry me because it will make them king, nothing more.'

Eperitus turned to see a white figure by the side door. A veil obscured her features, but he recognised her voice at once, even though he had not heard it for many years. He bowed low.

'My lady.'

'Autonoe, our visitor doesn't need your opinion about my suitors. Perhaps your time would have been better spent fetching him a little food and wine. And putting these tables and benches in some sort of order.'

'Yes, my lady,' she said, pausing to shoot Eperitus an accusatory look before disappearing through the side door.

'Will you sit down?' Penelope asked.

She crossed to a chair by the hearth, and Eperitus sat opposite her. The light from the fire shone on her veil, giving only a faint impression of the face beneath. His memories of her were vague, but he remembered her features had been beautiful then, made more so by the kindness and intelligence in her eyes. He wondered if that beauty remained, or whether it had indeed faded with sorrow, as she claimed.

'I'm sorry if Autonoe spoke out of place,' she began, her tone softening with the apology. 'It's easy for a hard-pressed slave to resent those who give her orders.'

'She spoke honestly. And if these suitors are as rude as your maid suggests…'

'They have high spirits. And high hopes.'

'Then you'd rather they weren't clamouring around you?'

'I'm under an obligation.'

'So your maid told me. It must be difficult to choose a husband from so many?'

'Yes,' she replied. 'I'm spoiled for choice.'

Autonoe arrived back carrying a small table and a platter of meat, followed by Eurycleia, who held a bowl of wine and two cups. Autonoe laid the table beside Eperitus and placed the food on top before moving over to straighten the benches the suitors had left in disarray. Eurycleia set the bowl down and poured wine for her mistress and her visitor.

'Leave us now, Autonoe, and go prepare a bath for our guest,' Penelope said.

Autonoe bowed and left, followed by Eurycleia.

'You'll stay in the palace tonight, of course,' Penelope said, looking at Eperitus. 'Before you move on to wherever it is you're going.'

Her words might have suggested he was unwelcome, but he understood her meaning. She was afraid the suitors would mistreat him and bring shame on her household.

'I'd like that, my lady. I only regret that when your suitors return and fill the hall with their feasting, our conversation will lose its intimacy.'

'Yes,' she agreed, a little ruefully.

He stood and poured a libation into the flames. The queen joined him, almost shoulder to shoulder. Her perfume was intoxicatingly feminine, drawing his gaze as she made her offering to the gods. Her nose and her long eyelashes were visible through the gauzy material of the veil, and he could see her lips moving in a silent prayer. They returned to their seats and he ate until his hunger was satisfied, all the time sensing Penelope's gaze on him. After a final swallow of wine, he placed his cup down on the table and looked at her, wondering how to say what was on his mind. She spoke first.

'You seem familiar. Have we met before?'

'No, my lady.'

'Perhaps if you lowered your hood...'

'I don't think you'd find me a handsome man.'

'And yet you talk of intimacy,' she smiled. 'But I can't expect you to reveal yourself if I keep my own face hidden, can I?'

To his surprise, she took the corners of her veil and lifted it back over her head. She was as attractive as he remembered her, with only a few additional lines around her eyes and mouth to mark the passing of the years. Her dark eyes bore the same intelligence and compassion that he had known so well. But the lightness in her spirit had gone, smothered by the great weight of her sadness.

'Your beauty is worthy of a hundred suitors, my lady,' he said. 'Though I wonder if your suitors are worthy of *you*. They lay a heavy burden on you, I think.'

'Would that the suitors were my only worry. But now, sir, I'd like to look on *your* face, if you please.'

Eperitus reluctantly took hold of the edge of his hood and tipped it back. A flicker of recognition crossed Penelope's brow, then passed away. She shook her head and smiled.

'You're too hard on yourself,' she said. 'Beneath those scars and that eyepatch is a handsome man. But I'm surrounded day and night by handsome men, with their oiled skin, their rich cloaks and their obnoxious self-obsessions. I prefer the company of a man who's seen something of the world.' She crossed her legs towards him, making circles in the air with her foot as she looked at him. 'Someone like yourself. Won't you tell me your name and what brings you to Ithaca?'

'My name is Theoclymenus, son of Polypheides,' he answered, 'and I came here to speak with you.'

'And what do you want with me, Theoclymenus?'

'I knew your husband, my lady. We fought alongside each other at Troy.'

She turned away to look at the fire.

'Friends of Odysseus are always welcome here. Though I've had many visitors claiming to have known him who did not.'

'What do you mean?'

'They've been coming for years now,' she said, looking him in the eye, 'saying they know where he is and that he is coming back to Ithaca soon. But he never has.'

'My lady...'

'My hopes turned to bitterness long ago, but I still let them come. I fed them and gave them new cloaks and staffs – not because I believed them any more, but because I *wanted* to believe them. My son and my servants told me to throw them out and deter them from encouraging others. But I *needed* them. I wanted so desperately to think that one day, one of them would be telling the truth. I held on and held on... and now it's too late. There is no hope any more. In a few days I'm to take a new husband, and no promise of Odysseus's return – true or false – can stop that. So, Theoclymenus, if you've come to tell me he's alive...'

'I've come to ask you to leave Ithaca.'

'To... to what?'

'I'm not here to buy your favour with lies, Penelope. Odysseus *was* my friend, though our parting was a hard one. So when I heard his wife was being forced to remarry because of an ill-judged oath she'd taken years ago, I came here to learn the truth for myself. And from everything you've told me, I can see the rumours were right. But your heart isn't in this. You don't want any of these men to be your husband, and yet you're going ahead because you think you're honour-bound to do so. I'm here to tell you you're not.'

'Is this some sort of joke?' Penelope asked, rising from her chair and staring at him. She walked to the edge of the circle of firelight. 'Have the suitors sent you here to test me? Or is this Eupeithes's work? Why else would a complete stranger want to save me from a trap of my own making? It doesn't make sense.'

He stood and walked towards her.

'What doesn't make sense? That I don't want to see my friend's name dishonoured? That I won't stand by while ambitious brutes take advantage of his wife for their own gain? That I refuse to let his kingship be given to a lesser man? You know as well as I do the throne should be passed to his son. *Your* son.'

'What do you know about it?' she asked, staring hard at him. 'I've fought for twenty years to keep my husband's kingdom intact, to guard our son's inheritance...'

'And now you're about to give it all away. You don't have to go through with this marriage. Come with me to the mainland and...'

'And what? Leave the throne empty for others to fight over? Let Ithaca divide into factions, family against family and island against island, until some tyrant murders his way to power? That's exactly what I've been trying to prevent.'

'But if you marry one of these men, then you *legitimise* them as king. There won't be any coming back from that.'

The anger in her eyes faded and went out, extinguished by the realisation of her own failure.

'You're right. I don't even know why I'm arguing with you. Of course you're right. I took a gamble, promising to remarry if Odysseus didn't return. I had to, or they'd have killed my son. But Odysseus didn't return, and now there's no way out of it.'

Penelope had always been strong. He remembered that from the ten years he had known her. That strength – reinforced by the hope that Odysseus would return – had carried her for another twenty years, helping her to stand alone against her husband's enemies at home. But time had run out. She reminded him of a doe caught in a net, her energy almost expended by struggling against her bonds, while coming ever nearer was the baying of the huntsman's dogs. He wanted to tell her that she did not have to continue alone, but the right words would not come to him. Instead he took her gently by the wrists. She looked at him, startled at first by his touch. But she did not pull away, even as his hands slipped down and took hold of hers.

'There is a way out,' he said. 'Go to Sparta, where you were born. Find allies for your cause. I can help you. There are still men who hold your husband's memory in high regard. Menelaus owes the return of his wife to Odysseus. Do you think he wouldn't send soldiers back with you to Ithaca, to support Telemachus's claim to the throne?'

'You speak like a warrior, not a politician,' she said with a light shake of her head. 'The people look to me as queen, and I will not abandon them, even for a day. As for my promise, if I don't keep it then I will lose all credibility in their eyes and the nobles will take the crown for themselves anyway – with bloodshed if necessary. To marry one of them is the only peaceful option, and if that's what the gods have decided must happen, then I won't go against them.'

Eperitus was tempted to tear off his eyepatch and reveal who he was. Surely then she would listen to him and end this reckless determination to go through with the wedding? But that would mean telling her Odysseus was dead. Could she take such a blow, even though she had assumed as much? And did he want her thinking of her husband when her hands were still in his? He could feel them trembling and knew she was as nervous as he was.

'I can't let you do that,' he said.

He moved his hands to her upper arms and leaned forwards, placing his lips against hers. They were soft and warm, and for a moment there was no resistance, only consent. Then she drew a sharp breath, as if waking from a dream, and stepped back. The palm of her hand flashed across his face.

'Who do you think you are?'

Tears came suddenly to her eyes. She took another step back and wiped her cheeks dry. But the look on her face was not anger or even shock. It was sadness. Sadness that she had been offered an escape, but knew she could not take it. She took a moment to compose herself.

'Because you claim to be my husband's friend – and because I believe your intentions towards me were honest and noble – I will not have you thrown out of my home. I have accepted you under my roof and I will not dishonour the gods. So my maid will bathe you and you are welcome to stay the night. But in the morning, you must leave and never return. Do you understand?'

'I understand, my lady. I understand why you won't leave Ithaca and why you feel you have to carry out your promise to take a new husband. But I can't stand by and let you destroy yourself.'

'You must!'

'Not if I formally state my intention to marry you. Penelope, consider me one of your suitors.'

-

Before Penelope could react, Autonoe arrived and announced that the bath was ready. With a last look at Penelope – her face tear-stained and thoughtful – he followed the maid out into the dimly lit passageway. She led him round several corners to a small room at the end of another gloomy passage, then pushed open the door. Warm, damp air enveloped him as he entered. There were no windows, just a single torch that fizzed and flickered in its bracket, casting a dim light around the room. In the corner was a bath filled with steaming water. A cloth mat was laid out on the stone floor beside it with a three-legged stool and a bucket close by.

Autonoe turned to face him and unclasped the brooch that fastened his cloak. She removed the garment and folded it neatly, laying it on a small table.

'You've upset my mistress,' she said, lowering her fingers to his belt.

'I didn't mean to.'

He had not meant to kiss her, either, or offer to become her future husband. One thing had followed another, and something deeply buried – perhaps from as far back as their liaisons in Sparta – had revealed itself. One moment he had been looking into her eyes, moved with sympathy for her desperate situation, the next his lips had been pressed against hers. Had she resisted immediately, he might have been able to control the hidden desire that had slipped beneath his guard and conceal it again. But she had not. As hot and sudden as his passion had been, hers had equalled it. And now he wondered whether that passion could ever be hidden away again.

As Autonoe coiled his belt onto the chair and knelt to untie his sandals, his mind opened itself to a flood of unanswerable – and unquenchable – questions. Did Penelope know she had been kissing her old friend? If not consciously, then maybe unconsciously? Could she overcome her pride and position and acknowledge the feeling behind her kiss? Or had it been nothing more than the confused reaction of a woman in a desperate predicament? A woman who had not seen her husband in twenty years and was ready to react to the first sign of genuine affection? In trying to save her from the suitors, would he not become an arch-suitor, avenging the death of Astynome by taking Odysseus's wife for himself?

'Don't worry,' Autonoe said. 'She upsets very easily nowadays. It probably wasn't your fault. It's the thought of this wedding.'

'We spoke about the suitors,' he said as she took the hem of his tunic and lifted it over his head and arms, leaving him naked. 'Tonight's feast should be revealing, if everything I've heard about them is true.'

'You shouldn't rush to meet them,' she said. Her eyes followed the contours of his muscles from his shoulders to his chest and down to his stomach before looking away. 'You'd be wise to wait until the morning, when they'll be less drunk. I'll make you a bed in one of the storerooms until then.'

He stepped into the bath and sat down, resting his forearms on his knees. The water was hot and smelled of herbs. Autonoe perched herself on the stool and pulled a sponge from the bucket, which she filled with water. Then she began washing his back.

'One of the other maids told me Telemachus's ship was seen arriving in the harbour earlier today. The suitors don't have much respect for his authority, but he'll give you all the protection he can when he comes to the palace. Avoid them until then if you can.'

'Don't worry about me.'

'It would pain me to see them abuse you or try to pick a fight.'

'I'm not afraid of them, Autonoe.'

'You should be. They respect neither gods nor men. And they're cruel…'

She fell silent and moved the sponge to his shoulders, squeezing out the water so it ran down over his back and arms. She refilled it and washed his chest, moving the sponge down to his stomach. As she did so, tears rolled down her cheeks and fell into the cloudy water.

'What is it?' he asked, cupping her chin in his hand and looking into her green eyes.

'It's nothing to concern you, sir,' she replied, her voice barely more than a whisper.

Then she dropped the sponge and raised her wet hand to his cheek. She looked into his eyes, her expression sad and uncertain. Slipping her fingers into the hair behind his ear, she pulled herself closer and placed her mouth against his. The kiss was hesitant and clumsy, but grew in intensity as her lips parted and her tongue met his. Then she pulled away, her eyes wide and her face aghast. He half expected her to slap him, as Penelope had done earlier. Instead, she stood and stepped backwards, almost tripping over the stool.

'I'm sorry,' she said, shaking her head. 'I'm sorry.'

The next moment she had gone, leaving the door open behind her, the cool air from the passage fanning Eperitus's skin.

Chapter Eighteen

Telemachus Returns

Eperitus woke from a disturbed and dreamless sleep. The windowless room was dark, and yet he sensed that dawn was close. He lay on his straw mattress with the thick furs pulled up over his shoulders and listened. Slowly he became aware of other sounds: a mouse squeaking among the sacks of grain in the storeroom where Autonoe had made him a bed away from the suitors; birds singing in the trees beyond the palace walls; a street dog barking; and, inside the palace, the scuff of sandals across stone floors and the clack of pots and cups as breakfast was prepared. He could smell porridge being heated and bread being baked, rich new scents to add to the earthy smell of the dirt floor in the storeroom, which contained the mingled odours of barley and mouse droppings.

As his mind slowly clawed its way to full wakefulness, his thoughts turned to the strange events of the day before. He asked himself whether he had been right to state his intentions of marriage to Penelope. It was not something he had planned as he had walked to the palace that morning, but when she had refused to leave Ithaca, it had suddenly seemed the only option. She could reject him, of course, but if she did then it was not because she was not attracted to him. There had been passion in her kiss, he was sure of that. There had been need, too: the need of a woman who had been too long without a lover; and the need of someone whose fortitude had been worn to breaking point.

She needed new strength to fight back with, and she needed a physical release from the trauma of her loneliness. Those were things he could offer her. But he could not take away her fear of the suitors or what their reaction would be if she picked an outsider to be her husband. It was almost certain that they would not give up their claim to the throne because of a newcomer from the mainland. And as a man who had sworn not to kill, he did not yet know how he would deal with an aggressive response from them.

But perhaps the greatest obstacle was that, sooner or later, he would have to reveal his identity to her – if she did not come to realise it for herself first. How she would react then he could only guess. But he accepted now that he had always had a suppressed attraction to her. Perhaps she had had similar feelings for him. Their separate loyalties to Odysseus had buried their treacherous desires for each other so deep that neither had dared to look at them, fearing what such an acknowledgement might mutate into. But Odysseus was dead and none of that mattered any more. He would tell her the truth about her husband and about himself. And then she would make her decision.

The mouse had stopped squeaking and was now gnawing at the bottom of a sack. Footsteps were approaching in the corridor outside, accompanied by the hiss of a torch. They stopped outside the storeroom, and he could see light flickering beneath the crack of the door. After a moment's hesitation, the door was pushed ajar and the torch was thrust into the room. A face followed, peering into the gloom. It was Autonoe. She saw him propped up on one elbow on the mattress and lowered her eyes.

'The queen sent me to ask if you will breakfast with her in the great hall.'

'Wait!' he said as she backed away and made to close the door. 'Wait, Autonoe. Come in, please.'

She entered the room, eyes still downcast. He pulled off the furs and stood. Taking the torch from her hand, he placed it in a bracket next to the door jamb.

'If it's about yesterday,' she said, 'I made a mistake. Please forgive me.'

'There's nothing to forgive. And I don't want you to feel embarrassed, or bad about yourself. I'm hoping to remain in the palace until the wedding – maybe longer – so I don't want you to feel you have to avoid me.'

'There are plenty of other maids who can serve you, my lord.'

'But I like having you serve me.'

She glanced up at him, her eyes questioning. Then she looked back down at the floor.

'My place is with the queen. I carry out other duties when she doesn't need me. That's why you found me in the great hall yesterday morning.'

'I thought you said there are plenty of other maids. Why weren't they clearing the tables?'

'Most were busy elsewhere. Others...'

'Others what?'

'Others were lying in the arms of the suitors. I sometimes help with the tasks they overlook.'

'No wonder you hate these men,' Eperitus said. 'At least you have the decency to refuse their advances.'

'Decency has nothing to do with it,' she said. 'No man would want me.'

'How can you say that?'

'All you see is a plain-looking slave girl who serves her household with loyalty,' she snapped. 'But you know nothing about me. Do you know why I ran away yesterday? *Do* you? Not because I kissed you and felt embarrassed. I kissed you because I like you – your strength, your integrity, the fact you're so different to *them*. I ran away because I'm not worthy of you. I kissed you on impulse, and then I became afraid you might kiss me back – that it might become something more. And then, eventually, you would find out the sort of woman I am, and you would reject me.'

'The sort of...? You are *not* a bad person, Autonoe. If you were I'd see it in your eyes. But all I see is misplaced guilt.'

'No man wants a dishonoured woman,' she scoffed

'And only the delusional expect virgins!' he replied. 'Desire can get the better of any woman, whether slave or queen.'

Autonoe shook her head, then picked up his cloak from a stool and threw it around his shoulders.

'We need to go,' she said. 'Penelope is waiting.'

Eperitus sat on the stool and picked up his sandals. Before he could place them on his feet, however, Autonoe knelt and slipped them on for him, laying each foot on her lap as she tied the leather thongs.

'I want to ask you something else,' he said.

'What is it?'

'What would you do not to see Penelope married to one of the suitors?'

'I'd do anything.'

'And to see Telemachus become king?'

She finished tying the last thong and stood. Placing a fist on her hip, she gave him an enquiring frown.

'These are the things my mistress wants above anything else, and so I want them, too. What's this about?'

'I intend to marry Penelope.'

'You...*what*?'

He plucked the torch from the bracket and left the room. The windowless passage was gloomy, its shadows pushed back by the yellow flames. Autonoe followed him.

'*You* want to marry the queen?'

'Would you rather see one of those suitors marry her?'

He followed the turns of the corridor to the same flight of stairs Autonoe had led him by yesterday.

'Have you told her this?' she asked.

'Yes,' he said, turning and holding the torch over their heads.

'What did she say?'

'Nothing. Before she could answer, you arrived and announced my bath was ready. It's obvious she hasn't said anything to you, either.'

'No.'

'But you're her maid. You know her better than almost anyone. What will she say?'

'How can I know that? Do you... do you love her?'

'I will. I know it.'

Autonoe took a deep breath and looked away, her expression forlorn.

'All I can say is she was happier after you arrived yesterday than I've seen her in a long time. Does that make you feel better?'

'It encourages me. Yesterday she said I had to leave this morning, but I hope she's taken time to reconsider. Maybe she's seen this for the opportunity it is and that's why she's invited me to breakfast with her. Not that I had any plans to marry Penelope when I arrived here. It just happened. I advised her to leave Ithaca and seek help on the mainland among her husband's friends, but she refused.'

'She would never leave Ithaca for the nobles to fight over and bring to ruin.'

'So the only way I could see of helping her was to beat the suitors at their own game – if she'll let me. Assuming the suitors and their families don't kill me first, or rise up and take the throne by force.'

He turned and walked round the next corner to the door that led to the great hall, where he placed the torch in an empty bracket on the wall. Autonoe followed and took him gently by the elbow.

'Why are you – a foreigner and a stranger – doing this? You owe us nothing. You seem to want nothing.'

'Because I hate injustice. I've hated it all my life, and when I heard about these suitors, I saw a reason for living – something I haven't had since Troy and… after. But there's something else, too. I think the gods have led me to Ithaca. It is my fate.'

'You have a noble character,' she said. 'But I think the world you want to fight for has gone. Perhaps it never existed.'

'You don't really believe that, Autonoe. You have a rare quality in this age – you have a conscience. But you're allowing it to hold you back, like your feelings of unworthiness because of your natural desires.'

'It wasn't desire,' she said, pushing open the door to the great hall. 'No man will ever want me again because I was raped.'

-

Penelope sat on her high-backed chair and stared at the hearth. Melantho had thrown more wood on the flames in her usual careless manner – causing ash to puff out onto the floor – and stoked the fire up into a proper blaze. Under Eurycleia's supervision, she, Autonoe and a couple of other maids had tidied away the mess left by the suitors the night before. They had removed the piles of bowls and cups, straightened the tables and benches, and raked the dirt floor until – for a while at least – the great hall looked as if the suitors had never polluted it with their presence. The queen had then commanded the servants to leave her, sending Autonoe to fetch Theoclymenus from the storeroom where he had slept the night.

As for herself, she had barely slept at all. In just one more day she would have to choose her new husband, a thought that sickened her. Ten years ago, the oracle had promised that Odysseus would return before Apollo's feast. But with a single day remaining, she knew that the Pythoness had been wrong. The priestess's hallucinatory prediction had bought her time, but now that time had run out.

Penelope had grown increasingly desperate with each passing day, but now a new light shone into that darkness. Theoclymenus's arrival brought her fresh hope. All night she had lain in bed staring at the moonlight coming through the thin curtains and wondering who he was – who he *really* was – and what had brought him to Ithaca.

The questions remained, stirring in her mind now as she stared at the flames. He was certainly not a beggar. Neither did she did think he was an opportunist who had heard of her plight and seen a chance to gain wealth and power. Even if he really had been a friend of Odysseus, her instincts told her he had not come to protect the honour of her husband's name. Had he not hinted at a conflict between himself and Odysseus? But whoever he was and whatever his motives, such thoughts would not have kept her awake through the night or occupied her mind into the morning. It was his kiss that possessed her.

Strange, she thought, that the simple meeting of his lips with hers should unsettle her so. That he should be so presumptuous, so *rude* as to force himself upon her did not, however, cause more than a false irritation in her. She had tried to make herself angry about it, but only ended up admiring his boldness. She had tried to convince herself that his rough appearance was that of a vagabond who could have no appeal to her, but again she found herself remembering the strength in his hands. She had not encountered such a man in many years. Not among the suitors, nor among the infrequent visitors to the island. Not since Odysseus.

And she needed a man. The realisation shamed her, but she could not dismiss it. Odysseus had been beyond compare – a husband and lover the likes of which no woman could hope for or deserve if she lived a thousand lives. But he was gone. Gone to the place of forgetfulness, where he would be unable to recall her face or remember the love they had once shared.

Now it was her turn to forget. *No,* she thought, *not forget. Move on.* She had desires, physical and emotional, that had been neglected for far too long. Antinous would never meet them; indeed, the thought of him repulsed her. But there was something about Theoclymenus that she could not easily reject. When he had kissed her she had momentarily forgotten she was a queen with status and responsibilities. He had made her feel like a woman again. And she had never promised to marry an Ithacan, so if she chose him she could still fulfil her oath and preserve her honour in the eyes of the people. And if the suitors and their families resisted her decision or tried to take the throne for themselves, she sensed there was a quality in Theoclymenus that had the power to defy them. In that much, he reminded her of Odysseus.

Perhaps it was because he reminded her of her husband that she had opposed the thought of accepting him. Her loyalty to Odysseus's memory remained. At least if she married Antinous there could be no comparison with her first and only love. Nothing to erode or replace her recollection of him. But did the oddly familiar man with the single eye have the ability to make Odysseus fade from her heart? It was a strange quandary, but it offered her a way to escape marrying one of the suitors; a way that did not involve the dark and desperate route she had been forced to contemplate before. The gods had remembered her at last. Hope had returned.

The door opened and Autonoe entered, followed by Theoclymenus. Penelope sat up at the sight of him and glanced down at herself. Hippodameia's efforts that morning had not been wasted, she thought with a soft smile. Her chiton was open almost to the hip, revealing the white skin of her thigh as she sat. The neck was low and exposed her cleavage to a degree she would never have contemplated with the suitors. Her pale flesh was visible through the light material of the dress, which was gathered at the shoulders in such a way that her throat and arms were clearly displayed.

Was she exhibiting a bit too much? She wondered about it briefly to herself before deciding she had spent too many years being prudish. Now was not the time to be coy or coquettish, but to use all her feminine assets. She raised a hand nervously to her hair, which Hippodameia had combed out, plaited and drawn up behind her head, leaving a curled lock hanging by each ear to frame her face. Her skin had been powdered to smooth away the lines that the years of grief and worry had traced there, and her eyes had been edged with black to make them stand out.

She remembered looking in the bronze mirror her maid had held up to her that morning and being pleased with the effect. It had felt strange to see herself looking so much prettier and more feminine. It reminded her of being young again, and she liked it. It was something she would never have done for the suitors, and the thought that she was defying them gave her a sense of childish excitement. And, of course, she wore no veil.

'Good morning, my lord,' she greeted Theoclymenus as he approached. 'Autonoe, please bring food and wine.'

The slave girl bowed and exited, leaving them alone in the great hall. Theoclymenus's gaze wandered briefly over Penelope, taking in the flesh exposed by her dress before admiring the beauty of her face. His eyes met hers and lingered for a moment.

'My lady,' he acknowledged, nodding briefly. 'You... you look like a goddess.'

She smiled at his clumsy praise. He was certainly no Odysseus in that respect, but his words pleased her nonetheless. She indicated a chair.

'Thank you. Please be seated.'

'No suitors this morning?' he asked, taking the chair and looking round.

'Some were too drunk to return to their homes and lodgings after last night's feast, but they've decided to go hunting.'

'So early?'

'Normally they hang around in packs all day long, playing dice or sports of one kind or another. But I wanted the hall to myself, so I asked one of them to bring me back a deer or a wild boar. Naturally, the rest didn't want him to earn my favour all to himself, so they all set off together.'

'Then I'll never get the chance to see these young nobles,' he said.

'What do you mean?'

'Have you forgotten your order to stay the night and leave in the morning?'

'Oh, that. But have *you* forgotten that you asked to join my suitors and compete for my hand? I can hardly throw you out now, can I?'

He ignored her light tone and drew his chair purposefully up to hers, almost knee to knee, close enough to reach out and touch her if he chose to. She felt her breath shorten.

'Then have you given my proposal any thought?' he asked, leaning towards her.

She looked at his ruggedly handsome features and suddenly all she could think of was the kiss they had shared the day before. The memory of it lingered like a wine that had been tasted, but not drunk. If she wanted to, she could reach out and pull his face to hers again, indulging her passions like the young woman she had once been. But instinct cautioned her against it. To do so would only encourage him, and she could not marry a man she knew nothing about just because her other suitors were monsters. Attraction was not enough, she told herself. And yet, did she really have a choice?

She leaned back in her chair, crossing her legs away from him. The thin material of her chiton parted across her knee and slid back to reveal the top of her thigh. She saw his good eye flick down at the bared flesh, but she made no effort to cover it up.

'Tell me again why you want to marry me.'

'To save you from a grave mistake, Penelope, and to prevent you spending the rest of your life in misery. And if good intentions aren't enough to satisfy you, then because you're beautiful.' He reached out and took her hand in his. 'And you *are* beautiful, in face, form and character. I won't stand by and let you marry someone you couldn't love.'

'Then you're suggesting I *could* love you?' she asked, trying to sound aloof and feeling anything but.

'I'd be a good husband to you if you'd have me. And if you did, it'd be up to me to make you love me. Would any of your other suitors promise that?'

The back of his hand as he held hers had come to rest on her naked thigh. The warmth of it penetrating her skin made her whole body tingle. She could not remember the last time a man had dared to touch her, but she was not going to play the distant queen now. She rubbed the side of his hand with her thumb, saying nothing.

'Or do you think I only want to marry you so I can become king in Odysseus's place?' he asked. 'Take the throne for myself and rule Ithaca as I see fit?'

'*Is* that what you want?'

He shook his head.

'No. If I had a kingdom, the palace would be a stone hut on a hillside, its walls a wooden stockade and my subjects the flocks of sheep and goats I kept. I dreamt of such a place a long time ago: a simple farm where I could live in peace and happiness.'

'It's a beautiful dream. Why did you give it up?'

'The gods took it from me. It seems to be the way of our world, for the strong to take from the weak. But I would never plot to steal your son's inheritance. Choose me as your husband and I will give the throne to Telemachus the day he comes of age.'

'Why would you do such a thing for someone you've never met?' she asked.

'I once knew a man who wanted power so much that he killed his rightful king to gain it. He paid for his ambitions with his honour and, ultimately, his life. But power does not interest me. I would rather give the throne to Telemachus, who it belongs to by right, and whom I consider a friend.'

'What do you mean?'

'I haven't been entirely open with you. I met your son when he visited Pylos. He told me about the suitors and all the wrongs they've done to him and to you, and that's when I decided to help him. We travelled to Sparta looking for news of his father, and then here to Ithaca.'

'I'd received word of his return. Did he tell you to...?'

'No,' Theoclymenus said. 'I insisted on coming here to see these suitors for myself and decide what could be done about them. When I couldn't persuade you to leave with me and go to the mainland, some god gave me the idea of asking you to marry me. So, will you take me as your husband?'

She looked down at her hand cupped in his and turned it so that their palms were pressed together.

'You're a far better man than any of the suitors, and I believe I could be happy being married to you. On top of that, you say you would give the throne to Telemachus, which is something I desire over all things, including my own happiness. I'd do anything to keep Antinous or the others from ruling this island that I love so much. But maybe the suitors will kill you anyway and fight each other for the throne, regardless of what the people think or the consequences to themselves. Don't underestimate the greed of their ambition! And another question still remains before I can give you an answer.'

'What is it?'

'I know my son. He wouldn't have returned so early unless he'd received news of his father. What did he hear in Sparta?'

Theoclymenus stood and walked to the fire. He warmed his hands for a moment, then turned to face her.

'Rumours. It's for him to tell you what he's heard, of course, but I've heard different.'

'And what have you heard?'

He hesitated. She saw the concern in his eyes and felt a sense of dread, but indicated for him to speak.

'Odysseus died at sea seven years ago. I heard it from one of his crew, the only survivor of the last galley in his fleet. The rest perished.'

Penelope felt a sense of muted shock. A chill spread through her flesh and her eyes filled with tears. She dabbed them up with a fingertip, not wanting them to run and smudge her face powder.

'You're the strangest guest I've had in many years,' she said, sniffing back more tears and smiling at him. 'First you kiss me and ask me to marry you, then you tell me my husband is dead. Everyone else is so keen to convince me he's still alive and that he's coming back, but not you. Part of me wants to tell you to leave, but I can't. For some reason, I can't bear to have you go.'

He stepped forwards and knelt before her, taking her hands in his.

'I'm sorry,' he said. 'I should have kept it to myself.'

'No, you did what was right,' she said. 'You told me what you've heard and you've been truthful. It's up to me to decide whether I believe what you've been told, and how I come to feel about it. I only wish...'

'You only wish what?'

'That you had been him,' she answered, squeezing his hands and looking into his eyes. 'If only you'd been Odysseus. That would have made things so much simpler. And now the black around my eyes will have run and left channels on my cheeks.'

'No, no, it's hardly noticeable. Here.' He took a corner of his cloak and dabbed at her skin. 'You can hardly see any difference. You're just as beautiful as you were before. More so, perhaps, because you look suddenly... vulnerable.'

The door opened and Autonoe entered, carrying a small table and a basket of flatbread. Theoclymenus stood and retreated to the fire. Melantho and Eurycleia followed, carrying more tables, a board of steaming meat slices that smelled like pork, and wine. Autonoe set her table down before the queen, looked at her face, then gave Theoclymenus an offended stare. But Penelope could see she was not so much hurt over her mistress's upset as she was about the closeness between her and her guest that had caused it. It was clear Theoclymenus had found his way into Autonoe's affections, too. Penelope turned away before Melantho could see her face and come to her own conclusions about what had gone on – conclusions that would soon be spread all over the palace.

Then, as the food was placed on the tables and Eurycleia poured the wine, Penelope heard the gate in the outer wall open, followed by footsteps on the porch. The door to the great hall was edged inward and a figure stood silhouetted by the sunlight.

'Telemachus!' cried Eurycleia.

She almost dropped Theoclymenus's wine cup on the table as she turned and ran towards her master. Telemachus entered the shadowy hall and spread out his arms to embrace the much shorter and fatter figure of his old nurse, who reached up to plant numerous kisses on his cheeks and forehead. Autonoe also abandoned her duties and ran over to greet him, throwing her arms about his neck and kissing him. In their excitement to see him safe and well, the two servants pinned him with questions and more kisses until eventually they remembered their mistress and stepped away.

Penelope stood and looked at her son, his image distorted by the heat from the hearth and the fresh tears filling her eyes. She stepped down from the dais and circled the fire to meet him. He embraced her and kissed her on both cheeks.

'Mother,' he said, and rested his head on her shoulder.

'I feared for you,' she told him. 'You're becoming a man and I must get used to you taking charge of your own life. But when I heard you'd gone to the mainland, I was terrified you'd suffer the same fate as your father and not come back to me.'

'Well, I'm back now,' he said.

He placed his hands on her shoulders and looked at her. There was a smile on his lips and a new light in his eyes. The coldness and the blame of the past few years were fading. In their place, she could see a growing confidence and a new hope.

'Did you hear anything?' she asked in a whisper, glancing across at Melantho. 'Did you find out what happened to your father?'

'I heard a fantastic tale about a sea god spotting him on a distant island, kept there as a prisoner perhaps, without sign of galley or crew. But we've heard such rumours many times before, Mother. This is nothing new. Theoclymenus! You found your way here, then.'

He strode towards his friend, greeting him with a handshake and a fierce embrace.

'This island's so small I could hardly get lost, could I?' Theoclymenus replied with a laugh as he pulled away. 'But your mother has been a gracious host to me.'

He bowed to her, then turned and spoke in whispers with Telemachus. Penelope returned to her chair, pondering her son's response. He had always been so eager for news of his father, and his growing desperation for evidence that he still lived had forced his journey to the mainland. So to dismiss this latest rumour so lightly was peculiar.

'Melantho, prepare a bath for my son.'

The maid gave Telemachus a curious look and scurried off. Telemachus and Theoclymenus sat down and began to eat, while Penelope picked disinterestedly at a piece of meat.

'Where did you hear this report?' she asked her son.

'In Sparta.'

'From whom?'

Telemachus hesitated over his cup of wine.

'Menelaus.'

'Menelaus is hardly a beggar. Perhaps this new information has some truth about it. It might mean your father is still alive.'

She glanced at Theoclymenus as she said it. His gaze was unflinching.

'I've never doubted it,' Telemachus said. 'He is alive, Mother, and one day he will come back to claim his kingdom. Perhaps he's here already, plotting the downfall of the suitors.'

'I think we would know about it if he had returned.'

'Not if he was in disguise. The gods have the power to change a man's appearance as they please, and if Odysseus is as favoured by the gods as you say he always used to be, he could be anywhere among us. As for this report of him being held captive on an island somewhere, who knows?'

He placed a slice of meat in a piece of bread and bit into it. He was hiding something, Penelope thought.

'Your journey was wasted, then.'

'Not entirely. I met Theoclymenus, and he sympathises with our problems.'

'I'm aware of Theoclymenus's desire to help,' she said. 'In fact...'

Theoclymenus stared hard at her and gave a little shake of his head before raising his cup and tipping back the contents.

'In fact, what, Mother?'

But Penelope had fallen silent. She looked again at Theoclymenus, remembering her son's words that the gods could disguise anyone they wished. Was it possible, she wondered?

A clamour of voices now became apparent from beyond the wall of the courtyard. Some were raised in song, others were cheering and shouting. The gate banged open, and a few moments later, the double doors of the great hall were flung wide, admitting a crowd of young men. The hunting party Penelope had sent out that morning had returned, bringing with it several other suitors who must have attached themselves along the way.

Eurymachus's formidable bulk led them in, a deer over his shoulders with a feathered shaft still protruding from its flank. He was followed by Antinous, Elatus and several others, perhaps fifty or sixty in all. They pushed and shoved their way into the hall and began filling up the long benches. Eurymachus dumped the deer noisily onto one of the tables and hollered for a steward. Antinous nudged him in the ribs and pointed at the three figures seated on the other side of the flaming hearth. Eurymachus scowled and muttered something angrily in Antinous's ear.

'My lord Telemachus,' Antinous said in a loud voice that caught the attention of the other suitors. 'So, the rumour's true: you've returned from your journey. Did you find news of your father?'

He gave a friendly smile, but Penelope sensed his tension. The question of Odysseus's whereabouts haunted the suitors more than anything else.

'Just hearsay,' Telemachus replied. 'I'm no wiser about where he is or when he might return. Does that please you?'

There were a few shouts of 'yes', though Antinous hid any satisfaction he felt at the news.

'I'm a loyal subject of the king and would be as pleased as anyone here to see him back, just as I'm happy that you've returned safe and well. Still, with no sign of your husband, my lady, then there's no reason why the wedding should not go ahead tomorrow as planned. Have you made your...?'

He turned to face Penelope and fell silent. She remembered then that she was not wearing her veil. Antinous's gaze lingered on her face for a moment, then passed over her breasts and stomach to her leg. To Penelope's dismay, she realised the chiton had parted over her knee to reveal the full length of her thigh.

'My lady looks stunning this morning,' he said.

Two or three other heads were turning as they noticed her dress, her hair and the way her eyes had been emphasised by Hippodameia's skills. Then Leocritus rose from his bench to stand at Antinous's shoulder.

'Aphrodite's girdle!' he cried. 'Look at her legs!'

Sudden uproar filled the hall as the suitors turned to gawp at the queen, whom they had only ever seen in heavy woollen dresses, her beauty deliberately cloaked and veiled. Penelope tried to pull the thin material back over her leg, feeling almost naked as she looked round at the leering, laughing faces of the suitors. She wanted to run and hide. And for the third time that morning, tears filled her eyes.

Then, as she shrank away from their stares, she saw Theoclymenus rise from his chair and unclasp his cloak. He walked towards her and placed it around her shoulders. Then he turned to the crowd of suitors, his expression suddenly fearsome. For a moment, Penelope could picture him in the midst of battle, striking terror into the hearts of his enemies as he advanced. Some retreated before him, others stood their ground and were pushed aside.

Then he seized Leocritus by the tunic, and with one hand carried him past the benches to the open doors of the great hall. Leocritus, his legs pedaling freely in the air, grabbed at Theoclymenus's hand and tried to prise open the grip that held him, cursing him repeatedly. But it was to no avail. Theoclymenus reached the portico and, with a grunt and a thrust of his heavily muscled arms, he hurled Leocritus out into the courtyard beyond. He hit the floor with a puff of dust and lay still.

Penelope was standing and craning her neck to see above the muted throng of suitors. As Theoclymenus turned and walked fearlessly back through their midst, she wondered who he really was. Had Telemachus been suggesting something about their mysterious guest earlier? It seemed strange that he should appear out of nowhere and offer to help them on the day before she was to remarry – the day the oracle had said her husband would return by.

'Who do you think you are, throwing our friend out in the dirt like a beggar?' Eurymachus demanded, striding out of the mob of suitors to confront him.

'A guest in this palace, just like you,' Theoclymenus answered. 'And if anyone else disrespects our hosts, I'll throw *him* out, too.'

'I'd like to see that,' laughed Agelaus. 'One man against all of us.'

The others began to form a circle around them.

'Leocritus is just a little duckling,' Eurymachus said, pulling himself up to his full height and staring down at Theoclymenus. 'Anyone of us could toss him out on his backside. But I'm not so easy. Why don't you try throwing *me* out, friend? None of these others'll get involved if I tell them not to.'

Theoclymenus glanced around at the ring of suitors.

'You're their leader, are you?'

'Leader?' Agelaus scoffed. 'We don't have a leader, and if we did it wouldn't be *Eurymachus*.'

'He's the biggest and strongest,' Theoclymenus said, eyeing the brute before him. 'Why shouldn't he be your leader?'

'You heard him,' Eurymachus said, turning his scowl on Agelaus. 'I've got more brawn than any of you, and that makes me chief here.'

'More brawn, but no brains,' Agelaus retorted.

A few of the suitors laughed, causing Eurymachus to ball up his fists and growl.

'Besides,' Agelaus continued, 'I was one of the first suitors here – why shouldn't I be the leader?'

'Well, whichever one of you is in charge, it's obvious he should be the one Penelope marries,' Theoclymenus said, subtly backing out of the space between the two suitors. 'It makes sense to choose a natural leader to be the future king.'

'That'll be me then,' Eurymachus said.

'Leader or no leader, I'll be the one she picks,' Agelaus snarled, laying a hand on the pommel of his sword.

'Your guest is a clever man,' Antinous said. He had moved next to Penelope and was watching the confrontation develop. 'Very clever indeed. But I can't have him turning my friends against each other now, can I?'

He stepped down from the dais and walked towards the mass of young nobles, just as Eurymachus splayed his fingers over Agelaus's chest and shoved him backwards.

'You're not fit to be a beggar, let alone a king,' Eurymachus blustered. 'She's going to choose me. Everyone knows that.'

'This stranger is making fools of you all,' Antinous declared, forcing his way through the other suitors. 'And who can blame him? You attack him when you should be thanking him.'

'*Thanking* him?' Eurymachus said, turning his scowl from Agelaus to Antinous. 'What for? I was looking forward to smashing his skull to a pulp.'

Antinous hooked his arm through Theoclymenus's elbow.

'Our queen decides to display her beauty for us and what does Leocritus do? Speak to her as if she's a common whore. This stranger taught him a much-needed lesson, and for that I welcome him. And now, let's have some wine.'

Antinous signalled to the stewards, who had come to take the deer out to the kitchens to be butchered. They nodded and left, carrying the deer between them. As Antinous led Theoclymenus to his own table, Penelope stood. With his cloak still about her shoulders, she went over to her son and kissed him on the cheek. She gave the cloak to Telemachus, then walked to the door at the back of the palace, followed by Autonoe. After a final wondering glance at Theoclymenus, she entered the passageway and returned to her room.

Chapter Nineteen

Odysseus Comes Home

It was afternoon when Odysseus and Eumaeus turned a bend on the clifftop path and saw the harbour below them. The last time Odysseus had set eyes on the modest anchorage had been twenty years before, when he had led his fleet to war. Now the only vessels that sat at rest in the calm waters were a few fishing skiffs and a merchant galley, their sails furled and the spars and masts laid out on the decks. The sun was high up in the west, shining down from above the hilltops of Samos on the other side of the straits. It penetrated the clear, blue-green water in the harbour to reveal the brown shapes of plant life on the sandy seabed. The crooked wooden jetty was empty, and there was not a single person on the beach or the road that led up to the town.

'What is it?' Eumaeus asked, wondering why the old beggar had paused at the top of the cliff.

'I was just thinking how beautiful the place looks. All of it. The water, the sand, the sun on the backs of the trees...'

The swineherd stared down at the harbour as if expecting to see something new.

'You must have witnessed some dark and terrible places to find beauty in that.'

'I have, my friend. I have.'

They continued along the stony path, Odysseus leaning heavily on his staff with each step. His muscles ached and, despite the gentle warmth of the sun, he felt the coldness in his prematurely aged bones and joints. But he cared little for such distractions. He was *home*. He had seen his son and spoken with him, and had not been rejected. Now all that remained between him and peace was an army of young nobles. And Penelope.

The path began to descend, becoming a series of stone stairs as it led down to the northern end of the crescent-shaped beach. As he took each step with caution, his body complaining with every movement, his thoughts returned to Telemachus. He was heartened by the lad's determination to defeat the suitors, whom he hated passionately. And yet years of powerlessness had weakened his confidence. To Telemachus, the number of suitors, their aggressive temperament, and the fact that each one had been taught in the art of warfare since childhood – as all noblemen were – were obstacles his imagination just could not overcome.

It was then that Odysseus most regretted his long absence. It was not that Telemachus had lacked a tutor. Mentor had taught him all that was required to become a man of rank in Greek society, but a boy needed his father to teach him who he really was, to understand his roots and draw strength from them.

Worryingly, Telemachus had shown all the emotional and mental fragility of an orphan or a bastard. And yet Odysseus was surprised how quickly he had responded to his father's encouragement. Just being back on his home soil had helped Odysseus overcome the doubts that had undermined him during his imprisonment on Ogygia. So much so, that he felt confident – more, perhaps, than he should have done – that the suitors could be overcome. And as he had discussed with his son ideas for overcoming their great advantage in numbers, Telemachus's faith in their cause had also grown.

At first he had added small refinements to his father's plans, using his knowledge of the suitors' strengths and weaknesses to make them more effective. By the time evening had fallen, though, Telemachus was expounding his own strategies for victory. The change in him had been wonderful to witness, and it was then that Odysseus realised that he loved him. The baby he had deserted had become a man in his own likeness, and they would face the challenges before them as father and son.

But over the course of their conversation it had become clear that the suitors were neither the witless fools Odysseus had hoped they were, nor fainthearted in their ambitions for power. Despite the divisions among a small core of them over who would marry Penelope and become king, they were loyal to each other and would fight as a pack. They were powerful, too: numerous, fully armed, and well-trained. If they lacked experience in battle, they made up for it in self-confidence.

Confidence born out of arrogance could be a weakness, though, and as nobody was expecting Odysseus's return, he and Telemachus had surprise on their side. With a little cunning they could make up for much of the imbalance of power. Odysseus told Telemachus about the time he had entered the palace by subterfuge and murdered many of Eupeithes's Taphian mercenaries in their sleep, just as he and the Greek kings had infiltrated Troy in the belly of the Wooden Horse, then slipped out after dark to butcher the unsuspecting Trojans and take their city. But when he had suggested poisoning the suitors' food and slaughtering them in the same manner, Telemachus had objected, claiming it was dishonourable. He would rather look them in the eye as they fell beneath his spear, knowing he had taken his vengeance on them for the years of misery they had inflicted. In that, Telemachus reminded him of Eperitus.

What they needed was allies. The crew of youths who had manned Noemon's galley could not be relied upon to keep the secret of Odysseus's return. Though loyal to Telemachus, they were from noble families and several had blood ties to the suitors. Besides, they had not yet come of age, and Odysseus had insisted they were too young to fight. He excluded Peiraeus for the same reasons, a decision that Telemachus accepted willingly, not wanting to put his friend in danger. Odysseus did not mention that they would be all that remained of Ithaca's young nobility if the suitors were massacred, and therefore could not be risked.

Telemachus remembered Polycaste's promise that Peisistratus would provide soldiers if he needed them. But even if they could send a message first thing in the morning, it would not reach Pylos until evening at best. By the time a galley of Pylian spearmen had sailed to Ithaca, the wedding would be over and the kingdom would have a new ruler. There were others they could call upon for help, but they were too few and could only be approached on the day of the wedding to avoid news of Odysseus's return slipping out.

And so their plans to destroy the suitors remained brittle: too reliant on courage, fortune and the ignorance of their enemies. The young nobles might yet abandon their lust for power and go back home once they knew Odysseus had returned. But his instinct told him the gods had more violent plans in mind. What he needed was something to give him an advantage. Perhaps once he had returned to the palace and seen for himself the strengths and weaknesses of the suitors, an idea would come to him.

As they reached the beach, Odysseus looked down at the small white flower tucked into his rope belt. He kissed his fingertips and touched them to the petals of the chelonion. The one he had worn through all the years of the siege of Troy had been lost long ago. But he no longer needed a reminder of his homeland. The flower in his frayed belt was a symbol that he was going to war again.

They reached the bottom of the road that sloped up to the town from the harbour. Eumaeus waited for his struggling companion to catch up, then offered him his arm as support. Together they climbed the rough and pitted track to a bend where a grove of tall poplars grew. The air was filled with the sound of birds singing and the smell of woodland plants on the breeze. The gurgle of flowing water came clearly to Odysseus's ears and he remembered with a smile the spring and the small man-made pool it fed into, where the townsfolk often went to draw water.

As they approached the towering grove, Odysseus heard the bleating of animals and the murmur of voices. A dozen goats were munching grass or drinking from the fountain, while in their midst a man was berating two boys for some misdemeanour. At the arrival of the swineherd and the beggar, the man forgot his lecture and turned his small, dark eyes on the newcomers.

'What're you doing here, you old villain? Driven out by your own pigs because they can't stand the smell of you? And what in Hermes's name is *that*? Have you taught one of your pigs to walk? But he's not nearly fat enough to be one of your animals, is he? They take too much after you, Eumaeus.'

The two boys laughed and jeered, pulling faces at the swineherd and Odysseus. Then one of them stooped down, picked up a stone and threw it at the old beggar, hitting his leather satchel. The goatherd laughed, giving the boys licence to throw more stones. Odysseus did not flinch as they bounced off his limbs and torso, but Eumaeus gave an angry shout and chased them away, catching one on the back of his leg with his staff. The lad gave a yelp of pain and ran crying into the trees, followed by his friend.

'Hoi! What do you think you're doing, hitting my lads!' the goatherd shouted, raising his crook and advancing threateningly towards Eumaeus.

'They got what they deserved,' Eumaeus replied, seizing his staff in both hands, 'and you will too, Melanthius, unless you learn to hold that tongue of yours. You've never liked me because I'm no friend to those suitors you admire so much, but that's no reason to abuse a stranger. I'll never understand how a decent man like your father could produce such vile offspring as you and that hussy, Melantho.'

'You insult my sister again and you'll feel this across your back!'

He waved his crook at Eumaeus, who raised his staff and stepped menacingly towards the goatherd. Melanthius reeled back, a momentary look of fear on his features. But once out of reach, his spiteful arrogance returned.

'You wait until I tell Antinous and Eurymachus about you! I'm supposed to be taking these goats up for their evening feast, but instead I've got to wander through the woods and hillsides looking for those poor lads you scared off.'

'Don't worry, friend,' Odysseus said, hobbling up to the goatherd. 'They're just over there, hiding behind the bole of that tree.'

'Get away from me, you pestilent old skeleton! I suppose this oaf's taking you to beg at the palace, is he? You've obviously helped yourself to too many of his porkers and now he wants shot of you! That's the sort of grudging hospitality Eumaeus gives all guests. Well, may the gods be with you if you expect any mercy from the suitors. They know a good-for-nothing workshy when they see one. You'll be lucky to get away with a cuff round the head or a kick up the backside by my reckoning – if they can stand to dirty themselves by touching you. Now be off with you!'

He launched a kick at Odysseus's hip. Odysseus quickly tensed himself against the blow, and as Athena had promised, his strength returned to him in his need. Melanthius's sandalled foot hit hard, but Odysseus's stance was so firm that the goatherd was thrown backwards with flailing arms, tripping against the lip of the fountain and falling in with a loud splash.

Eumaeus released a bellow of laughter. He raised his hands to three small and crudely shaped figurines on top of the rock from which the spring issued.

'The nymphs are teaching you a lesson, Melanthius! Never abuse a stranger: you don't know who he might be, or what qualities are hiding beneath his filthy rags.'

The sound of more laughter from behind the trees turned the goatherd's humiliation into fury. He cursed the two boys vilely until they came out from their hiding place and helped him from the water. Gathering the docile goats together, they moved up the road towards the town. Melanthius scowled over his shoulder at the two men, though his most hateful stare was still reserved for Eumaeus, not daring to give the old beggar more than a fleeting glower.

'Are you hurt?' Eumaeus asked after the goatherd was out of sight. 'He really meant that kick.'

'I'm tougher than I look, my friend,' Odysseus replied. 'Shall we make our way to the palace?'

Before long they reached the edge of town. A few small children sat in the street playing with sticks and stones while their mothers stood talking or were busy indoors. Some larger boys saw the beggar and followed him up the road, calling him names until Eumaeus shooed them away. Three ancient figures on a bench stopped their conversation to greet Eumaeus by name. They nodded to Odysseus as he hobbled past, and he recalled that they had been old men even before he had sailed for Troy, barely strong enough to haul in a net full of fish, and certainly unfit for the demands of warfare. He did not remember their names.

They reached the marketplace – emptied of its stalls for the day – and for the first time in twenty years he looked again at his home. He leaned on his staff and felt the tears filling his eyes. The plaster on the outer wall needed repairing and whitewashing, and the gate – through which Melanthius was herding his goats – was open and unguarded. But it was still home. The upper storey of the palace was visible above the outer wall, and he could see the windows that marked each room. One had white curtains that were slightly parted. He wondered whether Penelope was sitting in the dark interior, staring out at the oblong of grass beyond the walls – spying him and thinking him nothing more than an old beggar.

Then he thought of the others who had longed to see what he was seeing now. Of Antiphus and Polites, Arceisius and Eurybates, even of Eurylochus and Elpenor. Everyone had gone down to Hades, leaving only himself and Omeros – and him a bard to a foreign king, with no memory of his past life. And then there was Eperitus. As Odysseus looked around, his emotions confused between joy at his return and regret for time lost, he wished his friend had been there to share what should have been his moment of triumph. But, in truth, it was a moment of doubt, and he longed for that old confidence he had always felt with Eperitus at his side.

'Not far now, my friend,' Eumaeus said.

Odysseus followed his companion to the gate. The once-familiar dung heap was still there, sprinkled with animal bones and rotten vegetables. And the corpse of an old dog. It must have been a magnificent hound once, but old age and neglect had left its fur patchy and its hide covered with sores. A swarm of flies was hovering over it.

'Is it a fit end for such an animal,' he asked, 'to be thrown on a dung heap to rot?'

'He's not dead, friend,' Eumaeus said. 'And I'd keep clear of the old beast, too, if I were you. He's been known to bite unsuspecting hands. The suitors used to kick him about for a bit of sport, but he left his mark on too many shins, so they leave him to himself now. About the only good purpose he ever served, if you ask me.'

'Did he have a master?'

'Oh yes – belonged to the king himself at one time. Just a puppy he was when Odysseus sailed away, but he loved him so much he's clung on to life ever since, waiting for his master to come home. Poor, stupid wretch. Someone should put him out of his misery.'

Odysseus turned to the dog.

'*Argus*?' he whispered.

The dog's head lifted a little.

'Careful now,' Eumaeus warned.

Odysseus moved slowly forwards, his staff clumping on the hardened dirt of the path.

'Argus? Is that you, boy?'

His voice was low, but the dog heard him and raised his head. Almost-blind eyes focused on the shadowy blur of the beggar, and somehow he knew his master. Slowly, and painfully, he pushed himself up from the foul-smelling manure and staggered forwards, his tail wagging stiffly. Odysseus reached down and touched the underside of Argus's jaw, then stroked his domed head and long ears. The dog raised his nose upward, pressing affectionately against his hand.

'You recognise me,' Odysseus said, his eyes damp with emotion. 'You've waited loyally for me all these years, and now I'm back. I wonder if others will be as happy to see me.'

Argus gave a whine and pressed his body against Odysseus's shins. His tail wagged for a little while longer, then he slipped down onto his side. He tried to lift his head up one more time to look at his master, but could not. Odysseus dropped to one knee and laid his hand against the animal's flank. The protruding ribs rose and fell, then moved no more.

'I don't believe it,' Eumaeus said. 'That dog hasn't let anyone come near him in years, other than Telemachus and Penelope.'

'Well, he won't bite anyone any more.'

Odysseus wiped the tears from his eyes and looked down at the dead hound, remembering him as a puppy. He had been the strongest in his mother's litter and had shown the makings of an excellent hunting dog.

Odysseus smiled to himself as he recalled those far-off days in the woods of Ithaca, with Iphitus's bow in his hand and Argus at his side, sometimes sniffing out a scent, and the rest of the time jumping up at his master for attention.

He paused. The memory faded, leaving him with a single image. As it so often did, inspiration had come upon him unexpectedly and given him the seed of an idea, a seed that was already putting down roots in his fertile mind. Within moments a new plan had formed that would give him the advantage he had been looking for in his fight against the suitors.

Filled with new vigour, he pulled himself to his feet.

'And now I must meet these men who've made such a glorious name for themselves.'

'I told Telemachus they're bullies and they won't treat you with kindness, old man though you are,' Eumaeus said. 'But he insisted I bring you here, and so here you are.'

'Telemachus will protect me. These men will respect their host, unless they want to bring down the curse of Zeus Xenios on their heads.'

Telemachus had gone before them that morning to let his mother know he had returned. Though he had advised his father not to come until the day of the wedding, Odysseus wanted to see for himself the men who had taken over his home and planned to claim his wife for themselves. He needed to know their strength should it come to a fight; and he wanted to find out who among his servants had remained loyal and who had given their hearts to the gang of interlopers. It would go hard on the latter if he regained his throne.

Above all, though, he yearned to see Penelope. He wanted to look on the face he had once loved so dearly, but which he could no longer recall. Was she still beautiful, as she had been in their youth? Would the love he had once felt be woken from hibernation at the sight of her – or would he learn it had died long ago? The thought terrified him. For twenty years his love for her – or the memory of it – had been the distant lamp that had guided him home through the fog. But what if that affection had faded to nothing? What if it no longer had the power to keep him here? And even if his own feelings held true, what of hers?

Since waking on the beach in the Harbour of Phorcys he had carried with him a gnawing fear that she had forgotten him and was ready to give her love to another man, if she had not done so already. All these questions would be answered when they came face to face. And that, more than anything else, was what terrified him.

They came to the open gate, where the setting sun cast long shadows across the courtyard. The familiar porch to the great hall stood opposite. Its doors were shut, but Odysseus could hear the clamour from within. Voices raised in song or raucous laughter. Vulgar shouts rising above the hubbub. The sound of a lyre and a voice struggling against the tumult, the anonymous bard denied the honour and respect his art deserved. Odysseus gripped the shaft of his staff tightly and moved slowly and resolutely to the porch.

As he mounted the first step, a hand on his shoulder stopped him.

'Let me go first,' Eumaeus said. 'Come in behind me and sit by the doorpost while I find Telemachus and ask him to give you a little food. If you beg from the suitors they'll only insult you or give you a beating.'

He opened the door and entered the great hall. The sound of the feast was much louder now as Odysseus lingered a moment on the porch, the smell of roast meat and fresh bread stirring his empty stomach to life. With the afternoon sunshine behind him, he could make out little in the shadowy hall other than the blazing hearth. Nevertheless, memories of how it used to look came rushing back to him, filling him with a quiet joy at being home.

He recalled the words of the Pythoness, given to him thirty years before: '*If ever you seek Priam's city, the wide waters will swallow you. For the time it takes a baby to become a man, you will know no home. Then, when friends and fortune have departed from you, you will rise again from the dead.*' And so the oracle had been fulfilled to the letter, just as the gods had decreed. His penance had been paid, and from this point forward he would decide his own fate, even though he returned home a nameless beggar that none but a dying dog would recognise as king.

He crossed the threshold and entered the gloom.

Chapter Twenty

The Beggar and the Hooded Man

A large number of spears were stacked on racks to Odysseus's right, so he moved to the left and sat with his back to the wall. As his eyes adjusted to the darkness, he counted six long tables with over a dozen men sitting at each, at least a hundred in total. From what he could see of them, they were young and fit, boasting physiques shaped by long days spent on the sports field or in weapons training. Few seemed to notice the old beggar, and none enough to be distracted by his presence.

The din was settling down as more of the suitors turned their attention to the song of their minstrel, which must have only been beginning when Odysseus first heard it. The bard sat on a stool against one of the pillars. He was a short man with a round stomach and bandy legs that were angled outward as he couched his tortoiseshell lyre on his left hip. One horn of the instrument was attached to his wrist by a leather strap, keeping it in place as he alternated between plucking at the upper half of the strings with the fingers of his left hand and picking at the lower half with a flat shard of bone.

The music resonated back from the animal hide that had been stretched across the shell, filling the lofty hall with gentle music which, once it settled upon the ear, demanded silence. The words that accompanied the tune were soft but clear, and it took Odysseus a few moments to realise that the bard was singing about the fight between Menelaus and Paris. Though the song was the interpretation of a man who had not been there – full of gaps, errors and embroidery – Odysseus's mind drifted back to the duel he had witnessed on the plains before the city of Troy.

He saw again the vast armies of the Greeks and Trojans seated on the bloodstained earth as Helen's lovers fought for her hand. It was curious that the events of the war seemed to mirror so much else in life. He looked about at the proud young Ithacans – his own subjects – and hoped that he would not have to face them in battle. Perhaps with the arrival of Peisistratus's men they would see sense and go home with swords sheathed, acknowledging him as king.

He looked from face to face as they listened to the song. They were handsome and strong, filled with the energy and optimism of their youth. Though the reports of their behaviour had filled him with anger, now that he saw them he could not bring himself to despise them. If they were arrogant, were they not just overly proud? If disrespectful to the gods, was it not simply inexperience? How many of their sires had gone with him to Ilium, leaving their sons without the guidance of a father? Was he, their absent king, not as much to blame for their faults as they were?

He glanced around the large chamber. Little had changed. The murals were more smoke-stained and the plaster in need of repair, but the fading images were the same. And yet it did not feel like the home he had left behind. That may have been because of the crowds of suitors, or the unfamiliar slaves who were probably the sons and daughters of the men and women who had served him with such loyalty. Perhaps he could no longer relate to a place that was so ordinary, so domesticated. In all his years of longing for home, he had never considered that he might have outgrown Ithaca.

Or maybe it was because Penelope was absent. From the moment Eumaeus had opened the door, his eyes had been searching for her amid the smoke and clamour, desperate – and yet fearful – to see her face. Without her, his home was incomplete. If home was where his heart had been for all these years, Penelope was the beat that gave it life.

His eyes were drawn back to the hearth. Eumaeus was talking to Telemachus, who was seated on the dais, their features blurred by the heat haze. A man was seated beside Telemachus. Despite his hooded features, Odysseus could tell the man was older by some years than the other guests in the hall. He had a powerful build and the poise of a warrior. Something about the way he sat – his self-confidence, his quiet awareness of his surroundings – told Odysseus that he had seen his fair share of battle. As Eumaeus spoke, he pointed back over his shoulder to the entrance. Telemachus looked and spotted his father sitting against the wall. Bidding the swineherd to come closer, he pushed a basket of bread into his hand and piled it up with as much meat as it could hold before sending him over to the beggar.

'Telemachus says you are to go around the suitors and beg them for food,' Eumaeus said, passing Odysseus the basket. 'I warned him they would give you a hard time, but he insisted. "The man's a beggar," he told me. "If he's not used to a bit of mistreatment by now, then he should learn a different trade". Most unlike him, I must say.'

Odysseus crammed a piece of bread into his mouth. Telemachus was giving him the opportunity to speak to as many of the suitors as he could to find out for himself the sort of men they were.

'Your master's right. After all I've been through in life, a few harsh words or the toe of someone's sandal isn't going to kill me. First I'm going to fill my empty stomach with your master's generosity, though.'

He picked a large slice of meat and bit into it. The grease oozed over his lips and tongue, filling his mouth with its flavour. Before long, he had eaten everything Eumaeus had brought to him.

'May the gods bless your master for his kindness. Now we will test the charity of his guests.'

Eumaeus stretched out a hand and helped him back to his feet before going to rejoin Telemachus. Leaning on his staff, Odysseus approached the nearest table. The bard had finished his song and was about to begin his own meal. Without his music, the suitors quickly resumed their loud feasting, and none noticed the beggar until his empty palms were thrust toward the nearest.

'Spare some food for a poor man cursed by old age and an empty stomach.'

'You'll be cursed by more than that unless you clear off,' the suitor said, turning his face away and wincing. 'You smell like a herd of goats have pissed all over you.'

'We can't send him away with nothing, Eurydamas,' said another, who was feeding a slice of meat to a dog. Pulling it from the dog's teeth, he tossed it across the table to the beggar. 'That'll put some flesh on your bones, old man.'

The others laughed. Odysseus smiled along with the joke, though he left the half-chewed mutton where it had landed.

'My lord is very amusing. How about you, sir?' he asked another. 'Will you have mercy on a man fallen on hard times? I used to live in a house just like this, but war and the gods robbed me of everything I had and left me the pitiful creature you see now.'

One of the suitors behind Odysseus was pulling faces in mimicry of the beggar, while his friends around the table were laughing into their wine or wiping tears of mirth from their faces. But the man Odysseus had addressed sat up and looked him in the eye.

'It's said the gods will disguise themselves as beggars and walk the earth, testing the hearts of mortals,' he said. 'But whether you're a god or just a victim of misfortune, you have my pity. Here, pass me your satchel.'

'Don't encourage him, Amphinomus,' said Eurydamas. 'There's grease on his lips and crumbs in his beard – he's already had his fill from somebody else.'

'Nevertheless,' said Amphinomus as he put a large piece of flatbread and some slices of meat from his plate into the bag, 'the gods require us to treat strangers with decency. Maybe if I bless this poor vagabond, they'll repay me with the hand of Penelope tomorrow. And should anyone accuse me of giving generously from another man's wealth, I'll give him my own belt to replace that piece of old rope around his waist.'

Amphinomus passed the satchel back across the table and began to undo his belt. Odysseus reached for the bag, but before he could take it, it was snatched up by one of the others. Odysseus looked at him, expecting him to throw the food to the dogs. Instead, he took a piece of bread from his plate and dropped it inside, frowning unhappily as he did so. The others followed suit, if reluctantly, and last of all Amphinomus passed him his belt. Odysseus nodded gratefully and fitted it around his waist, remembering to tuck the chelonion behind the buckle.

'My lord Amphinomus,' Odysseus said, 'you are a good man and do not belong in such company. But the gods have seen what these men are doing and vengeance is coming to them all. Leave now and save yourself, while you still have the chance.'

Amphinomus contemplated his words for a moment, then shook his head.

'Ithaca needs a king, my friend. If the gods are just, they will give the throne to me and spare Ithaca from the likes of these others. And so, I must remain.'

'But *you* can't,' said Eurydamas, waving a hand dismissively at Odysseus. 'Go and bother someone else with your stench.'

Leaning heavily on his staff once again, he stumped off to the next table and held out his hand.

'So, you old villain, you didn't heed my warning then?'

Melanthius sat at the far end of the table, his hair still damp and his face flushed from standing by the hearth to dry off.

'That's the tramp I saw with Eumaeus,' he told the others around the table.

'The one that threw you in the fountain?' said a handsome man with a prominent nose and grey eyes that regarded Odysseus disdainfully. 'He's hardly ferocious, is he?'

A pretty servant girl was sitting on his knee, her arms draped around his neck.

'Tell him to go away, Antinous. He's ugly and he smells, and if I have that reek in my nostrils later it might put me off... you know.'

'You heard the girl, stranger,' Antinous said. 'Piss off before I have Eurymachus there throw you out on your arse.'

He hooked a thumb at a large, cruel-faced man sitting on the other side of the girl. Melantho turned to Eurymachus, stroked his square jaw tenderly and placed a kiss on his lips. Antinous seemed not to care.

'Yes, throw him out, Eurymachus.'

'Is it the place of a slave to order the guests what to do?' Odysseus asked. 'Or are you gentlemen so enamoured that you will insult the gods because a maiden flutters her cow-like eyes at you?'

'Aren't there enough verminous plate lickers on Ithaca already without Eumaeus inviting another?' Antinous said, thumping the table and pointing at Odysseus. 'Get out now, old man, before we do you some harm.'

'You forget, Antinous, that I'm the master of this house,' Telemachus said. Hearing the commotion, he had left his seat and now stood behind the suitor. 'If you want peace from this beggar, surely all you need to do is fill his satchel with food and he'll leave you alone. After all, it's my bread and my meat you're enjoying.'

'For once the boy's right,' one of the other suitors agreed. 'Here, put this in your pouch and be grateful.'

He tossed Odysseus a piece of meat, which he caught and stuffed into his bag. A few others passed morsels of food, with one giving him the dregs of his wine, which he drank down immediately. Grudgingly and with a scowl, Eurymachus slid his whole plate of food across the table.

'Here. You've put me off my food anyway with your stench. Now get out of our sight.'

Odysseus took the plate and tipped the contents into his satchel. But he made no move to leave. Instead, he turned his eyes towards Antinous and stretched out his hand.

'What do you have for me, my friend?' he asked. 'A person of your noble appearance surely isn't the least of all these great men. Indeed, a fine, strong-looking youth like you must expect to be the queen's first choice for her new husband. And if you want to be king, shouldn't you give more generously than all your comrades?'

'*Reward* you for ruining our banquet with your vile presence?' Antinous blustered. 'Does your greed know no limits? For the last time, get out of my sight before I lose my temper.'

It was no wonder Telemachus had reserved his greatest contempt for Antinous, Odysseus thought. The man had his father's black heart and lust for power. But whereas Eupeithes was a duplicitous schemer with the patience to wait for his plans to mature, his son was brash and dangerously impetuous. Odysseus could tell his tolerance was thinning rapidly. All it needed was one more nudge.

'So, your true character is revealed,' he said, loud enough for the whole hall to hear. 'Your host encourages you to give freely of what he has provided, and yet you refuse charity to a man who has nothing. You may be handsome and well-born, sir, but beneath those fine looks you have the heart and mind of a dog!'

Antinous's face turned a deep shade of red. His whole frame seemed to tremble as he glowered at the beggar, too incensed to know how to respond. Then he smashed his fist onto the table, catching the edge of his plate and sending the contents over Melantho, who screamed and fell off the bench. Antinous ignored her. With a cry of pure rage, he reached beneath the table, picked up a footstool and hurled it at the beggar. Odysseus turned away and raised his arm across his face. The stool hit him on the back, just beneath the shoulder, and broke into pieces.

Silence fell throughout the great hall. Before, the suitors had found amusement in Antinous's argument with the beggar, but to harm him was going too far. It was an outrage against Zeus, who protected strangers and supplicants. Their eyes turned to look at the old man, who to their astonishment had not been knocked over by the blow. He pushed himself up on his staff and turned towards Antinous.

'Again, I say, you have revealed your true character. To do violence to a man who is threatening you or stealing your possessions is justified, but to injure someone driven to begging by the curse of an empty stomach! Zeus himself sees what you have done, Antinous. I say here and now that you will not marry the queen. No, before nightfall tomorrow, the Thunderer will take your life from you – and that of every man who remains here at your side.'

A murmur of voices now rose up from the benches, some concerned, others angry. Antinous stood and reached for the pommel of his sword. Then a strong hand settled on his shoulder and forced him back down to his seat.

'It was foolish to have harmed the beggar, Antinous, but if you murder him, Penelope will have no choice but to throw you out. Now, sit down and drink your wine.'

It was the man with the hood. He picked up Odysseus's leather satchel from the table, slipped his hand through the beggar's arm and helped him to a shadowy corner of the hall. Behind them, Odysseus heard Telemachus ordering the bard to strike up a new song. A light tune filled the air, and a hundred voices sprang up in heated conversation.

'You've caused a stir, stranger, no mistake about it,' the man in the hood said as he helped Odysseus down onto a stool. 'How's your shoulder?'

Odysseus laughed.

'I've been pierced by sword and spear in my time, so a footstool isn't much to be concerned about. Though I'd have felt it less if I'd had my old armour about me.'

Now it was the turn of the hooded man to laugh. He pulled up a stool and sat opposite him. Only the tip of his nose was visible, the rest of his face being lost in shadow. Strangely, Odysseus saw that the man wore a chelonion in his belt.

'I knew you were a soldier the moment I saw you,' the man said. 'Too old for Troy, I'm guessing.'

His voice was low and gravely, but there was something familiar about it that sparked Odysseus's curiosity.

'No, I fought there for ten years, though I was already ripe in years when we set sail from Aulis. Idomeneus, son of Deucalion, was my king. What about yourself? You fought with the Greeks, that much is clear. Who was your commander?'

'I was with the Argives, under King Diomedes.' Hearing footsteps behind him, he turned and called to a passing maid. 'Wine for me and my comrade. Listen,' he continued, returning to Odysseus, 'I'm sorry for the way those men treated you. I arrived here yesterday and didn't meet them myself until this morning, when they insulted me, too. They're arrogant brutes for the most part, none of them worthy of the woman they're courting. That's her son, sitting by the hearth; not yet a man, and already they've eaten him out of most of his inheritance. It grieves me to see what's happening here, with none of the local men brave enough to raise a finger against their injustice.'

Though Odysseus could not see the expression on the hooded man's face, he saw his hands ball up into fists as they rested on his knees.

'The gods will repay them, my friend, and sooner than you think. But tell me, what happened to the young man's father?'

'He never returned from Troy.'

'You mean he fell in battle,' Odysseus said.

'No, he survived the fighting and set sail for his homeland. He just never made it back.'

'What was his name? I might've heard something of his fate.'

The man shook his head.

'The sea claimed him long ago. But his name and reputation won't have escaped you, not if you've ever heard a bard sing of that bitter war. Where Achilles, Ajax and many others failed, it was *he* who gave Troy into the hands of the Greeks. He was a man of unsurpassed cunning and intelligence – and all the faults that go with such gifts. Odysseus was his name, son of Laertes, king of these islands.'

He turned round as the maid emerged from the crowd with their wine, though he could not possibly have known she was approaching. He waved her over and she handed them both a wooden cup, which she filled with wine from a skin.

Odysseus dipped his fingers in the dark liquid and shook a couple of drops onto the floor.

'Yes, I know of Odysseus. I saw him in the vanguard of every battle we fought against the Trojans. No doubt you did, too, if you were there. Perhaps if you removed your hood I might recognise your face.'

'I doubt it,' the man said, touching his wine and sprinkling a little on the floor before taking a draught. 'I don't recognise *you*, old friend, so why should you know me?'

'You're right, of course. I was just curious. You've heard that one of Diomedes's captains – Euryalos, son of Mekisteus – stole something of great worth from him and is being sought by the king? I saw the man once and would know him anywhere. If I could find him and tell Diomedes where I saw him, I'm sure he would reward me handsomely...'

'I'm not Euryalos, and I did not steal from Diomedes, if that's what you're implying,' the man said. 'But if it saves you a long journey to Argos, then I'll prove it to you.'

He leaned forwards and tipped back his hood to reveal long, dark hair touched with grey. Raising his head slowly, he looked at Odysseus. His face was in shadow and his left eye was covered by a large patch of rough leather, but Odysseus was not fooled by the disguise.

'Do I look like Euryalos?'

'No,' Odysseus replied, his voice little more than a whisper.

For a while all he was able to do was stare at his old friend, the man who until that moment he had believed was dead. His thoughts slowed almost to a halt, unable to comprehend what he was seeing. He became aware of the dull thudding of his heart and the heaviness of his breathing; and only the realisation that his cup was about to fall from his lax fingers snapped him out of his stupor. He caught the wine before it fell, spilling a little on his leg. As he looked down at where it had splashed, he wondered whether what he was seeing could be true. But when he looked up again, Eperitus was still there.

'Are you all right? You look pale,' Eperitus said, staring at him with concern.

Thoughts began to register in Odysseus's mind, like the first few raindrops hitting the calm surface of a pool, sending small ripples across his consciousness. Eperitus was alive. The friend who had endured so many ordeals with him was *alive*! A sudden moment of elation followed. He wanted to reach out and embrace him, reveal his true identity and celebrate with him that they were together again. They had survived everything the gods had thrown at them and had been reunited for the final test. But the thought was quickly stifled by another – the memory of their parting. The plunging, rain-lashed deck; the ring of their drawn swords; the crack of splintering wood. In that instant, before the mast had come crashing down, they had been trying to kill each other.

He had blamed Eperitus for slaughtering the cattle of Hyperion and incurring the wrath of the gods. Equally, he knew Eperitus held him responsible for the death of his wife and their baby, effectively murdered by his decision to anchor on the sun god's island instead of pushing on to Phaeacia as they had been told to. Odysseus's own anger had subsided years before and turned to regret. But what of Eperitus's? He had pursued vengeance against his own father for twenty years for killing their king; and only his oath to Clytaemnestra had prevented him from murdering Agamemnon for sacrificing Iphigenia at Aulis. He would not easily have forgiven the death of his family.

'Come here, girl,' he heard Eperitus say. Looking up, Odysseus saw a maid approaching. 'Fetch this man a blanket. And a thick one, too – not some threadbare sack.'

'But sir, he'll be covered in lice and fleas...'

'Do as I tell you!'

'I'm all right,' Odysseus said, placing a hand on Eperitus's arm. 'I just felt a little light-headed. I haven't drunk anything in so long, and this is good wine.'

'Yes, the suitors don't stint in sharing Odysseus's best vintage.'

'Did you know Odysseus?'

Eperitus hesitated.

'I knew of him.'

'But you talked of his faults.'

'I didn't mean to speak ill of the man in his own home. Forgive me.'

'What's to forgive if you speak honestly? Do I guess right that you didn't like him?'

Eperitus glanced at him through narrowed eyes, then looked away and took a swallow of wine.

'I didn't say that. If he had been my king, instead of Diomedes, I would have loved him. He was resourceful, brave, a great one to listen to... and yet he was... he appeared to me to be reckless.'

'Reckless?'

'I heard he would do anything to get home, to be here again. That desire gave him greatness. The rest of the kings would still be butting their heads against the walls of Troy now if Odysseus hadn't resorted to cunning rather than relying on courage. But it also made him careless about other people's lives. They say that when his father's throne was usurped, when Odysseus was a young man, he tricked his way into the palace and cut the throats of as many of the rebels as he could reach – murdered them in their sleep. I heard he did other things in Troy that few would have stooped to. Doubtless he was led by that same selfish and careless spirit on the voyage home. Perhaps that's why he never made it back.'

'Maybe if he did return, he would be a different man,' Odysseus suggested. 'Wiser and a little less… reckless.'

'He won't return,' Eperitus said. 'People here have been living in the shadow of that false hope for too long.'

'But it seems fear of his return has kept the ambitions of many at bay.'

'Only until tomorrow. Tomorrow Penelope will choose her new husband, and then who knows what will happen?'

Odysseus looked around at the suitors. Food and wine was still being brought out from the kitchens, and no amount of it seemed to satisfy their wolfish desire for more. And their appetites did not stop at his flocks of goats and pigs, or his wine cellar. They were hungry for his wife, and they were hungry for his throne. And if anything stood in their way, they would tear it to shreds.

Then he looked at his friend. Had Eperitus's anger towards him subsided? He had called him reckless; but that was not a word that resonated with hate or lasting bitterness. Time may have healed him of such feelings – time and the belief that Odysseus was drowned. But if he revealed that he was alive, would Eperitus's old hostility also be resurrected? Would he want still revenge for Astynome and their baby?

He hoped not. More than anything, he wanted his friend back. To have his old captain at his side would give him the confidence he needed to retake his throne and restore his family. In a fight with the suitors, Eperitus would be worth a hundred spearmen. But their friendship meant much more than that to Odysseus. Eperitus was a part of him. When their paths had been sundered seven years ago he had lost a piece of himself, just as he had been torn in two when he had left Penelope to sail for Troy. If Penelope was his heart and soul – his reason for living – then Eperitus had been his conscience and strength. He wanted them both back.

'You said you feel aggrieved by the injustices you see here,' he said. 'And yet you're an Argive, as much a stranger to Ithaca as I am. What are the queen and her son to you that you should be angered at their treatment by the suitors?'

'I lost my wife and child some years ago,' Eperitus replied. He took a deep breath and looked Odysseus in the eye. 'It left me empty. Without a purpose, if you like. Then I met Telemachus at Pylos. He told me about these suitors, and I decided I had to help him. I couldn't save my own family, so maybe I could save his.'

'And what will you do now you're here? Even a seasoned soldier can't fight all these men on his own, if that's what you were planning.'

Eperitus shook his head.

'I swore a long time ago never to kill again.'

Odysseus raised his eyebrows.

'Why would any warrior take such an oath?'

'Because he had seen too much death. I used to fight for honour and glory, until I saw there was little of either in war. I should have been a farmer instead.'

'But would ploughing soil and sowing seed deal with these suitors? The queen chooses her new husband tomorrow morning. If we're to save her from the suitors, we need to act quickly.'

'We?'

'You aren't the only man who hates injustice, my friend. But this isn't the time or place to make our plans. Will you meet me later, in the porch? I have something to say that will be worth your hearing.'

As he spoke, he noticed Eumaeus approaching through the crowd of suitors.

'You're in luck, stranger,' he told Odysseus. 'The queen summoned me after she heard of your treatment at the hands of the suitors, shamed that you should be so abused in her house. I told her...' He paused, glanced at Eperitus and bent low with his mouth to the beggar's ear. '...I told her that you have news about Odysseus. She wants to speak with you, but not with her suitors present. She will meet you here in the great hall after the suitors have left for the night.' He pulled away. 'And now I must return to my farm. My herdsmen are good, but the pigs miss me if I'm gone too long.'

'So, you have news about Odysseus, do you?' Eperitus said after Eumaeus had left, proving his hearing was as sharp as ever. 'Well, you were wise to guard it from strangers like me. But now that we are co-conspirators, perhaps you'll reveal all when we meet later. *After* you've spoken with the queen.'

'I'll tell you everything, my friend. You may like what you hear, and you may not; but I will keep nothing back.'

Chapter Twenty One

Irus

Eperitus pulled up his hood and returned to his seat beside Telemachus. As Odysseus watched him go, he recalled what he had been told by the Phaeacian hunchback, that Omeros was not the only man they had pulled from the sea. The other must have been Eperitus.

It still seemed incredible to him that his friend was alive. The knowledge filled him with joy and hope. He wondered what Eperitus had been through since their parting – how he had lost his eye, and how resolved he was never to kill again. If he intended to honour his oath, then he would take no part in any fight with the suitors, despite his clear loathing for them. But he was getting ahead of himself. It was possible that when Eperitus discovered Odysseus had also survived the wreck of their galley, his bitterness would return and he would refuse any attempt to restore their friendship. He might even take it on himself to kill the man he had once served so faithfully.

But Odysseus did not think so. Eperitus would have to choose between his loyalty to Astynome's memory – which he might decide could only be avenged with Odysseus's blood – and his former loyalty to Odysseus, the king and friend with whom and for whom he had suffered and endured so much. Yet he hoped the goodness in Eperitus's nature would prevail and that he would see that vengeance was an empty and destructive desire. Perhaps he could even rediscover his old love for Odysseus.

He picked a piece of bread from his satchel and saw a blob of mucus where it had been torn in half. A parting gift from one of the suitors, no doubt. He flung it aside and eyed the crowd of young nobles, their faces red with the heat from his own hearth and the wine from his own cellar. His hands curled into fists and he remembered his sympathy for them when he had first entered the hall. But now that he had glimpsed what Telemachus and Penelope had endured for three years, his sympathy turned to contempt.

They were thieves who disrespected the gods and the laws that preserved order in society. If their crimes went unpunished, then the thin and brittle barrier between civilisation and anarchy would be broken. But would their crimes be punished? They deserved death, and yet if there was a fight tomorrow they were likely to be victorious, living to enjoy their spoils while he and Telemachus lay dead in their own home.

Or they might see Odysseus and meekly slink back to their families, their lives spared to hatch new plots against the throne when the time and the opportunity were right. He almost hoped they would choose to fight, for a bloodless victory over Antinous and his companions would only postpone the inevitable clash. But even if they vacated the palace and agreed to compensate Odysseus for the livestock and wine he had lost, the day would not be entirely bloodless. If he was to restore his true form, Athena had said he first had to kill one of the suitors.

A shriek was followed by loud laughter. Odysseus watched as Antinous grabbed a serving girl by the waist and pulled her over the table, scattering the food and cups of wine. He pulled her dress above her waist and sank his teeth into her exposed buttocks, causing her to yelp in pain and shock. Somehow she fought her way free to the guffaws of Antinous and his cronies, and managed to escape back into the crowd, her eyes filled with tears as she tugged the hem of her dress back down to her knees. And as he watched, Odysseus knew which suitor would pay the price for their collective offences.

At that moment, the door of the great hall swung open and the figure of a man was silhouetted against the late-afternoon sunlight. He was so tall, and his chest and shoulders so broad, that Odysseus was reminded of Great Ajax. His huge arms stuck out like the handles of a jug, the muscles too thick to lie flat against his ribs. His legs, too, were large and densely muscled, so that when he entered the hall they were barely able to bend at the knee. Odysseus could feel the thud of each foot as it hit the floor.

He looked up at him in awe, but as the giant stepped from the sunlit porch into the orange glow from the hearth, Odysseus saw that he was dressed in filthy rags that barely stretched around his great torso and limbs. More surprising still was his face. The features were soft and childlike, and his expression was almost fearful, his wide eyes flicking anxiously from side to side. He was barely able to look at the others in the hall and quickly revealed a habit of raising his hand to his mouth, where his fingers would quiver nervously as they touched his protruding bottom lip. His beard was light and tufty, more like that of a youth, but his skin was deeply browned from a life spent under the sun. At the sight of him, the suitors raised a mocking cheer and the giant's simple face spread into an uncertain grin.

'Irus, you buffoon!' one shouted, to the laughter of his comrades.

Irus nodded and gave a slow, heavy laugh of his own before raising his fingers to his bottom lip again.

'Irus, look out behind you!'

This time Irus flinched, ducking and raising his forearm across his face as he half-turned to ward off the phantom attacker. This had the suitors in an uproar. When Irus realised there was nobody behind him, he joined in with their merriment, unaware it was at his own expense. It was shameful to ridicule the simple-minded, but the suitors – all bar a few – seemed not to care.

A female voice rose in protest, then Melantho was thrust out into the open space between the tables and the door. She frowned over her shoulder at Antinous, who just laughed and waved her forwards. Straightening her dress, she took a step towards Irus. Forgetting her irritation, she put her hands on her shapely hips and smiled up at the giant. He looked back at her with an anxious grin, hopelessly captivated by her beauty.

'Are you hungry, Irus?' she asked.

He gave a nod and stretched out his hands imploringly. She glanced over her shoulder at Antinous again. Thinking he had not been understood, Irus rubbed his stomach and touched the fingers of his other hand to his mouth. At his mute grunting, the suitors threw their heads back in laughter, some of them mimicking him. Melantho took a piece of flatbread from the table and, scowling at Antinous this time, inserted it into her cleavage.

'Here you go then,' she said, leaning forwards, 'come and help yourself.'

Irus raised his fingers to his bottom lip again and shook his head.

'What are you afraid of, you big turnip?' Eurymachus shouted. 'She's only a girl.'

Irus gave another shake of his head, then turning to another table, moved towards them, rubbing his stomach and gesturing towards his mouth. They shooed him away.

'Here, Irus,' Melantho said. 'Here's some bread for you.'

'Melantho!' Telemachus shouted, rising from his seat. 'Leave him alone and get back to your work.'

She made to remove the bread, but was heckled by the suitors until she put it back. Antinous pointed to Irus, and she moved closer to him.

'Come on Irus, take the bread. In the names of all the gods, will you just take the bread?'

He shook his head and backed away.

Odysseus had seen enough. He rose from his stool and pushed himself up on his staff.

'What you're doing isn't right, girl,' he said. 'Now, do as your master says and get rid of that bread.'

'Stay where you are, Melantho,' Antinous ordered. 'As for you, you old rogue, I warn you not to cross me again today.'

Irus turned and looked at Odysseus, noticing him for the first time. His childish expression had been replaced by a frown.

'What's the matter, Irus?' Melantho called up to him. 'Don't you like me any more? Come on, you overgrown baby – take the bread.'

She shook her breasts at him. Odysseus felt anger coursing through his limbs, filling them with strength. Walking up to the slave girl, he took the bread and threw it on the floor.

'Get your hands off me!' she shouted, drawing back in disgust.

Something slammed into the side of Odysseus's head, lifting him from his feet and throwing him across the room. He crashed into a group of seated suitors, who pushed him to the floor. He lay there for a moment, his head suddenly very light. Small bursts of light popped before his eyes, and when he tried to push himself up onto all fours he fell immediately into the dirt again. Laughter rang out all around him. Then he felt strong hands lifting him back to his feet.

'Are you all right, old man?'

He turned to see Eperitus's hooded face next to his. Telemachus had his other arm.

Odysseus nodded and tried to stand. His legs seemed weak at first, but quickly regained their strength. He shook his head and looked at Irus standing a short distance away. His huge hands were clenched into fists, and his foolish, timid expression had turned dark with rage. Melantho was behind him, staring at Odysseus with a grin that was both impressed by Irus's strength and pleased that the old beggar had been the victim of it.

Antinous now left his chair and reached up to place his hand on Irus's shoulder.

'That's it, Irus. Don't let him hurt Melantho. He wants her for himself, you know. He wants to kiss her and put his filthy hands on her tits.'

'Be quiet, Antinous,' Telemachus warned him.

'Or what?' Eurymachus said, moving to stand beside Antinous.

'It's all right,' Odysseus told Telemachus in a low voice. 'I can handle this.'

'That's what he wants, isn't it, Melantho? To have his wicked way with you,' Antinous continued. Melantho nodded and feigned fear by shrinking back. 'Are you going to let him do that, Irus? Are you going to let that old crone touch Melantho like that?'

Irus shook his head.

'Don't listen to him, Irus,' Odysseus countered. '*He* is Melantho's lover; him and Eurymachus there.'

'And probably half a dozen others,' he heard Eperitus whisper beside him.

'It's not true,' Melantho said, laying her hand on Irus's forearm. 'The old beggar's a liar. He tried to kiss me before you arrived.'

The suitors were all clambering off their benches now, forming a wide circle around Odysseus and the giant. Irus gave an angry growl and stepped forwards, raising his great fists as he scowled down at Odysseus.

'He hit you with his left, so assume that's what he'll lead with,' Eperitus whispered in his ear. 'I don't think you can afford to take another hit from him, so play it clever and you might survive. May the gods be with you.'

He patted Odysseus on the shoulder and retreated. Telemachus gave him a concerned look, but his father indicated for him to follow Eperitus. The suitors were clapping and shouting with excitement, overjoyed at the thought of seeing the old beggar beaten to death. And if the simple-minded Irus came within reach, they would get their wish.

Odysseus felt his old strength returning to his body. He straightened his back slowly and pulled his fists up before his face. Irus advanced and threw a clumsy punch at his opponent. Odysseus moved his head to one side and let the blow pass over him. Then he stepped in to punch Irus twice in the ribs. Any other man would have been sent staggering backwards, gasping for breath. But Irus's torso was sheeted in thick muscle and he barely seemed to notice Odysseus's knuckles pounding his flesh.

Odysseus fell back, conscious of the wall of suitors behind him, and Irus came on again. His dull-eyed fury was terrifying to look upon, but his slow wits enabled Odysseus to guess his intentions and outthink them. Splaying his fingers and spreading his arms wide, Irus rushed at him with the aim of seizing him and crushing the life out of his body. To the surprise of the suitors behind Odysseus, who had expected his reactions to be slowed by age, he slipped beneath Irus's right elbow, turned and kicked him in the behind. He gave a grunt and fell headlong into the crowd, bundling four or five to the floor.

Oblivious to their complaints, Irus regained his feet and made another charge at Odysseus. Despite his bulk and slowness of mind, he was quick on his feet. As Odysseus tried to sidestep the attack, Irus's right fist caught him on the shoulder and sent him reeling against one of the tables. He jarred his back painfully and fell. As he lay among the pieces of discarded food in the dirt, he saw Irus halt and turn. Spying the old beggar, his face contorted into a snarl and he stomped towards his helpless victim, the floor thudding with each footfall. Odysseus tried to crawl under the table, but one of the suitors grabbed his ankles.

'I've got him,' he called to Irus. 'Come and finish him off.'

Odysseus kicked out at the suitor, but the man's grip was too powerful. Irus tossed aside a bench that was in his way and planted his feet either side of Odysseus's head. As he reached down to seize hold of him, there was a dull thud and the suitor fell unconscious across Odysseus's back. Odysseus glimpsed Telemachus's face as he was being hustled away by the other suitors, a wooden carving board in his hands. Then the body of the senseless suitor was being lifted from him. In the instant it took Irus to fling him aside, Odysseus rolled beneath the table and dragged himself away on his elbows.

He crawled as quickly as he could, expecting to feel the irresistible grip of Irus's hands on his legs at any moment. But it took the giant's slow mind a while to understand where his prey had gone. By the time the realisation came to him, Odysseus had already crawled three-quarters the length of the table. In two strides Irus was beside him. Seeing Odysseus, he stooped down and sent his long arm groping towards him. Odysseus did the only thing he could. He scrambled to his knees, flattened his hands on the underside of the table and pushed with all his strength.

It was large and heavy, but he managed to tip it over on its side, scattering plates of food and cups of wine across the floor. The weight of the table fell on Irus's arm and trapped it against the floor, pulling him down to his knees. Odysseus sprang up and, grasping the opportunity, drew his arm back and drove his fist into Irus's jaw. There was a crack followed by a gush of blood and two or three teeth from the giant's mouth. Then he slumped to the floor, unconscious.

The tumult of shouting and cheering that had filled the great hall gave way to sudden silence. Odysseus stepped back, pulling the table with him and righting it. He gazed about at the shocked faces of the suitors and saw Eperitus staring at him. There was a questioning look in his eye, but when Odysseus signalled him forward, he came without hesitation. Taking a shoulder each, they lifted Irus and dragged him to the door of the great hall. After Odysseus had paused to grab his satchel, they carried him to the gates of the outer wall and propped him against one of the posts.

'There's more to you than meets the eye, old man,' Eperitus said. 'I thought you were dead for certain, but you've still got some strength and speed in those limbs of yours. And not a little skill, either.'

'The gods were with me. Not that I take any pride in beating a child in a Titan's body. That Antinous has got a great deal to answer for, stoking this soft-witted soul's anger like that.'

'But who's going to *make* him answer?'

'The gods will see to it, my friend. The gods will see to it.'

Irus began to stir and groan. His head rolled from one side to the other, and then he opened his eyes. Both Odysseus and Eperitus edged back from him, but his expression was once more that of a fearful and confused imbecile. He raised his fingers to his bloody lower lip, then into his mouth, probing the gaps where three of his teeth had been. He looked at Odysseus, seemingly forgetful of the fact he was the one who had inflicted the wound upon him, and with a grunt held his hand out imploringly.

'Here,' Odysseus said, handing him the satchel of food. 'It'll hurt when you eat, so try and chew on the other side of your mouth. Do you understand?'

He touched the left side of his own jaw and made chewing motions. Then he stood and looked at the dusky eastern skies. Turning to the west, the sky was lavender in colour and the thin clouds were like a field of ploughed gold as they reflected the setting sun.

'I'll send one of my maids to tend to you,' he told Irus.

'One of *your* maids?' Eperitus questioned. 'You mean Telemachus's, of course. But the servants aren't likely to listen to a beggar, even one with delusions of grandeur. I'll find a girl; you stay with this poor fool.'

-

Penelope pulled the veil over her face and left her bedroom, followed by Autonoe and Hippodameia. She wore her thick woollen cloak, as usual, but instead of the plain dress that she normally reserved for her suitors, she had chosen a chiton that revealed her slender shoulders and arms. Its low neckline displayed her cleavage well, and the gauzy blue material would set any man's imagination roaming. Autonoe had cautioned her to wear something less flattering, reminding her of the embarrassment the suitors had caused her before. But she no longer cared about them; there was only one man whose interest she wanted.

Despite his rough looks, Theoclymenus was more of a man than the rest of her suitors combined. He reminded her so much of Odysseus that she had to fight the notion he was indeed her husband, disguised by the art of one of the Olympians. It was not a fight she had entirely won. Whoever Theoclymenus was, however, he would prove a better husband than Antinous. She had not forgotten Eupeithes's threat to have Telemachus assassinated if she did not marry his son, and if she spurned Antinous for Theoclymenus she had no doubt he would carry it out. But if Telemachus could once again seek sanctuary in Sparta until he came of age, then as king he would have the power to deal with Eupeithes once and for all. It was a slender hope, Penelope thought, but it was enough.

They reached the side entrance to the great hall. The sound of Phemius's lyre and his soft, enchanting voice had replaced the raucous shouting of the fight from a short while earlier, the noise of which had penetrated even to her upstairs chamber. She had been informed of the fresh abuses that Eupeithes's son had inflicted on the beggar who had arrived that afternoon, compelling him to fight Irus. At least poor Irus was too simple to understand the cruelties inflicted on him by the suitors. But if they had managed to rouse his temper, then she feared for the latest stranger to come under the protection of her roof.

She paused at the door, her usual feeling of dread at the thought of presenting herself before the suitors replaced by a touch of nervous anticipation. Was her girlish excitement due to Theoclymenus offering her an escape from marrying one of the suitors, or because she still felt there was a possibility he really was Odysseus? She chased the ridiculous thought away and opened the door.

Telemachus was seated in his usual chair by the roaring hearth. The place next to him, where Theoclymenus should have been sitting, was empty. For a moment she felt a terrible dread that he had left. Then she saw him talking to one of the maids and pointing to the main doors. The girl bowed slightly, gave the baskets of bread she was carrying to another servant, and left. As she opened the doors, a brief glimpse of sunshine splashed into the great hall, then was extinguished again.

By now, the few discussions in the hall had fallen silent at Penelope's appearance, leaving only the crackling of the hearth to compete with Phemius's song. She waited for Theoclymenus to return to his chair, then passed between the benches of suitors – their wine-eager eyes following her – and approached her own high-backed seat on the royal dais. Her maids followed. At a nod from Penelope, Autonoe unclasped the queen's cloak and took it from her shoulders. The sight of her naked arms and the glimpse of bared thigh for the second time in a day sparked whispered conversations among her audience. But with Theoclymenus present, and remembering what had happened to Leocritus earlier – he had since snuck back to rejoin the feast – there were no lewd comments thrown at her this time.

She glanced at Theoclymenus, the gleam of whose single eye she could see in the shadow of his hood, and gave him a discreet smile. He acknowledged her with a nod, though she could not see whether he returned the smile. Then she took her seat.

'What's this I hear about a beggar being abused in our house, Telemachus?' she asked, leaning towards her son. 'First Antinous throws a footstool at him, then he forces him to fight Irus. Why didn't you protect him?'

'I tried to, Mother, but I've no authority among these suitors of yours. Besides, the beggar can look after himself. He felled Irus with a single punch and is outside with him now.'

Penelope raised an eyebrow.

'Then my meeting with him this evening should prove interesting. But for him to be treated so shamefully in our home brings the judgement of the gods down on us. You shouldn't have let it happen, Telemachus. When he returns, bring him to sit by the fire near your feet so he can have both warmth and protection – or go sit with him yourself in the shadows.'

'As you wish, Mother. I'll go find the man now and see he wasn't hurt during the fight.'

Telemachus rose from his chair and crossed the hall to the double doors. Penelope watched him, regretting that she had driven him away.

'He's a good man,' Theoclymenus said, 'and he'll make a fine king one day, if the gods are kind. You would have felt differently, perhaps, if you'd seen him knock out one of the suitors who tried to help Irus.'

Spoken like a true father? she wondered.

'I know he tries his best, though I wish he had more faith in himself.'

'It's no surprise, surrounded by such a horde of tormenters,' Theoclymenus said. He looked at her from the shadows of his hood. 'Have you considered my offer?'

'I've thought of little else,' she said, lowering her voice. Her fingers brushed the top of his hand discreetly. 'And my answer is yes.'

He sat up and looked around at the nearest suitors. Though she could not see his face, she could sense his surprise.

'You've made the right choice. I won't let you down.'

'I know you won't, Theoclymenus. The funny thing is...' She looked around herself. 'How I wish we could speak privately and not be surrounded by these monsters! The truth is, I've been loyal to the memory of Odysseus all these years, and if he were to return I would do everything in my power to restore the loving marriage we had. But it's ten years since the war ended and I have to accept he *isn't* coming back. Until now I had resigned myself to marrying one of these suitors – or something worse. And then the gods bring you here. Didn't you say you'd been guided here by the gods? But the funny thing is, you remind me so much of him.'

'Of Odysseus?' Theoclymenus asked. 'But we are very different men.'

'And yet, to my mind, very similar.'

He leaned back in his chair and stroked his jaw. Phemius's song had ended and the suitors were calling for another. After a few moments of strumming at his instrument, he struck up a new tune and began to sing the story of Orpheus's journey to the Underworld to bring his wife back from death.

'I only have one worry,' Penelope continued. 'Eupeithes has threatened that if I don't choose Antinous, then he will have Telemachus assassinated. And he doesn't bluster when it comes to his ambition for power.'

'Then Telemachus must leave for the mainland, tonight if possible. He can seek sanctuary in Sparta again. If he stays there a few months until he comes of age, he can return as king. Eupeithes wouldn't dare threaten him then.'

Penelope smiled to herself, pleased that Theoclymenus's thoughts matched her own. It was then she noticed Antinous watching her from one of the crowded tables. He had a hungry look about him, knowing in his mind that tomorrow she would be his. Eurymachus was beside him, his forearms on the table and his large hands clasped around his cup. He, too, was looking at her with shameless lust, his wine-addled thoughts doubtless filled with desire for her. Penelope wondered whether it had been wise to wear such revealing clothing. She looked away, not wishing to further stoke the interests of either man.

'I'll speak with my son in the morning.'

'There's one other obstacle,' Theoclymenus said.

'Obstacle?'

'Before you commit to marrying me, there's something you must be aware of. I can't allow you to make your final choice until you know.'

She felt a stab of nervousness. Was he going to reveal his true identity? It had to be something to do with the strange, inexplicable feeling she had about him. She laid a hand on her chest and gave him a tense smile.

'What is it then? You *are* a spy sent by the suitors, after all?'

He shook his head, and she sensed him smiling beneath the shadow of his hood.

'I'll tell you tonight, after you've spoken with the beggar.'

'No, tell me now.'

Eurymachus banged his cup on the table, spilling the red wine over his hand.

'Listen to me,' he called in a loud voice, stilling the other conversations in the hall and giving pause to Phemius's song. 'We're here to pay suit to the queen, whose beauty is unrivalled across the islands of Ithaca, Samos, Dulichium and Zacynthos. And now that I see you in your full glory, my lady, I demand you put us out of our misery and tell us who your new husband will be. Most of these men have no chance of marrying you and they know it. They're just here to drink your late husband's wine and devour as much of his livestock as they can get their teeth into. But a handful of us are here for the true prize – your hand. And like rampant bulls, we may run wild if we are not harnessed to you soon. Which one of us will you have?'

Voices were raised in agreement and cups banged on tables. Many of those who had no expectations of winning the queen's hand joined in, not wanting to make their lack of ambition obvious. Several more were happy just to observe.

Penelope stood and raised her hands for silence.

'How can I choose between you when you don't act as suitors should? In every other country in Greece, a man who wants to win the woman he desires will bring his own sheep and cattle to slaughter at a banquet in her honour. They bring rich gifts, too, to impress the bride and her family. This is how men of noble blood have always courted the daughters of the rich and powerful. Why, even a lowly shepherd will bring a lamb for sacrifice at the home of another shepherd if he wants that man's daughter for a wife.

'But you! Every night for three years you've acted more like thieves than high-born princes. Odysseus was a man of great wealth – the only son of an only son, inheriting the undivided wealth of two generations of his family, not to mention that which he added himself. But you have whittled down his possessions with your excesses, and offered nothing in return. It seems to me there's no merit in choosing a rich thief over a poor thief, as I have received nothing from any of you.'

She sat down, turned to Theoclymenus and gave him a subtle wink.

'My lady speaks in jest, of course,' Antinous said. 'You wouldn't for a moment think of any but the highest born and richest among us.'

'Why not, Antinous?' she retorted. 'I've received nothing more from you than I have from Leocritus over there. Why shouldn't I choose him?'

Leocritus sat up in surprise, then with a broad smile raised his cup to the queen.

'To our union,' he announced, draining the contents.

There was a smattering of laughter from the other suitors, but it quickly faded away as Antinous rose to his feet.

'We both know you won't do that, Penelope. For one thing, Leocritus's family can't offer you more than an old goat and a moth-eaten cloak that once belonged to his dead mother, whereas I will send for a dozen head of cattle and a dozen more of sheep from my father's estate at once...'

'A dozen of each,' Penelope said in mock awe. 'And I thought Eupeithes was supposed to be wealthy.'

'Two dozen, then, and a dozen pigs, too. And for a gift, I will send for an embroidered robe fixed with a golden brooch, a dress fit for a queen of your beauty.'

He turned aside and whispered to his personal servant, who left at once. Eurymachus now staggered to his feet.

'I pledge you thirty head of cattle, another thirty of sheep, and another thirty of goats, to arrive by tomorrow evening,' he announced. 'And in the morning, I'll bring a golden necklace fitted with amber beads, an heirloom of my family that was made by the greatest craftsmen in Crete.'

Others now stood and pledged livestock and gifts, one after another, while slaves were sent running from the great hall to carry out their master's orders. Penelope acknowledged each vow and promised that she would make her choice at midday, after the gifts had arrived. The marriage would follow at sunset. As Phemius resumed his song and the suitors returned to their feasting, she stood. Bowing briefly to Theoclymenus, she turned and left, followed by her maids.

As she walked in silence to her room, she wondered how the suitors would react to her choice of Theoclymenus, especially after she had tricked them into pledging her livestock and gifts – though it was still only a small recompense for the amount the suitors had taken from her over the years. She hoped Telemachus would agree with her choice of husband, though she doubted he would want to go to Sparta and abandon his home at such a time of uncertainty. And then she began to speculate about the news Theoclymenus wanted to share with her. Would it make her question her choice? Or, as she hoped, would it reinforce it?

She entered her room and signalled for Autonoe and Hippodameia to leave. Sitting on her bed, she felt the coiled rope she had hidden beneath the mattress several days ago. She groped underneath and pulled it out. It was thick and coarse – a poor necklace for a royal neck. She looked up at the hook on the ceiling beam where, until yesterday, she had intended to hang herself from. It had been the only way of avoiding her oath to remarry; the only way to deny Antinous the throne and ensure it went to Telemachus when he came of age. But the gods had spared her. With the arrival of Theoclymenus she had been given another chance.

Standing, she walked to the window and considered tossing the rope out. The voices of slaves in the courtyard below deterred her. Instead, she dropped it in the basket where she put her dirty laundry. She would empty it herself tomorrow and discreetly dispose of the rope. Nobody need ever know what she had been thinking.

Chapter Twenty Two

Odysseus Unmasked

Telemachus fetched his spears from the rack by the entrance to the hall and gave one to his father. They walked past Irus, whose jaw was being reluctantly bathed by one of the serving girls, and out the palace gates to the manure heap. Taking Argus by his legs, they carried him under the shadow of the wall and began digging a hole with the broad-headed spear points. Telemachus could see the lice moving beneath the dog's fur as they lifted his body into the hole and began to fill it.

'He was a faithful dog,' Odysseus said, handing Telemachus his spear. 'If the Ithacan people had shown me the same loyalty, there wouldn't have been any need for bloodshed tomorrow.'

'Perhaps when the suitors learn who you really are they won't put up a fight.'

'Men of honour might respect their rightful king, but we're not dealing with men of honour. They will fight, and so we must change the odds in our favour. Remember what we planned.'

'Father,' Telemachus said, 'I've been thinking about the suggestion you made in Eumaeus's hut – that we should poison the suitors. It may not be honourable, but what choice do we have? I can still trust a handful of the maids…'

'No,' Odysseus said, shaking his head. 'I'm tired of disguises and subterfuge. If I'm to reclaim my homeland, my family *and* my name, then I'll do it openly, facing my enemies.'

'Then at least we'll die with our heads held high.'

'Son, never enter a fight unless you know you've got a fair chance of coming out of it alive. Ever since you and I decided to face the suitors, I've been trying to think of something that will give us the upper hand against them. Then it came to me. There's an old heirloom in the palace storeroom, and it probably hasn't been touched since I sailed for Troy. I need it for tomorrow.'

'What is it?'

Odysseus told him what was on his mind and Telemachus smiled.

'Can you get it to the great hall without arousing the suitors' suspicions?'

Telemachus thought for a moment and nodded. 'There is a way.'

'Good. And what about the messages I asked you to send?'

'They've gone, Father.'

They entered the shadowy great hall, Odysseus returning to his stool and Telemachus sitting next to Theoclymenus. Though the speed and strength Odysseus had displayed in the fight with Irus had faded away to leave him enfeebled and bent with age again, the suitors now eyed him with a grudging respect. Some of the maids still had the gall to laugh at him, while Melantho – annoyed that he had not been killed by Irus – sneered at the old beggar and insulted him. A harsh word from Odysseus sent her running, but before Telemachus could follow up his father's threat, Eurycleia caught her by the arm and ordered her away on an errand.

'You bone-idle old dog,' Eurymachus said, irritated by Odysseus's treatment of his lover. He stood and pointed a finger at the beggar, though his aim swayed drunkenly from left to right. 'What are you still doing here? You should be put to work and earn your crusts building walls or planting trees, but you'd rather be rolling around at a rich man's feet and begging for your food. Folk like you are parasites, living off the goodwill of others, but too lazy to lift a finger for your own good.'

'Says a boy who hasn't done a hard day's work in his whole life,' Odysseus responded. 'I could plough three fields in the time it took you to finish one; or take a sickle to the harvest at dawn and still be there at dusk, long after you'd given up and gone home. You're nothing more than the spoiled offspring of a rich father.'

Eurymachus stood and grabbed a footstool. He hurled it furiously across the great hall, missing Odysseus altogether and knocking a wine steward onto his back. The pitcher he was carrying smashed into pieces and sprayed its contents over the wall and floor. Amphinomus took Eurymachus by the shoulder and pulled him back.

'Stop this! Hasn't the old beggar received enough abuse at our hands today? And yet each time he comes out on top. Forget your anger, Eurymachus, and go home.'

Telemachus stood and held up his arms.

'Gentlemen, it's time we all went to our beds. Tomorrow my mother will choose one of you to be her husband, but what chance will you have if you turn up bleary-eyed and hungover? And when you come, leave your spears and shields at home. We don't want the hall looking like a barrack room during the marriage ceremony. Now, fill your cups and make an offering to the gods before you go.'

The suitors seemed reluctant to obey their host at first, but when Antinous poured a libation to the gods and drained his cup, the rest followed. Slowly they threw their cloaks about their shoulders, retrieved their weapons from the rack by the door and began to leave in twos and threes. Telemachus signalled to Eurycleia, who came shuffling over in response.

'Have a bed made up in the porch for the beggar. I'll escort Theoclymenus back to the storeroom where he slept last night.'

The two men left the hall through the side door and entered the dimly lit passageway, following it round to the room where Theoclymenus's mattress was located.

'Are you still hungry?' Telemachus asked, taking a torch from the passageway and fitting it in a bracket by the door. 'I can have one of the maids bring you something.'

'I've had my fill, thank you. But you and I need to talk. What are your plans for tomorrow? I thought you were going to call an Assembly and announce to the people your father is still alive; but when you spoke to Penelope, you almost dismissed Menelaus's news out of hand.'

Telemachus looked away for a moment while he gathered his thoughts.

'When we swam ashore yesterday, you said the suitors wouldn't care that he's alive and that it might push them to take power anyway. I think you're right. Even if the people believe me, they won't stand against all the noble families combined.'

'Then you've given up?'

'Of course not! I have something else in mind.'

'Is it to do with that old beggar?' Theoclymenus asked.

'Has he spoken to you? What did he say?'

'Nothing much. He wants to meet with me tonight to talk about some proposal he has. Whatever it is, it won't work.'

'But you saw the way he dealt with Irus earlier,' Telemachus said. 'I wouldn't be surprised if he couldn't take on the suitors all by himself.'

Theoclymenus laughed and shook his head.

'I doubt it. I'll listen to him all the same, but I've a feeling something else might happen to save your mother from this folly.'

'We'll see,' Telemachus said. 'Can I still count on your support tomorrow, whatever happens?'

'I'm here for you and your mother, whatever happens.'

–

Odysseus sat alone in the gloom of the great hall. The suitors and their servants had gone to their homes and lodgings. The tables and benches had been set back in their orderly rows and the dirt floor raked. The servants had cleared away the last of the bowls and cups. The hearth had been replenished with wood and stoked up. And a bed had been made for him in the porch.

He looked about at the walls with the faded murals he had once known so well. Gods fought Titans on the north wall and giants on the south, while lapiths battled with centaurs on the west. There were small alcoves in each wall, and though they were filled with shadow, he could see the effigies of the gods they housed. His eyes fell naturally on the crude representation of Athena. Her head was helmeted, and she carried a shield in one hand and a spear in the other, the tip of which had been broken off and not repaired. He said a silent prayer asking for her help in the morning, when his own fate and the fate of Ithaca would be decided.

'And be with me now,' he added aloud. 'Help me to rediscover the love I once had for my wife. I don't know if it's still there, but I want it to be. I *need* it to be if I'm to see this through. She's been like the setting sun to me these past twenty years: alluring and bright, but always on the distant horizon, beyond my grasp. And yet now that she's within reach, I feel doubt – doubt that I can't afford.'

The flames in the circular hearth rose suddenly upwards. Everything in the great hall was lit bright orange and a swarm of sparks flew up to the painted ceiling on a column of smoke. Odysseus felt the heat of it on his skin, even though he was seated by the south wall, and then the fire shrank back down again. He looked at the entrance to see who had let in the rush of fresh air, but the doors were firmly shut.

The goddess had heard his prayer, he thought. But what would the answer be? He felt sick with nerves. At any moment, Penelope would arrive to keep her promised appointment. The deep shadows of the hall reminded him of the Cyclops's cave, but he felt more afraid now than he had then. Polyphemus was an enemy he had the measure of. He had seen his horrid face, witnessed his terrifying brutality, and had known that he had had to defeat the monster or die. But Penelope?

He remembered the other women he had faced, Circe and Calypso, whose dangers had been subtle and cloaked behind feminine allure. They may not have had the violent natures of the Cyclops or the Laestrygonians, but they had caused him the greatest damage, imprisoning him for nine out of the ten years since he had sailed for Troy. What destruction might Penelope cause him? Did she love him? Had she been faithful or, like him, shared the beds of others? He recalled the image the Sirens had put in his mind years before, of his wife satisfying her lust with a group of young men, and try as he might, he could not drive it from his head.

The handle of the side door rattled and three women entered. The first was Eurycleia, his old nurse, whom he had recognised with pleasure as she had bustled about the great hall earlier, giving out orders to the other slaves and chastening the maids for lingering too long with the suitors. The other was one of Penelope's body slaves, who spotted him in the shadows and came towards him. The third – tall, elegant and veiled – walked to one of the high-backed chairs on the royal dais and sat down.

'My lady would like to see you now,' Autonoe said. 'Here, let me help you up. Lean on me if you need to.'

He gave her his hand and she lifted him onto his feet. How he cursed his aged body now, bent and aching with every movement as he approached his wife, reliant on the supporting arm of her maid. Still veiled, Penelope sat on the chair that he had made for her shortly after their wedding. It was inlaid with ivory and silver, the work of Icmalius, the greatest craftsman in the western islands, though little of his handicraft was visible beneath the thick fleece that had been draped across it. Then, as he neared the dais, the queen stood. Dismissing Autonoe with a nod, she took his arm in hers.

'No, my lady,' he said. 'You shouldn't defile your beauty by touching an old beggar like me.'

'Nonsense, sir. The only defilement I fear is an arrogant heart. Here, sit down beside me.'

The sound of her voice was magical, like finding something cherished that had been lost for too long. She helped him into a chair to her right and sat down facing him.

'Eurycleia, you may go to your bed. Autonoe, fetch some hot water to wash our guest's feet.'

'If you please, my lady,' Odysseus said, 'I would rather my feet remained unwashed than have a girl touch them. Youth is repulsed by old age and I wouldn't want to embarrass the child.'

'As you wish. Eurycleia, then,' Penelope suggested, signalling to Autonoe that she could leave. 'She's been in this household for many years, nursing my son *and* his father from when they were babies. There's little she hasn't seen or done in her lifetime, is there, Eurycleia?'

'No, my lady. I'll go heat some water now.'

The old nurse looked Odysseus up and down, gave a nonchalant shrug and followed Autonoe from the room. Odysseus turned his gaze now to Penelope. He could still feel the memory of her warm, soft hands on his wretched arm and smell the subtle aroma of her perfume in his nostrils. Her hair was covered by a white headscarf that left only a few dark locks of hair free. The veil that covered her face was of a thin material, but with her head turned towards him and the fire to her left, the dim orange glow did not penetrate to reveal the features he longed to see and remember again.

'Forgive me,' she said, seeing his lingering look. 'I forget I'm no longer in the presence of those suitors of mine. But I have nothing to fear from a man so long in years as yourself.'

She took the corners of the veil and lifted it over the back of her head. It felt like the sudden springing up of the sun at dawn, and light and colour streamed into the shadowy corners of his mind, restoring things forgotten and reviving memories that had dimmed to grey. Though only half-lit with the orange glow of the fire, her face was as beautiful and intelligent as it had been all those years ago, before the cobwebs of time had concealed it from him. Penelope had stepped into his life again, and he felt in that moment as if twenty years had been but twenty days.

And he knew with wonderful, resurrecting certainty that he had not stopped loving her. That he never would. He wanted to reach out and take her hand, and in that single touch impart to her how he felt. But he could not. All he could do was smile. Smile with love, relief, joy and the knowledge that his ordeal was almost over.

Penelope smiled back, a natural reaction to the warmth that had touched his aged features. He forced his eyes away to the walls, where the murals that before had appeared cold and lifeless now seemed warmer and more active as the firelight flickered across them.

'Forgive me, my lady,' he said. 'It is rare that I set eyes on such beauty.'

'Then you've been deprived of more than just food and warm beds, my friend. What you see now is only a remnant of the looks I had in my youth, when my husband was by my side and Telemachus was a babe in arms.

What beauty I had then has been ravaged by lonely grief since Odysseus sailed away to Troy.'

'If I look only on the shadow of what you were, then your husband was a fortunate man indeed. That is his throne, I assume.'

Odysseus nodded to the empty chair next to Penelope.

'It was,' she said. 'But tomorrow it will be claimed by another, though none could ever be as worthy of it as he was.'

A moth danced high over the flames, distracting them for a moment.

'Then do you still miss him?'

'After twenty years I've grown used to life without him. I can't really remember what he looked like now, or what his mannerisms and habits were. There are incidents I recall,' she said with a smile, making Odysseus wonder what those moments were that she still cherished after so long. 'Silly, trivial things more than anything. But he no longer haunts this place like he used to, those first few years apart.'

'And would you still love him, if he returned?'

The smile left her lips and she straightened up a little.

'I'm sorry, my lady,' he said, realising his mistake. 'I presume too much. It's… it's just I was thinking of my own wife who died many years ago. I was so fond of her. We were in love, you know, just as I can see you were.'

The queen relaxed again, believing his impertinence had just been the tenderness of an old man's heart.

'Then you've been blessed by the gods, sir, if you ever loved your wife as much as I loved Odysseus. But if he returned? I… I don't know the answer to that. Which reminds me of why I asked to speak to you in private. First, to give you my apologies for the treatment you received from my suitors.'

'They don't conduct themselves like suitors.'

'More like animals, I know. Did they hurt you?'

Odysseus gave a dismissive laugh.

'After all I've gone through in life, there's little they can do to increase the burden of my suffering. And I think I gave better than I got. Though I'm saddened by what I had to do to the giant.'

'Poor Irus,' Penelope sighed. 'I heard Antinous used Melantho to rouse his temper. She's his weak spot. In other circumstances, you'd have found him as gentle as a lamb. And yet you did well to survive his fury.'

'I'm a fighter, my lady, and not easily beaten – even in my old age.'

'And that's the other reason I wanted to talk with you: to ask where you come from and what brings you to Ithaca. And whether there is any truth in what Eumaeus told me – that you bring tidings of my husband.'

Odysseus repeated the story he had told to Eumaeus, from the old beggar's beginnings on Crete to the misadventures that led him to Thesprotia. Against his nature, he avoided prolonging his tale with embellishments and came quickly to the point where he became a guest of King Pheidon.

'It was he who told me about your husband. I'd seen Odysseus many times during the siege of Troy, but knew nothing of his fate after the war had ended. King Pheidon informed me that his voyage home had been a series of terrible encounters, in which he had escaped death and imprisonment many times, but had lost all his ships and every one of his comrades on the way.

'The king heard the story from Odysseus himself, whom the gods had led to Thesprotia only a few days before my own arrival. He assured me that Odysseus was planning to return to Ithaca – and that a Thesprotian ship was waiting to bring him here – but he had first set off to consult the oracle at Dodona to know whether he should come back openly or in disguise. As for myself, I was in a hurry to reach Dulichium, and took a ship that was sailing the next morning. But the crew proved treacherous and meant to sell me into slavery. By the will of the gods I escaped their clutches and ended up here, just as you see me.'

'You have my sympathy, friend,' Penelope said. 'Whatever help I can give you, I will. You only need to ask.'

'Thank you, my lady. But does my news please you? Your husband is coming back to Ithaca, I swear it before all the gods. And yet you seem uncertain about his return – about whether you could still love him if he did.'

She gave him a questioning look.

'I can't work out whether you are filled with compassion or effrontery, my friend. But I will tolerate it because I think your words are well meant. As for whether Odysseus is coming back, as you say, I've been told that too many times over the years to believe such rumours. And though you seem honest, you only *heard* Odysseus was in Thesprotia – you didn't see him with your own eyes. You could have been misled. But these are strange times, and you aren't the only visitor to have stirred me lately. For the first time in many years, I'm almost able to believe Odysseus *is* coming back. It's just that I'll be another man's wife by the time he does. Fate is cruel, is it not?

'Even if he did come back – if he were to step out of the shadows now – could I love him? Your question is like an echo of my own thoughts. I *should* love him. He would still be my husband, after all, and he hasn't done me any wrong – not of his own volition. And I *did* love him, all those years ago. But it's been so long. I can only remember what he looks like because I see his ghost in the face of Telemachus. We would be strangers now, so little in common any more. I mean, he's travelled to the ends of the world and been through a great war; and the gods only know what he has suffered since. What have I done? Sat at home, trying to keep his kingdom intact and his nobles divided. Watching the horizons for a dolphin sail. Crying a lot. We wouldn't know each other any more, let alone love each other.'

Odysseus wanted to tell her she was wrong, that none of any of that mattered. That they could start again. But perhaps that was just what *he* felt and wanted. Perhaps she thought differently. Perhaps she was listing the reasons why she did not want him to come back. And now that he was back, it was too late.

Penelope had paused to gather her thoughts, her eyes following the movements of the moth as it hovered over the flames, drawn irresistibly by the light and repelled in equal measure by the heat.

'But I would try,' she resumed. 'I would try to love him. I've never had another lover, and I don't want one. If he came back, I would want to make our marriage work again. Whatever he might think of me, however dull he might find me now, whoever else might have stolen his heart from me, I would do what I could to win him back. Even if he had stopped loving me, or I found I had stopped loving him, I would fight to restore what we had. Yes, that's what I would do. What else could I do?'

Odysseus fought back the tears that threatened to betray him.

'Spoken like a true queen,' he said.

The door swung open and Eurycleia backed into the room carrying a large tub. A towel was hung over her shoulder, and she was followed by two maids carrying bowls of steaming water.

'Shall I wash this man's feet now, my lady?'

'Yes, Eurycleia. Bring the basin here. Has a bed been prepared?'

'Telemachus ordered one made up in the porch. The maids prepared it earlier, with a mattress and furs fit for an honoured guest.'

'You shouldn't have troubled yourselves,' Odysseus said. 'I've become used to sleeping under the stars with nothing but hard earth or stone for a bed; I don't think a mattress of straw and furs to match will quite suit me any more.'

'Nonsense, my friend. That's how you shall be treated from now on – with the honour befitting your noble character,' Penelope said. 'But if you find a little luxury too uncomfortable, then the porch has a flagstoned floor,' she added with a smile.

Eurycleia set down the tub on the other side of the hearth and pulled up a chair. Ordering the maids to fill the tub and check the temperature, she came over to where Odysseus was sitting and offered him her hand.

'Will you come with me, sir?'

There was a hint of reluctance in the 'sir' and not a little coldness in her expression, but Odysseus took her hand and pulled himself to his feet. When he was seated again on the opposite side of the fire, Eurycleia dipped her elbow in the water, nodded to herself and dismissed the maids. She dragged the large tub next to his chair, then placed her hands behind his calves and lifted his feet into the water.

'I hope, sir, you haven't been misleading the queen about her husband,' she said in a low voice. 'Many beggars have come and gone with stories of Odysseus's imminent return, all of them untrue.'

'Old woman, I've said and done nothing to hurt your mistress's feelings. But why are you so doubtful the king will come back? I've heard there was an oracle that Odysseus would leave Ithaca and return after twenty years. And this is the twentieth year since he sailed for Troy. The gods reward the faithful, you know.'

'There've been none more faithful than I, old man,' she replied, soaking a sponge in the water and scrubbing the dirt from the soles of his feet. 'I've served this house since before the king was born – fifty years, more or less – and my loyalties to Laertes, Odysseus and young Telemachus have never swerved. Which is more than can be said for most of the younger generation of slaves in this household.'

She hitched Odysseus's rags above his knees and folded the hem back to the tops of his thighs.

'As for the king coming back twenty years after he sailed for Troy, I've heard nothing of that,' Eurycleia continued. She paused and looked through the flames at Penelope, who was gazing into her own lap. Her voice fell to a whisper. 'Though the queen did send men to Parnassus some years back to enquire about her husband's homecoming. It's said the Pythoness predicted he'd come back by tomorrow, or not at all. Personally, I...'

Eurycleia had lifted his foot and was sponging down his lower leg when something made her stop. She let the sponge slip back into the water and reached up to touch his right knee. Odysseus looked down with horror at the pink scar he had been given by a boar's tusk when he was just a boy. The old nurse's fingers were tracing its crooked course from the top of his knee to the middle of his thigh. Slowly, she raised her wrinkled face and looked into his eyes.

'*Master*?'

Her voice was barely a croak. Reluctantly, he gave a subtle nod of his head.

She sat back on her heels and released his foot, which fell back into the bowl and sent water splashing over the floor. With her eyes wide, Eurycleia looked across at Penelope – still lost in her own thoughts – and opened her mouth to speak.

Odysseus's hand shot out and covered her lips, stifling the words that were forming on them.

'*Silence*! If you're as loyal to me as you boasted you are, then you'll not give me up – not even to my wife. Not yet. Not until I've claimed back my throne. Now, can I trust you?'

Eurycleia nodded. He removed his hand from her mouth and she looked at him. There were tears in her eyes.

'Then the oracle was right. You've come home at last, my child.'

She threw her arms around his legs and kissed his knees.

'Eurycleia, my dear, beloved old nurse,' he whispered, urgently, 'keep your affections until I am back on my throne. If I am to reclaim my kingdom and frustrate the ambitions of the suitors, then we can't afford to let them suspect I'm back – not until the time of my choosing. Do you understand? If Penelope knows I've returned and acts any differently towards me, Antinous and the others will realise who I am and try to murder me before I'm ready to face them. Now, take up the sponge and finish washing my feet.'

'Yes, my lord,' she said, half-smiling, half-sobbing with joy.

No sooner had she finished sponging off the last of the dirt from his feet and lower legs than Penelope rose from her chair.

'It's getting late and tomorrow will be a long and trying day. Goodnight, my friend,' she said to the old beggar, 'and thank you for helping me to clarify my thoughts. Eurycleia, have you finished?'

The nurse nodded and, picking up her tub, followed the queen out of the hall. She shot a final glance at Odysseus and closed the door behind her, leaving him alone once more. He thought for a while about Penelope, relieved and happy that he still loved her after all this time. Then he looked at the scenes of battle painted on the walls and remembered that much blood would have to be spilled before they could be reunited again. The matter would be decided tomorrow, for good or bad. Despite his bravado in front of Telemachus and the plans they had made to defeat the suitors, he knew the odds of victory were almost zero. He had been in too many desperate fights to think otherwise. In all likelihood, he, Telemachus and anyone who had the courage to join them would be overwhelmed and butchered.

But there was another factor to be taken into account. At the time of Odysseus's greatest need, the gods had brought Eperitus back to Ithaca. With his old comrade at his side, the prospects of victory were less bleak. All he had to do was persuade him to fight.

Chapter Twenty Three

Odysseus and Eperitus

Eperitus lay on his bed and listened to the sounds in the palace. It was not long after Telemachus left him that the hubbub of the suitors' voices died away, followed a little later by the shifting of tables and the clattering of dishes as the slaves cleared up their mess. After that he heard nothing but the occasional passing of footsteps in the corridors outside, the voices of slaves amplified by the narrow space of the passageways, and the constant hiss of the torch in his room as it slowly burned itself out. When darkness eventually fell and everything in the palace had succumbed to stillness, he waited. Then, when he judged he had given enough time for the meeting between the beggar and the queen to have finished, he removed the warm fur that covered him and stood.

The passageway outside was dark, and the air chilly. With his fingers running along the wall to his right, he retraced his route back to the great hall. A faint orange glow flickered beneath the door and he could hear the low crackle of the hearth within, but there were no voices. Pushing the door open, he glanced at the fire and then around at the deep shadows about the walls. He was alone. Taking a fresh torch from its iron bracket, he lit it in the fire and walked to the main doors that led to the porch.

He had thought much about the strange beggar as he had lain on his bed. The old man had a strange familiarity that unsettled him. He did not seem as old as he looked, though Eperitus did not think he was a god in disguise. He had encountered Olympians masquerading as humans before, and the beggar did not have the same feel about him. Despite his impressive defeat of Irus, he still had an air of mortal vulnerability. And then there was the chelonion in his belt. The little white flower was a badge of pride for Ithacans during the siege of Troy, a reminder of their homeland. But what significance could it hold for a Cretan? And why was the beggar so keen to help Penelope? Nothing seemed quite right.

He had considered not keeping his rendezvous. After all, he had his own ideas for saving Penelope from the suitors. But he could not afford for the stranger's plans – if indeed he had any – to interfere with his own. He had to know what he was intending to do. The thought occurred to him that the old beggar's strategy might be better than his own hurriedly conceived idea. And if it made more sense than simply marrying the queen and hoping the suitors would go away, what then?

But something inside him had grown quickly used to the idea of having Penelope as his wife. To his mind, she was as beautiful as she was when the fleet had sailed to Troy all those years ago. The lightness in her spirit had been stifled, it was true, but that would return when the suitors were gone. And unlike Odysseus, her sharp intelligence was balanced by a powerful integrity. That was one of the qualities he had liked about her since the first moment he had met her. And he knew she had always liked him. She even seemed to warm to him in his current guise. Would that not deepen once she discovered his true identity? Could they not then learn to love each other? So, no, he would not encourage the beggar in his plans. Rather, he intended to discourage him.

He pulled open one of the doors and stepped onto the porch. The light from his torch spilled over the cypress columns and ashwood floor, where the old man was sitting on the mattress the servants had prepared for him. His arms were wrapped around his shins and he was staring at the gate in the outer wall. The sky was clear and the thin moon shone on the plastered walls, giving them a grey hue in the darkness.

The beggar turned and looked at him.

'You don't need your torch. There's a bracket inside the door, above the weapons rack. Then will you come and join me?'

Eperitus placed the torch in the bracket and closed the door behind him. He sat on the step next to the beggar.

'You intrigue me,' Eperitus began. 'Most of the beggars I've come across were lowly men, some of them scoundrels, and none with a single thought beyond their next meal. Yet when you fought Irus, you showed a cooler mind and better skill than some of the best warriors I saw at Troy. You were merciful, too – something the queen's suitors will never understand. There's a lot more to you than I can read.'

'The same could be said of you, my friend,' the beggar replied. 'It mystifies me that a fighting man should willingly take an oath not to kill. To go from having the power of life and death over others, to being suddenly impotent…'

Eperitus held up his hand.

'I hear voices.'

The beggar cocked an ear, then shook his head.

'I don't hear anything.'

Eperitus turned his head to the left, where a few moments later a side door in the palace wall opened and several maids stepped out into the courtyard. They spoke in low voices, interspersed with giggles as they walked towards the outer gate. He recognised one of them as Melantho.

'Ugh, it's that filthy beggar,' one of them exclaimed as they noticed the two men sitting in the porch.

'Mind your tongue, girl,' Eperitus warned her, 'or I'll tell Telemachus and he can cut you into a hundred pieces as a warning to the rest of you.'

The girl fell silent and hurried ahead of her friends to open the gate.

'And where are you all off to, leaving your warm beds so late in the night?' the beggar asked. 'To visit your lovers among the suitors? What will the queen think of that?'

'Be quiet, you silly old fool,' one of them called over her shoulder as she passed through the gate.

The others giggled at her nerve as they left the courtyard. But Eperitus noticed the figure of Melantho slipping back inside the door to the palace, sparing a last glance at the two men as she disappeared.

'I'm sorry they offended you, friend,' he said. 'This sort of moral decay is to be expected when the king is absent for so long.'

'Odysseus can hardly be blamed for that, can he?' the beggar replied. 'Unless you're suggesting he shouldn't have sailed for Troy in the first place?'

'He was honour-bound to do so. And even a man of his intelligence couldn't have foreseen the war lasting so long. But tomorrow there'll be a new king to restore order to Ithaca. Unless, of course, there's any substance to this plan of yours to save the queen from her folly?'

Eperitus faced the beggar, but the old man did not meet his gaze. Instead he raised his finger to his lips and pointed at the windows in the wall above the portico.

'You don't take me seriously then, friend?' he asked in a low voice.

'These suitors aren't like Irus. He has the brains of a child and he fought you alone. *They* are determined and ambitious men, and there are a hundred and eighteen of them. What can an ageing beggar do against such odds?'

'An ageing beggar? Nothing. Nothing at all. But I tell you now, tomorrow morning Odysseus will return to Ithaca, to his own palace, and he will call to himself all those who are loyal to his cause. If you are the friend to Telemachus that you claimed to be, will you put aside your oath and raise your sword alongside his?'

'Odysseus is dead,' Eperitus said. 'He's *dead*. Whatever rumours you may have heard, whatever lies people have deceived you with, they're false. Why don't you forget this phantom you're chasing?'

'Because it's not a phantom. Odysseus is alive.'

'No, he's not! He's not coming back because… because I witnessed his death with my own eyes.'

Something about the beggar's obstinate faith in Odysseus's return irked him. Let him live in his fantasy and see for himself that the king was not returning – tomorrow or ever. And if that was what his plan depended on, then the old fool would still be waiting for Odysseus when Penelope chose *him* to be her new husband.

He stood and moved towards the doors of the great hall. The beggar reached up and took hold of his wrist. His grip was surprisingly strong.

'Stay a little longer, friend.'

'We have nothing more to discuss.'

'You're wrong, Eperitus. We have much to talk about.'

Eperitus froze.

'My name is Theoclymenus.'

'Did you think I wouldn't recognise you, even with that eyepatch?'

Eperitus backed against one of the columns. He looked hard at the beggar now. What was it that was so familiar about the old man?

'Who are you? How do you know me?'

'Don't you know *me* yet, Eperitus? Look here.'

The beggar's hand was shaking as he reached down and lifted his tunic to his thigh. Eperitus looked at the wrinkled brown skin and the protruding kneecap. And then he saw it. A line in the flesh – white in the faint moonlight – curving slightly as it reached from the knee to the middle of the thigh. It was a scar. A scar he knew well.

'*Odysseus*?' he whispered.

His flesh slowly turned cold. It was not possible. Odysseus had drowned, sucked down into the depths of the ocean after Zeus had destroyed their galley with his thunderbolt. Nobody could have survived that terrible storm.

Except that he had. And Omeros, who had been picked up by the Phaeacians the following morning. And Eurylochus, who had dragged himself up onto Eperitus's piece of wreckage, and would have survived – if Eperitus had not murdered him.

'Yes, it's me.'

'I don't believe you. You don't look anything like Odysseus.'

'Athena gave me this disguise. She won't remove it until I've killed the first of the suitors.'

'Athena rejected Odysseus after he took...'

'After I took the Palladium. But I've served my penance for that, and now she's forgiven me.'

Eperitus seized him by the ragged remnants of his tunic.

'Where did we first see the goddess? If you're really Odysseus, you'll know.'

'By the sacred pool at Parnassus,' the beggar answered, looking him in the eye. 'She was disguised as Elatos, high priest of Gaea, before she transformed herself – a sight no mortal could ever forget.'

Eperitus recalled the priest's metamorphosis into the goddess, and how terrified he had been. And he remembered the words Athena had spoken to him, commanding him to be loyal to Odysseus and to follow him to the ends of the earth, if need be.

'We saw her a second time outside her own temple at Messene, after we'd killed the great serpent,' Odysseus added, to be sure.

'When she took the form of a shepherd, yes,' Eperitus said, as if to himself. He released his hold on Odysseus and fell to his knees before him. 'It really *is* you, isn't it!'

A surge of emotions cascaded through him, swelling every fibre of his body with a mixture of elation, disbelief and joy. For a moment, he did not know what to say or do. He saw the smile spread over the old beggar's face, and though he looked nothing like Odysseus, Eperitus knew it was him. The scar and the memories of Athena were evidence enough. But it was only as he looked into his green eyes that he finally knew. They were a little wiser, perhaps, and had lost some of their rashness; but beyond a doubt, they were Odysseus's. And as Eperitus looked at his old friend's face, he felt as if a part of himself had come back. As if he was finally waking from a long sleep.

Then he remembered Thrinacie. The island of the sun god, where against Eperitus's advice, Odysseus had weighed anchor. Where they had become storm-bound by the vengeful Poseidon. It was there that Astynome had been raped by Eurylochus, resulting in the death of their unborn child. She had died a short while later.

Eperitus lowered his gaze.

'How did you survive?'

'I clung on to the broken mast until I reached Ogygia, where I was held prisoner by the nymph Calypso for the next seven years.'

'Then what Menelaus heard was true.'

'Eventually the gods ordered Calypso to release me and I made my way to Phaeacia, and then here.'

'Home at last,' Eperitus said, 'and just as the Pythoness had predicted.'

'Yes, back from the dead with nothing but the rags on my back. But I hope she was wrong in one respect, Eperitus. I hope I'm not entirely friendless.'

'My wife and child would be alive today if you'd listened to me. Instead, you gave in to the demands of your crew. You knew the dangers of Thrinacie, but you harboured there anyway.'

'And I'll regret that for the rest of my life. If I'd been just a little stronger we might have made it to Phaeacia and safety. But I wasn't, and I'm sorry. I'm so sorry that my decision led to the death of everything you loved. For my own part, I lost another seven years of my life, and it seems I'm too late now to save my family. I also ruined the greatest friendship I ever had. But I hope you will forgive me. No, I *beg* you to forgive me. What I did, I did out of weakness and stupidity, never malice.'

Eperitus said nothing. Another thought had occurred to him: Penelope. The fleeting dream he had entertained of marrying her was crumbling before his eyes. With Odysseus back, there was no question now that she would accept a new husband. She would welcome Odysseus with open arms and forget her agreement with Theoclymenus; and he, Eperitus, would become an exile again, without home or family to provide the anchor his empty life so needed.

Why then had the gods brought him back to Ithaca? To mock him? Or to challenge him? All he had to do was put aside his oath not to kill, forget the years of friendship and loyalty and dash Odysseus's brains out against the hard floor. Nobody would care much for an old vagrant, and if suspicion fell anywhere, it would be upon the suitors he had so discomfited – or maybe Irus, the man he had humiliated before so many witnesses in the great hall. And Eperitus would have his vengeance at last. He could put to rest the ghosts of Astynome and their child, who had been so cruelly torn from him by Odysseus's feeble choices. The gods had given him the chance to release his years of anger and bitterness and find a new happiness with Penelope. It would all be so easy.

But as he looked at Odysseus there was no fury left. His rage at the past had gone, leaving only emptiness. An emptiness that could not be filled by revenge. As for Penelope, had he forgotten the oracle the Pythoness had given to him? As if speaking out of the depths of time, he heard her voice in the back of his head. *Ares's sword has forged a bond that will lead to Olympus. But the hero should beware love, for if she clouds his desires he will fall into the Abyss.* The priestess had given him a choice: friendship with Odysseus that would earn him undying glory, or a love that would lead to obscurity. Even if Penelope was that love, he would not take her at the price of Odysseus's life.

'Can we can be friends again, Eperitus?' Odysseus asked. 'Can we heal this division between us? It's haunted our lives for too long. When I recognised you in the hall today, for a moment I forgot that we had ever argued. I was so happy to see you, to know you were still alive; it felt like part of me had been restored. And I know you felt the same when you recognised me a few moments ago, before you remembered everything else. But you're greater than that, my friend. I know you are. Your pride is strong, and your honour is stronger still. But you aren't above forgiveness. Are you?'

He offered his hand. Eperitus looked down at it, a bridge of flesh and bone leading to restoration and healing.

'You asked me if I was ready to raise my sword in Telemachus's cause – your cause, as it is now,' he said. 'Well, I haven't forgotten the loyalty I swore to you, Odysseus, before Athena herself. Or the bonds of friendship that we forged in countless battles; a friendship that overcame every obstacle put before us. But those things aren't enough any more. I've changed. I threw my sword away when I took an oath never to kill again. And I haven't forgotten my grief for Astynome and my child. I can see the mound I made for their bodies, as clearly as if it was before my eyes now. *You* caused that, Odysseus. I may not hate you for it any more, but I can't forgive it.'

Odysseus's outstretched hand lingered a while longer, then fell and was withdrawn.

'Telemachus and I will fight the suitors tomorrow,' he said. 'We have no choice in that. With your help, there's a chance we might win. Without you we are certain to fail. If my poor judgement led to the death of your family, will the destruction of *my* family make that right? Even if you can't bring yourself to forgive me, Eperitus – if you're willing to see me die – can you stand by and watch Telemachus cut down and butchered, too? Will you allow Penelope to marry one of the suitors and fall into a life of misery? What have *they* done to earn such a doom? Think of the man you were: powerful, honourable, kinder and more honest than any other man I've ever known. Will you sacrifice that on the altar of your own *bitterness*? Or will you stay and be healed from the past?'

Eperitus knew he sat on a knife's edge between redemption and destruction. In his heart he felt the desire to forgive; the desperate yearning to turn his back once and for all on the past, to cleanse his soul of it and be whole again. As he looked at Odysseus he saw once more the friend with whom he had enjoyed and endured so much. But he also saw the man who had taken Astynome from him and was about to take Penelope, too. The bitter gall of his misery returned, insisting that to forgive was to insult the memory of the wife he had loved and the child he had not been given the chance to love. He stood.

'I'm happy you're still alive, Odysseus. Really, I am. But some things are beyond forgiveness. I can't fight for the man who took away my family, so I'm leaving in the morning and I'm never coming back.'

'You won't fight because you think there's no honour any more in killing; and you won't forgive because your sense of honour won't allow it. But if you run away tomorrow it will be the most dishonourable thing you've ever done, and for you that'll mean a life of misery and regret. Don't you understand yet, Eperitus? Have the terrible things that have happened in your life taught you nothing? Well, this is what I've learned: that the only things worth having in this world are bought with self-sacrifice. I refused to risk the voyage to Phaeacia and chose the false safety of Thrinacie, and it cost me seven years of my life and the greatest friendship I will ever know. You, Eperitus, must sacrifice your honour in order to regain it – exchange the falsehood you've fallen into for the truth you once knew. It's your only hope.'

Eperitus bowed his head. Odysseus's words cut to his very soul. But his soul had become seeped in darkness and would not listen.

'May the gods protect you, Odysseus,' he said. 'May they restore order to your home and repay you for the years that they stole from you. Goodbye, old friend.'

He walked through the door into the great hall. The orange glow of the hearth throbbed at the centre of the room, its flames a blur through the tears that filled his eyes.

-

Melantho was suspicious. The one-eyed stranger and that loathsome old tramp had no business whispering together in the porch after dark, so while the other maids distracted the two men, she slipped back through the side door and left it slightly ajar. Eurymachus's passions would have to wait a while longer – if he had not already expended himself on one of his father's slaves. With her back against the wall of the unlit passageway, she edged as close as she could to the gap in the door and concentrated on the two voices.

At first she could make out very little of what they were saying. She was too nervous about being caught, as well as excited at her good luck at being able to listen in on their conversation. She was curious for her own sake, of course; but Antinous had also told her to keep a watch on the stranger and the beggar, both of whom he distrusted. After a few moments, her pounding heart and stuttering breaths calmed down and she began to catch snatches of the whispered conversation between the two men. They were talking about someone, but she could not tell who. Then she heard mention of a plan and guessed they were hatching some mischief against the suitors. Her mind was distracted with thoughts of the reward she could extract from Antinous in exchange for her information. A new brooch. A dress of the finest wool.

'Odysseus is alive.'

The hissed words came distinctly to her across the courtyard. Images of brooches and dresses fell away and she turned and pressed her eye to the gap in the door. The one-eyed stranger was on his feet now and the beggar had seized hold of his wrist. Something was said that seemed to shock the stranger.

'How do you know me?' she heard.

Then the beggar called him by a name – Eperitus. But that was not the name the stranger had given to Telemachus and Penelope. Melantho rubbed her forehead a moment, then it came to her. Theoclymenus, that was it. Or *not*, it seemed.

The stranger – Eperitus – hissed something under his breath. Melantho did not catch it, but she saw that his face had turned pale and his single eye was opened wide. Melantho turned her head again so that she was looking into the darkness of the passageway behind her, but her ear was against the slight opening in the door.

'Athena gave me this disguise,' she heard the beggar say.

More mumbled words followed, then she heard the stranger say: 'Where did we first see the goddess? If you're really Odysseus, you'll know.'

Melantho's eyes widened and she pressed her hand to her mouth to stifle her sudden drawing of breath. Closing her eyes to focus entirely on her sense of hearing, she moved her ear as close to the gap as she could without nudging the door open any wider.

'How did you survive?' asked the stranger, Eperitus.

'I clung on to the broken mast until I reached Ogygia,' she heard the beggar say, 'where I was held prisoner by the nymph Calypso for the next seven years.'

It is *him*, she thought. *The beggar is Odysseus. The king has come back!*

She backed away from the door, her head reeling. It seemed impossible, but she knew it was true. In her heart, she had always known he would return. Then it struck her. Why had he come in disguise instead of openly, unless he knew about the suitors and had come to appraise their strength? That could only mean he intended to retake his throne by force and bloodshed. Melantho felt the panic rising up from the pit of her stomach.

'Think! Think!' she whispered to herself. 'Think straight, for once in your wretched, stupid life!'

What had he said? Something about clinging to a broken mast. Then he had been shipwrecked. Which meant he was probably alone. Was that why he was talking to the stranger, to recruit his help? Who else had he approached? Surely not many, Melantho thought, or he would risk someone telling the suitors who he was. And time was of the essence if he was to act before Penelope chose a new husband.

'So, he's lost his army, he's practically alone and he needs to defeat the suitors before tomorrow evening,' she told herself in a hushed voice. 'He doesn't stand a chance.'

The thought pleased her, but only briefly. She remembered the stories she had heard about the king as a young girl. That he was brave and an excellent fighter, but that above all he was clever and resourceful. Cunning, even. Was he not the one who had thought up the Wooden Horse as a way to deceive the Trojans? Then he would not rely on brute force alone, she thought. He had to have prepared some trick to give him the advantage against the suitors. What it was she could not guess. All she knew was she had to tell Antinous immediately. If the suitors were prepared, they could kill the beggar – the *king* – before he could act against them.

She returned to the gap in the door and peered through. The two men seemed to be arguing.

'But you aren't beyond forgiveness,' she heard Odysseus say in a pleading tone.

Melantho no longer had the patience to listen to any more of the conversation. She had to go to the servants' quarters and climb out the window, before running all the way to Antinous's father's house.

Then she heard a sound behind her. She turned and squinted into the darkness.

'Who's there?' she whispered.

There was no reply. Quickly, she hitched up her dress and – with a guiding hand against the wall – moved along the passageway. Suddenly she sensed a presence blocking her way.

'What are you doing, Melantho?'

A face emerged from the blackness. It was Autonoe.

'Nothing. I'm going back to bed.'

'What did you hear?'

'Hear? I don't know what you mean?'

'You were eavesdropping on the beggar and Theoclymenus. What did you hear them say?'

Melantho felt her anger rising.

'Who are you to make demands of me?' she hissed. 'I don't answer to *you*!'

Autonoe moved closer, her usually pleasant face suddenly stern.

'All I need do is shout and they'll be here in an instant,' she threatened. 'Are you going to tell me what you heard or shall I call to them?'

'Don't do that!' Melantho whispered, raising her hands for calm. 'But if I tell you, you can't let anyone else know. Swear it.'

'I already know everything. He needed an ally among the servants, someone to keep an eye on everyone, so he took me into his confidence as soon as he arrived.'

Melantho felt the panic rising again, like a deer with a pack of hunting hounds closing a ring around her.

'Tell me what you heard!' Autonoe insisted.

'I heard the old man say he is... he is Odysseus. That he was shipwrecked and kept prisoner for many years, but now he's back, disguised as a beggar by Athena. He seems to know the stranger, whose name isn't really Theoclymenus, but Eperitus. Wait... I recognise the name now. Wasn't Eperitus the captain of the royal guard? I've heard of him in the songs Phemius sings.'

Autonoe nodded mutely and Melantho carried on.

'Anyway, I think they're alone and they're planning to do something. I think they want to kill the suitors.'

Autonoe's anger had disappeared. Her expression was withdrawn, almost blank.

'Will you tell *them*?' she asked, quietly. 'Will you tell Antinous and Eurymachus he's returned?'

'N...no,' Melantho said. 'Of course not. I want the king back. He can kill every one of the suitors for all I care. It's not like they haven't deserved it. You'll tell him that, won't you, Autonoe? You'll tell him I wanted him back and the suitors dead, won't you?'

Autonoe nodded and reached up to take an unlit torch from its bracket.

'Go to bed now, Melantho. We'll talk about this in the morning.'

'Certainly. I'm so exhausted I'm sure I'll fall straight asleep. Thank you, Autonoe.'

Placing her hand against the wall again, she walked slowly towards the servants' quarters. And as soon as she was rid of Penelope's maid, she would slip out and tell Antinous all about Odysseus and his plans.

Book Four

Chapter Twenty Four

Morning Prelude

Telemachus woke to a sense of dawn. He opened his eyes to a grey half-light filtering through the window of his room. The air was chilly as he threw back his furs, forcing him to dress quickly. Crossing to the window, he pushed the curtain aside to look out at a ceiling of broken, rain-filled clouds and a blood-red sky in the east. An early shower had left puddles in the courtyard below. Several maids exited the great hall, oblivious to their master's presence above them as they carried clay jars out of the gate, heading for the spring at the edge of the town. A lone slave girl was hurrying across the empty space before the palace walls and roused a chorus of mocking laughter from her friends. Doubtless she had slept too long in her lover's arms and was busily contemplating the scolding she would receive from Eurycleia. There was neither sight nor sound of the suitors.

Telemachus returned to sit on his bed and tie on his sandals. As the sleep cleared from his mind, his thoughts began to race through the day ahead. The morning before he had been filled with excitement at the thought that his father would unveil himself and reclaim his throne, but now that the day had arrived, his desire for vengeance had dulled. Indeed, a mist seemed to have consumed all his dreams and aspirations, and he felt nauseous at the thought of what lay before him.

Odysseus had refused to be cowed by the odds against them and together they had finalised their plans for defeating the suitors. But Telemachus sensed he was putting on a brave face. As a seasoned warrior, he must have known that any attempt to destroy the suitors would be futile. He thought back to the only combat he had ever experienced, on the road to Sparta. He had not admitted it to Theoclymenus, but when the group of bandits had surrounded them he had been terrified. He felt the beginnings of that terror now. The knowledge that at some point he and his father, and possibly one or two others, would be fighting for their lives against a numerous and determined enemy made him sick with anxiety.

It was some consolation to know he would be shoulder to shoulder with his father, the best warrior on the whole island; and it helped to remember how his nervousness had left him the moment the skirmish with the bandits had started. But it did not give him greater courage or shore up his confidence. More than any other emotion, he felt sadness. Sadness that by midday he and his father would be dead. That they would never really know each other. He would never be able to sit at his father's side and listen to his tales of Troy and the voyage home. He would never see his parents together, or find a wife of his own to give them grandchildren. For a moment he thought of Polycaste and his promise to her that he would not return until he had resolved the difficulties he faced on Ithaca. It seemed now that he would never see her again.

But his spirit could at least go to Hades knowing he had died fighting, and that he had taken some of the detested suitors with him. If he could just bury his spear in Antinous's chest and see the light go out in his eyes, that would be satisfaction enough. But his fate was in the laps of the gods and there was no point in dwelling on what might happen. He had work to do. He must speak with his mother and suggest a test for the suitors that would determine who her future husband was to be.

Rising from the bed, he threw his cloak about his shoulders, took his spear from the corner of the room and opened the door.

-

Eurycleia entered the great hall and looked about herself. At the sight of her, the sleepy maids forced themselves out of their stupors and made a show of carrying out their chores.

'Come on, girls, make some effort. This is going to be a big day! The biggest most of you have ever seen. Your queen will be united with her husband and the throne will have a king on it for the first time in many years.' She fought back the smile that wanted to spring to her lips. 'Now, rake those floors and sprinkle them. Sponge these tables thoroughly and bring bowls and cups from the kitchens. Has anyone seen Thoosa or Melantho? You men, Telemachus wants all these spears and shields taking off the walls and back to the armoury. They're a disgrace, so blackened with smoke and mould. And you girls – what are you hanging around for? Didn't I tell you to get those jars filled with water? Hurry up, now. Once those suitors start arriving it's going to be chaotic in here.'

She watched the girls hoist the clay vessels onto their shoulders and file rapidly out of the hall, encouraging or cajoling each other to be quicker. After their voices had faded away, another maid entered, trying to slip discreetly into the shadows at the back of the chamber and join the maids sponging down the tables.

'Thoosa!' Eurycleia called.

The maid hurried over.

'Sorry, Eurycleia. I… I was working so late last night that…'

'You mean you were with that rogue, Agelaus. Who owns you, Thoosa? Whose household do you serve?'

'My master is Telemachus. I serve his household.'

'Then why were you sleeping with one of the queen's suitors?'

Thoosa decided that silence was her best hope and looked down at her feet. Another dreamer, Eurycleia thought, hoping some young nobleman would choose her for a wife if she jumped into bed with him. Shame. She was a big girl, but as pretty as a child. She could have found herself a decent, hardworking man with good prospects if she had kept her private parts to herself. Now she would be lucky to end up with a lazy, bad-tempered drunkard who was far too free with his fists. If she survived the day, that was.

'Go on with you, girl,' she said. 'You've missed your breakfast, and that's your own fault. And there's plenty of cleaning to be done in those kitchens. And before you go, have you seen Melantho?'

Thoosa shook her head and ran off to the kitchens. Eurycleia frowned to herself. Melantho was many things, and few of them good, but she was never late for her work. She thought for a moment of Chloris, who had become familiar with the suitors before disappearing. Eurycleia had had her suspicions about Chloris's fate, but it would have been no more than she had deserved. And no more than Melantho deserved, either. She shrugged her shoulders. They would get by better without her anyway.

She watched the men lifting the old weapons from the walls and carrying them away, leaving patches of clean plaster where the shields had been. Some maids had brought new logs for the hearth and were struggling to bring the flames back to life. She went over to help them until she heard the girls returning from the spring. They filed into the hall with their clay pitchers on their shoulders, and Eurycleia sent them off to the different parts of the palace where water was needed.

When they had gone, she put her fists on her hips and looked around herself. She pictured the hall in her mind's eye, filled with suitors feasting in their usual, unruly manner. And then she saw it piled with their dead bodies. Corpses slumped one upon another across the floor; lying in unnatural poses over tables and benches, their blood seeping like spilled wine across the polished wood while their pale, blank faces stared into nothing. She gave a shudder. It was a pitiable sight, a vision of horror that she would not have wished on anyone, even the suitors who had terrorised her master's house for so long.

But they had brought it upon themselves. They had thieved from the king's household for too long, slighting the gods with their behaviour, and with each misdeed building a wall that would one day collapse and crush them all. It was beyond her wit to guess how Odysseus planned to reclaim what was his, but she knew in her old bones that a day of violence and bloodshed had already dawned, and the doom of many was approaching. She just prayed that as the immortals served out justice, they would protect the king and guard his family from harm.

Loud squealing brought her back to her senses.

'Mantius,' she called to a slave with his arms full of spears. 'That'll be the swineherd bringing his pigs for the feast. Go and fetch him a cup of wine to slake his thirst, will you?'

And may the hogs he has driven to the palace be the last of Odysseus's livestock the suitors ever eat, she thought to herself.

–

'Hey there! Get on with you.'

One of the pigs had stopped to sniff at something at the side of the path. Eumaeus smacked its hindquarters lightly with his staff and it trotted ahead to join the other two. The trio of beasts grunted happily as they crossed the empty patch of ground before the palace walls, ignorant of the fate that awaited them. Eumaeus paused to look at the gates. Several of Odysseus's maids were going through, carrying clay pitchers on their shoulders. One glanced behind her at the sound of the pigs, then followed her friends into the courtyard beyond, leaving the gate open behind her.

A fine rain before dawn had made the grass sodden. Eumaeus's sandals were wet and slippery and his feet were cold, sending a chill up through his bones and into his legs. Soon he would be able to warm himself by the fire in the hall, but the prospect was marred by the thought the suitors would soon be filing in. At least their feasting would be over after today and the palace would be left in peace – though at a high cost.

He could not bear the thought that Penelope was going to marry one of those vulgar youths and live with him in his own home. If only the beggar was right, that Odysseus was just a short voyage away and would soon be arriving to claim his throne. And yet, if he did not come soon, there would be a new king to contend with and a bloody civil war would ensue. Eumaeus knew which side he would choose, but he could not say the same with certainty for his countrymen. In all likelihood, few would rally to Odysseus, and those that did would die in a short and bloody battle.

So be it, he thought, gripping his staff as if it were the shaft of a spear.

The sound of bleating to his right woke him from his daydreaming. Melanthius and his two boys were herding a group of goats along a track that opened onto the empty marketplace between two rows of houses. Eumaeus had no desire to wait around and be insulted so, with a shout to his pigs, he drove them through the gates. In an act of spite, he turned and slipped the bar into place behind him, then waved his animals off into the courtyard to scavenge for whatever food they could find.

'Greetings, friend!' he called, seeing the old beggar sitting on a bed in the porch. He walked over and took him by the hand. 'How did those suitors treat you after I left yesterday?'

'Exactly as you'd have expected them to.'

'That bad, eh? And…' The swineherd lowered his voice and peered through the open doors of the great hall to see that nobody was near. 'And did the queen speak with you?'

The beggar nodded.

'She's a good woman. She doesn't deserve this awful fate that's being forced on her.'

'I'd do anything to prevent it,' Eumaeus said, feeling a sudden surge of anger course through his veins.

The beggar put a hand around his shoulder. The old deerskin cloak that he still wore smelled of a mixture of stale sweat and woodsmoke. He looked Eumaeus in the eye and lowered his voice to a whisper.

'Would you fight for her, my friend?'

'What do you mean?'

'Would you take up arms against the suitors for her sake?'

Something in the old man's demeanour told Eumaeus he meant it. He tried to imagine for a moment taking one of the spears from the walls in the great hall and plunging the point into Eurymachus's foul heart. The thought was deeply pleasing; but he also imagined the other suitors drawing their swords and striking him down in revenge. How would his rash heroism serve Penelope or Telemachus then?

'My heart says yes, my head says no. Why do you ask?'

Before the beggar could reply, the gate was shaken furiously and Melanthius hollered at the top of his voice to be let in.

–

Penelope rolled onto her side, sliding her leg across Odysseus's and draping her arm across his chest. She felt the warmth of his naked flesh against hers, the gentle rise and fall of his ribcage as they lay together beneath the furs. She rested her cheek against his shoulder, kissed it softly and opened her eyes.

But he was not there. How could he be? And yet she closed her eyes again, hoping to drift back into the dream she had left too early. She tried to picture Odysseus beside her, to imagine his soft, hot skin again. But it was too late. He had gone, leaving only the damp trails of her tears as they rolled down her cheeks.

For too long she had fallen asleep with tears in her eyes and woken from her nightmares sobbing into her pillow. But what would tomorrow morning bring? Tears of bitterness as she woke beside Antinous? No, she would never wake to the sight of his face, or the faces of any of Ithaca's nobility. Indeed, she would not have woken at all – not in the world of the living – if that had been the only choice left to her.

But the gods had sent Theoclymenus to offer her a way out. Would she wake tomorrow to see his ruggedly handsome features on the pillow beside her? *Yes*, she thought. She would choose Theoclymenus and live, though the choice would bring new dangers from the enraged suitors whose ambitions she had thwarted. Not that she feared death for herself or Theoclymenus – a stranger before yesterday who she sensed was capable of defending himself. Only for Telemachus, whom she must send back to Sparta until the threat had passed.

But what if Theoclymenus was not a stranger? What if he was Odysseus, disguised by the gods and brought back to Ithaca in time to save her from the suitors and from her own hand? It was too good a hope to be true, and yet her instincts clung to it. And maybe tomorrow she would wake beside the husband whose face and voice she no longer remembered, and whom she might realise she no longer loved. Either way, it was better than opening her eyes to see Antinous staring back at her. Or not opening her eyes at all.

There was a knock on the door and Hippodameia entered, followed by Autonoe. Hippodameia walked to the curtains and pulled them open. A grey half-light filtered into the room, accompanied by the sounds of several slave girls passing into the courtyard from the town. She was reminded of their voices the night before, disturbing her already fitful sleep as they insulted the old beggar and were threatened by Theoclymenus. What the two men had been whispering about she could not guess, and sleep had taken her again soon afterwards.

'Time to wake up, my lady,' Hippodameia said, trying to sound cheerful. 'The day everyone has been waiting for is here.'

'Oh, be quiet, Hippodameia,' Autonoe said, sitting on the bed beside her mistress. She looked at Penelope with concern and dabbed at her wet cheeks with her thumb. 'Don't be afraid, mistress. I've got a feeling everything will work out for the best.'

'I hope you're right, Autonoe. Come what may, at least the suitors will go home and there'll be an end to these feasts.'

Autonoe stood and held up a robe. Penelope pushed aside her furs and rose naked from her bed, turning around so her maid could slip the robe about her shoulders. It was soft and cool against her bare skin. She crossed to a table next to the window and sat down. Sounds of grunting and bleating filled the courtyard below, and from somewhere in the town she heard the lowing of a cow. The sacrifices for the wedding banquet were arriving, and the suitors would not be far behind them.

Picking up a mirror from the table, she stared at her slightly distorted reflection. Her pale face was framed by her mess of black hair, the skin jaundiced by the polished bronze. The eyes that looked back at her were weary and listless, tired by many years of fighting alone against men who wanted to take her husband's place; of too long spent yearning for his return and pondering his fate. Today, one battle would end and a new battle would commence. Or maybe the gods would be kind and lift her burdens from her shoulders forever. By sunset she would know, one way or another.

Hippodameia came and stood behind her, pulling Penelope's hair back to show her face more clearly.

'I'm going to make you look so beautiful that the suitors are going to be *killing* each other to marry you,' she said.

'That would solve a lot of problems,' Penelope replied. 'But I doubt you'll succeed. Powders and paints can't put the smile back in my eyes.'

Before her maid could answer, there was a loud knock on the door. Penelope tightened the sash that held her robe together while Autonoe went to the door.

'The queen's dressing. Who is it?'

'Telemachus. I need to speak to my mother.'

Autonoe looked back at Penelope, who nodded. She opened the door and Telemachus strode into the room.

'Is this a convenient time?'

'Of course it is. I wanted to speak to you anyway. Hippodameia, Autonoe, would you leave us for a moment?'

Her slaves bowed and left the room, closing the door behind them. Telemachus pulled up one of two high-backed chairs that were against the wall and sat down opposite Penelope.

'Have you chosen yet, Mother?'

'No,' she lied. For some reason, she was reluctant to let her son know her decision. 'I'm afraid I find the selection on offer quite deplorable.'

'Then can I make a suggestion?'

Penelope nodded, intrigued by her son's clear agitation.

'Tell them you can't choose between them, so you've decided to set a test of strength. If they're serious about becoming your husband, they're bound to agree.'

'What test?'

He explained to her what he had in mind; an ancient trial of stamina and skill that was altogether beyond the skill of any of the suitors. Penelope shook her head.

'I still have to marry someone by sunset, though,' she said. 'I took an oath.'

'But it doesn't have to be one of the suitors.'

'What do you mean?'

'Perhaps somebody else will pass the test.'

Penelope shook her head.

'Why complicate things? If the suitors can't do it, there's not another man on Ithaca who can.'

'How do you know unless you give them a chance?'

She thought of Theoclymenus. He looked like he had considerable strength in his arms, and as an experienced warrior he would know how to handle any weapon. But what if he failed? Why take the risk when she intended to choose him anyway?

'I don't think it's a good idea.'

'But if there is a man who can do it,' Telemachus urged, 'at least he'd have proved he has the strength and skill worthy of marrying you and taking the throne. I would be ready to accept him as my new father and king.'

Did Telemachus know about Theoclymenus, she wondered? Was he trying to tell her something? Did he want Theoclymenus to take the test as a proof his true identity? Even if he failed – even if he was not Odysseus in disguise – it was almost certain nobody else would manage the task. The choice would then return to her anyway. And if she agreed to Telemachus's suggestion, perhaps she could persuade him to agree to hers.

'Well, if it's that important to you then I don't see what harm it will do. But you must do something for me, too.'

'What is it?'

She stood and went to the window. The courtyard below was wet and the grey clouds above promised more rain before midday. On the open space beyond the palace walls she could see the first knots of suitors approaching the palace.

'I want you to go back to Sparta and stay there until I send for you. You must go this evening.'

'Sparta? What for?'

'I didn't tell you before, Telemachus, because you didn't need to know, but Eupeithes has made another threat against your life.' He opened his mouth to speak, but she raised her hand for silence. 'Listen to me. He told me that if I did not pick Antinous to be my husband then he'd arrange for you to be killed. I was going to do it to save you, but… but perhaps your way is best. Let the strongest man win my hand. And it won't be Antinous, so you must flee Ithaca until I can find a way to deal with Eupeithes. I know it's not what you'll want, that you'll say you're soon to be of age and…'

'I'll do it,' Telemachus said. 'If you'll agree to set the test, I'll go to Sparta at sunset. A merchant ship arrived yesterday evening, heading to Crete. They'll take me if I pay them.'

'Good,' she said, surprised by his unquestioning agreement. 'That's good. And Telemachus, I'm sorry I've made such a mess of everything – taking that oath that brought these men into our house, selling your birthright…'

'It doesn't matter any more, Mother,' he said.

He walked up to her and put his arms about her. There was no coldness in his embrace, and as she laid his head on her shoulder, she felt as if she had her son back. *But much too late*, she told herself. *Much too late*.

'Our problems will be over soon,' he said, though his eyes seemed less certain. 'And now I can hear the first of the suitors arriving. Courtesy requires that I make them welcome on their last day in my home. And my heart compels me to check that our other guests have slept well and are not being abused by the newcomers.'

He kissed her on the cheek, then turned and walked from the room.

-

Odysseus pulled himself up with his staff and crossed the courtyard. He raised the bar from the gate and opened it, only to be greeted by Melanthius's angry face.

'What are you still doing here? Get out of my way before I give you a taste of my fists!'

He barged Odysseus aside, knocking him onto his backside in the mud. A flash of anger quickened Odysseus's limbs, but he contained it and waited for Eumaeus to come to his assistance. Ignoring them both, Melanthius ordered the two boys that were with him to tether the goats while he disappeared into the shadows of the great hall.

Eumaeus took Odysseus's hand and pulled him gently to his feet.

'There's one man's blood I wouldn't mind seeing spilled,' he said. 'Are you all right?'

'Don't be concerned for me, Eumaeus. Before the day's out we'll both have a chance to pay Melanthius and the suitors back for their hospitalities. Who's this now?'

He looked through the open gates at a man driving a heifer and a few more goats across the vacant marketplace.

'That's Philoetius,' Eumaeus said, peering over his shoulder. 'As good a man as any you'll find on these islands. He often brings cattle or goats for the suitors' feasts, though he has no more love for them than I do.'

'Aren't there enough beasts already, even for a wedding banquet?' Odysseus asked, indicating the swine and goats filling the courtyard.

'For some reason, Telemachus insisted that he should be sent for. Perhaps he thinks it's better to have too much meat than too little.'

They opened the gates wide to allow the animals into the courtyard. Philoetius followed – a tall, well-built man with a great black beard that seemed to swallow up the features of his face.

'Well met, Eumaeus,' he said, slapping the swineherd heavily on the shoulder. 'And who's this?'

He stared down at Odysseus, sizing the beggar up with his small, dark eyes.

'A stranger to Ithaca,' Odysseus replied, recognising in the man the youth he had left in charge of his herds on Samos twenty years before. 'I escaped a group of merchants intending to sell me as a slave and have been relying on the goodwill of others to feed this nagging stomach of mine ever since.'

'It's clear to eye and nostril that the gods have been hard on you, old man. But everything in its season: prosperity might follow mischance, provided you work hard and keep a courteous tongue in your head. There'll be a mighty feast this evening,' he said, hooking his thumb over his shoulder at the noisy livestock who were populating the courtyard. 'If you bring a bowl to myself or Eumaeus here, we'll see that stomach of yours stops growling. But a word of advice for you – stay clear of the queen's suitors unless you want to find insults and a footstool or two thrown at you.'

'Our friend has already found that out for himself,' Eumaeus said as a steward brought him a cup of wine. 'Be kind enough to bring another for Philoetius and our friend here, will you, Mantius?'

'So, you've met our kind-hearted guests, then?' Philoetius said with a laugh. 'Before they started arriving, my herds used to cover the hillsides yonder.' He pointed in the general direction of Samos. 'If the king had returned, he'd have found his property well-looked-after under my care, and multiplied many times from the cattle he left in my charge. If he came back now, though, he'd find fewer than when he left. A fine herdsman he'd think me, and he'd be in his rights to throw me off his land and give the job to someone else.'

'When the king returns, he won't be looking for cattle and pigs – he'll know whose bellies they've gone to feed over the years. What he'll be looking for are loyal men to stand beside him when he throws these suitors out of his home.'

'I reckon you're right, old man,' Philoetius replied. 'There's many a time I've watched those *noblemen* cavorting in the king's hall, eating of a better man's wealth without his permission, and thought of putting an end to one or two of them. All it'd take is to pull one of them spears off the wall and

I'll bet a few would be dead before they had time to piss themselves.' He stood up with a laugh and clapped his hands. 'But then the rest'd cut me down, and then who'd look after my master's livestock for his return?'

Mantius appeared with two more cups of wine. He gave them both to Philoetius, ignoring the old beggar altogether. The herdsman passed Odysseus his cup, dipped his fingers in his own and flicked wine on the ground before downing the remainder in a single draught.

Odysseus offered his own libation and raised the cup to his lips. Would the two herdsmen fight, he wondered? They spoke with devotion about their absent king, but how loyal would they be if he put spears in their hands and told them to fight the suitors? Even if their courage matched their words, what could three men really do against more than a hundred? He could still walk out of the palace gates if he wanted to. He could save his own wretched life and remain a beggar for whatever miserable years remained to him, leaving Telemachus to hate him for his cowardice and Penelope to share her bed with a new husband.

Or he could stay and die, effectively taking his son and the two loyal herdsmen to Hades with him. Why had Eperitus deserted him? Why now, at the pinnacle of their trials, after everything they had been through? But that was no longer a question for him to answer. He would face the suitors with what force he had, and many would die before the setting of that day's sun.

And then he heard voices of young men approaching the palace walls. The first of the suitors were coming.

-

Antinous crossed the grassy terrace where on most days the town's market was held. Today, though, the only people were the small knots of young noblemen heading towards the palace. For once respectful of Telemachus's instructions, none carried spears or anything more warlike than their short swords. Many, though, bore the marriage gifts with which they hoped to win Penelope's favour. *Poor fools*, he thought. The woman would never be won by such trinkets, though he had brought rich baubles of his own to offer.

No, Penelope was too intelligent to fall for offers of wealth or the flattery that came with them. She only understood cold, hard threats. And few of the others had the benefit of a ruthless and calculating father, as Antinous did. Eupeithes had assured him that Penelope would give him her hand in marriage, because he had made it abundantly clear to her that Telemachus's life depended on it.

'Antinous!'

He turned to see Eurymachus, Agelaus and Elatus. He walked to meet his friends, followed by his servant, who carried Penelope's gift in a bundle.

'I'm surprised you bothered to turn up,' Eurymachus said as they shook hands and embraced. 'You know I'll be the one in her bed tonight, giving her what she's been desperate for all these years.'

'But when you wake up in the morning, you'll find it was just another of those little serving girls you're so fond of,' Antinous responded. 'And then you'll be welcome to come to *my* palace and offer *me* allegiance as your new king.'

'*You*, the king?' Eurymachus grinned. 'I'd sooner bend down and kiss that disgusting beggar's feet than kneel before you, my friend.'

He slapped Antinous on the back – a little too hard – and the others laughed.

'Then I shall make that my first royal command, Eurymachus. As for you two, how do you expect to win the queen when your fathers are little more than glorified goatherds? Perhaps you'll persuade her with your fists, Elatus. And you, Agelaus – maybe you'll just rape her.'

Elatus frowned.

'At least our fathers never tried to take the throne by force, Antinous. The queen will never pick a son of Eupeithes.'

'We'll see.'

They reached the doors of the outer wall and joined another group of suitors, all talking excitedly about their prospects for the day ahead. At the sight of Antinous and the others – their faces red and scowling – they fell silent. Antinous barged his way through to the courtyard.

'Lunch has arrived,' he said, seeing the livestock in the courtyard. 'Eurydamas, Peisander – why don't you slaughter some of these beasts and get the banquet started? It's going to be a long day, and I've got an appetite like a hog. Steward, prepare plenty of wine! I'm in the mood to celebrate.'

The steward bowed quickly and ran off into the great hall. It was then that Antinous noticed the old wretch who had almost ruined his enjoyment of the feast the day before. He was leaning on his stick and staring at the newcomers with bold disdain, flanked on either side by Eumaeus and Philoetius. The swineherd's expression was one of cautious dislike, while the cowherd stood tall and arrogantly self-assured as he looked down at the suitors.

'Behold, the three Furies: Magaera and Alecto,' Antinous said, pointing first at Eumaeus, then at Philoetius. His finger turned last to the beggar. 'And you must be the Avenger, Tisiphone. Be wary, my friends,' he warned the other suitors. 'They'll hound us to death for our crimes. You, Eurymachus, for your arrogance; Elatus for your anger; and Agelaus for your injustices. And what about me?'

He turned to the beggar and arched an eyebrow, daring him to speak.

'How about murder?' the old man said.

The grin on Antinous's face melted away. In a fit of bad temper, he kicked the beggar's stick from under him. As he fell face-forward into the mud, Antinous felt his spirits spring up again.

'Come on, friends. A banquet awaits us and there's a throne to be had.'

Stepping over the beggar one by one, they filed into the hall, their laughter echoing from the walls as they entered.

-

Autonoe sat next to Hippodameia on the bench outside their mistress's bedroom. The sound of raised voices in the great hall below made her suddenly tense. She felt her hands begin to shake and clenched them into fists on top of her thighs. The thought of another day in the same room as the men who had attacked her made her want to be sick. She closed her eyes and saw the faces of Agelaus, Elatus and Leocritus leering over her.

'Are you all right?' Hippodameia asked.

Autonoe sniffed back a tear and nodded.

'Yes. Thank you.'

She had cried before dawn, too, but they had been tears of relief. Relief that her menstrual bleeding had started at its normal time. Relief that she was not pregnant.

'Last day today,' Hippodameia continued, guessing at the source of Autonoe's anxiety. And then, voicing an anxiety of her own: 'And then we'll have to start all over again in another man's house.'

'Who knows what the gods will bring.'

Autonoe sniffed again and thought of the beggar. Was he truly Odysseus in disguise? Would he take his revenge on the suitors for what they had done to his home and family? She hoped so. She hoped that in his rage he would strike down the men who had attacked her; that she would be free from the fear of them forever. But she knew it would not work like that. Their families were too powerful. Some compromise would be reached. Odysseus would receive compensation for his depleted livestock and the suitors would return home with their pride hurt, but their lives spared. That was how it was between the high-born. But she could never have her shame removed or be compensated for what she had lost.

Telemachus opened the door to the queen's bedroom, taking no notice of the maids as he strode away down the passage.

'Hippodameia, come and do something with this mess!' Penelope called, holding her hair on top of her head with one hand and looking in the mirror with the other. 'Autonoe, find that dress we agreed on, will you? Oh, and before you do – this basket of clothes needs taking down to the laundry maids.'

Autonoe followed Hippodameia into the room. Penelope's mood seemed strangely light considering she would soon have to choose one of the suitors to be her new husband. Did she know the beggar was Odysseus, Autonoe wondered? Surely she would have been unable to disguise her excitement if that was the case. As it was, she seemed more relieved than elated, though what had given her respite from her suffering Autonoe could not guess.

As for herself, her thoughts shifted between sceptical and hopeful. Anyone might claim to be Odysseus, and the old beggar seemed nothing like the broad-shouldered, muscular man she remembered from her childhood. Even if he had been disguised by Athena, as Melantho had overheard him say, it seemed too incredible to be true. But Melantho had been convinced the beggar was Odysseus. So much so that – fearful of what she might say – Autonoe had hit her over the head and tied her up in one of the storerooms.

She still wondered whether or not to tell Penelope what she had heard, but fear that she would raise the queen's hopes kept her from speaking out. If the beggar turned out to be another liar, the disappointment would crush what remained of her mistress's spirit. More importantly, if he *was* Odysseus in disguise, then he had kept his identity a secret for a reason. He would declare himself when he saw fit, and it was not Autonoe's place to reveal his secret before then.

She picked up the basket of laundry and carried it to the bed. It was too full of clothes to carry comfortably all the way down to the kitchens, so she began pulling out the items she felt her mistress needed most. As her fingers searched through the collection of dowdy dresses, she found her thoughts wondering back to Theoclymenus. Indeed, she had hardly *stopped* thinking about him since their first meeting – and the impulse that had driven her to kiss him.

His rugged appearance hid a character that was strong and true, not easily swayed by vice or temptation. She felt he was a man of courage and purpose, capable of overcoming any obstacle. The sort of temperament that put the suitors to shame, and – she fancied – could thwart their ambitions. That was why she had been so surprised to learn he was not a wanderer from the mainland, as he claimed, but an Ithacan – an old comrade of Odysseus himself. Surely if the beggar *was* Odysseus, then together the two men had a chance of defeating the suitors. All her hopes rested on it.

Her fingers closed on a dress of purple wool and pulled it from the pile. A coil of thick rope lay beneath it. Bemused by its presence, she picked it up. Glancing across at Penelope, who was discussing hairstyles with Hippodameia, she opened her mouth to ask how the rope had got there, then thought better of it. Perhaps the queen intended to escape out of the window that night, before her new husband left the wedding feast to claim his bride. Autonoe smiled at the thought and tossed the rope back into the basket with the clothes that did not need urgently washing. Bundling the rest under her arm, she left the bedroom and headed off to the kitchens.

–

Eperitus woke with a start. The windowless room he was in was still black, but his instincts told him the sun had already risen in the world beyond the palace walls. He had intended to wake ahead of the servants and leave before dawn, avoiding any need to say goodbye to Penelope, Telemachus or Odysseus. But the gods had kept him locked in sleep, soaking his dreams with the blood of the suitors as he pictured them lying slain in heaps on the floor of the great hall. A good omen for Odysseus and Penelope, perhaps; but one that he would not be around to see fulfilled.

He rose, slipped on his eyepatch and dressed quickly, hoping he might still be able to steal out of a side door or a window. He could already hear voices coming from the many rooms and corridors of the palace – mingled with the sounds of livestock in the courtyard – and he realised he must have slept later than he had feared. Then there was a loud rap on the door, which was opened a moment later by Telemachus.

'Good morning. The sun's up and the suitors are already gathering in the hall. I wondered if I might speak with you.'

Eperitus guessed what Telemachus was going to ask him.

'Telemachus, I'm sorry, but I have to leave.'

Telemachus's expression was confused.

'But I thought you were going to stay and...'

'I've changed my mind,' Eperitus said, moving past him into the dark passageway. 'I have to return to the mainland.'

He walked to the junction with the main corridor. Left led to a side door onto the courtyard, while right went to the kitchens, the living quarters, and ultimately the great hall. He turned left, but Telemachus slipped past and blocked his way.

'What's wrong? Why do you have to go?'

Eperitus turned back and followed the corridor to the right. He passed the noise and aromas of the kitchens and almost collided with a figure at the bottom of the stairs that led up to the royal bedrooms. It was Autonoe, a bundle of clothing clutched in her arms. She looked at him in surprise, followed by happy recognition. A moment later, Telemachus appeared.

'Then it has to be cowardice,' he said, angrily. 'You're leaving because you're scared of the suitors.'

'It's nothing to do with them,' Eperitus snapped back.

Autonoe still blocked his way, looking puzzled.

'You're *leaving*?'

'Yes, he's leaving,' Telemachus said. 'Abandoning us when we need his help most.'

'And what use could I have been to you, anyway? What good is a man who refuses to fight to anybody?'

'Resorting to your oath again, are you? How convenient. Or perhaps there never *was* an oath, because in truth you never *were* a fighter!'

Eperitus felt his hackles rise. He wanted to remind Telemachus of the ambush on their journey to Sparta, and how he had defeated three of the bandits – one of them their leader – without having to kill any of them. But what good would it do? Telemachus had been counting on his help, and his anger was justified. It was to escape that accusing look that Eperitus had wanted to rise early and leave unchallenged. To give in to his own temper now would only make matters worse, and he respected and cared for Telemachus too much to allow that.

'Telemachus, I have to leave. I can't tell you why, but you'll find out soon enough – if you don't already know. Try not to be angry with me for abandoning you in your moment of need. And... and please thank your mother for her generosity. Tell her I'm sorry to have let her down, but her disappointment will be short-lived. A better man than me has arrived to save her from the suitors.'

Telemachus narrowed his eyes, then shook his head.

'I thought you were a man of honour,' he said, 'but it seems you really are a coward. I'm only glad I've found you out now, rather than have you run away in the middle of a battle.'

He shouldered past him and broke into a run. Eperitus watched him go, disappearing in the shadows beyond the ring of torchlight at the foot of the stairs. He heard a door open and the sound of many voices leap out from the great hall before being stifled as the door closed again.

'Why are you leaving?' Autonoe asked. 'I thought you were Odysseus's friend.'

He took her by the arm and stared at her.

'What do you mean?'

'Last night in the portico,' she explained, her voice hushed. 'The beggar told you he was Odysseus, and he called you Eperitus.'

'Who else have you told?'

'Nobody. Not even Penelope. If the king really has returned, then it's up to him to reveal himself, not me. But I don't understand why you're leaving him. Why now, when he needs his loyal friends around him?'

'Then you didn't overhear everything that was said. Suffice it to say, we didn't part as friends when our galley was wrecked seven years ago.'

'Seven years is a long time to bear a grudge.'

'It isn't when you hold a man responsible for killing your family.'

'He *murdered* them?'

Eperitus shook his head.

'No, but he might as well have. I don't expect you to understand, but to me...'

He fell silent and Autonoe raised her hand to his cheek, stroking the twisted hair of his beard.

'I could never understand such a thing, because I've never had a family. But I know it must have been awful. I'm sorry for you, Eperitus.'

He placed his hand on hers, keeping her warm fingers against his cheek.

'That's why I'm going. I wish I could forget the burial mounds of my wife and baby, lying next to each other beneath a lonely tree in a place that I will never see again. I wish I could convince myself it wasn't Odysseus's fault they died. I wish I could withdraw my oath not to kill, even if only for one day, and take up a spear and shield in defence of this place and the people I care about. I wish a lot of things, Autonoe. But they won't happen.'

'You don't have to leave,' she responded. 'There's a home for you here, and rest from your burdens. With me, if you'd have me. But only you can overcome the struggle going on inside that proud heart of yours. Go if you must, Eperitus – the gods will take care of Odysseus and Penelope and Telemachus. But don't destroy yourself in the process. You deserve better.'

She stood on tiptoes and kissed him on the lips, her eyes full of tears. Then she gathered up the bundle of clothes hanging from her arm and ran to the kitchen. Eperitus watched her go, pondering the words she had said. Then he forced thoughts of a home with her on Ithaca from his head and went to the door that led into the great hall. He pushed it open and stepped inside.

The benches and tables were already crowded with suitors, and more were entering by the open doors. The smoky air was filled with the sound of their raised voices and ringing laughter, while dozens of slaves poured wine for them and served them food, helped by Eumaeus, Melanthius and another herdsman Eperitus did not recognise. A space had been cleared between the tables where animals were being sacrificed by some of the suitors. Other slaves flayed and carved up the carcasses and cooked the meat on spits over the hearth. Eperitus spotted Odysseus sitting at a small table by the weapons rack next to the entrance. To his surprise, Irus was sitting beside the man who had knocked out two of his teeth, sharing the scraps of food from his table. The giant's expression and demeanour were once again those of a child.

As Eperitus watched, Telemachus rose from his seat before the hearth and took a plate of meat from one of the carvers. He carried it over to where his father was sitting and laid it on the table before him. At his signal, a wine steward came over and poured a cup of wine for each of the beggars.

'Why should an old tramp receive as good as the invited guests?' Leocritus called out. 'Stop encouraging him, Telemachus, and send him on his way. He shouldn't be allowed to ruin the wedding feast.'

'Invited guests, Leocritus?' Telemachus said. 'Since when were any of you invited? As for this man, he remains under my protection and I won't have you or any of your friends abuse him again.'

Several voices were raised in mockery and one of the suitors – a man Eperitus knew to be called Ctessipus – stood up and banged loudly on the table.

'Listen to me. Listen all of you! Now, I respect the gods just as much as any man, and I'm glad to see Telemachus's newest lickspittle, that most pestilent old cadaver, being well-fed. But aren't you forgetting one of the most important requirements of any host, Telemachus? A guest needs a gift, doesn't he? The gods themselves command it. So I've saved the wretch something special, all for his own.' He picked up a cow's hoof that lay on the table before him. 'Enjoy *that*, old man!'

Ctessipus hurled the hoof at Odysseus, who ducked aside at the last moment so that it hit the wall with a thump. Uproarious laughter filled the hall, only to be silenced again as Telemachus balled up his fists and ran towards Ctessipus.

'You vile dog!' he shouted, seizing the suitor by his tunic and dragging him half across the table.

He pulled back his fist as Ctessipus fumbled for his sword, but both men were stopped by a shout.

'Leave him!' Odysseus called, his voice surprisingly strong. 'My lord, an old cur such as me isn't worth your trouble. Be content that the gods have seen the acts of these young nobles and will demand payment in their own time. Sit down, sir, I beg you.'

Telemachus contained his anger and released Ctessipus's tunic. The suitor let his sword slip back into its scabbard and dropped back into his seat, cursing and threatening his host in the vilest manner.

'What do you expect, Telemachus?' Agelaus said, rising to his feet beside Ctessipus. 'Your mother keeps us here like prisoners, waiting year after year for a decision. If we've given her any trouble, then she only has herself to blame. But now the day's finally arrived, we want to know who she's going to choose. Stop your delaying, boy, and go fetch her now.'

'Yes, fetch her!'

'Fetch the queen and let's be done with it.'

More voices were raised, demanding a decision. A sign, Eperitus thought, of the growing tensions in the hall.

'Am I my mother's keeper?' Telemachus protested. 'The queen will make her choice in her own time. Until then, watch your damned manners and treat my guests with respect!'

The suitors jeered at his helpless demands as he returned to his seat. Then a cloud passed over the sun, and the already thin light coming in through the open doors became suddenly grey and oppressive. Perhaps startled by the change in the light, a pig squealed as the sacrificial knife was set against its throat and leapt forwards. The suitor tried to restrain it and slit its throat at the same time, but failed to do either effectively. The animal fell awkwardly and rolled on its side, its blood squirting out in jets. Fine red droplets sprayed over the nearest suitors, speckling their faces and arms and settling over the baskets of bread and cheese on the tables before them. As the pig kicked out the last of its life before them, a shocked silence descended on the hall. The handsome, noble faces of the guests were strained and white, stricken with a sudden and inexplicable fear, as if Hermes had entered the great hall and spread his black cloak across them. At the sight of them, Eperitus was suddenly reminded of his dream. He stepped forwards and raised his arms.

'You shameful fools, listen to a final warning, if you have the wit to understand it. Last night I dreamed that a darkness had descended on this hall. The banqueting tables had been turned over and the wedding food scattered in the dirt. The walls and columns were splashed with blood, and upon the floor were many bodies, piled one upon the other like sacks of barley. From each corpse a spirit was rising, rising to join the exodus of ghosts streaming out of the open doors on their way to the Underworld. Vengeance is coming. If you have any brains at all, you'll leave the palace now, while you still have the chance.'

The suitors' stunned faces became fearful. A few started to rise from their seats, looking round uncertainly. Then a lone voice rang out in sudden, heavy laughter.

'How much did you bribe him to scare us off, Antinous?' Eurymachus asked. 'By the gods, it almost worked! Some of these fools are already half out of their chairs with fear.'

Those who had begun to stand sat down quickly, to the mockery of their companions. Other voices were raised in laughter – forced to start with, but becoming freer as relief drove away alarm. Some jeered at Eperitus, who marched across the floor and, without a further look at Odysseus, walked out of the great hall.

Chapter Twenty Five

The Bow of Iphitus

Odysseus felt a deep sense of sadness as he watched Eperitus leave. His joy at finding his friend alive again had evaporated, and his old feelings of loss had returned with a stinging freshness. He also knew that his last realistic hope of defeating the suitors had gone. But he could not allow himself to be disheartened. He would do what he had committed to doing, and do it without hesitation.

When the moment he had planned for came, he would reveal his true identity and face the men who had come to steal his wife and his throne – even if it meant death for himself and Telemachus. In all his years at Troy he had never shown fear or reluctance in battle, even though he had been fighting another man's war. Now he was fighting for his own cause – the only one that had ever really mattered – and he would not baulk at the final challenge. And though he loved his son and would never lightly endanger him, this was as much Telemachus's cause as his own. Even if they died fighting to take back what was theirs, it was better than living with the shame of never having tried.

He looked around at the suitors and their servants, whose ranks had swollen to their full complement. One hundred and eighteen men. The great hall was large enough to contain them all – and dozens of slaves besides – but there would be little room for manoeuvre when the battle started. He had chosen his position, though, and knew every detail of his plan. Telemachus had made sure the walls had been cleared of weapons and armour, and in compliance with his request the suitors had brought bridal gifts to the wedding feast instead of spears and shields. They still had their swords, of course – no nobleman would be without a weapon of some sort – but as long as Odysseus and Telemachus were the only ones armed with shields and spears they would have a powerful advantage.

The suitors' gifts sat like a hoard of plunder on a table against one of the walls. A large clay pithos had also been placed by the side door that led out to the outer passage, but none of the suitors seemed to have noticed its addition. Even the hard-worked servants had no time to pay it any attention. That was good, Odysseus thought.

'Here,' he said, passing Irus more meat. 'Eat up, my friend.'

Irus grinned stupidly and crammed the food into his large mouth, chewing noisily before swallowing. Odysseus had found him that morning peering sheepishly through the gates of the outer wall, hunger and fear competing equally in his simple mind. He seemed not to remember their fight of the day before, unless it was in his fawning attitude. Odysseus had taken him by the hand into the courtyard and fed him the few scraps he had kept from the previous day's feast. Since then Irus had stayed close by his side, barely leaving his shadow. But Odysseus's actions had not been motivated by pity alone. The moment he had seen Irus's strength, he knew that he would be better as an ally than a foe. And now the beggar was to have an important part in the downfall of the suitors.

The side door to the great hall opened and Penelope entered, followed by Autonoe and Hippodameia. A veil obscured the queen's features, but the memory of her face was still fresh in his mind from the evening before. Her black hair was combed back into a ponytail, with spiral twists before each ear. Across her temple was a band hung with golden threads that reached down almost to her eyebrows – an ornament he had given her shortly after they were married – and dangling from her ears were golden earrings that gleamed with the light from the fire. Her dress was pale blue, plunging low to her cleavage and clasped on either side of her neck to show off her white shoulders and long arms. The halves of the dress were held together by a golden belt, positioned high enough for the slit in the material to ride up to the top of her thigh. In her left hand she held a tall bow, while hanging from her right was a leather quiver bristling with arrows.

His heart beat rapidly at her sudden appearance, but his view of her was soon obscured by the suitors, who rose as one from the benches and crowded towards her like hungry dogs. Forcing his weak and weary body to its feet, he caught sight of her again through the press of young men. She was searching their faces, as if looking for someone. After a while, she set the quiver of arrows down and raised her hand.

'My noble lords,' she began, causing their voices to fall still as they hung expectantly on her words, 'ten years ago a deputation was sent to Parnassus to consult with the Pythoness about the return of my husband, King Odysseus. On Apollo's feast day, the priestess answered that he would return to Ithaca within ten years. I swore an oath then that I would remarry if he did not come back in that time, and thereby give the throne to my new husband. By the terms of that oath, I must be remarried by sunset today.'

A great cheer rose from the ranks of the suitors, followed by shouted comments about where her choice should fall. Some were almost self-mocking, others more confident or forceful. Of them all, only Antinous said nothing, folding his arms as he waited patiently for the announcement. Penelope raised her hand again, refusing to continue until the clamour had subsided.

'Some of you have made this palace your home for years now, others for just a few months, every one of you hoping to win me over by eating and drinking your way through my son's inheritance, or by your vile treatment of our servants, and not least through a combination of your base manners and feeble wit, thinly veiled behind a varnish of good looks and fine clothes.' By now, the last stubborn mutterings had died away to a stony silence. 'If a single one of you had possessed enough generosity to bring his own livestock to the nightly feasts, or the humility to treat our servants and other guests with respect and civility – let alone my son, soon to be the rightful master of this household – my choice might have been made easier. As it is, there is little comparison to be made between you, and nothing that appeals.'

She paused again and searched once more through the faces gathered before her, a look of growing concern infecting her movements. Odysseus had by now moved to the back of the crowd, close enough to see her black-lined eyes through the veil. The din of voices had resumed, this time angrier in tone. Beckoning to Telemachus, Penelope leaned down towards him and muttered something in his ear.

'Never mind Theoclymenus,' Antinous said, overhearing her words. 'He's gone and good riddance to him. A gloomy presence at the best of times. And if you've done insulting your future husband and his friends, my queen, perhaps you will do us the honour of naming Ithaca's new king.'

Penelope's arms fell to her sides and Autonoe had to reach out and catch the bow as it fell from her hand. She spared a concerned glance at her mistress, who for a moment remained staring at Antinous from behind the cover of her veil. Then, turning to her son, she took him by the hand.

'Telemachus, is it true? Has Theoclymenus gone?'

'Yes, Mother, he left shortly before you joined us. He thanked you for your generosity and apologised for letting you down. But whatever promises he may have made you, my advice is to forget them. The man is a coward.'

As he spoke, Telemachus looked at his father. His expression was angry but resolute. If Odysseus had suspected his son might baulk at the task before them both, he knew then that the lad was determined to go through with it.

'Choose!' a voice demanded.

'Who will it be, my lady?'

'It'll be me, of course,' Eurymachus snapped, his impatience getting the better of him. 'I'm the strongest and bravest of all of you.'

'My gift was best.'

'And my father's richer than half of yours put together! At least I can offer her the lifestyle she's used to, rather than living in the sties most of you call home.'

The bickering grew in volume once again. Penelope, who for a moment had seemed overwhelmed and was forced to lean against Telemachus for support, now pulled herself up to her full height. She took the bow from Autonoe's hand and faced the suitors once more.

'Why should I choose any of you?' she asked, bitterly. 'Indeed, choice isn't the word for this farce, for if I truly had a choice, I would choose *none* of you. And so I will let the gods decide.'

'What's this?' Antinous said. 'Don't fool with us, my lady. You know exactly who you must choose *and* the consequences of your choice.'

'I know who your *father* wants me to name, Antinous. But this is Apollo's feast day, so let the archer god himself pick between you.' She raised the bow above her head for all to see. One end of the string had been attached to the bow; the other hung down beside her. 'This was once Odysseus's, given to him by Iphitus, son of Eurytus. Only the man who can shoot an arrow from this bow through a dozen axe heads is truly worthy to be called my husband and our king. The competition is open to all, noble or poor, freeman or slave. But I will not stay to watch my fate decided. Eumaeus, take the bow and these axes' – she indicated the box at Hippodameia's feet – 'and come to me yourself when a winner has been found. I will be in my room.'

The swineherd moved forwards and took hold of the bow, moved suddenly to tears by the sight of his former master's heirloom, and by the realisation that a lesser man would soon take his place. She touched his arm gently.

'Bring news of my new husband to me yourself, Eumaeus,' she said. 'Don't let Telemachus come. Do you understand?'

He frowned uncertainly, but nodded. Penelope then turned and left the great hall, followed by her maids.

'Stop snivelling, you filthy peasant,' Antinous sneered at Eumaeus. 'Go off to some corner where we don't have to listen to your sobbing, or better still, go and cry for your old master outside in the courtyard.'

He snatched the bow from Eumaeus's hand and inspected it closely, checking for signs of woodworm before planting one end in the dirt and pressing down on the other.

'So, this bow is going to decide our fates,' he said. 'But there's more to this test than meets the eye. This is no ordinary weapon, my friends: it'll take strength and skill to string, and perhaps that's the point. She thinks no one but Odysseus can do it.'

'Then she's wrong,' said Eurymachus. He crooked an arm, making his oversized bicep bulge impressively. 'I'll have that antique strung in moments, but not until I've laughed at the rest of your puny efforts first.'

'She called on Apollo to choose, if you remember,' Odysseus said, moving between them with the help of his stick. 'And he'll make sure that only the rightful king can perform the task.'

'Maybe, if that's what you believe,' Antinous said. 'Though the test was to fire an arrow through twelve axe heads, *not* string the bow.' He turned about and tossed the bow to Telemachus, who almost dropped it, to the amusement of the suitors. 'Here, lad, why don't you try your hand? Doubtless you think the kingdom should go to you, so let's see if you're worthy.'

'I *am* the rightful king of Ithaca, or would be if my father is indeed dead,' Telemachus replied.

'Prove it then. String the bow and we'll all kneel before you.'

'Oh, great king!' Leocritus mocked, bowing low.

'Here's your chance to prove yourself, boy,' Elatus added.

The others jeered and laughed, and Odysseus saw his son's temper taking the bait. His ears turned red and his brow puckered into a frown. Gripping the loose end of the string, he tied a small loop around the bow, about two-thirds up its length. Then he put his left leg between the bow and the string, with the bottom end resting against the outside of his right ankle. Stepping back so that the weapon was tensed against the underside of his left thigh, he placed the palm of his left hand against the top of the bow and took the loop in the fingers of his right. Odysseus and the suitors watched in silence as he took a breath, then pulled down on the top of the bow. It moved a little at first, then stopped. Telemachus gritted his teeth and pulled down harder, but the upper tip moved no closer to the loop.

A moment later he let go and stood up to be greeted by more taunts from the onlookers, who were relieved at his failure. Resting the bow against his shoulder, he rubbed at the back of his thigh, flexed his fingers and then resumed his earlier pose. Another quick breath was followed by a further effort at bending the bow. Again it moved a little and stopped. Squeezing his eyes shut and blowing through pursed lips, Telemachus pulled harder. The muscles of his arms strained with exertion, the veins bulging beneath his skin. His cheeks turned red and sweat broke out on his forehead. The bow edged a fraction closer to the loop in his shaking fingers before he could take the strain no longer and stood up again. This time a handful of suitors clapped his endeavours.

'Come on, son,' said Agelaus. 'You've given it your best, but you're no king. Give the damned thing over to a real man.'

'No!' Telemachus snapped. 'One more go, that's all I need.'

For the first time, he glanced at his father. Odysseus gave an almost imperceptible shake of his head, but Telemachus – his blood up – frowned and turned away. Seizing the bow once more, he gave a loud grunt and pulled down on it. The loop between his fingers drew closer to the notch than on the previous efforts. Telemachus, his whole face now crimson and his limbs shaking with the effort, gave a shout and pulled harder still. Fearing his son might actually string the bow and throw their plans into confusion, Odysseus stepped forwards. But Antinous was quicker. As the rest of the suitors watched in silent awe, he brought his hands together in a slow clap.

'Bravo, Telemachus. You've proved your point, but enough is enough. The bow is unconquered.'

The distraction threw Telemachus's concentration. He released the bow and moved back to sit on one of the benches.

'You're right,' he gasped between breaths. 'I'm too young and weak to be king of Ithaca. I leave the competition to you men, and may Apollo choose wisely.'

He leaned the bow against the door jamb, then stood and picked up the box of axe heads. With an apologetic glance at his father, he carried them to an open space between the tables and benches. Throwing his purple cloak back over his shoulder, he drew his sword from its baldric and used the point to dig a long, narrow trench in the dirt. After checking it was straight, he took one of the bronze, double-bladed axe heads from the box and knelt down. Gripping it in the middle, he pushed it into the dirt at one end of the trench. He placed a second next to it, then scraped the earth back into the trench around them and trod it down.

While the suitors passed around the bow, testing it and arguing over who should get the first attempt at stringing it, Telemachus took one of the rakes used to smooth the dirt floor at the end of every evening and passed the handle through the holes in the axe heads where the hafts would go. He repeated the process until all twelve were perfectly aligned. Their axis lay between the main entrance to the hall and the small side door that led to the rest of the palace, just as his father had instructed him when they had drawn up their plan. Even if any of the suitors could string the bow of Iphitus, Odysseus knew none of them would have the skill to fire an arrow from such a low and awkward angle through a dozen axe heads. Indeed, he had only ever seen it done once, and that was by Philoctetes, the greatest archer in the Greek army.

As Telemachus finished, the suitors reached an agreement that they would follow the order in which they usually sat during their nightly feasts. A young man called Leodes, who sat at the furthest corner of the hall near the main doors and acted as priest for the suitors' sacrifices, now took up the challenge of the bow. Assuming the same stance as Telemachus earlier, he tried to bend the notched tip far enough down to reach the loop of string. Smiling to himself as he watched Leodes's face redden and break out in a sweat, Odysseus shuffled slowly back to his stool. Irus was still there, licking the grease from the wooden board that Telemachus had brought their meat on.

'Irus, would you like more meat? And a whole skin of wine to yourself?'

The giant – ridiculously large compared to the diminutive table he sat behind – nodded mutely. Odysseus heard the mocking laughter of the suitors behind him and guessed Leodes had failed in his attempt to string the bow.

'Can you stand on the other side of those doors and keep them shut? Can you hold on to the iron rings until I tell you to let go of them again?'

Irus just smiled.

'You see, the suitors are going to fight over who marries the queen, and some will want to be let out before the fight is over. You have to stop them. Nobody can escape until Telemachus or I say so. Do you understand? Good, then go outside and hold the doors shut behind you.'

The beggar rose to his feet and left. He closed the doors, shutting out the grey morning light and leaving the great hall in a tomb-like gloom, relieved only by the glow from the hearth. Odysseus picked up his stool and carried it to the opposite wall, setting it down next to the large pithos. The side door opened and Melanthius entered holding a block of white tallow, which he began warming by the fire. When it was ready he handed it to one of the suitors, who greased the bow vigorously in an attempt to soften the wood. But his dismal effort at stringing the bow was no more successful than Leodes's had been, and concluded in a torrent of curses.

The next man pushed him aside and, after adding more grease to the bow, stepped astride it and tried to bend it. His failure was met with chorus of catcalls. Odysseus did not wait to watch any more of their efforts. The time to act was approaching. Spotting Eumaeus and Philoetius on a bench at the back of the hall, he signalled for them to follow him.

'I can't watch any more,' Eumaeus said as he followed Odysseus out into the shadowy passageway and closed the door. 'One of them is sure to string the bow and claim the queen as his prize.'

'And what if none of them does?' Philoetius asked. 'Surely that was the point of the challenge?'

The swineherd shook his head.

'Penelope knows she's honour-bound to take one of them for a husband.'

'Unless your king returns,' Odysseus said.

Philoetius laid a hand on his shoulder.

'My friend, we've been praying for that ever since the first of the suitors arrived.'

'Ever since we heard the war was over,' Eumaeus corrected. 'If only the gods would answer us. But it's an empty hope. It always was.'

'Didn't the oracle say he'd return by Apollo's feast day – *today*? And it's not even noon. Anything can happen between now and sunset.'

Eumaeus shook his head.

'Your optimism is admirable, but you haven't spent ten years watching the horizon, excited by the least glimpse of a sail, only to be disappointed when it doesn't bear Odysseus's dolphin. No one loves the king more than I do, but even I have to accept he isn't coming back.'

'What if he came in secret?' Odysseus persisted. 'Counting his enemies and his friends; biding his time until the moment was right to strike? What would you do if he was here in the palace now, Eumaeus, waiting to face the suitors and reclaim his throne? Would you stand and fight with him?'

'You've had too much wine...'

'I would stand by him,' Philoetius said. 'I may have been young when he went away, but I remember he was a good king. Ithaca was a happy place then and I long for those days to come back. And I want to see Antinous and Eurymachus and the rest pay for what they've done in his absence. *I* would fight with him against the suitors, even if it were just the two of us. Even if it meant death.'

The passion in his voice pleased Odysseus. The cowherd had indeed been little more than a child when he had sailed for Troy, but his loyalty was beyond question. His words seemed to have moved Eumaeus, too, who looked at Philoetius in surprise. He gave a slow nod and looked down at his feet.

'You're right, Philoetius. If the king returned I would fight at his side. Of course I would. But not to bring back the old days or punish the suitors for their crimes. I'd fight because he's my master. Twenty years hasn't lessened my loyalty to him; twenty more could not do so.'

'Then I tell you he has returned,' Odysseus said. 'He is here on Ithaca. Here in this very palace.'

'If he was I'd know him, whatever his disguise,' Eumaeus said. 'Why do you say such things?'

'Because *I* am Odysseus.'

The two herdsmen looked at him uncertainly. Philoetius gave a shake of his head.

'The Odysseus I remember had short legs, a chest like a wall and shoulders out here. Nothing could change him into the man I see before me.'

'A god could, and did,' Odysseus insisted. 'Athena herself transformed me, and will change me back when I slay the first suitor. But any rogue can use the gods to justify himself, so I offer you a different proof. Eumaeus, do you remember I visited my grandfather on Parnassus when you were a young slave? Do you remember the wound I received there, and the scar I've borne ever since?'

'I remember this much: that the young prince was gouged by a boar. The beast's tusk ripped open his thigh from above the knee and left him with a mark that I would recognise anywhere.'

Eumaeus reached down and pulled aside the ragged hem of Odysseus's tunic. Even in the weak torchlight the pale scar was clearly visible. The swineherd's mouth slumped open. He fell to one knee and ran his fingertip along the crooked line of the old wound.

'Is it…?' Philoetius asked in a whisper. '*Is it him*?'

Eumaeus was shaking his head.

'I don't believe it. It's impossible.'

He stood, his hands shaking, and stumbled back against the wall. A roar of laughter came from the great hall, as if in mockery of the strange reunion. Then Eumaeus burst into tears and embraced his master.

'My lord, my lord.'

Odysseus kissed his forehead and stepped back. Eumaeus dropped to his knees and buried his face in his hands, his shoulders convulsing with emotion. Odysseus now looked at Philoetius, whose complexion had turned ashen and whose eyes were wide with confusion and joy and disbelief. He held out his trembling hands to his master, who took them in his own and kissed them. Tears streamed down Philoetius's face as he knelt before the returning king. Odysseus placed his hands on both men's bowed heads.

'Listen, my friends, you must still your tears and take control of your emotions. I have returned, but alone and without force of arms. If I'm to reclaim my throne and my family, then I have to destroy the suitors. I've observed them for a single day and know they won't accept me as king. They're arrogant, like their fathers, and they've developed an appetite for power that will only be satisfied by the throne. Only death will put an end to their hunger, and death is what they deserve. But Telemachus and I can't slay them all alone. Will you prove yourselves true and fight beside us, now you know that I am Odysseus? Even though we are all likely to fall?'

Philoetius wiped away his tears with the edge of his cloak.

'I'm no warrior, my lord. My life has been spent caring for animals, and I couldn't have asked for a happier one. But if it's my fate to die in battle, who am I to question the will of the gods? I will fight.'

'Me too,' Eumaeus said, raising his red-rimmed eyes to look at his king. 'I have no wife or children to feed, or to mourn me if I die. How can I long for your return for twenty years, then fail to stand by you now you've come back? We are yours to command.'

'And to reward, if the gods grant us victory. From this moment on you are free men, and if you are still alive when the sun rises tomorrow I will find you each a wife and build you both homes in which to raise families of little swineherds and cowherds. But now, listen to me.'

He took them by the arms and lifted them to their feet. Speaking quietly, he told them the plans he had made with Telemachus and how he wanted them to help. Philoetius nodded and ran off down the corridor. Eumaeus followed Odysseus back into the great hall. There they found more than half of the suitors sitting on the benches, looking despondently at those who remained on their feet. That so many could already have tried their hands at stringing the bow in such a short time showed how little opportunity they had been given – no more than a single attempt each, Odysseus guessed. And by the seditious looks on some of their faces it was clear they were not happy with the bullying methods employed by those who remained standing. The friends with whom they had enjoyed years of riotous feasting had shown themselves to be selfish and ruthless in their ambitions.

Leocritus was at the centre of the remaining suitors, holding the bow at a safe height above the hearth in the hope the heat would make the wood more supple.

'Enough now,' Eurymachus said, sounding bored. 'Time to test your strength against the bow or sit down with the rest of these weaklings.'

He took Leocritus by his shoulders and pulled him away from the flames.

'Get your hands off me!' Leocritus snapped. 'I've had my hopes set on the queen just as long as you have, feasting every night at the same table as you and Antinous. Why should I surrender my chance to be king just because some oversized thug I *used* to think was my friend rushes me through the test?'

Eurymachus seized Leocritus by his mass of curly hair, forcing his head downwards. As he squealed with pain, Antinous bent down and looked him in the eye.

'Really, Leocritus? What chance did you honestly think you had of becoming king? A king's fool, perhaps! Now, take your turn or take your leave. We don't care either way.'

Eurymachus released him and he stood, scowling at his assailants as he rubbed his head. Positioning himself astride the bow, he pinched the loose end of the string and stretched it upwards, while with his other hand he pulled down on the upper tip of the weapon. He strained loudly for a while until he was red in the face, but the wood had barely moved. Then Eurymachus took him by the tunic, snatched the bow from his hand and pushed him towards the benches. The defeated youth sat down among the others and spat in the dirt.

'Hasn't anyone managed to string that old antique yet?' Odysseus said, lowering himself onto his stool by the door. 'Come on, Eurymachus, what are you waiting for? String it now and put us all out of our misery. You're strong enough, aren't you?'

'For once, something worthwhile has come out of that stinking dog's mouth,' Eurymachus said. 'I'm tired of watching you little sparrows chirping and flapping your wings and getting nowhere. It's time the eagle claimed his throne!'

'It isn't your turn!' shouted a young nobleman, moving through the crowd of onlookers. 'We agreed to follow the order of seating, and I'm next.'

Eurymachus spread his hand across the man's chest and pushed him backwards into the crowd of other suitors. The man leapt back to his feet, pulling his blue cloak aside to reveal the sword at his hip. But before he could lay a hand on the hilt, the point of Antinous's blade was against his chest.

'Don't be a fool, Demoptolemus. It's Eurymachus's turn to try the bow. Phemius! Phemius, where are you?'

'Here, my lord.'

'Play us all a tune to soothe our nerves, will you? Tempers are getting strained, and we don't want bloodshed.'

The bard took his lyre onto his knee and began to play, the soft notes easing some of the tension in the great hall. Antinous nodded for Eurymachus to continue, though as Eurymachus hooked his thigh over the lower half of the bow and took a firm hold of its notched upper end Odysseus saw the anxiety on Antinous's face. He also noted that he kept his blade ready in his hand.

Eurymachus tested the strength of the wood with his right hand, then spat on his palm and rubbed it against his tunic before taking hold again. Sucking in through his teeth, he pushed down on the top of the bow with his left hand, while with his right he drew the loop upwards. After a moment, the bow began to move. Slowly the loop edged towards the notch. Eurymachus's teeth were gritted hard and sweat was gleaming on his forehead and the bulging muscles of his arms and legs. Antinous's eyes widened, while around him some of the suitors began to shout encouragement. Those on the benches came forwards to watch and Telemachus stood on his chair to see over their heads.

Odysseus was sitting on the edge of his stool, his gnarled hands clenched tightly into fists as he watched the loop creep closer to the top of the bow, even to within a finger's breadth. A hair's breadth. Now it was touching the narrow pinnacle of wood, bumping against it with each tremor of Eurymachus's muscles as he tried to lift it over and onto the notch.

Chapter Twenty Six

Penelope's Choice

'Athena,' Odysseus whispered. 'Is this the man you want to rule Ithaca in my stead? Have you brought me back home just to witness the bastard son of Polybus take my wife and my throne from me?'

Eurymachus's arms were shaking uncontrollably. He gave a shout of rage and tried to force the loop over the notch. It missed, and with it the last of his strength gave out. The bow sprang up again and Eurymachus crashed backwards at the foot of the royal dais. In a fit of rage, he hurled the bow at the fire. Antinous reached out and caught it.

'Come now, Eurymachus. You've had your turn and failed, but the rest of us still have to have ours.'

Antinous reached down and offered him his hand. Eurymachus took it with a scowl and pulled Antinous closer to him.

'It's impossible,' he growled. 'Not even Odysseus could string that bow.'

'Well, one of us must,' Antinous replied, dragging him to his feet. 'For now, though, I propose we take meat and wine to strengthen ourselves before we continue with the test. Where are the stewards?'

He looked about the great hall, but the only servants present were the eight they had brought themselves and Medon, the herald.

'Medon, pour wine for everyone, if there's any left,' Antinous ordered. 'Telemachus, where are your slaves? This may be the last day you entertain us, but will you insult us by making us wait on ourselves?'

Telemachus exchanged glances with his father, but said nothing. Antinous's face was crossed with concern as he looked around the great hall, the bow still in his grip. Eurymachus picked up a cup of half-drunk wine that had been left on a table and drained it before throwing it in the fire.

'What's the point any more, Antinous? We all failed,' he said, indicating the men who had returned to their benches, 'and if *I* can't do it, what makes you think you can? I'm twice the man you are, Antinous, and ten times stronger than anyone else here.'

'Strength has nothing to do with it,' Antinous responded. 'If it had, Eurymachus, you'd have succeeded. The point is this: Penelope set the challenge for the *gods* to choose between us. If they'd wanted you to be king, you'd have strung the bow *and* shot an arrow through those axe heads over there. Even Leocritus could have done it, if Zeus wanted him to. And so I won't just give up. I will have some food and wine, and then I'll take the test. Where are those slaves?'

'I'm with Eurymachus,' Agelaus said. 'This is just another of Penelope's tricks, like Laertes's shroud. I say we go upstairs and *make* her pick one of us.'

'You're wasting your time, Antinous,' Eurymachus said. 'I tell you there isn't a man alive that can string that bow.'

'Then how about one who is dead?'

They turned and looked at Odysseus.

'You don't, I hope, mean *yourself*?' Antinous said.

'Am I not as good as dead in your eyes? Indeed, my name used to be feared and honoured by the great, but my long sufferings have brought me down into shadow. I've been forgotten by the world, little more than a ghost to haunt the dreams of children. But come now, what harm will it do to let me try my ailing strength on the bow? What are you afraid of?'

'We're afraid of nothing!' Antinous snapped. 'Least of all a miserable wretch like you. The truth is you have no right to try stringing that bow. Your audacity is breathtaking. You should be content to sit in the presence of your betters, eating our food and drinking our wine, and listening to the wisdom of our talk. But *you* have the nerve to consider yourself our equal, maybe even our better! Do you expect to heap humiliation on our failure by achieving a feat many of us have already found impossible? Or perhaps you intend to take the Lady Penelope as your own wife.'

The others laughed at the suggestion and launched pieces of bread and meat at Odysseus. One threw a wine cup that hit him on the knee, splashing him with its dregs. The narrowing of Odysseus's eyes was the only sign of his anger. Slowly, he pushed himself up from the stool.

'Why would I compete for any woman's hand when I already have a wife? All I ask for is the chance to prove myself. But if you're scared I will disgrace you all...'

'If any man here has the right to say who can or cannot handle the bow, it's me,' Telemachus said. 'Until my father returns, this house and everything in it is mine. There's no question this old beggar is going to string the bow, so calm down and amuse yourself at his efforts. Eumaeus, pass him the bow.'

The swineherd took the weapon from Antinous's fingers and handed it to Odysseus. As their eyes met, Eumaeus gave a small nod and left the hall through the side entrance. Odysseus tested the weight of his old bow. He had not handled it for many years, but it felt familiar and comfortable in his grip. And yet, as he held it, he felt his hand shaking.

The weak daylight that had filtered in through the smoke-hole in the ceiling became suddenly dull and grey, turning the atmosphere in the great hall oppressive. He heard the hiss of heavy rain outside and smelled its dampness in the air. He looked round at the insolent, angry faces of the suitors and realised the time had come. This was the moment he had anticipated for twenty years, for which he had faced so many trials; the moment in which he would reclaim his kingdom and his family. But as he weighed the number of the suitors in his mind and felt the feebleness of his aged limbs, he began to doubt. In his youth there would have been no pause for thought. Even in the prime of his years he would not have been daunted by the task ahead. In those days he would have understood there could be no turning back. But now his heart quailed.

'Well, what are you waiting for?' called a voice

'Ha!' Eurymachus snorted. 'Where's your bravado now, old fool?'

The expressions on the suitors' faces began to change. Where before there had been nervous anticipation – a fear that the man who had unexpectedly defeated Irus might surprise them all again – now there was relief and mockery. He was the joke they had always believed him to be. Odysseus looked at Telemachus and saw the hope in his son's eyes wavering. Soon the admiration that he felt for his father would turn to disgust. He closed his eyes and saw Calypso's mocking face. His plan to slay the suitors was futile. It had been easy to hope when only Telemachus had known his identity, easy to talk about killing over a hundred young men. But his hopes were baseless. The truth was that if he did not put down the bow and shuffle out of the hall to the laughter of the suitors – and the hate of his son – then he was doomed to die, and take Telemachus and the two herdsmen with him.

When he opened his eyes again he saw a slave girl standing before him. She looked like Autonoe, only taller. None of the others seemed to notice her.

'Odysseus,' she said. 'Do you remember Philoctetes? Do you remember how he had been marooned for nearly ten years? Forgotten by the Greeks who stranded him there, until the gods said Troy could not fall without him? And when you brought him back to the army, did he fail in his task?'

'No,' Odysseus whispered.

'The Olympians haven't forgotten you either, Odysseus. Do not fail us. Do not fail yourself. Remember Philoctetes.'

'Somebody take the bow from him,' shouted Antinous. 'I thought he was at least going to provide us with some amusement, but he can't even do that. Leocritus, bring the bow to me and then go find some slaves to bring us food and wine.'

Odysseus wiped the tears from his eyes. The goddess had gone, and he knew in his heart he would never see her again. But he had made up his mind. As Leocritus approached, he sat up and stood one end of the bow in the dirt.

'You shall have your entertainment, my lords,' he announced.

Leocritus looked at Antinous, who signalled him back to his bench. Odysseus turned the bow around, checking for signs of woodworm or other damage. Finding none, he stood and put his left leg over the bow. His bones and muscles complained at the movement, but nevertheless he sensed a strange warmth returning to his shoulders and arms.

Telemachus moved to the edge of his chair and the suitors' chatter faltered into silence. The soft music of Phemius's lyre faded away and every eye became fixed on Odysseus. He gripped the top of the bow and pinched the looped end of the string, pulling it taut. Whereas the others had kept their legs straight, he leaned into the bow, using his weight to add pressure. He felt the sudden strain of the upper end against his palm. At the same time, he sensed the strength returning to his arms. With barely a grimace, he bent the bow inwards and slipped the loop over and into the notch.

Odysseus allowed himself a brief smile, then looked up at his audience. Some eyes were wide with shock, others narrowed in disbelief. Mouths hung open, aghast at what they had witnessed. Even Telemachus shook his head incredulously. Then Odysseus pulled his leg back through the bow and plucked at the string. It sang gently, for a moment the only sound in the room. Then a clap of thunder rumbled menacingly from the skies above the palace, followed by a hundred voices erupting as one.

'We shouldn't have let him try!'

'What now?'

'It's a trick!'

Telemachus stood and picked up the quiver of arrows. He brought them over to Odysseus and laid them at his side.

'Do it now, Father,' he urged.

'Not yet.'

'The herdsmen will be waiting for us. The time to act is *now*.'

'No, Son. I have one more thing to do. I let your mother down, and now I must win her back.'

He took an arrow from the quiver and fitted it to the string. Telemachus shook his head, but Odysseus motioned for him to back away to the door.

'What are you doing?' Antinous shouted. 'You've proved yourself by stringing the bow, now give it back to me.'

'Why you?' Eurymachus demanded. 'Now the bow's strung, we should all have a chance at completing the test!'

More voices joined the clamour, and for a moment Odysseus was forgotten. He counted the arrows in the quiver. Twenty at the most. Had Philoetius done as he had been asked? None of it mattered any more, he thought. It was in the laps of the gods.

He looked at the row of axe heads. The rings for the hafts were at shin height. Any archer hoping to shoot through them had to bend over while kneeling. That was how it had always been done, but the difficulty of balancing while aiming made the shot impossible even for the best of men. Indeed, he had never achieved the feat himself. But he had seen it done. He recalled the evening before Philoctetes had duelled against Paris in front of the gates of Troy. Menelaus, angry that the gods had chosen Philoctetes to fight Paris, wanted to prove he was not the great archer others believed him to be. He challenged the best men in the army to shoot an arrow through a dozen axe heads, the ultimate test of any man's skill with a bow. Prizes were offered, but even silver and gold were no match for the honour of being named the greatest archer in the Greek army.

Several men had tried and failed. When it came to Odysseus's turn, his arrow had skimmed through the first axe head, nicked the next and – driven off course – crashed into the blade of the third. Then came Philoctetes. But rather than kneeling and bending over to fire, he had placed a footstool in the sand and leaned back across it. With his body at the level of the rings, he had shot his arrow through all twelve and claimed both the prizes and the glory.

The sound of Phemius's lyre began to fill the hall again. As the arguing voices mellowed and died away, Odysseus set his stool down on the axis of the rings and – with some difficulty – lay across it so that it supported his back.

'Hey! What's he doing now?'

He looked through the axe heads and adjusted the position of his body until he could see a clear line through them all. Resting the arrow on the bridge of the bow, he drew back the string. More voices were raised in protest, but he paid them no heed. He steadied his breathing, closed his left eye, and released the string.

–

'What is it, my lady? What's the matter?'

'Can't you guess, Hippodameia?' Autonoe asked. 'How would you feel if you were being forced to marry one of those louts?'

'But they're handsome and high-born. Some of their families are rich, very rich indeed...'

'That'll be all, Hippodameia,' Penelope said, sitting on her bed and wiping her eyes. 'Leave me. You too, Autonoe.'

'Yes, my lady,' Hippodameia said, giving the queen a final, concerned look before leaving.

Autonoe was about to follow, then turned and knelt at Penelope's side.

'I know you thought Theoclymenus was a way out of this, my lady. But it wasn't the will of the gods.'

Penelope reached out and stroked her cheek.

'Then the gods truly are cruel.'

'Sometimes. Perhaps to the unworthy, or to strengthen us. But your time of testing is coming to an end. You won't have to marry one of those men, I promise it.'

Despite the weight of her sadness, Penelope managed a smile. Autonoe had a good heart and was bright with the hope that youth instilled in her.

'I know,' she said. 'The gods won't make me share my bed with one of those men, or give them the throne they hanker for. Not if I don't want to. They'll provide a way out.'

They already have, she thought, leaning forwards and kissing her maid on the forehead. Autonoe stood and smiled weakly.

'They will,' she said.

She closed the door behind her and Penelope felt suddenly and terribly alone. The sombre daylight that filtered in through the thin curtains was grey and oppressive. The air was chill, and she felt the goosebumps rising on her naked arms. Why had Theoclymenus abandoned her? She would never know, and it mattered little now. Her last chance to take back control was gone. Now only two choices remained, and she had already resolved she would not give herself or her son's rightful inheritance to the suitors.

Her gaze fell on the washing basket. Then she remembered asking Autonoe to take the clothes to be laundered. Fearing death would cheat her, she ran across the room and tore the few remaining clothes out of the basket. And there it was. The rope.

She breathed a sigh of relief, and immediately thought how odd it was she was pleased she still had the means to kill herself. A strange last glimmer of treacherous joy in a life that had suddenly plunged into cold shadow. Taking the rope in her fingers, she rubbed her thumb against its coarse weave. Then she went to her dressing table and sat down. Propping the polished bronze mirror against the wall, she held the rope to her neck as if she were trying on a necklace. It was rough and horrible on her soft skin. Tears clouded her vision. Clutching the rope to her chest, she stumbled to her bed and fell across it.

She lay there sobbing for a while, hoping someone would come and stop her. But the corridor outside was silent, and the only sounds in the palace were the muffled shouts and laughter of the suitors. For a moment she entertained the thought of going to the kitchens, finding a knife and taking it to the great hall. She could stab Antinous and maybe Eurymachus before they overwhelmed her. But insane though they might think her, one of them would still force her to marry him and take the prize that only she could give.

No, there was only one escape. She turned over on her back and stared at the hook on the ceiling beam, beckoning to her like a curled finger. She sat up and tied a loop big enough to fit over her head, though it was difficult with shaking hands and tear-blurred vision. Then she dragged the chair from her dressing table and positioned it below the hook. Standing on the chair and reaching up on tiptoes, she estimated the length she would need and hitched the rope securely over the hook. It was a knot she had asked one of the fishermen in the market to teach her, and she knew it would hold.

Carefully, she turned about and was almost surprised by the closeness of the loop to her face. She stared through it at her room. Everything seemed alien, as if it was not the place she had slept and dressed and hidden from the harshness of her world in for so many years. The grey light robbed it of its comforting brightness. Outside, it began to pour with rain.

She put her hands around the rope and slowly pulled it over her head. It rubbed harshly against her neck. Tears spilled from her eyes, making the room a blur. She wondered whether Eumaeus would be the one to find her, or maybe Autonoe. She should have asked Autonoe to come back after a certain time. She would understand. Not that it mattered, as long as Telemachus did not find her.

She reached out with a foot. The chair wobbled a little and she tightened her grip on the rope as it sat round her neck. She realised then how easy it was to lose her balance. How easy the whole thing would be. She brought the foot back. And then she thought of Odysseus. Was he dead, she wondered? Would they meet again in the Underworld? Would they remember each other there? A peal of thunder tore through the skies above the palace, startling her and almost knocking her from the chair. Her tears flowed faster now. She imagined the way the black powder around her eyes would leave stains on her cheeks. Was there no dignity in death?

What did it matter?

She rested her toes on the edge of the chair and pushed it away behind her.

Chapter Twenty Seven

Slaughter in the Palace

Eperitus sat on the edge of the jetty and looked at the waiting merchantman. He had tossed his eyepatch onto the compost heap as he passed through the palace gates, relieved to no longer have to hide his identity. The galley captain was glad to let him work his passage for as far as he wanted to go, and so shortly he would leave Ithaca for the last time. He did not care where he went after that, though he felt no temptation to spend the rest of his life as a sailor on a merchant ship. He has seen more than enough of the sea in his lifetime.

He watched the crew cover the cargo with tarpaulins against the rough weather ahead. The skies were darkening and Eperitus could feel the fine spots of rain on his skin and smell the coming storm in the air. Out in the straits that separated Ithaca from Samos, two men were rowing a small boat over the choppy waters. They would be lucky to make it back before the rain caught them.

He tried to think where he would go. Not back to Pylos, where he guessed his return would not be welcomed. Nor Sparta, with its memories of the courtship of Helen and the founding days of his friendship with Odysseus. Perhaps Crete.

'What does it matter?' he asked himself.

He flicked a pebble off the jetty. It landed in the undulating water with a plop, leaving a trail of bubbles as it sank. He did not care where fate took him now. He just wanted to think of something other than Odysseus and their bitter parting; or of his betrayal of Penelope and Telemachus. Or of Autonoe and her offer of a home. Such things were not for him. His life was doomed to be one of strife, unhappiness and discontent. How different to the naïve dreams of his youth.

He lifted his eyes to the straits again. The rowing boat was closer now. A heavily built old man was at the oars, his broad back facing Eperitus and obscuring the man in the stern. Even at that distance he could discern odd snatches of their conversation between the gusts of wind and through the chatter of the sailors on the merchantman. Then he distinctly heard mention of the suitors and Penelope.

'We should have done more to stop them, years ago, when they first started gathering.'

'Aye – like vultures. We failed because we believed he'd return and...'

A tarpaulin came lose in the increasing winds and flapped loudly until it was secured by swearing sailors. So, some of the islanders, at least, shared his sense of guilt. Penelope had done everything in her power to defend her husband's kingship, but when the worst of the noble families – led by Eupeithes – had smelled a chance to seize the throne for themselves, few had aided her. When she had promised to remarry, none had asked why. When there should have been uproar about the actions of the high-born suitors, there was only a cowed silence. Penelope and Telemachus had been betrayed by their own people, both high-born and low.

More than that, they had been betrayed by the gods who brought about the war that had robbed them of a husband and a father – that had robbed a whole generation of their husbands and fathers. But who could question the gods? he thought. They decided whether a man succeeded or failed, whether he lived or died. Odysseus had always believed a man could decide his own fate, and yet the prophecies about him had been right. Despite everything he had achieved, either by feat of arms or his use of cunning, he had only returned in the twentieth year since he had sailed for Troy – alone and destitute, just as the Pythoness had foretold.

And yet she had said nothing of what would happen next. The oracles had been silent about whether he would then return to being a king, husband and father, or whether he would be murdered in his own palace, knowing that his wife and throne would be usurped by another. Perhaps that part of his fate had been left to himself to write.

The waves lapping against the shore were now pitted with raindrops. Eperitus felt a bump against the end of the jetty and heard a voice call out for someone to catch a rope. From the corner of his eye he saw the captain of the galley reach down and help the two men from their little boat.

What of his own fate? he wondered. Did the gods care enough about him to decide how his life would go on from here, and how it would end? Did the small and unimportant men and women feature in the thoughts of the immortals? It was a question beyond his understanding. All he knew for sure was that the narrative of his life had already been woven into a heavenly tapestry, vast enough to encompass every human existence since the creation of the earth to the end of time.

But the ending of his story made no sense. Why had he been put through so much suffering? Why had he overcome so much, changing beyond recognition from the youth who had been exiled from Alybas so many years before? Surely all those things had a purpose? Had the gods really planned for him to die alone and unloved in some distant corner of the world, looking back in bitterness? Or was he writing that ending himself?

'Theoclymenus?'

He turned and saw Mentor standing at the end of the jetty. Remembering he had thrown away his eyepatch, he pulled his hood over his head so that his face was in shadow. He stood as Mentor approached.

'Are you leaving already?'

'Yes. The captain there has offered me passage, if I work for it.'

'And where will you go?'

'Crete, probably.'

'I'll be sorry to see you leave. So will Telemachus. He thought a lot of you. Forgive me, this is my friend, Halitherses.'

Halitherses, the figure Eperitus had seen rowing the boat, stepped forwards and offered his hand. Eperitus took it. He had not seen his former captain for twenty years, and the glimpse he caught of the old warrior from beneath the edge of his hood brought back memories of Ithaca when he had first known it.

'I was hunting on Samos, but Halitherses came to bring me back,' Mentor continued. 'Telemachus wants us both to go to the palace as quickly as possible. Probably concerned about the reaction of the rest of the suitors when Penelope makes her choice. Come back with us, Theoclymenus. The merchant won't be leaving for a while yet.'

'I can't risk them sailing without me.'

'You seem familiar,' Halitherses said. 'Throw back your hood, man, and let's see your face.'

Eperitus was taller than both Mentor and Halitherses and knew he could not hope to hide his identity from them for much longer. Reluctantly, he took hold of his hood and tipped it back. The rain was coming down much harder now, hissing in the water on either side of them. It quickly soaked his hair and beard and penetrated his double cloak and tunic.

Mentor wiped the rainwater from his eyes and stepped forwards.

'Your eye! Where's your leather patch?'

Thunder boomed across the open skies. Halitherses took hold of Mentor's arm.

'Zeus's beard. I knew I recognised that voice. It's Eperitus!'

-

The bow hummed and the arrow sprang from the string. To Odysseus's eye it appeared to shrink rapidly, like a stone dropped from a great height. It disappeared through the first axe head and he saw no more. There was no sound of metal upon metal, no thump of a heavy axe head falling down in the dirt; only the silence of the suitors and – a heartbeat later – the thump of the arrow as it buried itself into the far wall.

Odysseus sat up and released the breath he had been holding.

'He *did* it!' said Leocritus, rising slowly from his bench. 'I don't believe it. The arrow passed through all twelve axes.'

'It can't have.'

'I saw it with my own eyes.'

'We all saw it.'

'Who *are* you?' Agelaus demanded, rising from his seat with his wine cup clutched in his hand. 'No beggar can do what you've done.'

Odysseus pushed his aching body up from the stool and stood in front of the side door. He glanced at Telemachus, who gave a nod and came to stand at his side.

'I didn't let you down, Son,' he said in a low voice. 'I've failed you for twenty years, but not this time.'

'You've never failed me. When Palamedes put me before the plough, you turned aside, didn't you? And you've fought every day since to come back home. You've done everything a true father would do.'

'I asked you who you are,' Agelaus repeated. 'You've strung the bow and won the contest, and you've made a fool of all of us in the process. Now, tell us who you are so we can decide what prize to award you.'

All around the great hall the suitors were staring at Odysseus. Their shocked expressions were morphing into looks of anger. They had been disgraced by an old beggar, a humiliation few of them wanted known outside the muralled walls of the chamber. And Odysseus could guess at the prize they intended for him. He stood the quiver at his feet and removed an arrow. Fitting it to the string, he pulled it back to his cheek and took aim at Agelaus.

'That's not funny...' the suitor began, holding up a warning finger.

The bow sang for a second time. The arrow flew fast and hard, passing through Agelaus's soft throat until it was stopped by the fletching of black feathers. Dark blood pumped from the wound, spilling down over his chest. He choked briefly, spraying blood over the suitors nearest to him, then instinctively raised a hand halfway to his neck. Before his fingers could touch the wound, he dropped his wine cup on the table and fell sidelong in the dirt.

Cries of shock and fury rose up from the crowd of suitors.

'You clumsy oaf!' one shouted, pointing at Odysseus. 'You've *killed* him!'

'You can't worm your way out of this one, old fool,' Eurymachus snarled. 'A hunting accident with a bow is one thing, but *this*! You'll die for what you've done and your body will be food for the vultures.'

'Somebody take that bow out of his...' Antinous began, then fell silent.

The rage that had stirred up the crowd of suitors began to ebb as more faces stared in dumb alarm at Odysseus.

Almost from the moment the arrow left the bow, Odysseus had felt his body fill with warmth. It began in his chest and radiated outward, driving the cold stiffness of age from his flesh and filling each muscle and joint with a rush of burning energy. The pain that had imprisoned his body lifted from him, like the removal of heavy armour after many days of battle; and his shrunken chest and limbs expanded to their former dimensions. Strength and suppleness were restored to every part of his body, and he felt the power return to his hand as it clutched the bow. He stared down at himself. The beggar's rags were still there, but now they were stretched tight over his broad, muscular torso and limbs. Athena had kept her word. He was himself again.

'Father?' Telemachus asked, staring at him in disbelief.

Odysseus nodded.

'It's me, Son. The father you've never known has come back to claim what is his.' He turned his gaze on the suitors, a smile on his lips. 'Do you know me now, noble lords? I am Odysseus, son of Laertes. Even in your darkest nightmares, you never imagined you would see me here again. You've helped yourself freely to what you knew to be mine: my livestock; my wine; my maids. You even plotted to steal my wife, and with her my throne! But the rightful king of Ithaca has returned. Your fate has been sealed.'

He fitted another arrow to his bow and the crowd of suitors shrank back before him.

'Wait! Don't be hasty, my lord,' said Antinous, edging forwards with his hands raised before him. 'Everything you say is right. We were wrong to feast at your expense and set our ambitions on your wife – even if we were only here because she promised to remarry if you didn't return. But Agelaus – the man you slew – was the one who led us. His heart was set upon your throne, not ours. Be satisfied that you've had your revenge in full, and let the rest of us go. Killing us will solve nothing. But if you let us live we will compensate you for everything that we took. Twenty oxen per man!' He looked at the king expectantly, but saw his hard expression had not softened. 'We'll give you bronze and gold, too. Tell us what you want and let's discuss terms.'

'That's your father talking, Antinous,' Odysseus replied. 'Do you forget that I've been among you for two days, observing your ways, noting your crimes – deciding who are the ringleaders and who are the lackeys? And for all his arrogance and the blackness in his heart, Agelaus wasn't chief among you. Even Eurymachus can't claim that title, much though he would like to. *You* were, Antinous. As for your offer of compensation, I don't want your oxen, or your gold and bronze. The payment I demand is the lifeblood of each and every man here. So, fight or die – the choice is yours.'

As he spoke he was aware of Ctessipus moving slowly through the crowd to his right. A blade gleamed in the firelight.

'Then we fight!' he yelled, dashing forwards.

Odysseus turned and let his arrow fly. It hit Ctessipus between the eyes, knocking him backwards into the dirt. He lay there with his foot twitching, though his spirit had already left him. The suitors now ran in different directions, crying out in panic. Some hurled themselves against the double doors, but were thrown back. Confused that the doors would not move, despite the bolts and bar being on the inside, they tried again. Odysseus's next arrow hit one of them in the back and he fell dead against the doors. The others scattered.

Some of the suitors had run to the walls where shields and spears had hung for many years, but which they now found empty. Others overturned the heavy wooden tables – scattering cups, dishes and food across the floor – and threw themselves down behind them. Seeing there was only enough cover for half the suitors, vicious fights broke out. Odysseus calmly fitted another arrow, took quick aim at a tall youth who seemed at a loss where to hide, and shot him in the chest. The force of the arrow threw him back against the wall, where he slumped to the floor in a lifeless heap. Two more fell in quick succession as they fought to pull others out from behind the cover of the tables.

A small group now formed behind the hearth, with Amphinomus at their head. Drawing their swords and shielding themselves behind footstools, they circled the flames and advanced hesitantly upon Odysseus. His first arrow hit one of them in the groin. The man gave a muted grunt and staggered sideways into the fire, where he thrashed out the last of his life screaming among the burning embers. Another threw down his stool and ran back, diving over one of the upturned tables. Odysseus aimed his next arrow at Amphinomus but, remembering the kindness he had shown him when he was a beggar, he wavered and switched to the man beside him. The arrow leapt from the bow and drove into the corner of his mouth. The force of it smashed his teeth and pierced his spine, bringing him down in the dust.

The others now cast aside their cumbersome footstools and rushed forwards. The nearest fell with an arrow in his heart. The second raised his sword and ran directly at Odysseus. With no time to fit another arrow, Odysseus tossed his bow up, caught one end in both hands and swung the other into his attacker's face. His nose broke and blood poured down over his mouth and chin.

As he fell, Amphinomus – the last of the group – lunged at Odysseus with his sword. There was no time to bring the bow back across and parry the blade, but as Odysseus gritted his teeth against the inevitable impact of the sharp bronze passing into his chest, he heard a clang and saw the suitor's blade driven upward and aside.

Telemachus moved past his father, driving Amphinomus back with the ferocity of his attack. Their weapons clashed loudly and Amphinomus's was sent flying from his hand. A moment later the point of Telemachus's sword was at the base of his throat, pushing through the flesh so that his dark blood flowed down the blade. Amphinomus reached up and seized the weapon with both hands, more blood oozing from his fingers as the sharp edges cut through the soft skin. He stared up into Telemachus's face, then the light left his eyes as he slid from the cold bronze to the floor.

Odysseus picked up the dead man's weapon. The remaining suitor, his face a mask of blood from his broken nose, staggered back to his feet and groped for the hilt of his sword. With a powerful stroke, Odysseus swept his head from his shoulders. The body collapsed, pumping blood over the floor. Sliding the blade into the belt Amphinomus had given him, Odysseus took up his bow again and fitted an arrow. Antinous and Eurymachus had left the cover of the tables and were encouraging the others to form for another attack.

'Are you just going to hide here until he picks us all off?' Eurymachus shouted. 'Come on! We'll rush him.'

Several nobles rose from behind the tables and drew their swords. Odysseus aimed at Eurymachus, who saw the bow turn towards him and pulled another of the suitors in front of himself. The look of surprise was still on the man's face as Odysseus's arrow pierced the middle of his chest. Eurymachus pushed his body aside and urged the others forward with a shout. Two were shot down as they clambered over the tables, and the rest dropped back under cover again, Antinous among them. Eurymachus cursed their cowardice, saw Odysseus fit another arrow, and joined them.

'Go tell Eumaeus and Philoetius to bring in the weapons,' Odysseus told Telemachus. 'The suitors will soon find their courage again.'

He looked sidelong at his son, who was staring down at the body of Amphinomus. The suitor's blood was still dripping from his blade.

'I shouldn't have killed him,' he said. 'He was a good man. He treated me with decency, unlike the others.'

Odysseus remembered his own hesitation when he had aimed an arrow at Amphinomus, and how it had nearly cost him his life.

'I told him to leave the palace before the gods took their vengeance, but he chose not to listen. His own foolishness killed him, Son, not you. Now, fetch the others before the rest of the suitors find their courage.'

Telemachus disappeared through the side door and Odysseus turned his gaze back to the shadowy hall. More suitors had managed to squeeze themselves behind the overturned tables, while others were crouching in fear, ready to run the moment he raised his bow again. A few had gathered by the large double doors and were trying to push them open, but Irus's strength held them fast. Odysseus shot two before the rest gave up and threw themselves on the floor or tried to hide in the shadows. He fitted another arrow and saw that only two more remained in the quiver. Reaching into the pithos that Telemachus had placed by the door the day before, he felt the fletches of at least another forty. Grabbing a handful, he dropped them into the quiver.

The side door opened and Telemachus, Philoetius and Eumaeus appeared, carrying shields and spears brought from the armoury. Both herdsmen wore leather helmets, but despite their armour and weapons, neither man looked the least bit warrior-like. Odysseus would have smiled at the sight of them were it not for the seriousness of their expressions. They were pale with fear, knowing death was close, and yet they did not recoil from the fight before them. Eumaeus propped an old, mildewed shield and two spears against the wall behind Odysseus.

'I'm sorry we took so long, my lord. We moved the other weapons away from the armoury to another room, just in case. But we're ready now.'

'You've done well. The suitors will soon realise they have no choice but to attack us. When they do, overlap your shields to form a wall and hold them off as long as you can. And if you feel like running, *don't* – not unless I tell you to. Turn your back in battle and it's the last thing you'll ever do.'

He raised his bow again and shot a tall, heavily built man in the shoulder. He spun round and crashed into the wall, knocking out a section of the plaster as he fell. A second shot brought down another suitor, and a third another still. In their terror, some of those without cover fought to hide behind each other, or lifted the bodies of the dead to act as a shield from the deadly arrows. The more aggressive pulled at the ones crouching behind tables. Punches were thrown and heads stamped on in their fright, as Odysseus picked off several more. In desperation, one drew his sword and thrust it into the back of a man hiding behind the edge of a table. He pulled the body away and took his place.

The targets were fewer now. Some suitors feigned death, lying among the fallen, but most were crammed behind the tables. Leaving his son and the herdsmen by the door, he placed the last of the arrows from the pithos into the quiver and hung it over his shoulder. Moving to his right, he found new targets at the edges of the tables, slaughtering more of his terrified foes. Four men sprang up from the nearest group and dashed at him. The first fell with an arrow in his eye. The second was pierced below the ribs and crashed into the dirt, tripping one of the men behind him.

The fourth was a handsome youth with the physique of an athlete. His rich clothing was torn, his oiled skin smeared with dirt, and his elegantly styled hair now hung in dishevelled locks over his forehead. He carried an expensive sword with a golden hilt that had never been intended for battle. He threw himself at Odysseus, arcing the blade towards his neck in a blow that would have swept his head from his shoulders. But Odysseus's fighting instincts had anticipated his attack. He ducked beneath the blade and jabbed the end of his bow into his attacker's stomach, knocking the wind out of him. In the next instant, Odysseus pulled his sword from his belt and brought it down on the man's wrist.

Hand and weapon fell to the floor and a jet of blood spurted from the stump. The young noble gave a cry and fell to his knees, clutching at his wounded limb. Only then did Odysseus notice the other suitor, who had recovered from his fall and now sprang towards him with the point of his sword extended. In the same moment, a spear thumped into his chest and carried him back against the wall. Turning, Odysseus saw Eumaeus, his empty hand still outstretched, staring in disbelief at his first kill.

'Ready your other spear,' Odysseus ordered.

He glanced at the rest of the suitors, some of whom were emerging from the cover of the tables. Sword still in hand, he drew another arrow from the quiver and half-fitted it to the bow. They quickly withdrew again.

He looked down at the wounded man before him, his severed wrist held tightly into his torso.

'Mercy, my lord,' he whimpered. 'Have mercy on me. I only joined the others three months ago. My father will recompense you if you let me live.'

Odysseus felt suddenly uncertain of what to do. He had killed many enemies in cold blood before, but the lad before him was barely more than sixteen or seventeen years old. He slipped his sword back into his belt.

In the same moment, the youth drew a dagger from his belt and lunged at Odysseus's ribs. Odysseus twisted away from the deadly thrust, but the blade cut through the leather strap of his quiver and spilled the arrows over the floor. Odysseus jumped aside, drew back his remaining arrow and fired it into the base of the suitor's throat. Blood erupted from his open mouth and he fell dead at Odysseus's feet.

Seeing the arrows scattered over the floor, the other suitors gave a triumphant roar and jumped to their feet. Odysseus slipped the bow over his shoulder and snatched Eumaeus's spear from the body of its victim, before sprinting back to join the others by the door. Telemachus threw him his shield as he approached and, fitting it over his arm, he turned to meet the onslaught.

Chapter Twenty Eight

The Armoury

Autonoe left her mistress and went downstairs. She paused to listen to the clamour of the hated suitors. Duty told her to go and help the other slaves in the great hall, but a sudden and intense hatred held her back. She hoped Odysseus would kill them all! But there were too many of them, even for him. And if they defeated him, what then? A new home and lives of misery for the queen and for herself. Sometimes she wished she had a man's strength, to take a sword and murder the men who had defiled her. But she was just a woman, and a slave at that, good only for dressing her mistress and styling her hair.

How she had wanted to tell Penelope that her husband had returned. She had been distraught that Theoclymenus – as she knew him – had abandoned her and left her with no option but to marry one of her contemptible suitors. Autonoe considered returning to the bedroom to comfort her, but Penelope had asked to be alone and Autonoe dared not disturb her.

Then she remembered Melantho, tied up in a storeroom in one of the less-frequented parts of the palace. She despised the girl, but she did not have the heart to leave her for much longer without food or drink. Resolving to take her a cup of water and some bread, Autonoe made her way to the kitchen. To her surprise, the room was filled with household servants, very few of them doing any work. Hippodameia was there, sitting on the lap of one of the stewards. As Autonoe poured a cup of water and snatched up a basket of bread, Hippodameia held out a hand to stop her.

'You're not to go into the great hall,' she said. 'Telemachus's orders: whatever we might hear, we're to remain out of the way. It's a bit odd, considering the wedding's today, but we're not complaining.'

Hippodameia and the steward giggled and fell into a kiss. Autonoe ignored them and slipped out into the dimly lit passageway. She chided herself for having forgotten Melantho. If she had not tied her up and gagged her, she would surely have revealed Odysseus's identity to the suitors, but she felt sorry for her all the same. She would be terribly thirsty and hungry, and the ropes around her wrists and ankles would have chafed her skin raw.

Autonoe stopped. Rope! Why had the queen hidden a rope in her laundry? What could she want with it, unless…? She paused. It was a ridiculous thought. The queen would never do such a thing. She was not afraid of the suitors, even if she hated them, and she would not abandon her duty to Telemachus or Ithaca.

'Telemachus,' she said to herself. 'But that's the point! If she kills herself before she's forced to marry one of her suitors, her oath will be meaningless and Telemachus will become king when he's of age.'

She put the cup and the basket of bread on the floor and turned around. She wanted to run to the bedroom, but forced herself to walk. It was ridiculous to think Penelope would ever think of hurting herself. All that would happen was she would be told off for bursting in on her mistress when she wanted to be alone. And yet as she reached the stairs to the upper floor, she took them two at a time and almost ran along the corridor to the bedroom. A loud clap of thunder brought her to a momentary halt, and in the pause she heard the scrape and clatter of a falling chair.

'Aphrodite save her,' she gasped, and ran for the door.

She threw it open and dashed into the room. The bed was empty and the curtains were blowing inward on a cold breeze. Then she saw Penelope, the rope pulled tight around her neck as she hung from a ceiling beam. Her face was red and she was gagging. Autonoe ran to her and seized her legs, lifting her up to relieve the pull of the rope. Seeing the chair nearby, she reached out with her foot and pulled it towards her. Somehow she managed to set it back onto its legs. Resting the soles of Penelope's sandals on the seat, she climbed up beside her and slipped the knot from the hook on the ceiling beam. Penelope slumped into Autonoe's arms. Carefully, she lifted her down and carried her to the bed.

The queen's eyes were closed and her face bloodless. She was breathing, but the movement of her chest was so slight that Autonoe feared she would yet slip away. She begged the gods not to take her mistress, to let her live. Gently, she untied the rope from around Penelope's neck. It had left a red lesion on her pale skin, the sight of which brought stinging tears to Autonoe's eyes. She wiped them away and began stroking her mistress's hair.

'My lady?' she whispered. 'My lady, can you hear me? Penelope? Oh, mistress Aphrodite, what should I do?'

She kissed the queen's forehead. The gods had brought her back in time to save Penelope from strangulation or serious damage, but her spirit was already fading – slipping away into a darkness from which it would not return. She had finally accepted that Odysseus was not returning, and did not want to go on any more without him.

'But he's back!' Autonoe sobbed, holding her mistress's hands in hers. 'If you'd waited just a little longer, you'd have seen it for yourself. I couldn't tell you, though I wanted to. But Odysseus *is* back! He's here in the palace, after all this time. He's come back for you, my lady.'

Her words fell on ears that could no longer hear. The queen lay still on her bed, and the faint rise and fall of her chest had faded away. Still holding on to one of her hands, Autonoe rested her head on Penelope's chest and closed her eyes. Through her tears, she offered the gods her own life in exchange for her mistress's, but they refused to listen, or felt the bargain a poor one. Autonoe could feel her own frightened heart beating rapidly, but there was no sound at all from Penelope's.

She laid there a little while longer, eventually pulling herself away and sitting back on her heels to regard the queen. In the great hall below the suitors were shouting loudly to each other, disturbing her mistress' peace; but Autonoe cared nothing for their ill manners any more. Penelope was dead. Whatever happened today – whether Odysseus unveiled himself and slaughtered the young nobles who had laid siege to his wife, or whether their numbers overwhelmed him and sent his mighty spirit down to Hades – Penelope would still be dead. A new wave of tears burned Autonoe's eyes and flowed down her cheeks. Not knowing what else to do, she reached out and folded her mistress' hands across her stomach, praying that her spirit would find the balm of forgetfulness in the Underworld.

Then Penelope's hand reached out and took her by the wrist. Her eyes flickered open.

'Is he here?' she said. 'Has Odysseus really returned?'

–

The suitors gave a furious cry and fell upon the narrow wall of defenders. One threw himself at Odysseus and was impaled on his outthrust spear. Odysseus dragged his weapon free and the man's entrails spilled out over the floor. Ashen-faced, he staggered backwards into his comrades, his hands desperately trying to stem the flow of blood and intestines.

At Odysseus's side, Philoetius planted the head of his spear into the shoulder of another attacker, piercing the sinews and nearly severing his arm. The suitor stared down at his limb as it hung uselessly at his side, the blood pouring from the wound. A second attacker now threw himself at Odysseus. He slipped inside the point of his spear and aimed a blow at the king's head. Odysseus raised his arm and deflected the blade with his shield before pushing it into the suitor's face. The man fell back, stunned, and Odysseus plunged his spear into his chest, breaking through his ribs and puncturing his heart. A third man advanced at him, but slipped in the entrails of the first suitor and was easily finished off. The rest fell back.

Glancing to his left, Odysseus saw Philoetius ram the boss of his shield into another suitor and knock him backwards. He followed it up with a thrust of his spear, but the man turned the blow aside with his sword and retreated. Eumaeus and Telemachus, though, were engaged heavily. A man lay dead at their feet, but three more – Eurymachus among them – were trying to find a way between their spears and bring their swords to bear.

At a signal from Eurymachus, one of the men sprang forwards. At the last moment, Telemachus's spear point caught him in the hip and he collapsed in the dirt. Close on his heels was Melanthius, the goatherd. Avoiding a defensive thrust of Telemachus's shield, he slipped behind him and reached the side door. A dagger gleamed in his hand. Afraid he would stick it in Eumaeus or Philoetius as their backs were turned, Odysseus brought his spear up to his shoulder and hurled it at Melanthius. But the goatherd's instincts were quick. He ducked down and the spear clattered off the wall behind him. Then he opened the door and escaped into the shadowy corridor behind.

'Shall I go after him, my lord?' Eumaeus asked.

Odysseus spared a glance at the suitors, who had left their dead and retreated back to the line of tables.

'No, let him go. If Zeus grants us victory, then justice will catch up with him sooner or later.'

-

Melanthius pulled the door shut behind him and ran. The torches had fizzled down to glowing stumps, leaving the passageway in almost total darkness. Terrified he would be followed, he fumbled his way forwards in the direction of the storerooms. A thread of light ahead of him marked the door to the kitchens, and as he passed it by he heard the gathered slaves talking within. With no sounds of pursuit behind him, his sense of panic lessened and he began to ponder his situation.

Antinous and Eurymachus had contrived the attack in the great hall so that Melanthius could slip around the defenders into the corridor and make his way to the armoury. Once there, he was to find as many shields and spears as he could carry and bring them to the main entrance. After removing whatever obstacle had been placed against the doors, he was to give the weapons to the suitors and go back for more. The hardest part of their plan had succeeded – at a cost in lives – and yet Melanthius was not sure he could go through with the rest.

He had enjoyed privileges from the suitors, who had allowed him a place at their feasts and treated him almost like one of themselves. And he felt confident that when Antinous, Eurymachus or one of the others married Penelope and became Ithaca's new king, his loyalty and service would not be overlooked. But the shock appearance of Odysseus had changed everything. Armed with just his bow, he had single-handedly killed over twenty of the suitors without hesitation or qualm, and showed every intention of murdering the rest. Perhaps if Melanthius was to sneak back and reveal Antinous's plan to Odysseus, he would save his own life and earn a generous reward. Or, as was more likely, they would simply kill him there and then.

And what of his beloved sister, Melantho? Her disobedience and arrogance towards Telemachus and Penelope had surprised and concerned him, and it would not go unpunished. Perhaps he could persuade her to run away with him? Find a boat to the mainland and start a new life there. But he knew Melantho would never accept that. Ever since she had been a little girl – her looks as irresistible then as they were now – she had dreamed of being a lady. Spoiled by the queen, she had grown up almost thinking of herself as one of the royal family, rather than a slave girl born to a slave father.

She still expected to gain a husband among the suitors, letting several of them sample her delights in the hope one at least would acquire enough of a taste to marry her. The fact that nobles did not wed slaves did not deter her, and Melanthius knew he could never persuade her to leave Ithaca with him as long as any of the nobles still breathed. And so he must remain, too. He would fetch arms for the suitors and pray they were victorious.

He sensed a change in the air to his left and, stretching out his hand, found the opening to one of the corridors that led to the storerooms. On the floor ahead of him was a strip of light, flickering brightly in the blackness. It came from the armoury. Pressing his ear against the door, he listened for a moment and entered.

The torchlight was almost blinding after the blackness of the corridor, but his eyes adjusted quickly. He had only been in the armoury once before and he remembered it being filled with piled shields, racks of spears, bundled swords, daggers, bows, quivers full of arrows, and helmets heaped like skulls. But to his astonishment, the room was empty. He pulled the torch from its bracket and held it over his head, letting its light shine into each shadowy corner. All that remained was a bronze cap and a broken leather strap.

'But that's *impossible*!' he shouted, kicking the helmet against a wall. 'This whole room used to be *filled* with weapons. Antinous will kill me if I go back empty-handed.'

He fell to his knees dejectedly. And then he heard a thump. As he lifted his gaze from the dirt floor, he heard it twice more. He stood up and shone the light around the room. A sound like a muffled voice was coming from behind the wall to his right. Mystified, he pressed his ear to the plaster and heard more thumping and muted shouting. He left the armoury and went to the neighbouring storeroom, nudging the door open cautiously. It was dark inside and smelled of barley. A scuffing sound was followed by more mumbling. He stepped inside and held up his torch. A woman lay on her side by one wall. Her ankles were tied with thick rope and her hands had been bound behind her back. A cloth was wrapped around the lower half of her face.

'Melantho!'

He jammed the handle of the torch upright between two sacks of grain and undid the gag. Melantho took a deep breath then broke into a fit of coughing. After untying the ropes from around her wrists and ankles, he slipped his arms under hers and lifted her into a sitting position. Her head slumped on his shoulder and she draped her hands around his neck.

'Who did this to you?'

'Autonoe,' she rasped in reply.

'The queen's maid? But why?'

She said nothing, but as her strength returned she began to sob. He could smell the heady perfume she sometimes wore – a gift from one of her lovers – mingled with the tang of fresh sweat.

'How long have you been here?'

'Since last night. Do you have anything to drink?'

'I'll fetch you some water from the kitchens.'

He picked up the torch, but she refused to let go.

'No, don't leave me.'

He took her arms from around him and kissed her on the forehead.

'I won't be long.'

He left the storeroom door open behind him and set off along the corridor. Before he reached the kitchens, though, he found a basket of bread and a cup of liquid on the floor. Who had left them there and how he had missed stumbling over them in the dark he did not know, but he picked them up with his free hand and walked quickly back to his sister. She drained the cup in one draught and followed it with a piece of bread.

'Why did she do this to you?'

Melantho paused briefly to think. Suddenly her eyes widened and she clutched at her brother's arms.

'Quick Melanthius! Find Antinous and Eurymachus and tell them that he's here! Odysseus has returned to Ithaca and is planning his revenge.'

The goatherd removed her hands from his arms and held them.

'We know. He has the suitors holed up in the great hall. He picked off twenty or thirty with a bow, and now he and Telemachus – with the help of Eumaeus and Philoetius – are guarding the only way out with shields and spears. I managed to slip past them, but when I went to the armoury to find weapons it's been emptied.'

'What about Antinous? And Eurymachus?' Melantho asked, her eyes wide with sudden fear.

'They were alive when I left them. But they won't be for much longer unless I can find something to arm them with.'

'I heard Eumaeus and Philoetius emptying the armoury earlier,' Melanthius said. 'But they didn't take the weapons far, judging by how rapidly they were coming back and forth. They could only have moved them to another storeroom along this corridor. Here, help me up.'

Melanthius took his sister by the arm and lifted her to her feet. She almost collapsed at once, but he caught her and held her upright while the blood returned to her weakened limbs. Soon she gave him a nod and they left the grain store and inspected the other rooms along the corridor. As they opened the last door the torchlight was met by the gleam of bronze from the shadows. Melanthius fitted the torch in a bracket by the door and looked around. The room housed stacks of clay tablets – the palace records from decades past – and several wooden chests, which, when he opened one, contained reams of different-coloured cloth. The rest of the room was filled with shields and spears and a host of other weaponry.

'Are you strong enough to carry a couple of spears?' he asked.

'I'll do anything that helps stop that bastard taking back his throne,' she replied.

Melanthius hung a shield over his sister's shoulder and gave her two spears. For himself, he took two shields on his back, another on his arm and four spears in his hands. They both wore bronze helmets. With some difficulty, they exited the room and fumbled their way along the narrow passage in the darkness. They found the main corridor and followed it to the left until they saw daylight framing a door at the end. This led out into the courtyard, where they blinked against the grey light that filtered through the dark clouds above. The worst of the rain had passed, leaving a fine drizzle that quickly left the surface of their clothes damp.

Melanthius looked over to the pillared threshold and was surprised to see Irus leaning with outstretched arms against the doors of the great hall. One knee was bent and the other leg was firmly planted behind him. He seemed oblivious to their arrival.

'Irus!' Melanthius shouted. 'What in Hermes's name do you think you're doing? Men are dying in there because you've prevented them from escaping.'

Irus paid him no attention. Then Melantho approached the portico.

'Irus, listen to me. We need to get into the great hall.'

He turned and looked longingly at her. But he did not move.

'Come away from the doors,' she said. 'Melantho and I want to go inside. It's raining and we have gifts for the suitors.'

His eyes rested on her a few moments longer, then he shook his head.

'Get out of the way, you damned oaf!' she yelled.

Melanthius shed the shields he was carrying and all but one of the spears. Moving past his sister, he rammed the head of the spear hard into Irus's side. The sharp bronze sliced through the layers of muscle and between the ribs, piercing his chest. Irus threw his head back in a silent cry of anguish and pulled one hand away from the doors. Blood gushed from the wound onto the floor of the porch, but slowly he moved his hand back to the door. Melanthius pulled back the spear and plunged it this time into Irus's neck. More blood spilled over the bronze and down over the giant's chest. He clutched briefly at his throat, and fell dead on the threshold. With some difficulty, they pulled his body aside and opened the doors of the great hall.

-

Antinous had held back during the fight, urging the rest of the suitors on from the rear and watching in dismay as they fell to the spears of the defenders. But between the to and fro of the melee he saw Melanthius dodge past Telemachus and escape through the side door. At a signal from Eurymachus, the mob of suitors – they could hardly be described as anything else, Antinous thought – fell back.

'He's through,' Eurymachus said, arriving at Antinous's side. 'The question is, do we trust him not to run off?'

'He'll think about it, but he'll realise he doesn't have that option. If we don't find proper weapons to fight with then we'll all die.'

'That's going to happen anyway,' said Leocritus from behind them. 'The gods want revenge. We've flaunted the rules of xenia and now they've brought Odysseus back to make us pay for it.'

Elatus joined them. His tunic and left arm were sprayed with gore, but he did not appear to be wounded.

'Believe that if you want, Leocritus, but then you never were much of a man. The gods listen to those who offer them the most sacrifices, and we've been slaughtering cows and goats before them every night for three years.'

'And doomed ourselves with every drop spilled,' Leocritus retorted. 'Whose animals were they, you idiot? Every one we killed was accounted to Odysseus's credit, not ours!'

Elatus stepped forwards with clenched fists, but Antinous placed a hand on his chest and pushed him back.

'The gods can favour whom they please, but in this battle, there's only one thing will decide the outcome: numbers. We've lost a few, a quarter of our number perhaps, but we still outnumber them twenty to one or more! Besides, they've spent all their arrows and we'll soon have spears and shields to match theirs. Then we'll see who gets the upper hand.'

'Victory will be ours,' Eurymachus said, staring at their opponents' shield wall. 'Nothing is going to rob us of that. And when she sees her husband's corpse, Penelope will have to marry one of us.'

'And there'll be fewer of us to choose from,' Antinous added.

He looked at the bodies strewn across the great hall. He had seen murals of battles and heard descriptions of combat with spear and sword, but they had not prepared him for the sheer brutality of it all. Mulius – Amphinomus's attendant – lay in an unfeasible pose at the foot of one of the columns, his legs folded under his body at the knees in a way that would normally be impossible for a living man. The black-shafted arrow protruding from his chest had made it possible, though.

Another, Demoptolemus, lay on his back with his stomach ripped open like a gaping mouth. His entrails were strewn and tangled along the dirt floor. Poor Eurydamas had joined the suitors a few months before, but now lay face down with his arm attached only by a flap of skin, his blood forming a puddle around him. The sight of their corpses, among so many others, was enough to fill any man with fear and revulsion. For Antinous, it only increased his desire to kill the man who had returned from the dead to reclaim a throne he had effectively surrendered twenty years ago.

Both sides stood facing each other across the hall. Neither was capable of renewing hostilities – Odysseus and his small band too few in numbers to take the fight to the suitors, and the suitors lacking the weapons or armour to attack their enemies' shield wall. Then Antinous heard voices outside the porch. A moment later the doors were being pulled open and Melanthius and Melantho appeared bearing shields and spears. Eurymachus pushed the other suitors aside and collected weapons for himself, Antinous and Elatus. Grinning at their change in fortunes, Antinous hung the shield on his arm and took up the spear in his other hand.

'For this I'll make you chief herdsman to my flocks when I'm king,' he told Melanthius.

'As will I when I'm king,' Eurymachus countered. 'Now, go and fetch us more so we can put an end to this little uprising.'

'I'll go help,' Leocritus said.

'You're not skulking off while we take all the risks,' Antinous said, grabbing him by the shoulder and indicating for Melanthius and his sister to go. 'If any man wants a place in the *new* Ithaca, he will stay and fight.'

Leocritus pulled his arm free.

'Not me,' he said. 'I haven't got a chance of becoming king, so why should I risk my life for *your* ambitions? I'm going back to the safety of my father's house while I still can.'

A few voices murmured in agreement. Leocritus turned and crossed the threshold, pausing briefly to look up at the rain. As he stepped out onto the puddled morass that was the courtyard, Antinous's spear thumped into his back. He lurched forwards, blood surging from his lips, then fell face down.

'Does anybody else want to go home?' Antinous asked, staring at the other suitors.

The handful who had edged forwards now melted back into the ranks of their comrades. At that moment, Melanthius and Melantho reappeared with more shields and spears. Several suitors jostled for possession of them.

'Come on,' Antinous said to the others as the goatherd pulled his spear from Leocritus's back and handed it to him. 'It's time we convinced Odysseus that he should never have come back.'

The eight suitors with shields and spears formed a line. Another four with spears stood behind them, while those with swords spilled out across the flanks. Odysseus and his comrades crouched lower behind their shields.

'You men will cast your spears on my command,' Eurymachus said, touching six nobles on the shoulder as he passed behind them. 'You can't miss – they're like fish in a net. Now, put an end to their puerile ambitions so we can get on and decide which of us is going to take Penelope to his bed tonight.'

He raised his arm and brought it down again with a chopping motion. Six spears flew through the air towards their enemies. Two thumped into the door behind them; another pair clattered off the walls. A fifth buried itself into the floor at Telemachus's feet, while the sixth tore into Eumaeus's shield, almost ripping it from his arm. It pierced the fourfold leather and carried him back against the door, but to Antinous's dismay the swineherd pulled the bronze head from his shield and rejoined his comrades, a little shaken, but unharmed.

'Again!' Eurymachus commanded, raising his own spear to his shoulder.

Antinous dashed across and laid an arresting hand on his arm.

'No, Eurymachus. We only have six spears and Melanthius hasn't come back with more yet. Besides, I have an idea that might prevent more bloodshed.'

Eurymachus gave him a puzzled look, but Antinous turned and walked towards Odysseus, his palm outstretched in sign of parley.

'You know you can't win this fight, Odysseus,' he said. 'Even if you kill another ten, twenty or even thirty of us, sooner or later we will overwhelm you. Your arrows are expended and now we have shields and spears. So let's talk terms, man to man. You'll find I'm fair-minded.'

Odysseus lowered his shield.

'Other than your worthless lives, I don't see what you have to offer me,' he replied. 'But I will listen to your pleas.'

'Pleas? I'm not the one who needs to plead, my lord. You have three men at your side and no hope of other help, unless you intend to arm your maids. But there are more than eighty of us. We could kill you all if we wanted to – not just you and your two slaves, but your son, too. Be sensible, now; is that what you want? Indeed, what *do* you want? What is it you desire, Odysseus? I doubt you've suffered ten years of war and another ten years trying to get home just to be butchered in your own palace, your lifeblood mingling with that of your son and your servants. You came back to be reunited with your family and reclaim your throne. As for us, each one wants to marry Penelope and become king of Ithaca. So let's compromise and prevent the spilling of any more blood.

'We will allow you, Telemachus and your servants to live, and we will surrender Penelope to you, giving you our word that no man among us has touched her. In return, you and your household must swear to leave Ithaca forever and find a new home on the mainland. You can take your slaves, except Melanthius and Melantho, and all your wealth, and we will add to that gold and silver to compensate you for the loss of your home and lands. But you must announce before the people that their new king will be chosen by the Kerosia, and that he and his line will be their new rulers forever. Show wisdom now, Odysseus, and agree to our proposals. The alternative is death.'

Antinous stepped back to rejoin the ranks of the suitors, many of whom patted him on the shoulder and spoke words of enthusiastic encouragement. Odysseus could not refuse such an offer, some said. It was his only hope. And it was a more than reasonable proposal. Antinous agreed. He had spoken fairly and justly, like a true king should. And when he *was* king, he would make certain Odysseus and Telemachus were never able to return and challenge his rule. They would die in some ambush on the mainland, and their slaves and gold would be brought back to swell his own wealth. To Penelope he would give the choice of becoming his wife or becoming his whore, and he cared not which she chose.

Odysseus stepped forwards.

'I agree with Antinous,' he began, to the triumphant celebrations of the suitors. 'I agree that the only alternative is death. *Your* deaths! Antinous has proved once again your arrogance. You have insulted the gods, and the only appeasement they will accept is the sacrificing of your lives.'

He raised his spear and hurled it at Antinous. The suitor ducked aside at the last instant and the spear took the life of the man behind. Telemachus, Eumaeus and Philoetius cast their own spears, hitting two more of their enemies, who fell with pitiful cries among their comrades.

Antinous retreated to the line of the tables. Eurymachus gave a shout of rage and threw his spear. It passed the edge of Telemachus's shield and found its target, eliciting a cry of pain. Antinous gave a victorious shout as he saw Odysseus's son fall. Another volley followed from the suitors, hurling their remaining spears along with the ones they had taken from their dead. They clattered from the walls and punched through shields, and this time Eumaeus fell.

'Kill them!' Antinous shouted, drawing his sword.

The suitors gave an exultant cry and rushed forwards.

Chapter Twenty Nine

The Battle in the Courtyard

Eumaeus heard the whoosh of the heavy spear and the cry of pain as Telemachus fell. A moment later more spears came spinning out of the gloom, their bronze points gleaming with deadly menace. He felt one thump into the floor by his foot and heard a second as it pierced Odysseus's upheld shield, penetrating the layers of hide and splitting the wicker framework. More hit the walls and the door behind him. The last he did not see at all. It struck him like a giant fist, glancing off his left collarbone and cutting through the upper flesh of his shoulder. Intense pain sliced through him and he felt his legs folding up, followed by the feel of the soft earth beneath his buttocks and lower back, and then the slamming of his head against the door.

What followed was a blur. He heard a shout of triumph erupting from many voices. Then a powerful hand seized his upper arm. The door was opened behind him and he was dragged into the cool darkness of the passageway, where he was dumped hastily against the wall. Someone leapt over him, followed by another who stumbled into his legs and fell with a grunt. Then the door was slammed shut and two figures threw their weight against it. An instant later there was a corresponding thump from the other side as the suitors hurled themselves against the wood. The door gave a little, then was pushed shut again.

'Get up, Eumaeus.'

He gazed up. Odysseus was standing with one heel against the back wall and both hands on the door, looking down beneath his armpit at him. Philoetius was beside him. Eumaeus tried to push himself up on both hands, but was undone by a sudden bolt of pain from his left shoulder and collapsed back against the wall.

'It's just a graze, Eumaeus. Stand up and tear off a strip of your cloak to stem the flow of blood.'

Eumaeus raised his fingers to the wound and felt the blood flowing warm from where the spear had sliced through the flesh. A hand's breadth lower and it would have punctured his heart. He uttered a quick prayer of thanks to the gods then gingerly clambered to his feet, picking up his shield and spear as he did so. Glancing down, he saw Telemachus propped against the wall, tying a band of cloth from his cloak around his lower forearm.

'It's nothing,' he said, noticing Eumaeus's look. 'A flesh wound.'

He pulled the knot taut with his teeth and knelt beside Eumaeus. He lifted the hem of the swineherd's cloak and tore off a length of cloth. The door rattled again as more suitors tried to force their way through.

'It won't be long before they think to ram the door with one of the benches, or just come through the courtyard and enter the passage from there,' Odysseus said.

'What will we do?' Telemachus asked, lifting Eumaeus's arm and winding the cloth as best he could under his armpit and around the wound, wincing at the pain from his own injury as he did so. 'This passage is narrow. We could hold it against any number of men.'

'For a while, maybe, but not long if they attack us from both sides. And we can't go deeper into the palace and draw them after us – I don't want the fighting anywhere near Penelope. We have to get out into the open where there's more room to manoeuvre. I'll hold them here while you and Philoetius head for the courtyard; we'll take our chances there.'

'What about me?' Eumaeus asked.

'I want you to go to the place where you hid the weapons and stop Melanthius. He's already brought them a dozen shields and spears; we can't afford for any more of them to be armed. Once you've dealt with him, rejoin us as best you can.'

Eumaeus looked at the king uncertainly, then gave a nod and ran past him up the unlit corridor. As it bent round to the right he paused and tried to move his left arm. It was painful, but the spear had not pierced his muscles. And yet he could feel a grating inside his shoulder that made him suspect his collarbone was broken. For a moment, he wished Odysseus had accepted Antinous's offer. If the choice had been his, he would have taken it. But the king was proud and determined, and would rather accept death than the shame and dishonour of giving up his throne to the suitors. And that was why Eumaeus loved him and would obey him to the very end.

He slipped his shield from his shoulder onto his right arm and readied his spear. Behind him he heard the crash of the door being flung open, followed by angry shouts and a sudden clash of arms. Eumaeus quickened his pace towards the storerooms, using his spear to feel along the walls in the blackness.

Soon he reached the side-passage that led to the storeroom where he and Philoetius had hidden the weapons and armour. He could see a patch of orange light on the wall at the far end, and from the open door heard the clack of wood and the sound of voices. Fear rose up through his chest, momentarily immobilising him. In the great hall he had stood shoulder to shoulder with Odysseus and Telemachus and his nerves had been soothed by their presence. Here he was alone, reliant on his own courage rather than that of others. And Melanthius had help, in all likelihood another suitor. Ignoring the pain in his shoulder, he grasped his spear in both hands and advanced.

'That's enough,' he heard Melanthius say as he neared the door. 'Hurry up! I'll follow with the shields.'

Eumaeus felt his hands shaking. He wondered if he should go back and find help among the servants, who he had heard in the kitchens as he passed. Then a figure emerged from the storeroom. He was silhouetted black against the flickering torchlight and three or four spears were clutched in his hands. Driven by panic, Eumaeus lunged with his spear, felt the resistance of flesh and bone giving way to the sharp bronze. The figure released a terrible shriek, but to Eumaeus's horror, it was not the cry of a man, but a woman. The spears dropped from Melantho's hands, clattering loudly on the floor, and she stumbled backwards, clutching uselessly at the blood spilling from her chest. Then she fell, dead before her body hit the floor.

Melanthius thrust his head and shoulders through the open doorway, saw his sister and dropped to her side. He gathered her up into his arms, looked for a moment into her lifeless eyes, then buried his face in her neck.

'Melantho, Melantho,' he sobbed, not caring that her murderer was within striking distance of himself.

Eumaeus felt sick. He wanted to throw down his arms and run away, to find somewhere in the palace to hide until the fighting was done. But he could not. Neither could he kill his helpless enemy. Turning the spear around in his hands, he brought the shaft down with a crack on Melanthius's head.

–

Odysseus handed his spear to Telemachus. With one hand still on the door, he drew his sword.

'Philoetius, go with Telemachus to the door that leads out to the courtyard. I'll follow when I can.'

'Yes, my lord.'

Odysseus watched his son and the cowherd ready their weapons and disappear into the darkness. The press of bodies from the other side of the door was now so great that he expected any moment to be thrown back against the wall and crushed. Quickly, he sprang aside. The door crashed open and several men tumbled to the floor. A sweep of his sword almost beheaded the uppermost. The others screamed and squirmed as his warm blood gushed over them. One he stabbed through the ribs, and then a shield was thrust at him as more suitors clambered in through the doorway, driving him back.

He slipped his own shield from his shoulder to his arm and forced back the tide of new arrivals. They fell over the men who were still in a heap on the floor. Odysseus plunged his sword point through the exposed throat of the first. Though the suitors wore no armour, his instincts sought out the vulnerable points where a man was not protected by his breastplate or greaves. As the remaining suitors clawed their way back out of the passageway, he stabbed one in the groin and hewed the arm from another as he tried to pull one of his friends free.

Taking his chance from the chaos he had created, Odysseus turned and fled. For a moment he was running into darkness, then the door at the end of the passageway opened and grey light came flooding in. Blinking against the brightness, he saw Philoetius and Telemachus silhouetted in the doorway. Then there was a shout and several men appeared in the courtyard beyond. One drove his sword through Philoetius's chest, where it became jammed between his ribs.

As the suitor tried desperately to pull it free, Telemachus plunged his spear into his stomach. He fell with an agonised cry, but Telemachus was forced to spring back from the furious attacks of the man's comrades. Feeling the battle rage come upon him, Odysseus sprinted the remaining stretch of the corridor. Two men now filled the open doorway. Odysseus ran past his son and rammed his shield into them, pushing them back out into the courtyard where a dozen more suitors stood in a semicircle before him. They hesitated a moment too long and he dashed forwards, driving his sword through the nearest man's chest before he could bring his spear to bear. He fell into the mud, his blood spilling into the brown puddles left by the earlier downpour.

A second man brought his sword down at Odysseus's head. Odysseus warded off the blow with the rim of his shield and lunged blindly with the point of his sword, finding flesh and hearing the crack of bone. The man fell dead beside his comrade and the remainder fled back to the porch, where Odysseus saw Irus's corpse face down on the ground. They were met by a crowd of other suitors led by Antinous.

Telemachus had hooked his hands beneath Philoetius's armpits and was dragging him back into a corner of the courtyard. Odysseus slammed the door shut behind them and helped his son prop the wounded herdsman up against a wall. The hilt of his attacker's sword was still buried in his chest, but somehow he was clinging on to the last of his life.

'Am I going to die?'

Blood frothed over his lips as he struggled to speak.

'Yes, my friend,' Odysseus said. 'And you will be held in honour in the Halls of Hades, as are all brave men.'

He remembered the horror of the Underworld – its ranks of phantoms, devoid of hope, forgetful of all that had brought them joy on earth, desperate for another taste of the life that had been ripped from them. And soon, he realised, he would be joining Philoetius there.

So be it, he thought.

'Brave or foolish, my lord? But I thank you for letting me die a free man. May the gods protect you.'

His head rolled onto his chest and they knew his spirit had left him. They stood and Telemachus handed Philoetius's spear to his father. Then the side door burst open and more men poured out, Eurymachus and Elatus among them. Joining with the throng leaving the great hall through the main entrance, they formed a wall of armed men – sixty or seventy strong – that trapped Odysseus and Telemachus in the corner of the courtyard. At last, the magnitude of Odysseus's folly was clear to him. He turned to his son.

'The messages you sent – are you sure they were received?'

'I don't think it matters now, Father. If they were coming, they'd be here by now. Not that they could have made any difference.'

'Then I'm sorry, Telemachus. I gambled with our lives, and I lost. I should have taken Antinous's offer.'

'You know as well as I do he'd have found a way to betray us. Besides, what value is there in a life without honour?'

Odysseus laughed.

'You remind me of an old friend.'

He looked at his son with pride. He had not shirked from his duty or shown weakness in the face of death. Indeed, he was now a man. But more than his pride, Odysseus felt a genuine love for Telemachus, and he knew Telemachus loved him back. He regretted more bitterly than ever now the years he should have spent with his son and all the lost moments that had been taken from them. Intimate memories of Telemachus's first steps and his first words, of carrying him on his shoulders and playing with him, and later of teaching him how to be a man and how to be a king had been denied him. All he had to look back on were times of war and hardship. But the gods had been merciful, too: they had allowed him to see his son before he died, and even to glimpse his wife's beauty. At least he could face death with satisfaction.

He levelled his spear and turned to face the throng of their enemies. Several carried shields now, and had formed a wall that was impassable. He thought of throwing himself at the wall and killing as many suitors as he could before they overwhelmed him, in the hope Telemachus might escape. But Telemachus would not run, even if he ordered him. Then a hard-faced suitor at the centre of the line, a man Odysseus knew as Polyctor's son, Peisander, lifted his spear above his shoulder. He barked a command and a dozen more spears were levelled at Odysseus and Telemachus. The two men raised their shields in a futile gesture, knowing full well that on Peisander's next command their bodies would be torn apart by the force of the bronze spear points being aimed at them.

Then Peisander staggered forwards, his weapon slipping from his fingers. His eyes were wide with shock and blood was spilling from his mouth. He pitched forwards onto the sodden ground, the shaft of a spear protruding from his back.

-

As the suitors streamed out into the courtyard, Elatus edged his way into the shadows at the back of the hall. The others may not have seen it, but there was a quicker way to resolve this fight. A way that would not require any more of Ithaca's young nobility to die. The floor was littered with their bodies, thirty at least. Some lay curled up, others with their limbs spread and their mouths screaming silently at the heavens. Many had arrows protruding from them. A few he had known well, and he remembered them shouting and laughing rowdily at the lavish banquets that they had enjoyed at another man's expense, never realising the price he would demand on his return. But no one had expected him to return.

One of the corpses propped up against a pillar moved.

'Phemius?' he asked.

The bard was still clinging to his lyre, his eyes wide and his face ashen. Elatus walked over to him and gave him a kick.

'Get up and join the others.'

'Why should I? Was I competing for Penelope's hand? No, I'm only here because the rest of you made me come.'

'You still ate the food and drank the wine though, didn't you?' Elatus reminded him. 'Now, get out there and earn your keep, unless you can raise a tune that'll wake these poor souls from their slumber. You made them dance once, Phemius, so why not again?'

Reluctantly, the bard got to his feet. Elatus picked up a discarded sword and tossed it to him. He caught it and trudged out into the courtyard, where the rain had started falling again. Climbing over the bodies that wedged the side door open, Elatus entered the unlit passageway and found his way to the stairs that led up to the queen's chamber. He paused for a moment, listening. Somebody was sobbing quietly up there. Slowly, he drew his sword and climbed the stone steps.

He had never visited the upper floor in the three years since he had made himself a guest in the palace, but guessed the sobbing would be coming from Penelope's bedroom. He followed the sound along a short passage to a door with two benches outside.

'Be quiet now, Hippodameia,' said a voice from inside that he recognised as Autonoe's. 'The queen hasn't suffered any harm.'

'But what about the sounds of fighting in the hall? What if Telemachus has been harmed?'

'Shouldn't that be my concern?' asked the queen. 'And yet I'm not crying, Hippodameia. There will come a time for questions and answers, and for counting the dead; but that time isn't now. We must keep ourselves out of harm's way and await the outcome of the battle, as women have done since time began. Now, go back to the kitchen and thank Eurycleia for the food and wine. And tell her to keep the servants out of the way until all of this is over.'

'Yes, my lady.'

The door opened and a round girl with a large chest and curled black hair looked up at him in surprise. Then her mouth opened and she let out a sudden, high-pitched scream. Elatus ran the point of his sword into her stomach and pulled it out again, cutting the scream short. The girl looked at him in pained confusion, then flopped against the doorpost and slid down to the floor. He stepped over her body into the room beyond, where Penelope was seated on her bed with Autonoe beside her. For a moment they looked in shock at the body of Hippodameia, then Autonoe stood and placed herself between her queen and the intruder.

'Stand aside or I'll do the same to you,' he ordered.

Penelope rose to her feet and stepped forwards.

'Is the fight over, then?' she asked as sternly as she could, despite the tears in her eyes. 'Is this man who my maid claims to be my husband dead? And... and my son with him? Have you come to summon me before the suitors and force me to make my choice from among you?'

He heard the fear in her voice and saw that her hands were shaking, and there was something about her unfamiliar vulnerability that aroused him. She was afraid that all her hopes had been revived again, only to be dashed; and most of all that her husband and son had perished. There was fear in the face of her remaining maid, too. But that was a different kind of terror. She looked at him and remembered the storeroom where he had taken her by force. She remembered the strength in his arms and the confidence to take whatever he desired. But did she fear him for her own sake, or for her mistress's? Of course, he could take either woman or both, if he wished. It was not lust that had brought him to the queen's bedroom, but now the thought was in his mind, it amused him to play with it.

'Then you doubt the man who strung the bow and wreaked havoc among the suitors is your husband?' he asked.

'Any man can claim to be something he isn't. But I ask you again, is he dead? Has Telemachus fallen with him?'

'Both men live, for now,' he said, watching the queen take her maid's hand and squeeze it tight. 'They have murdered many of my friends in the great hall, and I fear more will fall before the end. That's why I'm here. To take you with me before your husband and son and demand they lay down their weapons. If they don't, I will kill you.'

'Then I won't come.'

'You'll do as you're told!'

He sheathed his sword and stepped forwards, seizing her by the wrist. Penelope brought her hand up to slap his face, but he caught it and twisted her arm behind her back, making her cry out in pain. Autonoe threw herself at him, her fingernails reopening the scars on his cheek that they had made days before. He lashed out with the back of his hand, sending her sprawling across the floor.

Penelope fought against his hold, but he threw her face down on the bed. She pushed herself up on her hands and knees and tried to crawl away. Snatching the hem of her dress, he pulled her back, enjoying the feel of her powerlessness. As he did so, the split at the side of her chiton parted to reveal her long, shapely thigh. He stalled at the sight of her white flesh. What did it matter now? he thought to himself. The palace was in chaos and half of Ithaca's young nobility had been killed. He had already struck the queen, so why not go further? He dropped to his knees on the bed and wrapped his arm about Penelope's waist, pulling her towards him. She screamed. Pulling her dress aside, he lay his hand on her thigh and moved it up to her buttock. She twisted round and lashed out at him with her fist. Laughing, he caught her forearm and twisted her onto her back.

Autonoe leapt at him again, pulling his hair and dragging his head backwards. He yelled out, shocked by the sudden pain. Raising himself to his full height, he threw the maid onto her back and straddled her, taking her wrists in his powerful hands.

'Remind you of anything?' he sneered.

He snatched the dagger from his belt and held it against her throat, enjoying the feel of its razor edge upon her soft skin. She looked at him wide-eyed, expecting death at any moment. Then he slipped the blade back into its sheath.

'The next time you interfere, I *will* kill you. Do you understand?'

'Take me,' she said, suddenly. 'I won't resist you.'

'Take you instead of your mistress, you mean?' He laughed. 'What sort of offer is that? A slave for a queen? And why would I want *you*, anyway? I've had you, and you were pathetic. I could've got more response from a corpse.'

She took him by the tunic and pulled herself up, pressing her mouth to his. Her hand moved down between his legs, touching his manhood. Suddenly aroused, he took hold of her waist and ran his hands over her ribs to her breasts, feeling their softness beneath the wool of her dress. And that was when she slipped the dagger from his belt and, with her lips still against his, pushed it into his stomach. The bronze burned hot as it sliced through his flesh. A surge of pain drove up through his body, overwhelming his senses. He felt his blood gush out of the wound as Autonoe withdrew the blade. Then she pulled her face away from his, her expression calm, a slight frown the only indication of her emotions. She stabbed him again, higher this time. And again.

'You took something from me, Elatus. You took away a part of who I am. You made me feel small and weak and worthless. But you didn't destroy me. I won't *let* you destroy me. And I won't let you do the same thing to my mistress, or anyone else, ever again.'

She pulled the knife free and pushed him backwards, his head connecting hard with the floor. As he stared up at the ceiling, his vision began to darken. His body seemed strangely light, as if it was shedding the weight of flesh and bone. The pain faded away, too, and for a moment he felt as if he was rising upwards, a pleasant sensation, like the releasing of a great burden.

And then a shadow fell across him and he felt cold. Suddenly and horribly cold.

Chapter Thirty

Unexpected Help

The gates were unguarded as the three men stole up to them. In the courtyard beyond, the sounds of fighting had died away. Eperitus clutched the shield and spears Mentor had given him, praying to Athena that they were not too late. Halitherses reached the gates and turned to the others. They nodded that they were ready, and he eased one of the heavy doors open.

A crowd of men filled the courtyard to their left, their backs turned to the gates. A handful of bodies were scattered over the sodden mud, and through the open doors of the great hall Eperitus could see many more lifeless shapes in the shadows. There was no sign of Odysseus or Telemachus among the living or the fallen, but the tension in the air told him the battle was not over yet.

'Ready!' a voice shouted.

A man raised his spear to his shoulder. Several others followed his command, and in an instant Eperitus understood what was happening. The suitors' backs were still turned, unaware of the arrival of the three men behind them, and through the wall of their shields he could see Odysseus and Telemachus. Another moment and a volley of spears would end their lives.

'May the gods forgive me,' he said.

Raising one of his spears to his shoulder, he launched it at the man who had given the command. He had not thrown a spear in anger for many years, but his aim was true and the point passed through the man's back and out of his chest, sending him forward with a splash into one of the puddles that littered the courtyard floor.

Mentor and Halitherses hurled their own weapons into the mass of suitors. Both found their marks, killing one man instantly as the bronze point split open his head; the other was caught in the hip, his leg almost torn from its joint. Forgetting Odysseus and Telemachus, the others looked behind themselves in shock and confusion.

Eperitus drew closer to Mentor and Halitherses and they locked shields to present a wall of oxhide. The rear rank of suitors turned hurriedly to face them, two or three of them armed with spears and the rest with swords. Only one carried a shield, while two more held footstools in their hands. Halitherses uttered the command and the three men charged. A large youth threw his footstool at Eperitus's head, then turned to run. Eperitus leapt after him and lunged with both hands on the shaft of his spear. The tip caught the man in the ribs, piercing his flesh and knocking the strength from his legs. He fell onto his back, his face a mask of pain. Seeing Eperitus above him, he clasped his hands together imploring mercy. Eperitus drove his spear into the angle between his throat and his chin, killing him instantly.

He stared at the dead man for a moment, but felt neither pity nor remorse. He felt no sense of guilt, either, for having broken his oath to the gods. As he watched the man's lifeblood seep into the ground, all he felt was satisfaction – the satisfaction of a man who has ended a long period of fasting. He was a warrior by instinct, whether he liked it or not, and the man he had killed had been a threat to all that he held dear. And Ithaca and its king *were* dear to him. They always had been.

He had realised that on the jetty when he had explained to Mentor and Halitherses that Odysseus had returned. Their jubilation at the news was how he should have felt, how he *would* have felt had he not blamed Odysseus for the tragedy that had happened to his wife and child. But he had been wrong to blame his friend. His family had died because the gods had willed it. That truth had taken him a long time to learn, but he understood it at last. And he believed it was the will of the gods that he should fight for Odysseus now, forsaking his oath not to kill and honouring instead the promise he had made to Athena thirty years before – to follow his king always.

He looked up to see that Mentor and Halitherses had killed their opponents, while Odysseus and Telemachus had launched an attack of their own, killing two more. But instead of pursuing the suitors, who were retreating in disarray, Mentor and Halitherses ran to the man they had not seen for twenty years. They fell to their knees before him and he laid his hand on their shoulders before pulling them to their feet and embracing them. Then, as the others took up their shields and spears again, he turned to his old friend. Eperitus felt the shame of his earlier anger, his betrayal of Odysseus and Telemachus and their cause. He fell to one knee, and then

Odysseus was speaking to him, calling him friend and pulling him to his feet and into his arms.

'Can you forgive a stubborn fool?' Eperitus asked.

'There's nothing to forgive,' Odysseus replied. 'I'm just glad to have my friend back. But you swore you would never kill again. What changed your mind?'

'You did. Last night you told me I had to sacrifice my honour to regain it. And you're right: I've allowed my sense of honour to become something rigid and immovable, a stick to beat myself and others with rather than an instinct to do what's right. But your cause *is* right, Odysseus. To turn my back on you and Penelope and Telemachus would be more shameful than breaking an oath taken out of anger and confusion.'

'Even though the gods will punish you for it?'

'Even if it means I pay for it with my life.'

'That's not what they brought you back here for,' Odysseus said, frowning. 'I'm sure of it. You're here to help me win back my wife and my home. Are you with me?'

Eperitus stared at the suitors as Antinous and Eurymachus ordered them into lines before the entrance to the great hall. Still more than half of them remained and, of those, almost two dozen had shields and spears. These formed the first rank, with the rest in the ranks behind them. Their losses had been terrible so far, but they still had confidence in their numbers and the fact many were now fully armed.

'I'm with you,' he answered.

The rain began to fall again. It hissed in the puddles that had already formed across the courtyard and rattled on their shields. Eperitus's damp cloak became sodden and heavy. The rain collected in his hair and beard and ran in rivulets down his face and neck.

'If they attack, they'll fold round the sides and surround us,' Halitherses said, squinting against the downpour. 'We must fall back to the gates. That way they can't flank us, and we still have an escape route if we need it.'

'We'll defend the gates,' Odysseus said, 'but I haven't come back home just to run away again. If any of you wants to escape, then go with my blessing. I'm staying to the death – mine or theirs.'

'My place is at your side, alive or dead,' Eperitus said.

'Everything I have is here, Father,' Telemachus said. 'I'd rather die than see it in the hands of Antinous or one of those others.'

'We'll fight it out together, then,' Mentor said.

He looked at Halitherses, who nodded. Together they retreated to the gates, and Eperitus thought it lucky that the suitors had so few spears, or a couple of well-aimed volleys might have seen the end of them. Instead, realising they had to take the fight to Odysseus, the suitors began their attack. With time to organise themselves, they now drew on the weapons training they had received since boyhood and advanced towards the small band by the gates, marching in step with their spears levelled. Then, at a signal from Antinous, they broke into a run.

Eperitus had moved to the left flank, with Odysseus on his right and Telemachus in the centre. Mentor and Halitherses held the right of their short line. He hated fighting with his back to a fixed obstacle, leaving no room for manoeuvre, but it was the only way to keep from being surrounded.

The front rank of the suitors crashed into them, shield clattering against shield, spear points deflected upward by the thick oxhide. They were driven back almost against the gates by the force of the attack, restricting their ability to move even more. Eperitus was hardly aware now of Odysseus by his side or the others beyond him. Amid the press of bodies – the pushing and shoving behind thick shields, the grunts and oaths, the smell of wet wool and bad breath – he focused on the two men who were pushing against him.

One was a handsome youth with a scrubby growth on his chin, the other older with fierce eyes and a thick beard that seemed to sprout from the neck of his tunic and cover every bit of skin below his earlobes. He was strong, too, and together with the younger suitor they were trying to crush Eperitus against the gatepost. He felt his sandals slipping in the quagmire below and knew that soon they would have him crammed into a position where he could not move or defend himself.

But they had not experienced the bitter struggle of a fight to the death, as he had many times over. All they knew of battle had been learned in the safety of their own courtyards at home, with wooden weapons and opponents who were there to help them, not dismember them or slash them to pieces with sharpened bronze. Eperitus looked into the eyes of the older suitor.

'You can still save your life if you turn and run now.'

'Run?' he laughed. 'Why would I…?'

Eperitus scraped his sandal down the man's shin and slammed his heel onto his toes. The suitor cried out and stumbled backwards. Throwing all his strength behind his shield, Eperitus opened up the man's defences and pushed his spear into his opponent's exposed abdomen. He felt the once familiar tug of sharpened bronze piercing skin and sliding into soft flesh. The man gave a grunt and fell dead.

The second attacker panicked and tried to turn, slipping in the mud as he did so. Eperitus's spear pierced his upper chest and he collapsed over the body of his comrade. A third suitor dashed forward and brought his sword down against Eperitus's shield, where it stuck fast in the rim. Eperitus tore the shield aside, pulling the blade from the man's hand, and plunged his spear into his groin. He collapsed into the glutinous mud, pulling Eperitus's spear from his hands as he fell. Others pushed forward and, as Eperitus tugged his sword free from its scabbard, a figure dashed past him and drove his spear point between the nearest suitor's eyes, killing him instantly.

'Just like old times, eh?' Odysseus said, giving his friend a blood-spattered grin

Eperitus smiled back, realising how much he had missed the excitement of battle. But the smile froze on his lips. By the other gatepost Halitherses had struck down a lad probably a third his own age, sinking his spear in his chest and releasing a jet of dark blood as he pulled it out again. But another figure loomed up beside him, as large and fierce as Halitherses himself. Though his features were blurred by the curtains of rain, Eperitus knew it was Eurymachus.

Mentor shouted a warning, but too late. Eurymachus's spear pierced the side of Halitherses's head, spattering Mentor with pieces of brain and skull. The old warrior dropped to his knees, before falling slowly forwards into the mud. Eurymachus gave a shout of triumph, raising the tip of his bloodied spear to the heavens. The corpse was dragged into the crowd of suitors, who laughed as they hacked at it with their swords.

Mentor rushed at Eurymachus, who turned his spear aside with his shield before retreating to the safety of his comrades. Eperitus saw no more. Encouraged by Eurymachus's victory, the ranks of suitors now renewed their onslaught, shouting as they leapt over the bodies of their fallen comrades.

If the joy of battle had filled him before, Eperitus was now consumed by a fierce lust for revenge. He met his first opponent shield to shield, knocking him aside and stabbing him through the liver. Beside him, Odysseus brought down another suitor. Two more threw themselves against Eperitus, crashing their shields against his. They were close enough for Eperitus to smell the meat and wine on their breath. One was half a head shorter than Eperitus, the other slightly taller. The latter's beard had been neatly cropped in readiness for the day of the wedding and he wore a purple cloak made of the finest wool. It was clasped at the shoulder by a golden brooch depicting a charging boar. As they struggled against each other, Eperitus found himself wondering whether the man was from Samos, where boar hunting was popular among the nobility.

Casting the thought aside, he butted the suitor in the face and split the bridge of his nose. As the man staggered backwards, Eperitus sank his sword into his stomach and he fell dead. The shorter man shoved against Eperitus with all his strength, cursing him and spitting in his face. Swordsmen from the second rank pushed into the opening created by the fall of the first suitor, forcing Eperitus to retreat. Odysseus, too, had been driven backwards by the number of suitors. He threw down his spear and drew his sword.

'Blade work, I think,' he said.

Eperitus nodded, and together they hurled themselves back into the fray. Eperitus hacked down over the upper rim of his shield, cleaving the skull of the nearest man, who joined the growing wall of bodies at his feet. Another suitor dropped his unwieldy spear and tugged at the sword hanging from his side. Eperitus stabbed him through the eye and he collapsed back into the mass of his comrades.

More suitors pressed forward. One tried to bring his sword down on Odysseus's skull and was brushed aside with a sweep of the king's shield. A second aimed a clumsy thrust at Eperitus's stomach, which he parried easily before cutting the suitor's face open with a diagonal slash of his blade. But each step of the fight, whether defending or attacking, had drawn them away from the gates. Three men now appeared to Eperitus's left. Seeing the danger, he tried to move back. One of the suitors stabbed at him with his spear, forcing him to raise his shield in defence while one of the others slipped round behind him.

They attacked simultaneously. Using his shield, Eperitus threw the man to his rear back against the wall. The move opened his guard to the others. One leapt at him with the point of his sword, which Eperitus managed to turn aside an instant before it pierced his groin. Another lunged with his spear. Instinctively judging its mark, Eperitus twisted away and the point glanced over his ribs and became snared in his cloak. But in dodging the blow, he had overbalanced and now fell back into the mud.

He looked up into the falling rain. His ribs ached and the flesh stung where the spear had broken the skin. Two men appeared above him. One was the spearman, who tugged his weapon free from Eperitus's cloak. The other raised a sword over his head to deliver the final blow. Then he threw his head back and arched his chest. The weapon fell from his fingers, and at the same moment blood gushed from the front of his tunic, followed by the head of a spear emerging from his ribcage. The other suitor stared at his comrade in confusion, and in that instant Eperitus thrust upward with the sword that was still gripped in his hand, driving the point up through the man's genitals. He fell back into the mud, clutching at the wound and screaming. Eperitus struggled back to his feet and finished him off.

Eumaeus was pulling his spear from the body of the first suitor. Where he had come from, Eperitus could not guess. To their right, Odysseus, Telemachus and Mentor stood wearily, but with their shields and weapons at the ready. Their faces and arms were spattered with blood that was being slowly diluted pink as it was washed away by the rain. About their feet was a thick layer of bodies. Most were still, but others twitched in the last throes of life or tried to drag themselves away through the mud. The remainder of the suitors were retreating towards the great hall. Two of them took hold of the doors and began to shut them. Telemachus levelled his spear above his shoulder, took quick aim and launched it into the chest of one of the men. He was thrown back into the shadows. The other fled, leaving the doors half open.

'After them!' Odysseus shouted. 'We can't let them escape into the rest of the palace.'

'They're not going anywhere, my lord,' Eumaeus said. 'When I returned from the storerooms and heard the fighting in the courtyard, I decided to bar the side door. The suitors are trapped.'

'You've earned your freedom many times over today, Eumaeus,' Odysseus said, laying a hand on the swineherd's shoulder. Then his smile faded. 'But Philoetius has fallen. I'm sorry.'

Eumaeus's expression hardened and he said no more.

'Come on, Father,' Telemachus said. 'Before they try to close the doors against us again.'

Odysseus glanced across at Mentor, who was crouched over the body of Halitherses. He rose to his feet slowly, wiping the tears from his angry eyes, and nodded to the others. Together they approached the shadowy entrance to the hall.

Eperitus heard the crackle and hiss of the hearth, but no voices. He could smell the woodsmoke and the dirt floor, mingling with the aromas of roast meat and wine. Raising his shield, he moved ahead of Odysseus and the others, waving for them to stay behind him. Stepping over the body of Irus, he crept between the large doors, his senses reaching out before him. His nostrils could now discern the smell of blood, and in the shadows before him he saw the humped shapes of corpses littering the floor. Then he heard the sound of strained breathing and realised the last of the suitors were hiding among the dead.

Suddenly they jumped to their feet. One threw a spear at Eperitus, but the aim was hasty and he deflected it with his shield. The others dashed at him, swords and spear points gleaming in the firelight. The first raised his sword and swung at Eperitus's head. He ducked beneath the blow and hewed the man's arm off below the elbow. Then Odysseus and the others dashed into the hall, killing a number of the suitors and driving the dozen or so that remained back towards the hearth.

A man dashed forwards, tossing his weapon aside, and fell to his knees before Odysseus.

'Have mercy, my lord,' he said. 'I never set my heart on your wife. I'm a priest – Leodes, son of Oenops – forced by Antinous and the others to preside over their sacrifices. If you kill me, you'll bring the wrath of the gods down on your own head.'

'I've had the wrath of the gods hanging over me ever since I left the shores of Ithaca. But they've forgotten their anger and allowed me to come home. Indeed, I am now the *instrument* of their wrath! As for you, Leodes, if you were the suitors' priest then you must have prayed many times that I would not return to Ithaca.'

'No, my lord, never. I swear it...'

Odysseus struck him in the neck with his sword and his head rolled away into the shadows. Shrugging off his shield and sheathing his weapon, Odysseus now took the bow from his shoulder and plucked an arrow from one of the bodies lying nearby. The other suitors scattered, but not before one had fallen with the arrow in his back. The others cowered behind tables. Seeing a figure crouching at the foot of one of the pillars, covered with the recently flayed hide of one of the cattle that had been sacrificed that morning, Odysseus found a second arrow and fitted it to his bow.

'No, Father!' Telemachus cried. 'It's Phemius, the bard. The suitors forced him to attend their feasts, and his music has been a comfort to me in the presence of those men. If you spare any, spare him.'

Odysseus nodded and signalled to Phemius, who threw off the hide and came running over to kneel at Telemachus's feet. In the same moment, Eurymachus stood and leapt over one of the tables. Odysseus fired his arrow, but Eurymachus caught it in his shield and ran on. Odysseus reached for his sword, but too late. The suitor brought his blade down in an arc toward the king's neck, only for the blow to be checked at the last moment by Mentor's shield.

He hurled Eurymachus back and the two men stood glaring at each other, their chests rising and falling heavily. It was then that Eperitus noticed the fresh blood running from a wound on Mentor's shoulder that must have been inflicted in the earlier fighting. He swayed a little, weakened by blood loss and the exhaustion of the battle. Odysseus also noticed the injury.

'Leave him to me,' he said, laying his hand on Mentor's other shoulder and pulling him back. 'You're in no state to...'

Mentor shrugged him off angrily.

'He killed Halitherses. They dragged him away and hacked at his body like it was a piece of meat!'

'The old fool was no friend of ours, always haranguing us in the Assembly,' Eurymachus said. 'He got what he deserved. And you're about to go the same way. The last time we met I promised I'd kill you if you crossed swords with me again. It seems you don't know how to take good advice.'

He grunted as he swung at Mentor's head. Mentor checked the blow with his blade and the clash of their swords rang from the walls.

'When I'm king, I'll hang your weapons on my palace wall,' Eurymachus growled as they faced each other, 'right next to Halitherses's. Together in death, just as you were in life.'

'Still dreaming of becoming king?' Mentor snarled back. 'A wiser man might have begged for mercy when he realised the true king had returned. But you've never been able to see beyond your own arrogance, have you?'

He threw the suitor back and brought his sword down at his head. Eurymachus deflected the blow with his shield and dropped back, smiling. Then his expression changed to a scowl. He spat in the dirt and leapt at Mentor, hacking down at him repeatedly with his sword as if he would drive his opponent into the ground. His hatred gave him strength and Mentor fell back beneath it, step by step, until the wall stopped his retreat. Eperitus moved forward, though he was powerless at this distance to help his old comrade. But Mentor's rage at Halitherses's death was still fresh. Using the strength of his anger, he locked blades with Eurymachus and began pushing him back. Every eye was upon them, watching as both men's arms shook with the intensity of their contest. Then Eurymachus began to weaken, slowly at first, and then more quickly as he realised he was beaten. With a last effort, Mentor swept the sword from his hand and pressed the point of his blade to the base of the suitor's throat.

'Mercy!' Eurymachus begged, taking hold of the sharp bronze with both hands. 'In Zeus's name, have mercy.'

'For three years you've flaunted the laws Zeus gave us,' Mentor sneered. 'Stealing, raping and murdering until you became an offence to the very gods you now ask mercy from. Well, they hear you. And the answer's *no*!'

He pushed his sword through Eurymachus's neck, severing his windpipe and spine. His head rolled backwards and dark blood gushed up Mentor's blade as he withdrew it.

Knowing they would receive no mercy either, the other suitors launched a final assault. Four of them drove Eperitus and Odysseus into a corner of the hall, while Antinous led five others against Telemachus, Eumaeus and Mentor. Eperitus raised his shield and Odysseus drew his sword, but their opponents made no effort to attack them.

Behind them, Eperitus saw Eumaeus – still angered by Philoetius's death – brush aside a sword thrust with his shield and drive his spear into his attacker's liver. Two more suitors, both armed with shields and spears, backed him against a wall. Mentor, seemingly exhausted, was pushed back by two others, leaving Telemachus alone against Antinous. Their swords met with a loud clang and Antinous retreated before him. Eperitus could see it was a feint, designed to draw Telemachus away from Eumaeus and Mentor. But Telemachus was driven by a lust for revenge against the man who had made his life a misery for three years, and angrily pursued him back across the hall, their shields and swords clashing repeatedly.

Then Telemachus's sword was swept from his hand and the point of Antinous's blade was pricking at his neck. He indicated for Telemachus to drop his shield, then grabbed him by the shoulder and pulled him back against his chest, holding the edge of his sword against his throat. The other suitors fell back again to form a line before the hearth.

'Odysseus!' Antinous called. 'Tell your men to drop their weapons.'

'Don't do it, Father!' Telemachus shouted. 'They'll murder us all and take the throne for themselves.'

'Throw down your weapons and I swear I'll let you all live,' Antinous said. 'You'll have to leave Ithaca, of course, and declare me king in your place.' Two or three of the other suitors glanced at him, but none of them said anything. 'But I'll still let you take Penelope and all your wealth with you, just as I promised the first time.'

'Don't listen to him,' Telemachus insisted. 'I'd rather die than let him rule Ithaca.'

But Odysseus shook his head and threw his sword into the dirt.

'No, Son. They've won.'

Still holding his empty bow, he signalled to Eumaeus and Mentor. Reluctantly they let their weapons slip to the floor. Then he turned to Eperitus.

'I know you can hear me,' he said, his voice low and his lips barely moving. 'Place your shield and spear slowly on the ground. Then pull the arrow from the body by your feet and throw it to me.'

'It's too dangerous,' Eperitus said, his voice audible to all.

'Just do as you're ordered!' Antinous said.

Slowly, Eperitus lowered himself to one knee. Looking down, he saw the black-feathered arrow sticking up from the throat of a young noble. He glanced across at Antinous and Telemachus, silhouetted against the flames of the hearth. This was not like shooting an arrow through axe heads. It was too dark, the consequences of missing too dangerous. If his throw was poor or too slow, or Odysseus mis-caught it, if there was the slightest delay in fitting it to the bow, aiming it or shooting it, Antinous's blade would slice through Telemachus's throat in an instant. And yet the alternative was to make Antinous king, after which he would surely kill them all anyway. Using his shield to cover his movements, Eperitus reached across and plucked out the arrow.

'Hurry *up*, damn you!' Antinous exploded.

Eperitus threw the arrow with a flick of his wrist. It spun towards Odysseus, who caught it deftly. In a single motion he fitted it to the string and tensed the bow. In the moment of time that it took Antinous to understand what was happening, he took aim and let the arrow fly.

Chapter Thirty One

The Final Test

The bowstring sang in Odysseus's ear. He could hear his own heart thudding against his ribcage as he watched the long black arrow winding towards its target. Antinous's head snapped back as the point pierced his eye and the sword fell from his hand. For a moment his dead body clung to Telemachus's shoulder, then dropped slowly to the floor. Telemachus stooped down, retrieved Antinous's sword and drove aside an attack from one of the other suitors.

Odysseus ran forwards to a cluster of bodies, knelt beside them and pulled out another arrow. Telemachus had killed the first suitor and was engaged in combat with two more, one of whom toppled forwards with Odysseus's arrow in his stomach. The second fell to a thrust from Telemachus's sword. Eperitus rose to his feet, a spear balanced over his shoulder. An instant later it had found its mark in the chest of one of the surviving nobles, throwing him back against one of the columns.

Mentor and Eumaeus joined the fight at Telemachus's side, spears and shields at the ready as they clashed with three of the remaining suitors, making quick work of them. The last man threw down his sword and ran to the side door, pulling at the handle and pounding on the wood, screaming to be let out. Odysseus shot him in the back and he fell against the door, blood frothing from his mouth. His feet struggled briefly for a grip in the dirt, and then his corpse sank to the floor.

Odysseus looked about at the carnage. He felt no sense of exultation or accomplishment, no elation that the last obstacle on his long journey home had been overcome. Rather, he felt sick. Sick that his return had to come at such a cost, bathed in blood and the destruction of so many of his own people. He looked down at his hands. Despite the rain in the courtyard, they were still dark and sticky with the blood of his victims. Indeed, his whole body was spattered with their gore. He felt it caking up on the skin of his thighs and arms, and sensed the stiffness in his beggar's rags as it dried. And he felt a great weariness. Staring at his silent, motionless friends, he saw the tiredness in them, too.

'What about the wounded?' Mentor asked.

A whole generation of Ithaca's nobility lay slain around them. Here and there a humped figure would try to raise a head or a hand and, finding the effort too much, would drop back down with a groan. Two or three emitted low moans, punctuated with an occasional gasp of pain.

'Leave none alive,' Odysseus replied.

He looked each one of them in the eye and they nodded their understanding. As they laid down their spears and shields and drew the daggers from their belts, he knew they realised that what they had taken part in had been terrible and inglorious; not a triumph, but a thing to be ashamed of. Perhaps this closing episode of the battle – the murder of the wounded – was the hardest and dirtiest part.

But it was necessary. The suitors had coveted the wife and throne of a man whom they had assumed to be dead, but whom death had been unable to claim. Worse than that, their insolent ambition had been a stench in the nostrils of the gods. And so the Olympians had brought the rightful king home, and he had wrenched back his throne with blood-drenched hands. For all Odysseus's schemes and stratagems on his long journey home, for all his successes and catastrophes, it was by the will of the gods that he had finally found his way to Ithaca. And it was by their will the suitors had been slaughtered. The guilt did not belong to him.

He watched Eumaeus in his slave's clothing crouch down by a richly dressed figure, pull back his head and slit his throat as if he was slaughtering one of the swine on his master's farm. Another raised an imploring hand towards Mentor, who dropped to one knee and slipped his dagger into the man's heart. Even Telemachus showed no remorse as he bent over a wailing suitor – his cloak falling like a curtain to hide the pitiless deed – and silenced him. Three years of their arrogant bullying must have deadened his compassion towards them, just as the deaths of Philoetius and Halitherses had hardened the hearts of the others. Odysseus had just as much cause to finish off the men who had expected to marry his wife and take his throne. But it was not like murdering Taphian invaders as they slept. For all their conceit, these men were still Ithacans.

'What about the families?' Eperitus said. 'They're more powerful than we are and they'll want vengeance.'

'They are and they will, but I'll worry about them tomorrow. For now, we must see that the bodies are removed and the palace cleaned of blood. We'll need sulphur to get rid of the smell, too. It seems so strange, seeing them all dead. I can remember the older ones when they were still boys, chasing each other around the marketplace with no thought for the future.'

He knelt down and turned a cloaked figure onto this back. His dead eyes stared vacantly up at the ceiling, his throat drenched with blood. Another man lay with an arrow protruding from his chest, his handsome face relaxed as if in sleep.

'Do you remember the battlefields of Troy?' he asked, looking up at Eperitus. 'The dismembered corpses in their many hundreds lying in lines before the city walls, clustered where the fighting had been thickest, as if some monstrous tide had washed them ashore. Do you recall the missing limbs and disembowelled stomachs; the mouths, eyes and nostrils crawling with flies? How they would rise up in the air if you tried to brush them away, then settle back again a moment later? A soldier learns to expect such things on a battlefield. But this isn't a battlefield; it's my home. It makes the sight much worse, *much* worse. Only this morning these same men were eating and drinking at these tables, served by maids and wine stewards...'

'*Your* maids and stewards,' Eperitus reminded him, laying a hand on his shoulder. '*Your* tables, *your* food and wine.'

Odysseus turned to him.

'Why did you come back, Eperitus?'

'Because this is a *just* fight. Never forget that. If you do, you'll not be able to rule Ithaca again. Now, let's do as you say and clear away this mess. Penelope should not see this.'

Odysseus stood.

'Yes, the sooner the better. Telemachus, fetch Eurycleia.'

Telemachus nodded to his father, and with the side entrance still barred, followed Mentor and Eumaeus out to the courtyard, where the rain had stopped and there was a glimmer of sunlight. After a last look at the great hall, Phemius went with them. A little while later, Odysseus heard the bar being lifted from the side door. Eurycleia entered, staring in open disbelief at the blood-splashed walls and the bodies that lay in heaps about the great hall.

'Praise Zeus and all the immortals,' she said. 'Our misery is over at last.'

'It is indeed,' Odysseus said.

Eurycleia looked at the king and raised her hands to her cheeks. Tears welled up in her eyes and she bowed her head.

'My lord and king, it really *is* you. I… I thought maybe it would all prove a dream. But you did it. You killed them! You killed them *all*! This is a great day. Many will celebrate the destruction of the suitors.'

'And many will mourn their deaths, too, old woman. This is a tragedy. There can be no other word for it, and there will be no exulting over what has happened, even if these men deserved to die. But Ithaca has lost a generation of its best men – or men who should have been its best, if war had not robbed their land of order and discipline. And two honest men have also died – Philoetius, the herdsman, and Halitherses, my old captain and good friend.'

'I didn't mean to cause offence, my lord,' Eurycleia said, bowing lower while glancing up at Odysseus and Eperitus. 'I will fetch the queen at once…'

'No! First the great hall must be cleaned. The bodies must be washed and removed to the courtyard, the filth scraped up with shovels and replaced with fresh earth, the walls and pillars washed of blood, the air purified with sulphur. Do you understand, Eurycleia? I want the tables and benches returned as they were, torches set in the brackets and the fire built up. It has to look as if there had never been a battle, as if the suitors themselves had never sullied my house. As if… as if I had never left.'

'I'll fetch the other servants at once.'

Odysseus shook his head.

'Not all of them. Just the ones who were disloyal to me, the ones who gave themselves to the suitors. Let them wash the blood from their lovers' bodies and lay them out by the courtyard walls. They can clean away the mess their chosen masters have made of my house.'

'And what of the bodies?' Eurycleia asked. 'Should I send word to their families to come and collect them?'

'No. No one is to leave the palace, no one at all. My return must remain a secret to those beyond our walls – for now at least. Some in the town will have heard the clamour, but the rain will have dampened the sound and kept people indoors. Besides, they're used to the noise of the suitors; perhaps they'll assume they were celebrating the marriage to Penelope. Now, Eurycleia, go and send the maids here to me.'

She bowed again. Then, despite the blood that covered Odysseus, she threw her arms about him and showered his head with kisses before turning and bustling out of the hall.

'The families of the suitors are bound to come, though,' Eperitus said. 'By tomorrow at the latest they'll want to know which of their sons is the new king.'

'I know,' Odysseus nodded. 'And we will be ready for them when they come.'

-

The palace had been silent for some time now. The clash of weapons and the cries of dying men had faded away, as had the drum of the rain on the roofs. Autonoe had insisted on finding out what had happened and Penelope had reluctantly let her go, leaving her alone with the agony of not knowing who had proved victorious. If it was the suitors, then Autonoe would have been better letting her end her own life – though she had taken the rope with her to ensure there was no second attempt. But if it was the beggar, what then? How would she know he was Odysseus? If the gods could transform the man she had once loved into such a wretched old crow of a figure, could they not also transform someone else into the form of her husband?

And then there was the other question. If he could prove himself to be Odysseus, what then? She felt no excitement at the thought he might be in the great hall, and that concerned her. But neither did she feel any joy or relief at the thought she might have been released from the threat of the suitors. All she felt was tension – deeply coiled and as hard as rock, stiffening every nerve, joint and muscle in her body until she wondered that she could take any more of it.

Earlier, as the fighting had spilled out into the courtyard, she and Autonoe had glanced fearfully out of the window, but they had been unable to make out anything clearly in the rain and the confusion of the melee; and it had only taken the sight of one man being impaled on a spear to send them scuttling back into the shadows. After the fighting had stopped they heard voices, too low to recognise, followed by the sound of wounded men groaning or crying out as their lives were brought to a sudden end. The possibility that the voices might belong to the suitors, and the dying moans to her son and his comrades, had defeated the temptation to go to the window again.

But then, as she awaited the return of her maid, she heard something strange and unexpected: the weeping of women. Unable to fight her curiosity, she left her bed and went to a corner of the window. The rain clouds had all but cleared away and the last of the sun shone brightly on the treetops and the roofs of the town. She saw two of her maids in the courtyard below, staggering under the weight of a body – one holding the ankles, another the arms – and laying it down against the outer wall. More maids followed carrying more bodies. It reminded her of the times she had seen the suitors carrying their drunken comrades out of the great hall.

But there was no mistaking that these men were dead. All were naked, their pale bodies sponged clean and displaying the marks of battle. Some wounds were less obvious: slits like tight-lipped mouths where a sword, spear or arrow had pierced the soft flesh. Others were plain to see and terrible to look at: a severed limb or missing head, the detached part laid on top of the cadaver; or a gaping cavity where the torso had been ripped open and the organs had spilled out. And as the maids carried each corpse – a horrid and seemingly unending procession – their weeping barely paused for longer than the time it took to draw breath.

All the time, Penelope had dreaded the sight of Telemachus's body being brought out, or even the beggar's, but by the time the gruesome parade had ended, every corpse had belonged to a suitor. That did not mean the suitors had not won – perhaps the bodies of her son and the others had been stacked elsewhere, or been desecrated in some way. But it soon became clear to her that the task of removing the dead had been given to the same eleven slaves, girls whom she knew for their insolence and their willingness to sleep with the suitors. And by that measure alone she knew they were being punished for their treachery, and that therefore the suitors had been defeated.

The door opened and Autonoe entered. Her face was bright with excitement but, knowing her mistress's doubts, she was trying to contain her joy.

'My lady, the suitors are dead and Telemachus is alive!'

Penelope felt the bronze fist around her heart release its grip. Tears of relief flowed down her cheeks as she stood. Autonoe dashed over to her and they embraced each other tightly.

'And the beggar, the man who calls himself my husband?'

'He *is* your husband! I know it, and he's alive too. I haven't seen him, but Eurycleia has. She swears he is the king and that he now wears the likeness of Odysseus.'

Penelope looked at her maid, her expression filled with doubt and confusion.

'Do you really think it's him, Autonoe? How can you be sure? Oh, how can I be sure of anything any more?'

She sat down and rested her forehead in her hands. Autonoe sat beside her.

'It's him, I just know it. I can't say any more than that, my lady.'

'Then what do I do now? Do I go to him? I suppose I have to, though the thought terrifies me. What if it *isn't* him? I will know. And if it is, what if… what if he's changed?'

'He's bound to have changed, but…'

The sound of voices outside the window stopped her. They were followed by the wailing of women. But these were not the grief-stricken cries of earlier. Now they were filled with terror, the anguish of people afraid for their lives.

'What's happening?'

'Don't listen to it,' Autonoe said. 'Put your hands over your ears if you have to.'

'Tell me what they're doing. What did Eurycleia say?'

'Odysseus asked which of the servants had been faithful and which… and which had not. You'll know the ones she named, the ones who would sit on the suitors' laps at the feasts and sneak out after dark to be with them. They're going to hang them, and Melanthius, too.'

A great shout of horror and panic erupted across the courtyard, followed by pleas for mercy. Penelope ran to the window and yanked aside the curtain. She saw figures by the stables. Telemachus was there with Eumaeus. Kneeling around them were several maids, all of them young and pretty; girls who until that morning had gloried in the attentions of the suitors, thinking themselves beyond the reproach of even their own mistress.

Then she saw a row of nooses hanging from the tops of the stable doors. Two were already occupied, one with the dismembered body of a man whom Penelope was barely able to recognise as Melanthius, the other with one of the maids. As Autonoe joined her mistress, Telemachus ordered another of the girls to stand, and when she refused, pulled her to her feet. Penelope wanted to shout down to him to stop, but closed a hand over her mouth and stepped away from the window.

'No, I can't,' she said. 'I can't tell him to stop. He's a man now, whether he has come of age or not. He knows what he's doing and it's not my place any more to give him orders.'

Autonoe took her hand.

'What choice does he have? Those girls were foolish, but they knew what they were doing. They betrayed their old masters for those they thought would become the new. Just like the suitors showed no loyalty to Odysseus, trying to take you and his throne for themselves. They stole his wealth and showed no respect for him, his family or the gods. If he'd compromised with them, shown mercy of any kind, then they'd have seen him as weak. Their ambitions would have stayed alive with them and there would never be peace on Ithaca. Odysseus is the king, my lady, and Telemachus will be king after him. They have to show their authority.'

'Maybe,' Penelope said, listening to the continuing screams from the courtyard. 'But he's not the king I knew.'

'No, he's not,' Autonoe said. 'He's not the king any of us knew. But he *is* the man you've prayed for all these years, and you must accept him as he is.'

-

When the time came, Penelope put on an old dress that she had ordered brought up from the storerooms, a simple blue chiton that Odysseus had always liked to see her in. She covered the marks Elatus had left with powder and wound a thin scarf around her neck to hide the bruising left by the rope. Both would fade in time, but she did not want to draw attention to her own sufferings when she faced the man who had freed her from the suitors.

As she stepped out of her room accompanied by Autonoe, her eyes fell on the bodies of Hippodameia and Elatus, laid side by side in the passageway with a sheet spread over them. Patches of blood had seeped through the cloth, but Penelope turned her face away and continued to the top of the stairs and down towards the great hall. She stopped before the side door and laid her fingers on the handle, but did not turn it. She wanted to return to her bedroom, but her courage would not let her. And yet it took Autonoe to open the door and guide her through with a hand about her waist.

She winced slightly at the lingering smell of sulphur as she entered the great hall, but it was mostly masked by a strong aroma of flowers. The room was warm and shadowy. Through the open doors at the far corner of the hall she could see the last traces of twilight in the evening sky. Looking around, the tables and benches stood in orderly rows and gleamed in the light from the handful of torches on the walls and the glow from the blazing hearth. Their polished surfaces were spread with lilies and a fresh layer of dirt had been raked over the floor. Even the muralled walls had been sponged clean. If pieces of the plaster were newly missing here and there, few others would have noticed it as she did. The shields and spears that had been absent that morning were now back in their places.

Two figures rose from the chairs around the fire and came towards her. For a moment her heart raced wildly. Then she recognised her son and – to her surprise – Theoclymenus, recognisable despite his face being shadowed by his hood. She embraced her son, who held her tightly for several moments before pulling away and kissing her cheeks.

'Perhaps things can start returning to normal now,' he said. 'Whatever that is.'

'I wonder,' she replied, caressing his cheek. 'Perhaps this is normal – right now – and tomorrow will see this momentary peace brought crashing down on our heads. But I thank the gods you're alive, Telemachus, and that they've delivered us from the tyranny of the suitors.'

'The gods and my father,' he said.

He passed into the corridor and Theoclymenus stepped forwards. Then, as he tipped back his hood, she saw that it was not Theoclymenus at all, and never had been. Eperitus bowed before her, and taking her hand, kissed it.

'Whatever passed between us, whatever I may have said or done, it was all to save you, my lady. But now you are saved, and I'm your servant again.'

'No,' she said. 'No, Eperitus. You're my friend, just as you always were.'

And as he took Autonoe by the arm and closed the side door behind them, she knew then in her heart that her long wait was over, for wherever Eperitus was, there her husband would be also. She dabbed the tears from her eyes – careful not to smudge the black lining – and looked over at the hearth. There was her husband's high-backed chair, turned away from her to face the flames. An elbow was draped over the armrest, and two muscular legs, crossed at the ankles, were stuck out before it. Pulling her veil down over her face, she walked past Odysseus's chair without looking at its occupant and sat down on a stool on the other side of the hearth. She fixed her eyes upon her knees, but not before she had stolen a glance towards the seated figure. He was a blur, his features lost behind the heat haze.

They sat like that for a while, neither speaking, listening to the rage of the fire as the last of the twilight faded to blackness outside.

At last he moved, pulling himself up in the chair.

'Have you become so hard-hearted in my absence, Penelope, that you will not even speak to me?'

His voice was deep and soft. It almost seemed that it was inside her head, a memory from years before. The very sound of it moved her, sending fissures through the hard layers she had built around her emotions.

'I don't know what to say to you, sir,' she replied. 'I don't even dare to look at you.'

'Because you've forgotten the love you once had for me?'

'Because you might not *be* the man I loved. I could not stand that, not after all I've been through.'

He moved to the edge of his seat.

'Then don't you trust the evidence of your eyes or your ears? Do a few grey hairs – the symbols of my long labours – deceive you so?'

'I do not believe because my hopes of your… of *his* return have been dashed too many times. I've been alone too long, fighting to defend my husband's kingdom with just my wits. It has made me careful. Some might think cold.'

'A cold heart can be thawed,' he said. 'You know, Penelope, there's not been a single day in the past twenty years that I haven't longed for you, or regretted those actions of mine that sent me to fight in another man's war. I'm truly sorry for abandoning you and Telemachus. Will you not forgive me? Will you not even look at me?'

Stung by the anguish in his voice and dismayed at her own hardness, she lifted her gaze. Perhaps it was the bravest thing she had done in all the years since he had gone away, to look into the eyes of the man she had once loved so deeply and confront the truth of whether that love still existed.

He sat perched at the end of the throne, the firelight shining golden on his oiled skin, giving definition to his muscular arms and legs. He wore a purple tunic and a white cloak that had belonged to her husband. His hair and beard were red, if shot through with strands of grey. And as she looked at his face, though the air between them rippled with the heat of the fire, something within her moved. A doorway had opened in her terrible loneliness, and beyond it a warm, familiar light was shining. The burdens that had fallen on her so heavily over the years, suppressing her gentler emotions, seemed to lift. She remembered who he was, and who she had been, and what they had had together. And she wanted to cry. But the caution that had come to control her character demanded one more proof before it would surrender. She took command of herself once more.

'It is true your appearance is now like my husband's, and I see nothing of the old beggar with whom I spoke last night. My maid tells me you were transformed by a god. And yet how can I know that the same god has not changed a stranger into the likeness of the king? But if Odysseus *did* return, there are ways that I would know him that go beyond mere appearance. Signs that only we two know.'

'Then test me, my lady,' Odysseus demanded, rising from his chair.

She looked out at the darkness beyond the doors.

'It is late; the test will wait until tomorrow. For now, come with me and I will show you your quarters. You have rid me of the suitors, and so I will not have you sleep on the floor like the beggar you were. You shall have a room to yourself, with a bed.'

She stood and walked across the great hall to the side door. Removing a torch from its bracket, she signalled for him to follow her, then entered the passageway. She moved swiftly, her heart beating faster as she heard his footsteps behind her. With every stride she told herself that he was not Odysseus, fearing still that he might prove otherwise – something that would surely now destroy her. But she would know soon enough.

After several turns in the corridor they came to a wide door. It looked old and forgotten, its handle heavy with dust and casting a long shadow in the torchlight. She reached out and turned it. The door opened stiffly onto a large room where pieces of furniture were covered with white sheets that in turn were layered with dust and cobwebs.

'Here,' he said, taking the torch from her hand.

Their fingers brushed against each other, sending a sudden thrill through her body. She dared a glance at him, but he was busy fitting the torch in a bracket by the door. Then he placed his hands on his hips and stared round at the room.

'I think I prefer the great hall,' he said.

'I admit it hasn't been used for some time. No one has slept here for twenty years.'

'No one?' he asked, his eyes briefly catching hers. 'That's a long time. Too long. Makes the place feel like a... like a mausoleum, a place for dead memories.'

'Slumbering memories,' she corrected. 'But if you don't like the way it looks, you can always move things around until you feel comfortable. Why don't you push the bed away from that central column and closer to the window? The air's fresher there.'

'Perhaps I will.'

Her spirit sank within her and she looked down at the floor.

'Or I would,' he continued, 'if that was just an ordinary column. But it's the bole of an old olive tree that stood here when I built the bedroom around it all those years ago. I used the tree for one of the bed posts, and so I couldn't move that bed without tearing it to pieces first.'

He took her by the hand and led her toward the bed.

'Look, there's even a new branch at the top,' he said, reaching up and touching the leaves that had grown from it. Then he turned to her and laid his hands on her waist. 'Have I passed your test, Penelope?'

'Only one man could have known that,' she said. 'My husband.'

She put her arms around his neck and looked into his eyes, trying to read what was in them. There was no point fighting back the tears any more – tears of grief for what had been lost, mingled with tears of joy for what had been found again. And through it all she felt a lightening in her spirit, as if the bonds that had held in all her joy had been broken.

'I still don't know what to say to you,' she said, smiling through her tears.

He kissed her forehead.

'Why say anything? It's enough for me to be with you after all this time. Perhaps if I hold you long enough it'll start to feel real.'

'But won't there be this gulf between us?' she asked, suddenly afraid. 'We've both changed so much. So much has happened to us individually. Will we ever be able to bridge that?'

'We loved each other once, Penelope. The memory of that love brought me back to you. Even if the gods took the past twenty years from us, we have more than enough time ahead of us still. But we mustn't try to claim back the love we had, for the old you or the old me. Let's learn to love each other for who we've become. Start over again. You're still as beautiful to me as you were then, and how difficult can it be to fall in love with the intelligent, funny, kind-hearted woman I know is still inside you? You've carried too great a burden for too long, but you don't have to any more. I'm back. We'll carry the burden together. That's what a man and wife are meant to do, isn't it?'

And then she realised that learning to love him again would be easy. She leaned forwards and placed her lips slowly against his. The kiss was uncertain at first, awkward and yet exciting. His powerful hands moved up behind her shoulders and pulled her body into his. For a moment they remembered the old passion they had once known; then they relaxed and pulled away to look into each other's eyes again. He smiled then for the first time, and it seemed as if years of care were removed from his face.

'Lie down with me,' she said, pulling the sheet from the bed.

Chapter Thirty Two

The King Returns

The next morning, Odysseus woke to bright fingers of sunlight streaming through the gaps in the heavy curtains. He looked down at his sleeping wife and smiled. The nightmare was over and the dream was beginning. Only one barrier now remained between him and the life he had sought for so long.

He dressed and went to find Telemachus. His son was in the great hall with Eperitus, Mentor and Eumaeus, eating a simple breakfast. As Odysseus joined them, they greeted him with smiles and jokes about the comfort of his bed and whether he had slept much.

'I had as much sleep as could be expected,' he replied, grinning.

A steward poured him a cup of wine and a maid brought him a bowl of hot porridge and a basket of flatbread. Recognising Autonoe, he took her by the hand and brought her close.

'I saw the mark on Penelope's neck,' he said in a low voice. 'She told me it was you that saved her, Autonoe. For that I will always be grateful. And if there is anything I can give you for what you've done, you just have to name it.'

Autonoe's gaze fell briefly on Eperitus, who was sat on a high-backed chair with a small table beside him, talking with Telemachus.

'My lord, there is nothing I want that is in your power to give, unless it is to serve my king and queen for the rest of my days.'

She bowed her head, collected up a few empty bowls and cups and went off to the kitchens. Odysseus noticed Eperitus's eyes follow her out and smiled to himself.

'Well, old friend,' Mentor said, 'the chariot of the sun has left Ocean's stream and will soon be showing itself above the hilltops. By noon at the latest the suitors' families will arrive to find out which of their sons married Penelope and has become king of Ithaca. What are your plans? When they find out every one of their sons are dead they'll want revenge.'

'The household servants will lay the bodies of the suitors outside the walls, then bar the gates. As for us, I haven't set eyes on my father in twenty years and he doesn't even know I've returned, so as soon as breakfast is finished I intend to visit his farm. And when we return, we'll see what awaits us.'

'At the very least we should go to the armoury and equip ourselves for a fight,' Eperitus said. 'Breastplates, greaves, helmets and all – even for Eumaeus here. The rest I'm happy to leave to your scheming mind.'

As the sun edged above the hills, it found them climbing the stony path towards Laertes's farm. Odysseus had been deep in thought, remembering the pleasures of his reunion with Penelope and pondering the things they had shared from their years apart. The most difficult had been his infidelities with Circe and Calypso. And yet Penelope had accepted the revelations with grace, believing him when he said he had been given little choice but to share their beds. Indeed, she almost seemed relieved at his confession, afraid perhaps that he might have kept such things from her and built their future relationship on a lie. And the shadow of it did not mar their lovemaking or their happiness at being together again.

After a while his thoughts had turned to what would happen when the families of the suitors discovered their sons were dead. He had forbidden the servants to leave the palace – other than to lay out the bodies in the empty marketplace before the walls – and on pain of death not to mention to anyone that the king had returned. Ithaca's nobles would discover the truth soon enough, and at a time of his choosing. Then, as they had neared Laertes's farm, his thoughts drifted to the pending reunion with his father. Telemachus had described how frail Laertes had become, and Odysseus was afraid of what the shock of learning his son had finally returned would do to him.

They passed through terraced vineyards where workers in wide-brimmed hats watched the approach of the armed men nervously, until they recognised Telemachus and waved greetings to him. Remembering one or two of them, Odysseus pulled up his hood so that his face was shaded. Then he saw his father's cottage at the top of a low hill. It was stone-built and sturdy, surrounded by ramshackle outhouses and orchards where the trees were dotted with immature fruits. There was a strong smell of manure, and from somewhere he could hear the grunting of pigs and the mingled bleating of goats and sheep. Soon they approached an old man on a ladder against one of the trees, his head and shoulders lost among the leafy branches.

'That's him!' Telemachus said. 'He'll be overjoyed to see you again after all this time. Shall I call him?'

'No! The shock will most likely kill him. I'll go myself and speak with him, and Eperitus will come with me. Here, take our shields, spears and helmets and go wait for us in the cottage.'

Signalling for Eperitus to draw up his hood, Odysseus led the way into the orchard. Though once a king, his father wore a patched and grubby tunic, cowhide leggings and thick gloves. His goatskin hat lay on the grass amid a pile of leaves and branches. As they approached, Odysseus heard the snapping of shears and saw more clippings drop to the floor, followed by the shears.

'Damn it!'

Odysseus turned uncertainly to Eperitus, who signalled for him to go forwards. The rickety ladder creaked as Laertes descended.

'Here,' Odysseus said, retrieving the shears and handing them to him.

He looked at his father and felt tears come to his eyes. The old man's skin was deeply tanned and leathery. His nose seemed to have grown with the years and his cheek bones formed prominent ridges beneath his cloudy eyes. His lips were the same brown colour as his skin and deeply lined, like the rest of his face. His white hair was so fine that a puff of wind might have blown it away. He still had a broad chest and the muscles in his arms were solid, though the skin was taut over his shoulders and elbows. And yet the man was unmistakably his father.

Laertes stepped off the last rung. Removing his gloves and putting them in his belt, he took the shears from Odysseus's hand. He narrowed his eyes at the newcomer, then shook his head; Telemachus had warned him that Laertes's eyesight was still good at a distance, but everything was a blur to him close up. The old man pointed to the hat on the ground.

'Spare me the trouble, will you?'

Odysseus picked it up and handed it to his father, who pushed it down onto his head.

'Where is your master?' he asked. 'I'd like to speak with him.'

Laertes peered at him closely, sparing a glance also for Eperitus.

'The master is busy. What do you want with him?'

'He knows me well and would be pleased to see me.'

'His eyesight's not so good any more; he might not recognise you. Tell me your name and I'll go see if he remembers you.'

'He will,' Odysseus said. He placed a hand on the bole of the tree, feeling the texture of the bark and letting his mind wander back to a time many years before. 'He once brought me to this same orchard when I was just a boy. I remember the sweet scent of the blossoms and how they had made a carpet of white on the grass. He gave this very tree – all thirteen trees in this row – to be my own. Apple trees, too, in the orchard adjacent to this one, and forty fig trees on the other side of the cottage...'

'Odysseus?' Laertes said, his voice barely a whisper. 'Odysseus, can it possibly be you?'

'Yes, Father. It's me.'

He embraced the old man and for a while they said nothing. Then Laertes pulled away and tipped the hood back from his son's face, his milky eyes looking directly into Odysseus's.

'I can't make out your face any more, Son, not this close up. But your voice hasn't changed, and who else would know about the trees? Thank the gods! But why couldn't they have brought you back a day earlier? Penelope took an oath to remarry on Apollo's feast day if you hadn't returned. By now she'll have chosen one of the vile suitors who've occupied your home for the past three years.'

'They're dead,' Odysseus said. 'I slaughtered them to a man yesterday, with the help of Telemachus, Mentor and Eumaeus. And Eperitus here.'

He indicated Eperitus, who removed his hood and bowed. Laertes reached out with a gnarled hand, which Eperitus took. They discussed the battle, and though Laertes was moved to more tears at the news that Halitherses and Philoetius had fallen, he could not suppress his joy that the suitors had been overthrown.

'I haven't been to the palace since they arrived,' Laertes said. 'Turning my old home into a den for fools and braggarts. I'd very much like to see it again now they're gone, if seeing is the word with eyes like mine. And Penelope, too. She used to visit me at least once a week, but since those wretched men took over the palace I've been lucky to see her once or twice a season. Damn them! But have you thought about their families? Killing their sons is enough to start a blood feud that'll go on until you or they are dead. And there's far too many of them, even for you, Odysseus. What about the fleet? Are they anchored nearby, and can you get a message to them in time?'

'The fleet was destroyed years ago,' Eperitus said. 'We can expect no other help, unless Odysseus calls an Assembly of the people.'

'That would mean civil war,' Odysseus said, 'assuming any of the ordinary folk still felt any loyalty towards me. Don't forget that most of them lost sons, husbands, fathers and brothers under my command. Either way, I don't want to bathe the throne in the blood of more of my people, if it can be avoided. But now we must return to the palace and discover whether the families have found the bodies of their noble sons yet.'

'Then I will come with you,' Laertes said. 'I still have my weapons and armour, and the strength to wield them. And you'll need every spear you can get if that fool Eupeithes is there.'

-

The sound of wailing voices came to them on the breeze as they approached the town. Odysseus and Eperitus exchanged glances.

'I hope you know what you're doing, Odysseus,' Eperitus said.

'I hope so too.'

Before they reached the edge of town, they heard a horn blowing from the skirts of Mount Neriton. It was the call to the Assembly.

'That'll be the families of the suitors,' Telemachus said. 'They're not content to fight this battle on their own; they want to justify their cause to the rest of the island and win the support of the people.'

'Eupeithes's work, no doubt,' Laertes said, spitting on the grass. 'Be careful, Son. He's going to use the Assembly as a bid for your throne.'

'I expected as much,' Odysseus replied. 'Let's go and hear what he has to say. Raise your hoods and speak to no one.'

They soon joined many others – farmers, shepherds, fishermen; young men and old – streaming in from the fields and beaches and villages to the foot of the mountain. It was here the Assembly traditionally gathered to hear important news or make collective decisions. Only men of noble blood could call the Assembly, and as head of the Kerosia, Eupeithes would command the attention of every man there. Odysseus and the others were among the last to arrive, sitting on the slopes to look down at the nobles gathered below. Five or six hundred had answered the summons, men who might soon be persuaded to join Eupeithes's cause. The old merchant stepped forwards and raised his arms for silence. Even at that distance, Odysseus could see that his eyes were red and his cheeks stained with tears. His rich clothes – the finest he owned, worn in confident expectation that his son would greet him as the new king of Ithaca – hung in shreds, ripped in grief by his own hands.

'Men of Ithaca,' he began, his voice broken and difficult to hear. A servant brought him a cup of wine and he took a swallow. 'Men of Ithaca, hear me. A terrible crime has befallen us all. The noble youth of our four islands – Ithaca, Samos, Dulichium and Zacynthos – were gathered in the royal palace at the request of the queen, hoping to win her hand in marriage, and through her, become our new king. You've witnessed for yourselves the qualities of these men, the best of all our kingdom's youth: their strength, their godlike looks, their thirst for honour and glory. Any one of them would have provided us with a fine king, and you know as well as I do that Ithaca desperately *needs* a king!'

Eupeithes had found his voice quickly enough, and now his persuasive powers were gathering momentum. There were nods and murmurs of agreement from the crowd.

'The last king deserted us for a foreign war and perished on his return, taking many of your sons, brothers and fathers with him.' More rumblings of anger and discontent. 'I have done my very best to rule Ithaca through the Kerosia, and yes, I admit it, we've prospered and enjoyed unbroken peace, unlike many of the kingdoms on the mainland. And yet we still need a king, and you, like me, had hoped that one of those young lions who've been paying court to Penelope would take on the mantle of power. I won't lie to you and pretend I had not hoped my own son, Antinous, would sit on the throne. But...'

He faltered and swayed. His servant caught him as he fell and helped him to steady himself. Laertes muttered something inaudible, but Odysseus knew that the anguish that had unmanned Eupeithes was genuine. And it only gave power to his speech.

'But not one of those men will now become your king. Not one of them. They were lured into a trap by Penelope and now lie dead! Murdered by Telemachus and his slaves.' Cries of shock and dismay erupted from the crowd, followed by shouts of anger. Eupeithes had to raise his arms again to silence them. 'Not a single man remains alive. We, their fathers and brothers and uncles, arrived this morning excited at the thought one of our sons would be married and Ithaca would have a king again. Instead, we found the corpses of our sons lined out on the marketplace, their bodies stabbed, slashed and dismembered in the most horrible ways.'

The clamour rose up again and Eupeithes's raised arms could not stop it, forcing him to wait for quiet before resuming his speech.

'Telemachus hatched this scheme with his mother – a scheme worthy of Odysseus himself – and carried it out ruthlessly. Why? Because *he* wants to be king! He has hated every moment that our sons graced his tired and shabby home, knowing that his mother had sworn to marry one of them by Apollo's feast day. He hated that Ithaca should have any king other than himself, even though any one of his mother's suitors would have made a much better ruler. So I ask you: will you have him as your king? Or should another be chosen? Chosen here and now, by the Assembly of the people?'

'We should choose,' shouted one man, jumping to his feet.

Many voices were raised in agreement, whipped up by Eupeithes's rhetoric. Odysseus looked at Telemachus, whose eyes burned with a fierce anger as they glared at Eupeithes from beneath his hood. Then he glanced at Eperitus, who shook his head and nodded back the way they had come.

'Eupeithes should be our king!' said one of the nobles, stepping forwards from the gathering at the bottom of the slope. 'Eupeithes for king!'

A few shouted their agreement from the Assembly and several more nodded. Then a man stood – a shepherd by his fleece jacket and the staff in his hand.

'Eupeithes for king!' he echoed.

Others took up the call, and though many refrained, there were more who stamped their feet or clapped in agreement. Then Odysseus rose to his feet.

'Ithaca already has a king.'

His voice rang out loud and clear, bringing an end to the clamour and drawing all eyes to himself. Eupeithes, whose grief had been somewhat consoled by the support for him to take the throne, stared indignantly up at the hooded man on the hillside.

'The last king died years ago, and his son is a murderer who will pay for his crimes with his life.'

Odysseus looked around at the men seated on the hillside below him. He understood their support for Eupeithes. All men needed a leader, someone to make decisions and bear the responsibility for them; and Eupeithes was claiming to offer them that. But the rich merchant was a liar and cared nothing for the people he was deceiving. That was his greatest fault. Odysseus, too, was a liar. He had cheated and tricked his way through many dilemmas, some of them much more dangerous than the situation before him now. But few had been more important. And if he was to become king again, he knew he could not do it with cunning. If he was to rule Ithaca, it had to be because the people chose him for who he was, not because he had fooled them with falsehoods and empty promises. Unlike Eupeithes, he knew that any king of worth ruled by the loyalty of his subjects. Nothing more.

'It's true Telemachus killed many of the suitors who had invaded his home,' he said. 'But what he did was prompted by the gods, who were enraged by their disregard for the rules of xenia. They stole his livestock, drank his wine and raped his maids, and they received a just punishment. But whose fault was that? Look no further than yourselves! Were you not called to other Assemblies by Mentor and Halitherses, who implored you to demand that the suitors refrain from their folly and leave the palace? You knew that what these young nobles were doing was wrong, but you allowed them to continue, increasing the wrath of the gods against themselves. Telemachus only did what you would have done in your own homes, and *should* have done to protect the palace of your queen. Their blood is on all your hands.

'And as for that man's claim to be king,' Odysseus continued, pointing at Eupeithes, 'are your memories so short? He talks of peace, but he was the one who led an army of Taphian pirates to these shores and stole the throne from King Laertes. And if Odysseus failed you in anything, it was in allowing that serpent to live. Indeed, he thought he might appease him by offering him a place on the Kerosia. But you weren't content with some power, were you, Eupeithes? You wanted *total* power. You cajoled Penelope into swearing an oath to remarry, and threatened to murder Telemachus if she did not choose Antinous, the son by whom you intended to rule Ithaca.'

'That's a lie!' Eupeithes shouted. 'Who are you to come before the Assembly and insult me? Who are you to insult the glorious names of our murdered sons?'

'Who am I?' Odysseus said, tipping back his hood. 'I am Odysseus, king of Ithaca. I have come to reclaim my throne.'

There were gasps from the Assembly, followed by cries of recognition. Men stood and stared, while Eupeithes withdrew into the group of nobles, looking up at Odysseus in disbelief. As they started arguing among themselves, a voice from among the people called out.

'Where are our sons?'

'Where's my father?' asked another

'And my lad? Have they returned with you from Troy?'

Now the real test came, Odysseus thought. If they chose to, they could rise up and strike him down. He would die, not beneath the blows of a hundred arrogant young nobles, but at the hands of ordinary men, who were driven not by political ambition but by anger at the deaths of their kinsmen. His final victory had to be to win back their loyalty, a decision that was theirs to make and not his to impose. And if he failed, then perhaps he deserved such a death.

'Your son was brought down by a Trojan chariot,' Odysseus said, moving into the crowd and laying a hand on the first speaker's shoulder. 'I saw him kill an enemy spearman, only to fall prey to Hector himself. Be proud, Thrasymedes: your son died an honourable death. And you, Ilus, your father also fell on the plains of Ilium, after we had driven the Trojan army back across the Scamander and under the shadows of their own walls. He fought bravely, to the last. They all did, and many of them survived the war to sail with me back to Greece. But the gods had other plans for us. The fleet was destroyed and only myself and Eperitus here made it back to Ithaca.'

'What of my boy, Antiphus?' said an old shepherd. 'Did he die a warrior's death, though his place should have been tending flocks with his father and brothers?'

'Aegyptius, it was not the will of the gods that Antiphus remain with his family. And I'm glad he didn't: your son was one of my best men. He won renown and became like a brother to me. All your sons and brothers and fathers were like my own flesh and blood. They fought bravely and to the best of their skill, and not one of them brought shame on the name of their homeland. Not one. Now you must choose how you want to honour their memories. Though the throne is mine by right, I am prepared to surrender it to Eupeithes if that is your will. Choose your king.'

The men of Ithaca talked quietly among themselves, some looking from Odysseus to Eupeithes and back again. Telemachus, Eperitus and Eumaeus removed their hoods and stood by Odysseus, leaving their spears and shields on the grass. Odysseus looked at the groups spread across the hillside, all of them ordinary men whose wisdom was with the plough or the fishing net, not the rhetoric and deception of politics. But their minds were guided by their hearts, and their hearts were true. After some time Aegyptius hobbled forwards, using his staff for support, and lowered himself to one knee before Odysseus.

'I choose Odysseus to be king of Ithaca,' he said, bowing his head.

Thrasymedes knelt beside him.

'Odysseus, king of Ithaca!'

One by one others began to kneel, then in twos and threes, and rank upon rank until the whole hillside knelt before him. And then, from among the families of the suitors, men came forwards, drawing their swords from their sheaths and presenting them on bowed knees before the king. They had lost sons, but they remembered the oaths of allegiance they had retaken when Odysseus had succeeded his father to the throne. Many more, though, withheld their swords, the memory of their dead kinsmen fresh in their minds and Eupeithes's words still ringing in their ears, drowning out the calls of loyalty and honour.

Eupeithes signalled for his servant, who brought him his armaments.

'We do *not* acknowledge you as king, Odysseus,' he declared, slipping the bronze helmet over his head and tying it under his many chins. 'We know now that you were the chief slaughterer of our sons, and for that you will pay. Your reign will end in war and bloodshed!'

With that, he raised his spear and hurled it up the slope at Odysseus. For a merchant his aim was good, the head burying itself in the turf at the king's feet. But before Eupeithes could take his second spear from his servant's hand, Laertes stood and threw his own weapon. The point passed through Eupeithes's cheek, almost decapitating him. The merchant fell dead on the grass, a pool of dark blood spreading out around him.

Epilogue

The Final Wound

Eperitus sat on the stone wall of his sheepfold and looked across the fields and orchards towards the sea. It sparkled in the sunlight, calm and unthreatening, as if a man might freely walk across it to the horizon. He could hear the bleating of his sheep on the hillsides behind him, and the squeal of his pigs in the sty he had built beside the cottage. Inside the walls of his little farmstead he could hear little Iphigenia crying for her mother's milk, and Autonoe's gentle laughter as she picked the child up in her arms. Arceisius had finally learned to walk and was somewhere among the fig trees, playing with Ajax.

'Let me at least sing you a part of the song. If you don't like it I promise I'll take you out entirely and stop bothering you about it.'

Omeros sat on a stool beside the wall. His lyre was on his lap and he was staring at Eperitus's farm as if his dead eyes could see each tree, shrub and blossom. He had been back on Ithaca for over a year now. After Ocyalus had revealed his real name and the other details about himself that Odysseus had told him, Omeros's memory had slowly returned. When it was fully restored, he had asked the Phaeacians to take him back to Ithaca, and since setting foot on his homeland again he had been working on his song.

'I'm not that stupid, Omeros. You'll sing me part of this new poem of yours and it'll be so wonderful I won't want you to change a thing. So the answer is the same as it's always been: no, I don't want to be in your song.'

'Do you know how difficult it's going to be to tell Odysseus's story without you in it? The king won't be happy.'

'Odysseus understands.'

'But I don't. I can immortalise you, Eperitus.'

Eperitus heard Ajax barking and looked over at the rows of fig trees for a sign of his son. The puppy came running out onto the stony meadow, followed by the small, hobbling figure of Arceisius. The boy fell over and cried a little, but forgot his tears as soon as Ajax came bounding back and began to lick his face. Eperitus smiled.

'When I was a young man,' he said, 'all I wanted was to be in a song. I wanted to kill my enemies, strip their armour for trophies and have my deeds immortalised by a bard. Even if it was only by a bard with a fraction of your skill, Omeros. I wanted my name to live forever, just as you're offering me now. But I was young and naïve, and I was wrong. We've seen the Underworld, you and I; we've witnessed what eternal life really looks like. You remember Achilles. He would've given it all for another moment of life. They all would have.'

Arceisius saw his father and limped awkwardly towards him, falling once over his own feet and then again when Ajax tripped him. Eperitus dropped down from the wall and lifted his son in his arms.

'You see, life isn't a story,' he continued, 'and stories are not life. People in songs are not their real selves, not as they were in life, with all their faults and their weaknesses. When a man enters a song, no matter how skilled the bard, he becomes set in stone, like one of those statues of the gods. I don't want to become like that, Omeros.'

'So all your glorious deeds will just be forgotten?'

'He is my glory now,' Eperitus said, kissing his son's cheek.

'But the poor lad's lame.'

'That was my punishment from the gods for breaking my oath. But it's also a blessing. He'll never have to be a warrior and face the horrors you and I had to. But he can still become a farmer, or a fisherman if someone will teach him. Or maybe a bard! And don't forget Hephaistos is lame.'

Omeros nodded and smiled.

'That he is. And Arceisius is more fortunate than many. He has the love of his father.'

'Him and Iphigenia, and all the others that will come after them,' Eperitus agreed. 'And why not? I've found immortality in my children and contentment in their love. So let my family remember me as I am, not frozen in some song.'

He heard something and looked up the hill, where the road led past the cottage and over the ridge towards the town.

'He's coming,' he said. Turning to the cottage, he cupped his hand over his mouth. 'Autonoe! Bring my sword.'

'How long will you be gone?'

'He didn't say. As long as it takes, I suppose. The final wound must be healed: he still has to appease Poseidon's anger.'

'And how will he do that?'

'Ask him yourself.'

A shout came from the ridge, where Odysseus's familiar outline was silhouetted against the afternoon sky. He gave a wave and continued down the track towards them, a long oar carried over his shoulder.

'Well, Penelope finally let me go,' he said, taking Eperitus by the hand and smiling. 'It was hard on her, what with Telemachus sailing to Pylos yesterday to court Polycaste, and now me leaving her all alone. But she's a strong woman.'

'The strongest I know,' Eperitus agreed. 'And we'll be back soon, won't we?'

'Back from where? Back from what?' Omeros asked.

He held out his hand. The king took it and pulled him into a one-armed embrace, his other hand holding the oar. Omeros reached out with his fingers and found the smoothed wood, feeling it up and down.

'An oar? Why are you carrying an oar?'

'You remember Teiresias? In the Underworld he told me to carry an oar inland until I met a man who would ask me why I was carrying a winnowing fan. Once I'd reached a place so far from the sea that the people don't know an oar when they see one I'm to build Poseidon an altar. Then, when we've made the proper sacrifices, it'll all be over and we can come home.'

'The curse of a god isn't an easy thing to live with,' Omeros said with a nod. 'But don't worry, I'll cheer Penelope up with my songs about your adventures, while she keeps me happy with meat and wine!'

'A fair exchange, so long as you don't overstay your welcome.'

Autonoe emerged from the cottage with Iphigenia, Eperitus's baldric hanging from her shoulder. She gave Odysseus and Omeros as much of an embrace as she could with a baby in her arms, and invited the bard to eat with her when the others had gone. He accepted with a smile. Then she looked at Eperitus.

'Say goodbye to your daughter.'

'Goodbye, little Iphigenia,' he said, kissing the baby on the forehead.

He kissed Arceisius, too, and handed him to Autonoe, who gave him his sword in exchange. Then he kissed his wife, a long and passionate kiss that obliged Odysseus to turn away and look at the sea.

'I'll miss you all.'

Autonoe's eyes welled up with tears, which she brushed away before shaking her head, as if dismissing her emotions.

'We'll miss you. Just don't take twenty years to come home.'

He brushed her damp cheek and smiled. But the thought struck him hard. When he had sailed for Troy all those years ago he had been embarking on an adventure to find out who he really was. And now, at last, he knew. But Odysseus had not set out on a voyage of self-discovery. He had known who he was all along. He had seen himself in Penelope's tears and in the face of the child in her arms. His war had been a war to come home again, to return to himself. And as Eperitus stared at his own family, he understood more than ever how his friend had felt, and why he had done the things he had.

Odysseus placed a hand on his shoulder and together they turned and walked up the track to the ridge. Eperitus spared a final glance at his family and home, then plucked a pair of chelonion flowers from beside the road and handed one to Odysseus. They tucked them into their belts and set off.

Author's Note

It's eighteen years since I started researching and planning my *Adventures of Odysseus* series. To quote an article from *The Telegraph*, it has been "an act of endurance worthy of Odysseus himself". It has also been a great pleasure. There are few, if any, characters from antiquity as unique and fascinating as the Ithacan king, so it has been a privilege to have retold his story over six novels. I only hope I've been able to do him justice.

In this final instalment, I've tried to remain true to the events in the *Odyssey*, while, as ever, giving them a modern sensibility. Homer is one of literature's greatest storytellers. His second great work (the first being the *Iliad*) is packed with wonderful characters, thrilling events and sophisticated themes that are often as relevant today as they were thousands of years ago. And yet his poems were aimed at a very different audience to today's, so—as with the other books in this series—I've adapted my retelling with this in mind.

The *Odyssey* is, essentially, the tale of Odysseus's return to Ithaca, twenty years after he sailed for Troy. But it is not his tale alone. It also concerns his wife, Penelope, and her weakening attempts to fight off the attentions of her suitors; and also Telemachus, whose journey to manhood is defined by his struggle against the suitors who have taken over his home. In my version, there is a fourth character: Eperitus. Readers of other books in the series will know that he is my own invention, put there to add an element of unpredictability to a famous and much-loved tale. Although he doesn't appear in the original myths, I believe he has been an important addition to *The Adventures of Odysseus*. Indeed, Odysseus would have found life much more difficult without him—and a lot lonelier.

Homer's *Odyssey* begins with the gods deciding Odysseus should be released from his imprisonment on Ogygia. It then switches to the royal palace on Ithaca, where we see the selfish and anarchic suitors making merry while an indignant and helpless Telemachus looks on. Goaded by Athena, he sets out to find out what happened to his missing father, travelling to Pylos and Sparta in search of news.

Up to this point, Odysseus has been an off-stage figure. When we finally meet him, he is a shadow of the great man Telemachus has heard about from the lips of others—alone and weeping on an island, where he has been held prisoner by a nymph for seven years. At the news that he is to be released, though, we begin to see a transformation. He builds a sturdy raft with his own hands, sails it for many days, and survives a storm sent by the vengeful Poseidon. He then impresses the Phaeacians with the tales of his voyage from Troy, so much that they load him with gifts and take him back—at last—to Ithaca.

Disguised as a beggar by Athena, and warned about the dangers facing him at home, Odysseus sets out to size up his enemies and find out who his allies are. The suitors quickly prove themselves to be arrogant, ambitious and impious, their lack of respect for the customs of xenia—and hence the supremacy of the gods—making them worthy of their ultimate fate. After revealing his true identity to Telemachus—who has since returned from the mainland—Odysseus brings his son into his plans for a showdown with the suitors. Together they trap the young nobles in the great hall and slaughter them to a man, sparing only their bard and their herald. Further ruthless vengeance is then taken out on the traitorous servants, who gave their loyalty to the suitors, rather than to their master's household.

Only when their bodies are hanging in the courtyard does Odysseus go to Penelope, his beggar's disguise discarded and his looks enhanced by Athena. But their meeting is a strange one—certainly to modern minds, at least. They are cautious, testing each other and admonishing each other's apparent emotional coldness. It is not until final proof has been given that Odysseus is who he says he is, that we get the Hollywood ending: the tears; the embrace; the kiss.

Other than the inclusion of Eperitus and his influence on events, I've made a few changes for dramatic effect. Homer didn't require Odysseus to earn his passage from Phaeacia to Ithaca, but I felt that, after his lengthy, unwelcome and demoralising sojourn on Ogygia, he needed to prove something—to himself as much as to the Phaeacians. In the *Odyssey*, Telemachus can sometimes feel a little passive in his reactions to the bullying suitors—at least until then end, when he kills several of them—so I've tried to demonstrate the frustration he must have felt by making him more confrontational. The brutal response of the suitors to their host also lays bare that these men are not simply misguided youths, but are ruthless, ambitious thugs.

In the *Odyssey*, although they plan to ambush and kill Telemachus on his return from Sparta, he lands on Ithaca without being spotted. I decided to make things a little less easy for him by ensuring the suitors' trap was sprung. Another of their victims is Autonoe. She barely receives a mention in the original tale, but I felt that Penelope needed some moral support. Autonoe provides more than this, of course, and—after the terrible tragedies Eperitus has been through—I thought she would be a worthy new wife to help him enjoy his well-earned peace.

For all her suffering over the long years of Odysseus's absence, Homer's Penelope does not attempt suicide. Nevertheless, her unhappiness is clear in the *Odyssey*, and I don't believe such an act would have been beyond her. She weeps regularly over the loss of her husband, and the thought of being forced to marry one of the suitors would surely have proved intolerable, had Odysseus not returned in the nick of time.

For me, the strange reluctance of their final reunion reveals a great deal about the long ordeal they have both been through. It does not put a question mark over their love. Rather it confirms it, and confirms that the *Odyssey* is, ultimately, a love story. Penelope is cautious because she can't bear to think that this man, who looks so much like her husband, might *not* be him. And he is wary because he can't be sure, after all this time, that his wife still loves him. After all he has been through—all that men, monsters and gods have thrown at him—the possibility that her love for him might have died, has to be the thing he has feared the most.

But she does still love him and, after a bit of mopping up, Odysseus's life is back where it was twenty years before. Except he isn't the man he was back then. He has lost many friends, and every night his dreams are filled with the horrors he has witnessed. Perhaps more than anything, he regrets the lost years that should have been spent with his family, enjoying the closeness of his wife, and watching his baby son grow up. And if he is respected and revered for all he has achieved, hasn't that also put a gulf between himself and everyone else—even those closest to him? For what do they know of his experiences? How many battles have they been in? How many gods have they spoken with? How many monsters have they fought against?

But for those times, he has Eperitus. For now, at last, they have earned the right to sit down by a glowing hearth, with meat and wine to hand, and look back over their adventures in the knowledge they have endured more than most. And survived.

Glossary

A

Achilles – renowned Greek warrior

Acroneos – Phaeacian guard

Aeolus – ruler of the Winds

Aethiopes – peoples from northern Africa

Agamemnon – king of Mycenae, murdered by his wife on his return from Troy

Agelaus – Ithacan noble, son of Damastor

Ajax (greater) – king of Salamis, killed himself after being sent mad by the gods

Ajax (lesser) – king of Locris, drowned by Poseidon

Alcinous – king of Phaeacia

Alybas – home city of Eperitus in northern Greece

Amphinomus – Ithacan noble, son of Nisus

Antinous – Ithacan noble, son of Eupeithes

Antiphus – Ithacan guardsman

Aphrodite – goddess of love

Apollo – archer god, associated with music, song and healing

Arceisius – Ithacan soldier killed at Troy

Arete – queen of Phaeacia

Artemis – moon-goddess associated with childbirth, noted for her virginity and vengefulness

Astynome – wife of Eperitus, who died after childbirth

Athena – goddess of wisdom and warfare

Aulis – sheltered bay in the Euboean Straits

Autonoe – Penelope's body slave

C

Calypso – island-dwelling demigoddess

Charybdis – a monstrous whirlpool

chelonion – flower native to Ithaca

Chloris – Ithacan maid

Cicones – northern allies of the Trojans

Circe – witch possessing the power to turn men into animals

Clytaemnestra – queen of Mycenae and wife of Agamemnon

Ctessipus – Ithacan noble, son of Polytherses

Cyclops – one-eyed giant

D

Demeter – goddess of agriculture

Demodocus – Phaeacian bard

Demoptolemus – Ithacan noble, suitor to Penelope

Diomedes – king of Argos

Dodona – oracle in northern Greece, where the will of the gods was interpreted through the rustling of a great oak tree

Dolius – Ithacan slave

Dulichium – one of the Ionian islands under Odysseus's rule

E

Elatreus – Phaeacian noble

Elatus – Ithacan noble, suitor to Penelope

Elpenor – Ithacan soldier

Eperitus – captain of Odysseus's guard

Eteoneus – squire to Menelaus

Eumaeus – swineherd loyal to Odysseus

Eupeithes – member of the Kerosia

Euryalus – Phaeacian noble

Eurybates – Odysseus's squire

Eurycleia – nurse to both Odysseus and Telemachus

Eurydamas – Ithacan noble, suitor to Penelope

Eurylochus – Ithacan soldier, cousin of Odysseus

Eurymachus – Ithacan noble, henchman to Antinous

H

Hades – god of the Underworld

Halitherses – former captain of the Ithacan royal guard

Hector – Trojan prince, killed by Achilles

Helen – queen of Sparta and wife of Menelaus

Hippodameia – Penelope's body slave

Hyperion – god of the sun

I

Ilium – the region of which Troy was the capital

Iphigenia – daughter of Eperitus and Clytaemnestra, sacrificed by Agamemnon

Iphitus – Oechalian prince who befriended Odysseus and gave him a bow

Irus – Ithacan beggar

Ithaca – island in the Ionian Sea

K

Kerosia – Ithacan council meeting

L

Laertes – Odysseus's father

Laestrygonians – race of giant cannibals

Laodamas – eldest son of Alcinous, King of Phaeacia

Leocritus – Ithacan noble, son of Euenor

Leodes – Ithacan noble, son of Oenops

lotus eaters – a people addicted to the lotus fruit

M

Malea – cape on the south-eastern tip of the Peloponnese

Mantius – Ithacan steward

Melanthius – Ithacan goatherd and henchman of Antinous

Melantho – Ithacan maidservant

Menelaus – king of Sparta, brother of Agamemnon and husband of Helen

Mentor – close friend of Odysseus, given joint charge of Ithaca in Odysseus's absence

Mycenae – most powerful city in Greece, situated in north-eastern Peloponnese

N

Nausicaa – Phaeacian princess

Neoptolemus – son of Achilles

Neriton (Mount) – highest point on Ithaca

Nestor – king of Pylos

Noemon – Ithacan noble, son of Phronius

O

Ocyalus – apprentice Phaeacian bard

Odysseus – king of Ithaca

Ogygia – island home of Calypso

Omeros – Ithacan soldier and bard

P

Palladium – sacred image of Athena's companion, Pallas

Paris – Trojan prince, killed by Philoctetes

Parnassus (Mount) – mountain in central Greece and home of the Pythian oracle

Peiraeus – friend of Telemachus

Peisander – Ithacan noble, son of Polyctor

Peisistratus – son of Nestor

Peloponnese – southernmost land mass of Greek mainland

Penelope – queen of Ithaca and wife of Odysseus

Phaeacia – island on the cusp of the known world

Pheidon – king of the Thesprotians

Phemius – bard to Penelope's suitors

Philoctetes – Malean archer

Philoetius – herdsman loyal to Odysseus

Phorcys – sea god known as the Old Man of the Sea

Polites – Ithacan warrior

Polycaste – daughter of Nestor

Polyphemus – a Cyclops, son of Poseidon

Pontonous – Phaeacian steward

Poseidon – god of the sea

Priam – king of Troy

Pylos – city in south-western Peloponnese

Pythoness – high priestess of the Pythian oracle

S

Samos – westernmost of the Ionian islands under Odysseus's rule

Scylla – six-headed monster

Sirens – monsters with the body of a bird and the head of a woman

T

Taphians – pirate race from Taphos

Teiresias – blind seer

Telemachus – son of Odysseus and Penelope

Theoclymenus – false identity used by Eperitus

Thesprotia – region in north-western Greece

Thrinacie – island where Hyperion keeps his cattle

Thoosa – Ithacan maid

Troy – chief city of Ilium

X

xenia – the custom of friendship towards strangers

Z

Zacynthos – southernmost of the Ionian islands under Odysseus's rule

Zeus – the king of the gods

Lightning Source UK Ltd.
Milton Keynes UK
UKHW040708250820
368797UK00004B/1341